## PRAISE FOR *BLUE COL*

"Catherine McLaughlin evokes a lyrical sense of place and time in her novel, *Blue Collars,* set in New Bedford's South End during the 1950s, '60s, and '70s, while reminding readers that the past wasn't always rosy."

—Maureen Boyle, award-winning author of *Shallow Graves: The Hunt for the New Bedford Highway Serial Killer*

"*Blue Collars* is a powerful work of fiction. From the first page to the last, the story is both real and relatable. Finn Kilroy and her supporting cast of characters jump right off the page, making *Blue Collars* a page-turner that kept me up late into the night. Highly recommended!"

—Steven Manchester, bestselling author of *The Rockin' Chair* and *Twelve Months*

"McLaughlin's work never fails to leave the reader enthralled. *Blue Collars* is no exception. We journey the streets, backyards, and factories of New Bedford in the late 1950s throughout the fevered '60s as seen by McLaughlin's young heroine, Finn. We watch hopefully as Finn overcomes one dilemma after another—problems too heavy for her slender shoulders to bear, and we, the rapt reader, look for solutions alongside her. We are her cheerleaders, her shoulder to lean on. McLaughlin's collection of poetry, *Under a Circus Moon,* left me breathless; *Blue Collars* resurrected the same emotion."

—Patricia Gomes, award-winning writer and poet laureate of New Bedford, MA

"The author breathes life into the characters; they are our neighbors in a vividly portrayed New England city in the midst of economic depression and changing values. But mostly, this is a story about a secret that gnaws at Finn throughout her childhood and adolescence—one that she believes could tear apart her tight-knit family. Like the hurricane dike protecting the harbor of New Bedford, Finn builds a wall of silence to protect her family. But the specter of guilt and shame leaves its imprint on the young girl. A riveting read!"

—Elizabeth Pimentel, essayist and freelance writer

"A must-read for anyone who grew up in New Bedford in the mid-20th century, an absorbing read for anyone who didn't get the chance—despite the painful story. McLaughlin at once manages to evoke a sense of nostalgia for old New Bedford, and to tell Finn's heartbreaking story, so timely in the light of the #MeToo movement. With dialogue that rings true, *Blue Collars* delivers a sweeping family drama, a bildungsroman of a young Finn Kilroy, and a story with New Bedford itself as a main character. From Clarks Cove to Hazelwood Park, we smell the salt water, the *malasadas,* the Portuguese 'pops'. We see the millworkers, the ice cream trucks, the neighborhood ball games. McLaughlin speaks SouthCoasters' language."

–Lauren Daley, *BookLovers* columnist for *The Standard-Times* of New Bedford

"From describing the family set-up in a triple-decker in the South End to the fun of Lincoln Park, *Blue Collars* is a compelling look-back to the time when factory jobs were plentiful, kids could roam free, and everyone knew their neighbors' business. Yet, there is a dark side to this story – abuse, tenuous race relations, alcoholism, family arguments that turn violent. Through it all, the close-knit Irish-American family at the center of the book powers through with love and respect. I enjoyed it very much."

–Gail Roberts, director of Joseph H. Plumb Memorial Library in Rochester, MA

"McLaughlin captures not just the marrowed scintilla of significance in Finn as she grows up on these dear streets of New Bedford, but with practiced hand she culls and reimagines the exotic amid the New England quotidian life. We feel an eerie familiarity with these sometimes not-familiar-at-all stories—thus is the compelling power of McLaughlin's prose. You've never read New Bedford like this."

–Corey Nuffer, theologian and contributing writer to *South Coast Almanac*

# Blue Collars

# Blue Collars

by

Catherine McLaughlin

*Spinner Publications, Inc.*

New Bedford, Massachusetts

New Bedford, Massachusetts 02740
Printed in the United States of America
Support provided by the Massachusetts Cultural Council

**Front cover:** "Blue Collars," etching by Catherine McLaughlin
**Back cover:** "South End Garden, New Bedford," watercolor etching by Jim Sears
Photograph of Catherine McLaughlin by Zachary White

**Author's Note:** Unless otherwise attributed, all poems in this novel are the author's and appear in her volume of poems, *Under a Circus Moon,* published by Old Seventy Creek Press, 2015.

Library of Congress Cataloging-in-Publication Data

Names: McLaughlin, Catherine, 1951 - author.
Title: Blue collars / by Catherine McLaughlin.
Description: New Bedford, Massachusetts : Spinner Publications, Inc., [2018]
Identifiers: LCCN 2017031611|
ISBN 9780932027320 (hardcover) | ISBN 9780932027252 (softcover)
Subjects: LCSH: Families--Massachusetts--Fiction. | Domestic fiction.
Classification: LCC PS3613.C5745 B58 2017 | DDC 813/.6--dc23
LC record available at https://lccn.loc.gov/2017031611

*For Ma and Dad,*

*with love*

# Acknowledgments

First, always first, I wish to thank my children: my son, Conor, who provided my website photos, and my daughter, Caitlin, who designed and created the website (www.creativelycatherine.com) along with her partner, Erin. They are my lifeblood whose love sustains me.

I also wish to thank my immediate and far-flung family for their support and belief in me, especially my sister, Mary Elaine, and her husband, Armand, and my brothers, Kevin, Charles, and Chris. Special thanks to the women of Women's Week—Mary Elaine, Ro, Susan, and Sue—for their early reads and helpful criticisms, and to Ayaan Agane for her reading of multiple drafts and meticulous editing as well as the blessing of her friendship. I am also grateful for the encouragement I received from Ann Sheehan and Pat Gomes.

At Spinner, I would like to thank Sue Grace for all her hard work and suggestions; Natalie White for long hours spent with the manuscript and for her advice and great effort to make this book the best it could be (she wouldn't let me get away with anything); Claire Nemes for her proofreading and suggestions; Jay Avila for his help with book design; and finally, my publisher, Joe Thomas, for his encouragement, work, and belief in this book.

# Contents

# *Blue Collars*

*On the outskirts of New Bedford,*
*a jumble of mills, bricks, and turrets,*
*bars, diners, and churches*
*surrounds rows of triple-deckers.*
*In a third-floor tenement,*
*a woman dressed in black, dark hair graying,*
*dusts gilt-edged bric-a-brac from glass closets*
*and the framed bleeding heart of Jesus*
*nailed to the wall. The daughter*
*sits under the slanted eaves on a bed*
*layered with handmade patchwork quilts,*
*a frayed afghan across her shoulders,*
*writing a language her mother cannot comprehend*
*and rarely speaks, the shape of new words*
*too sharp against the soft palate*
*of age and the old world.*

*The hall smells of spice and linguiça,*
*but outside, the air tingles with the promise of snow.*
*In that hour after the sun, before the moon,*
*schoolboys play ball against brick walls*
*suffused with pink and purple shadow.*
*Red-cheeked, blood stirred with vague longings,*
*they laugh and curse and yell in vibrant chorus,*
*delighting in their strong limbs and raucous company.*
*From church to church the deep bells reverberate*
*and the men released from work appear,*
*lunch pails, caps and cigarettes.*
*The mother, sighing, rises to fix the family supper;*
*the tower clocks of the mills tell the hour,*
*steeple, chain and spire.*

# Prologue

**September 1995**

My mother is leaving home for the first time in her 80 years of life. The house is hollow.

A spoon rattles in the teacup as my mother stirs her tea and drinks in her empty kitchen, this the only expression for a silenced voice, silent with the weight of years, the heft of an unsaid goodbye to the tenement of her childhood and mine. I am Fiona (a.k.a Finn), the fourth youngest of five siblings. Now I look to the sentiment in boxes and plastic bags, the old chairs with worn-down arms, tables scratched with our growing pains. On a wall inside my old bedroom closet, my father's whimsical sketch of Kilroy will not be erased with scrubbing and spray, and there, by my bed, is still the wide patch of plaster covering the hole I'd picked at nightly, trying to reach my brothers' room. I never did break through, but the excavation yielded strips of '60s contact paper, shades of '50s stippling, sheets of generations-ago wallpaper, and, finally, chips of rosedust-colored paint from 1910, until I'd reached the slats in the wall and could go no further.

Boxes are everywhere. We have gathered—my siblings and I—to ease the transition: My older sister, Molly, with her husband Richard, my older brother Tom, and our younger brother, Skip. Only my brother Drew, also older than me, is missing, unable to get away from his research in Los Angeles. Fortunately, my children and my nephews have come to help out.

Ma has never lived anywhere else. She was born in this house and grew up here with her parents and her sister. She set down her married life here, raised her children here, with her parents above and her sister and her family below. Granny's tenement one floor up is still very much as she left it on the day she died, right down to the knife, spoon, and fork set out with a placemat at the table, teacup and saucer waiting for the kettle to boil. We still need to pack that up. Downstairs, where Aunt Joan and her husband, Callan, used to live, stands empty, cleaned out by my cousins after their mother died a few months ago. My mother is the only one left living here, and now she, too, is leaving the neighborhood where she once knew everyone and now knows almost no one. Ma has recently turned 80, the decade has slipped into the

1990s, and the city no longer seems a safe place for her as sometimes drugs and violence intrude on the peace. The house has been sold.

I stand amid boxes in the kitchen, hearing the echoes of laughter and shouts and tears. The living noises of 13 people inhabit my head. While Tom goes about packing with a goofy lampshade stuck on his head, I remember him at 16...

*Tom stands in the kitchen in his khaki Eagle Scout uniform, all dimples and freckles and red hair, thrilled that he has moved up to the highest rank in Boy Scouts.*

*"Take another picture for posterity," my mother says.*

*My father groans and complies, his nervous, arthritic hands shaking the old Brownie camera. I'm proud of my big brother in his uniform with the dark green sash that has all the badges sewn on meticulously by my mother. Tom is my hero. He doesn't tease me as much as the other boys, and he always picks me up without laughing at me when I fall off my bike.*

As we pack up our mother's dishes, the lampshade slips off Tom's head and hits the bare floor. He's doing his best to add comic relief, but his eyes tell a sadder story. I flash back to him at 21...

*He is in uniform again, during the Vietnam War, and at 15, I am ironing his Navy whites ever so carefully while he sits in the rocking chair spit-shining his shoes. I put the iron down on the leg of his pants, and steam rises with the strong smell of hot cotton. Our brother Drew sits in the other rocker playing "Peg o' My Heart" on his harmonica. I hum the bass line to his tune, and he is pleased.*

*"Finn, how do you DO that?" Drew asks me as a September breeze wafts through the open window and steam hisses from the iron. I just grin. Harmony has always come easy to me.*

Molly is in charge of boxing up the living room bric-a-brac. She takes the ceramic Robin Hood statue off the mantle and is inspecting it when my mother yells to her from the kitchen, "Be careful with that. It's an antique."

"Of course, it's an antique. These are all antiques. They're yours," Molly shoots back.

Suddenly I can see a much younger Molly, sitting in the well-worn recliner next to the phone...

*It's a warm night in May, and Molly comes down from our bedroom with the intention of taking a bath. She has her journal with her. Before she can get into the bathroom, however, she gets a phone call from her best friend, Bridie. She puts her journal on the table and goes to answer the phone. While she is talking to Bridie, I see Ma edging her way toward the journal. Molly sees her, too.*

*Just as Ma is about to open the cover, Molly says, "Bridie, hang on a minute." Then, to distract Ma before she can open a page, Molly lets out a positively blood-curdling scream. Ma is so shaken, she throws the book in the air and wets her pants, whirling around to the front door to see if we are being invaded. Molly calmly retrieves her journal and goes back to the phone to Bridie, who is terrified, thinking something horrible has happened. Even I, witnessing the whole event and knowing what Molly is doing, feel chills go up my spine.*

*"You're crazy!" Ma says to Molly when she recovers.*

*"It was the only thing I could think of to get my journal back before she had a chance to read anything," Molly says to Bridie, laughing. "It worked."*

*Meanwhile, there are fast footsteps on the stairs, and Aunt Joan rushes in.*

*"What happened? Is everyone all right?"*

*Oh, we're all right, I think. Just recuperating from another episode of Molly's madcap madness.*

We clear out the pantry shelves.

"God, how many thousands of plastic containers do you have in this pantry?" Skip mutters as he bags them.

"They're useful," Ma says. A child of the Depression, Ma can't throw anything away. She has rubber bands wound up in a ball, bits of multicolored string tied around a piece of newspaper, and stacks of used, flattened, and washed tin foil, all waiting for some unspecified use.

Skip twirls a few lids in the air as we sort through bowls and bins in the kitchen, and I can vividly recall him at age 10...

*He is standing in front of me in the kitchen trying his best to get his wooden top to spin. He will not give up. Like Tom, Skippy has red hair, freckles, and dimples. He looks comical with his tongue sticking out in determination, his blueberry eyes focused on his task. He patiently winds the string around the top, snaps his wrist back, yanks the string, and lets it fly. The top hits the floor point down and buzzes across the linoleum. He grins.*

With a touch to my hand, Ma brings me back to moving day.

She wants me to bring the oversized picture of the Sacred Heart, the one that has always hung on the parlor wall. It's huge and looming, Jesus staring down at us with a bloody, dripping heart below eyes that follow you everywhere.

"I'm sorry, Ma, but this isn't coming to my house," I tell her gently.

She protests. I say I have nowhere to put it.

She tries to foist it off on my other siblings, but no one wants it.

Ma just shakes her head, and I quickly head off more Sacred Heart requests by ducking into the master bedroom, which is just slightly larger than the girls' and the boys' rooms. My parents' room was a comfort zone, where we went when we were really sick, with high fevers and mumps or measles. My poor father had to sleep on the couch those nights, while my mother tended to us in their room. It still feels peaceful and safe in here.

"Has the stove been disconnected?" I hear my mother ask, and I think it's safe to head back into the kitchen without the Sacred Heart coming up again.

Tom checks the gas line on the Humphrey heater to make sure it's disconnected and capped off correctly.

"Let's put the kitchen table in the van—it's going to my house," I say to my nephews. I want to get this move over with, but memories manage to hijack the moment…

*Ma is clearing the last of Thanksgiving from the kitchen table, which doubles as a Ping-Pong table after holiday dinners. Tom and Drew string out the net across the middle of the table, and the games begin.*

*Tom grabs his paddle.*

*"Come on, Dad, let's go," he says, handing my father the other paddle.*

*The white ball pings furiously around the kitchen. Dad usually wins the first game, and he does tonight, too. Laughing, he hands his paddle to Drew; after that, we're in for a few hours of taking turns playing the winner.*

I look around at the emptiness. Nothing left but the mantle clock, still ticking.

My mother turns her back on her home and slowly goes out the door, followed by Tom and Skip. My nephews hang back with me to do a last walk-through and videotape the abandoned rooms. I tearfully unplug the mantle clock. For this family and this place, time has run out.

The boys back out of the tenement, filming as they go. I follow them out, shutting the door and turning the key for the last time. As I walk by his car, I see Tom hunched over the wheel crying like the boy he once was. We drive away slowly, a procession of packed cars and a U-Haul van, my mother in the lead with me. Dry-eyed, she looks straight ahead as we leave the block.

"Goodbye, my life," she says, quietly.

She does not look back.

---

We lived in New Bedford, Massachusetts, a city scarred by its fall from grace as the once-proud "Whaling Capital of the World." Some called it New Beffid. Others jokingly called it New Beige—why, I am not sure.

Call it what you will: It was home.

New Bedford is a city with its mills and factories, its railroad tracks going nowhere, its secret shames and poor self-image, its steeples and spires and Seamen's Bethel perched on Johnny Cake Hill, but its lifeblood beats through its half-dozen or so ethnic neighborhoods.

Ours was the working-class section of the South End, where blocks of tenements once housed mostly French Canadian, English, and Irish immigrants, replaced in later years by waves of Portuguese, Puerto Ricans, and Central Americans. We lived tight among the other tenements.

Our home was on Winsor Street near Clarks Cove. The sea sounds and brackish smells, the mourning of the foghorn, the reeling gulls, the hum of the mills all haunt my dreams. They make up the soundtrack of my childhood and the backdrop of my striving and struggling family.

At the top of our street was County Street, a main thoroughfare hosting corner drug stores, shoe stores, lunch counters, and soda fountains. At the New Bedford Bakery, you can still get Portuguese sweet bread, airy rolls called Portuguese pops, sugary fried dough called *malasadas,* and custard-filled pastry. Dad used to stop there for a loaf of bread and always asked the girl for "One Portagee, sliced." Further down was the Z Club, the barroom where my father hung out with his cronies: Jimmy-the-Crutch, Manny-Me-Nuts,

Quarter-of-a-Man, Joe Second Street, Odds & Ends, and Copper. I always thought the Z stood for the ending sound in Portuguese, pronounced by locals with heavy emphasis on the "eeezzz" at the finish.

One time, the guys got together and rented a bus to go see a Bruins hockey game at Boston Garden. When they got back, they were so drunk they couldn't recall who had won. Dad went into the Z Club to pee, asking the bartender for the key. And then the toilet paper. And the light bulb. Nothing was safe. Though how Dad, in his condition, negotiated screwing in the bulb to the socket is anyone's guess.

After, the crew tried to get Jimmy-the-Crutch home. Partially paralyzed in his legs, he was wobbly on the best of days, and more so after too many beers. He lived with his mother on the second floor of a house across from the club. Joe Second Street, Manny-Me-Nuts, and Odds & Ends tried to get him up the stairs, but only made matters worse. Unstable themselves, they kept dropping him. Dad stayed at the bottom of the stairs with Quarter-of-a-Man, who was too small to be of much help. They laughed as time after time Jimmy came sliding back down the stairs. His mother yelled epithets from the top. Finally, Jimmy took charge. He had strong arms and upper body strength, and despite still being somewhat drunk, he managed to pull himself up the stairs using the banister and dragging his legs. Dad thought it was hilarious. Of course, when he finally got home, my mother was not amused.

At the other end of our street was Crapo Street, where the Fosters lived: Connie, Freddy, Fremont, Little Nicky, and their widowed father. I liked the Fosters. Theirs was one of the few African American families living in the neighborhood. When I was growing up, it was mostly Portuguese, French Canadian, Lancashire English, and Irish.

The area further south, where the beaches are, was considered more upscale. New Bedford's south peninsula sticks out into the water like a stubby thumb with beaches on either side. While our neighborhood was jammed with three-story tenements, sitting on close-together lots, single-family homes lined the boulevard that encircled the most southern tip of the peninsula.

Where the beaches begin, a hurricane dike emerges at the shoreline from the north. Fashioned from giant granite boulders harvested from nearby towns, the dike rises more than 20 feet high and spreads 30 feet wide. When it was built, its primary purpose was to protect the mills, the fishing fleet, and the harbor, along with rows of tenement houses situated in their shadow.

The dike cut off the poor man's view of the ocean in the South End, and with that, the poetry of the inscrutable sea. The smell of tide and seaweed was and is still strong here. As an adult, when I came home for visits, I fancied I could see my father walking into the fog, round shoulders hunched, head bent as if into a strong wind, carrying a paper lunch sack. The foghorn in the harbor lighthouse moaned. The ocean water lapped lazily at the shoreline.

Across from East Beach is where Acushnet Park once stood. I don't remember it, but the adults always spoke fondly of this amusement park and pavilion—the clam bakes, big band music, and dancing every weekend. My parents courted here. My dad held my mother's hand for the first time on the Ferris wheel. The park was wiped out three separate times by hurricanes, and after Hurricane Carol in 1954, the owners gave up rebuilding it. (I was only three when Carol roared through, swelling the waters and flooding the South End. I distinctly remember watching from the window and seeing boats float down our street. The strangeness of it frightened me badly, and I retreated into the kitchen, where the hurricane lamps were lit. In an attempt to make Drew's glow-in-the-dark plastic skeleton glow brighter, I held it atop the lamp's flame. It melted, of course, and Drew was furious.)

At the top of the peninsula and along the shores of Clarks Cove, people launched motorboats or sailboats. The long stretch of Municipal Beach abuts this area.

Municipal Beach was our beach as kids, and almost every day in summer, we'd walk about 10 blocks from home to get there. Directly opposite the beach is Hazelwood Park. Many years ago, when he was a young man and not yet broken by the mills, my father played tennis here. Once, he was even named city champion.

The hurricane dike on this side ran behind the old Kilburn Spinning Mill, a complex of red-brick buildings housing several garment factories and warehouses. This was where I had my first job, at 16, and where my father retired from after being laid off from the Berkshire Hathaway.

---

Our clapboard, three-decker house was like much of the city's housing—New England-style tenements occupied by related families on all floors. In our case, my mother's sister Joan and her husband, Callan Murphy, lived on the first floor with their twin sons, my cousins Little Cal and Patrick, known to us as the Twins Downstairs. Granny and Grandpa lived on the third floor. The seven in my family—my parents, Fay and Jack Kilroy; my three brothers, Tom, Andrew, and Skippy; my sister, Molly; and I—were sandwiched in the middle floor.

A squat, gray metal gas burner called a Humphrey heater warmed our home. It sat in the main room, which was our kitchen, along with the white porcelain Magic Chef cook stove and cream-colored Frigidaire with its door rounded at the top. You had to listen for just the right clicking sound every time you shut the refrigerator because it didn't latch right. In the middle of the room stood our dining table and as many chairs as we could cram around it. This was the space you walked into when you entered from the back door, which is the door we always used. The refrigerator was on the right, and straight ahead was the glass cabinet that held special dishes, a fancy clock, and two ceramic dogs.

For much of my childhood, we were without hot running water and a phone, but we did have a small TV in the parlor. It sat on a television stand in the corner. To get to the parlor, you had to pass through the kitchen. We took company into this room, with its tall bay windows overlooking the street. A cedar chest sat in front of the windows in a little alcove, and this spot was where all family formal pictures were taken—proms, graduations, anniversaries, even Eagle Scout promotions. The room was also furnished with a couch and twin rocking chairs, one almost always occupied by Tom, who loved to rock while listening to records on the hi-fi that he and Molly had bought. At Christmastime, the cedar chest would be moved to make room for the tree.

A door from the parlor opened to an elaborate staircase that led downstairs, to the front door, which we almost never used. We always came in from the backstairs. The front staircase was used mostly for storage. It had a musty odor and many, many wall hooks filled with winter coats. Shelves lined one wall containing a huge assortment of canned goods. On top of the shelves were extra Army blankets and pillows. A short barrel held the potatoes, another the onions.

Our tenement had three bedrooms. I shared the middle bedroom with Molly, who was the eldest. In addition to a three-quarter bed, two bureaus, and a narrow closet, it had a two-shelf bookcase on the wall near the bottom of the bed. The shelves were stuffed with Louisa May Alcott novels and such classics as *Five Little Peppers, Skippy,* and many more, which I devoured by the light that bled in from the kitchen. There was that recurring hole in the wall next to my side of the bed, which I worked on every night, picking with my fingernail, like a prisoner plotting an escape: I was trying to break my way into my three brothers' room. Periodically, Dad would slather thick plaster of paris over the hole. Undeterred, I'd be right back at it the next night, sometimes even before the plaster had dried.

Off one side of the kitchen sat a small bathroom with toilet, sink, and clawfoot tub, and off the other side was tucked a very narrow pantry, which had cupboards and shelves and a long, shallow, porcelain-enameled, cast-iron sink. Here was where we kids had our baths when we were young, and where Ma did the washing with water warmed on the stove: the clothing of five children, the towels, sheets, and bedding, her dresses and aprons, Dad's blue-collar work shirts for the mill and his rugged chinos and all of our bathing suits. After she scrubbed them clean, she'd string them out on the clothesline from the pantry window, which overlooked the backyard. I spent countless hours daydreaming at this window, wondering about life beyond Winsor Street. From here, I could see the sun setting, with its reflection in the windows on the block. I could look out at the green steeples of the Portuguese church, the slate spire of the French church, and the gray steeple of our grand Irish church, St. James, on lower County Street. Truth be told, St. James was the "shanty Irish" church—St. Lawrence's, on upper County, was for the lace-curtain Irish, which we certainly were not.

This was our New Bedford.

This is how we lived it.

# 1. Overture

**Late 1950s**

"Molly-Tom-Andrew-Fiona-Skippy, all come in now for the Rosary!" Ma screeched out the second-floor bay window, her head bobbing like a mop. I was seven. It was May, the month of devotions to the Blessed Virgin Mary. When my mother called, we slunk away from our friends on the street and ran up the stairs to say the ritual springtime Rosary. We each rushed to our rooms to get our rosary beads. Mine were brown. I grabbed a pillow to kneel on and a chair to lean against in the parlor. Saying the Rosary could take quite a while.

All of us began reciting the Rosary, though little Skippy didn't know all the words to the Hail Mary prayer. I knew all the words by heart, but I got bored after the first decade and started to run the volume of my voice up and down to make it more interesting, until Ma shot me a look. We would be celebrating the coronation of Mary at church on Sunday. The girls would line up outside in white dresses, each holding a carnation, which we would put on Mary's altar inside the church, and the boys would dress in white shirts and ties. Birds would sing, too, and the sun would be warm upon our faces. We would sing, "Bring flowers of the fairest, bring flowers of the rarest..." as we processed into church. One girl would be chosen to place a crown of flowers on Mary's statue. The rest of us children would sit together in our pews and in our innocence. But amid the white blooming flowers, one child would sit in a solitary, uneasy darkness.

That summer, Ma had signed us up for swimming lessons at Municipal Beach. After Tom and Drew outgrew what our old instructor, Mrs. Trembley, could offer, it fell to Molly, poor thing, to shepherd me and Skippy there at eight in the morning. Skippy was not quite four—Ma believed in starting lessons at a young age. I thought Mrs. Trembley was ancient, with her sun-browned, wrinkled skin and sun-bleached hair, though she was probably only in her early 40s. Sometimes Molly's best friend, Bridie from Welcome Street, joined us. If Molly was a stick, and she was, Bridie was only marginally bigger. Every bone on Bridie stuck out. Still, her angular face lacked severity, and her eyes, an unusual shade of blue-gray, were deep-set and compassionate even at the tender age of 17. Her dark hair was short-cropped and mussed, like she had just gotten out of bed. I liked Bridie a lot. She was what Ma would call "a good egg."

Rain or shine, cold or warm, the lessons went on.

"What's a little rain? You're going to get wet anyway," Mrs. T would say to anyone who dared to protest.

Monday through Friday, we stood in a bedraggled line in shallow water, knock-kneed, in ill-fitting bathing suits and stupid swim caps. Skippy—so thin his ribs stuck out—wasn't too steady on his feet. Dad said he hadn't gotten his sea legs yet. Even small waves could knock him over, and Mrs. T spent most of her time plucking him out of the water and setting him upright again. She was determined to teach us how to float. She demonstrated by flipping Skippy over like a rag doll and laying him atop the water, with one hand under his bum and the other under his head. Though Skippy's eyes were huge with fright, he never said a word. I think he was too afraid to open his mouth lest the seawater get in. When the lesson was over, we stood shivering by the beach wall while Molly wrapped us in hooded terrycloth robes. When the Pony Boy truck came by selling Popsicles, ice cream, and frozen Zero bars, we immediately stopped shivering. We begged.

Eating my blue Popsicle, I'd stare over at the right side of the bathhouses, considered mostly the "colored" beach. No signs anywhere said white beach or colored beach. It was more an unspoken segregation. No one seemed to mind if anyone strayed from one side to the other, though, and people did at times, and without incident. Some days, I'd look at the different shades of glistening bodies on the beach and wonder at the mystery of it all.

One day, as we walked toward home in the heat, I was particularly cranky and miserable and tired. I had sand in my bathing suit and my PF Flyers sneakers chafed. I tried hard with my spindly legs to keep up with Molly's fast pace. Bridie carried Skippy. About a quarter of the way home, we stopped at Bridie's house. I was grateful for the rest but anxious to be back and into some soft, dry clothes.

Bridie gave me a large bag full of old toys from her family. Periodically, Bridie's mother went a little berserk and did a random purge of the house. She threw away anything lying about, regardless of its owner or worth. It fell to Bridie and her older sister to cull through the castoffs when their mother was distracted and save those items that had sentimental and practical value. In the bag she gave me was a matted, well-loved, brown teddy bear that smelled peculiar, and I fell in love with it. The bear looked lost and forlorn, and my tender heart went out to it. Holding it under one arm, I trolled through the other toys, piling up items that might interest Skippy. Bridie's 14-year-old brother, Robert, who had a limp as a consequence of polio, came into the room and said something teasing to me. Tender heart notwithstanding, I deliberately kicked him in the shin of his bad leg. I wanted to be home and out of my damp, chafing bathing suit. I wasn't in the mood. I was a brat.

Molly, for her part, was mortified. "*Fiona!*" she hissed at me, knowing I hated to be called by my full name, preferring the nickname, "Finn," that Dad had given me. I scowled. Molly apologized for my kick and pushed me toward the door. She was less than happy. Now she had to deal with a bratty little sister and a cranky baby brother while dragging a big bag of toys home. Bridie agreed to come along and help.

We ambled on to South Water Street, in those days a bustling area with two movie theaters, a shoe store, Woolworth's 5 & 10, and other optimistic shops. An A&P supermarket filled the street with the aroma of Eight O'Clock Coffee. In years to come, urban renewal would turn it into a ghost street full of rubble. But, for now, the street was busy and crowded. We cut through the 5 & 10 and emerged from the back door, opposite the City Mission on South First Street, much closer to home.

We walked up Division Street, crossed County, and went over to Winsor, the street where we lived, a short street of side-by-side tenements with a couple of cottages thrown into the mix. This day, as we made our way along, we could see Ma in the parlor window with her three-foot-long, glow-in-the-dark rosary beads. When we got to the backstairs, Skippy wiggled to get down so he could run to her.

"Hello, everybody," Aunt Joan said through her screen door as we passed the first floor. Molly and Bridie said hello back. I just hurried past.

"Where have you been all this time?" Ma said as we all trooped in.

"At my house," Bridie said cheerfully.

"I might have known," Ma said. "Get out of those wet bathing suits—"

"—and rinse them and put them on the line," Molly finished. "I know the drill, Ma."

I went to our bedroom where there was just enough space to walk between the bed and the bureaus. I wriggled out of my bathing suit, which kept sticking to my damp and sandy body. I kicked it out of the way and dried off with a towel before changing into clothes fresh from the clothesline, smelling of sun and wind. It was a great relief to feel comfortable and cozy. I brought my bathing suit and towel to Molly, who was helping Skippy get dressed. She rinsed the stuff in the pantry sink and hung it on the line to dry.

This time of year, I loved the smell and feel of clothes fresh off the line. In winter, though, it was a different story. Everything on the line would freeze and have to be dragged in by numb fingers snapping the legs of trousers in half to get them in through the small pantry window. Then they would be hung on the rack above the Humphrey heater to thaw and dry. If Dad was asleep in his cozy chair by the stove (or passed out, Ma would say), Molly would hang the clothes on him, too: socks draped over his arms, facecloths on his head, dish towels in his lap. When he'd finally get up to pee and go to bed, the clothes would drip off in a trail. While Dad muttered expletives, we would try to muffle our laughter.

Back in my room, I sat on my bed and wiggled my toes to get the sand out of them, then put my socks and sneakers back on, but not before dumping the sand from my shoes onto the floor. I went out to the kitchen and slumped in a chair.

"Want to play Parcheesi?" I asked Molly and Bridie.

Before either could answer, Ma said, "Molly isn't playing any game. She has to clean her closet."

"Ma," Molly protested, "I've been up since the crack of *dawn* to take these kids to their swimming lessons, and I'm *exhausted*."

"Don't be so dramatic," Ma said. "Clean your closet."

"I'll help," Bridie offered.

"Why does it have to be today?" Molly said.

"Because it's a pigsty in there. Clean, or you won't be going out later."

"Come on, let's just do it," Bridie said.

They went into the room and closed the door.

"Here, Finn, take this upstairs to Granny," Ma said. She handed me a plate with some unidentifiable meat on it. "Ask her if she wants that for her lunch."

I was glad to do the errand. I loved visiting my grandparents upstairs.

"Hallooo, Finn!" yelled Grandpa when I walked in. He sat in his big overstuffed chair by the TV. He was nearly deaf, and a stroke had left him paralyzed on his left side.

Granny had just finished feeding him. I went over and gave him a giant hug.

"Here, Gran. Ma sent this up for your lunch, if you want it."

"Sure, I'll have it," Granny said. She took it into the small pantry to make a sandwich.

The tenement had low eaves, dormer windows, and a skylight through which the chimney had fallen during the 1938 hurricane. Their kitchen setup was similar to our tenement below, though the pantry and bathroom were smaller, the latter able to hold only a very small sink and a toilet with its tank up near the ceiling. No tub or shower. Under one of the kitchen eaves was a tiny storage closet that adults had to stoop to get into, as Granny was doing now to retrieve a box of Fig Newtons to go with her sandwich.

"Are you hungry? Did you have your lunch yet?" she asked.

"No," I said.

"Come on, Finn, have a little bit of my sandwich. It's good for you."

To please her I took a small bite. It was bland.

"Want some of my tea?"

"Sure."

She poured tea into her saucer and gave it to me to drink. I loved drinking tea from a saucer.

"Here, now, have a cookie. Fatten up them skinny legs of yours."

Granny listened to my stories of the beach (though I omitted the part about kicking Robert). After lunch, I helped her put clean sheets on the couch in the parlor, where my brother Tom slept. Granny needed him to help her with Grandpa during the night.

The parlor and bedrooms also had steep eaves. I thought Granny's room was enormous. She had a trestle Singer sewing machine, and the bedroom furniture had been their wedding present in 1908. It was made of walnut, the grain showing through in beautiful warm patterns complemented by elaborate carvings. The patterns on the head and footboards were repeated on the vanity and chest of drawers. (The entire set would come to me as a gift on the occasion of my divorce many years later.)

Grandpa dozed in his chair. A big man, mostly bald, with a ready smile, he loved nothing more than a good joke. He wasn't very good at telling them, however. He would laugh so hard in the telling that he would never make it to the punch line.

One time he awoke from a nap frantic, looking everywhere around his chair.

"What's wrong?" Granny shouted.

"I can't find myself," he said, terrified.

It took a lot to snap him out of it.

Grandpa had already had his first stroke and retired from the mills by the time I began developing memories. He and his people had come to New Bedford from Ireland via Liverpool. As a young man, he used to visit Granny's brother Liam at their tenement for an evening of song. He had a good bass. Grandpa, Liam, and a couple of other fellows from the mill would practice singing quartets, and Grandpa's favorite song was "My Gal Sal." Granny was 16 and Grandpa 21 when they began stepping out together. Two years later, they married and moved into the tenement on Winsor, owned by Grandpa's father. My mother and her sister Joan were born here and never left.

When I was three and four, Grandpa would take me on long walks, often to Bum's Park or to Joseph Francis Playground by Clarks Cove. He told interesting stories but never spoke about their pre-American lives. Most of what I learned about that came from Granny and Ma. I always got the female side of our family's history. The men remained silent.

Grandpa's second stroke, when I was five, devastated him. Granny took care of his every need, with a little help from Tom. It was the end of our long walks together.

For her part, Granny was born in Dublin, Ireland, to peasant stock. She was a toddler when her family set sail for America. When the ship ran into foul weather during the crossing, the captain came down to steerage and asked if anyone had been born with a caul (part of the membrane found on a baby's head). Granny's mother said yes, her daughter had. Then, said the captain, "This ship will be safe." (Folklore has it that those born with the caul—a rare event then or now—carried with them extraordinary good luck and the gift of second sight. Families saved the cauls to ward off evil, and fishermen took them to sea to protect against drowning.) Granny's family had kept her caul, dried it out on a newspaper, and had it safely packed with their belongings. It still bore the imprint of *The Irish Times.*

Granny had waist-length gray hair that she braided every morning and folded around her head like a crown. Her eyes were pale blue, clear, merry. The skin on her face was soft, smooth, and free of wrinkles. She washed every morning at the pantry sink with cold water and Palmolive soap. She had a gentle smile and false teeth, which she used to pop out of her mouth and scare the hell out of us. Short and just this side of plump, she loved dancing to Lawrence Welk on Saturday nights. And how she loved flowers! Put simply, Granny was a strong woman with a happy outlook. But you dared not mess with her garden. It was her pride and joy, a small patch set aside in the backyard where she grew an enormous variety of vegetables and flowers.

"Granny, do you want me to pick the raspberries for you?" I asked.

"You're too late, love. I picked them early this morning. Would you like some?"

She opened the door of the ancient refrigerator and withdrew a small bowl. I took only two, though I loved them, because I knew she loved them, too. They nearly melted in my mouth, and juice ran down my chin. Granny laughed at me and wiped my face with a tissue. Thank God, she didn't spit on it.

"I love you, Gran."

"I love you, too."

"Thanks for the goodies."

"You're welcome... Finn?"

"Yes, Gran?"

"Is everything okay with you?"

I felt myself turn scarlet.

"Sure, Gran. Why?"

"Just wondering." She looked at me, but I could not hold her gaze.

"See ya," I said and went downstairs, bypassing Grandpa, who had fallen asleep.

Halfway down the stairs I paused at the window to look at the backyard and collect myself. My heart was beating hard, my face still warm. I tried to focus on Granny's garden, in full bloom with plants laden with string beans and tomatoes. Bright green lettuce added dashes of startling color. And up against the fence, so many lovely flowers in splashes of red, purple, white, and yellow. What could Granny have seen? In the dirt part of the yard, I noticed the area where Drew, the Twins Downstairs, and I had made roads with the push broom for our Matchbox cars. There were complicated intersections, even an overpass made of sticks and pieces of wood. Little wooden houses from our Monopoly game lined the streets.

Could Granny see guilt imprinted on my face? Was it in the way I talked? Walked? I would need to be careful around her. No one else seemed to notice—not as far as I knew.

When I thought I had it together, I went the rest of the way downstairs and popped into my tenement.

"Want your lunch?" Ma asked.

"No, thanks. I ate with Granny," I said. Then, hearing footsteps, I retreated to my bedroom. I heard the door open, and Aunt Joan said hello to my mother. She came up every day after meals.

"Get out of here," Molly said pleasantly when I walked in.

She was on our bed writing in her diary. Her baby-fine hair was all askew. Heaps of clothes covered our bed, and shoes littered the floor. Another shoe came sailing out of the closet. I could barely see Bridie's rump as she rummaged.

Molly was what Ma called "petite." She took a size two or something, and I always felt chunky around her. But looking at her shoes, it made me feel better that she had big feet.

"Want to play Parcheesi now?" I asked.

"No. I'm busy."

"You're just writing."

"No, I'm not. I'm cleaning my closet."

"Who's cleaning the closet?" came a voice muffled by clothes.

"Just one game?"

"You're going to pester me, aren't you?"

I nodded. "Why are your feet so big?"

"I do not have big feet," Molly said, wiggling her toes.

"I have cute little feet," I observed.

Molly rolled her eyes.

"Set up the board. I'll be right out."

"Bridie, want to play?"

"Sure, Pip. I don't want to get stuck in this closet."

Happily, I dashed through the kitchen.

"Hi, Aunt Joan."

"Hullo, Finn, what's the rush?"

"Molly's playing Parcheesi with me. And Bridie," I said over my shoulder as I dragged a kitchen chair into the pantry. Climbing up onto the sink, I reached the upper shelf where the games were kept. Parcheesi was right on top. I brought the game to the kitchen table and began setting up.

"Molly should be cleaning her closet," Ma said.

"It's ready," I called out.

"How was swimming this morning?" Aunt Joan asked.

"Okay. Mrs. Trembley's a terrent."

"A what?"

"A terrent. She yells all the time."

"Tyrant," Ma said.

"That's what I said. Molly, you coming?"

Molly came out of the room and slipped into a chair. Bridie followed.

"Coffee. I need coffee," Molly said.

"I'll get it," I said eagerly.

"Ma, I can't stand getting up at the crack of dawn for these swimming lessons. I'm tired all day."

"Go to bed earlier, then," Ma said.

Molly shot her a look but said nothing.

"Besides," Ma said, "it's only for a few more weeks."

I poured the cold coffee, adding sugar and evaporated milk, and handed Molly her mug. Skippy wandered in from the parlor, where he'd been playing happily, stacking wooden alphabet blocks on top of the set of Funk & Wagnalls encyclopedias that he'd emptied from the bookcase.

"Can I play?" Skippy asked.

"No, you're too little," I said.

"I want to play," he said.

"You can play when you're older."

Ma could see a tantrum coming.

"Come on, Skippy. I'll read you a story," she said. He ran to the parlor bookcase and returned with an ancient-looking, fat book.

"Which story?" Ma said.

"'Cruel Paul,'" Skippy said and snuggled in the chair close to Ma's ample bosom.

"Oh my God, not that one," Molly said. "It's a wonder it doesn't give little Oedipus nightmares."

Aunt Joan looked over my mother's shoulder. "Which one is that?" Aunt Joan asked.

"Who's Eddy Puss?" I wanted to know.

"It's the one where this kid named Paul is cruel to animals, pulls off the wings of flies, crushes ants, does all sorts of horrible things, and one day the animals revolt and attack him. They pluck out his eyes and tongue and hair and everything," Molly said. "It's disgusting, and it's illustrated! The whole book's full of stories like that."

"That's awful," Aunt Joan said, but she was laughing. "I'm going back to the salt mines. Dishes."

"Who's Eddy Puss?" I asked again.

"Me too," Ma said. "I've already heated the water four times, and I can't seem to get to them."

"Read," Skippy said.

"Who's Eddy—"

"Play," Molly said.

I rolled the dice, deciding to ask again later.

"'Once upon a time, there was a boy by the name of Cruel Paul,'" Ma began.

Aunt Joan left. She'd be back. She was in and out of our tenement a half-dozen times a day.

Aunt Joan was slender and about the same height as her husband, Callan ("God made 'em, God matched 'em," Granny said). She had an oval face and eyes I had trouble reading. Her dark hair was streaked with gray. Callan was short and powerfully built, with pale skin and a military crew cut. His eyes were brown and cold. Their identical twins were 12, my brother Drew's age. Where Pat was quiet and thoughtful and rather sweet, Little Cal was a hellion. Each twin had black hair in a crew cut, which their father gave them, brown eyes, and lithe bodies.

I was afraid of my aunt. She took it upon herself to discipline us as if we were her own children, which I resented mightily. She would come upstairs every morning with her coffee to visit with Ma. They would exchange aches and pains and whatever bad news was going around (Dad used to mutter that they sounded like the soap opera *As the World Turns*). If she came up at night, and I was in bed trying to sing myself to sleep, she came to my door and yelled, "Stop all that noise in there! Turn your face to the wall and go to sleep!" Then she'd close my door tight, which I hated, for it left me in total darkness. I have often wondered why Ma let her interfere like that.

If Aunt Joan scared me, her husband terrified me. He lost his scattershot temper easily and beat his kids, and I was always afraid he'd do the same to us. In fact, he was used as the household threat: "Stop [whatever we were doing] or I'll call Uncle Callan!" He was the bogeyman. He'd served in the Army and was stationed in France during World War II. Now he had a civil service job, working at city hall, which paid pretty well compared to blue-collar mill jobs. He also took care of most of the repairs needing to be done around the house—painting, shingling, seeding the "lawn," pouring cement, building a fence, or a garbage coop. He was multi-talented in these areas, where Dad was simply not interested in being the handyman. Maybe he got too much of that at work. At home, Dad's toolbox consisted of a hammer, a couple of rusted screwdrivers, several bent nails, some random wrenches, and umpteen unidentifiable broken and abandoned things. Uncle Callan had an entire workshop in the cellar, including a workbench with a vise attached, saws, power tools, all sorts of equipment Dad didn't want anything to do with in his off-work hours. So even if Uncle Callan was the family bogeyman, having him around had some benefits. For me, though, he was more than just the threat of a bogeyman. He was a predator. And for most of my childhood, I was his prey.

# 2. Generations

My father was a thin man with sinewy muscles and thick hair that was a dark red. His eyes were green, and he had a devilish cleft in his chin. He worked the overtime 6 a.m. to 5 p.m. shift at the Berkshire Hathaway. He tended and fixed looms all day, keeping them running smoothly, allowing the weavers to turn out cloth unhindered. Loomfixers were at the very top of skilled workers in a textile mill. Some oversaw hundreds of looms at once, ensuring quality and productivity in the manufacture of fine cloth. It was all tedious work, and the bosses were not always kind. They shouted, they swore... and firing was always their threat. Dad had to submit to the constant pressure to be on top of the looms, making sure they did not snag. And, after being on his feet for 11 hours, he had to walk about three-quarters of a mile home, regardless of the weather.

Rising at 5 a.m., he'd put the coffee on to perk, start the fire in the Humphrey if it was winter, and get dressed in the pre-dawn darkness. Then he'd sit with his mug of fresh coffee, enjoying the quiet, peaceful time before his day at the mill began. Or did he worry about the bosses being on his back all day? Did he face that walk to work with dread? He was a humble man, and I've often wondered if he ever felt appreciated, or if he felt like the lonely breadwinner on the outskirts of his family's life, unthought of as we slept in our beds. What strength did it take for him to unwrap his swollen hands from around his mug, leave that chair, rinse his cup, and grab the paper lunch sack with his name penciled on it from the refrigerator? Sometimes, when I was a young child, something would wake me, and I would venture out into the kitchen, blind with night, and crawl into Dad's lap while he had his coffee. He would hold me for a while, then carry me into his room and lay me down in the bed next to my mother.

"I'm leaving now," he would whisper.

And Ma would respond, "Be careful, Jack. Come right home after work." He rarely did.

What were his last thoughts as he pulled the door closed, passed down the stairs, and went out into whatever the weather? Did he long to stay home with us, just once?

This was his routine his entire working life. As poet Robert Hayden asked, what did we know of love's lonely offices? We only knew that when we got up from under our handmade quilts shivering, we could huddle in front of the Humphrey to get warm, our bare feet cold on the linoleum floor, and the tenement smelling deliciously of coffee. Did we even think of him as we planned our day, walking in heavy rain or blowing snow, or sub-zero temperatures, while we stayed sheltered, drinking the coffee he had made?

After work, Dad always stopped in at the Z Club for a couple of five-cent beers. He told of times when there were collections taken up in the club for someone's misfortune, and all he was able to contribute was a quarter—part of his meager spending money—and it embarrassed him deeply that he could not give more. After drinking his beers, he would make his way down the street, the air heavy with sea-smell from the cove, and Ma watching from the parlor window with her infamous, illuminated rosary beads dangling from her hands. By this time, it would be 6 o'clock. We'd be delighted to see him, as he almost always had gumballs or Chiclets in his pocket for us.

Just as often, there would be the inevitable fight between my parents over his going to the Z Club. Dad would eat his supper (or not), then collapse into the easy chair between the Humphrey and his beloved radio, set to a station that played only big band music. Ma would look at him scornfully. Drunk again was the assumption, and it's what we grew up thinking. Yet with the perspective of hindsight, I think the poor man was dead on his arthritic feet. He was, undeniably, a heavy drinker. But he had also worked an 11-hour shift, walked all the way home, and he had stopped for a couple of beers. Who wouldn't be exhausted?

And what did we know of love's lonely offices?

"Look at him," Ma said, disdain dripping from her voice. "His false tooth has fallen down."

*Just this once,* I thought, *let's give him the benefit of the doubt and speak softly in his presence.*

Yes, my sympathies were often with him, and I often felt torn between both parents. Dad never missed a day of work in his life, except once, and even that wasn't a day but a shorter shift: One October day, when I was a little older, I came home from school stunned to find him there, sitting in the parlor with the TV on. It was a gorgeous, mild sunny afternoon and quiet in the neighborhood, as the grammar schools hadn't let out yet. And there was my father. I asked my mother, was he sick?

"No," she said with a laugh. "It's the World Series. He's watching the Red Sox." That was the only day in my life I can recall my father being home in the afternoon on a workday.

---

I was four, and Dad let me sit on his lap at the kitchen table while he helped me learn to color. I had picked out a green crayon—well, the stub of a green crayon, as there was never a whole one, and most had streaks of other colors in them. Dad had just returned from visiting hours at the hospital, where Ma had gone to get my new brother. He was a late baby, maybe a surprise for my parents, who were in their 40s. I wanted to know why Ma wasn't here. Why she couldn't just pick him up and bring him home was beyond me. Instead, she had to stay there almost a whole week with him.

The reason this memory is so vivid wasn't the anticipation of a new brother. Rather, it was the only time that I recall coloring with my father. As a child, I loved the softness and fresh smell of his white tee shirt, and that day I wanted desperately to impress him with my skill. His hand over mine was gentle, bony, and warm. It was November, and the raw wind blew trash and debris down the dark street. It whistled under the ill-fitting door and rattled the windows on their ropes. But when I sat with my father like this, it calmed me, and I didn't miss my mother so much.

The apple we were coloring had a stem with small leaves. I wanted it all green, that being my favorite color.

But my brother Drew sidled over and said, "Hah. Whoever heard of a green apple? Are you color-blind or what?"

"Don't be so fresh, young man, or so quick to judge," Granny said. She had been minding us while Dad was at work or the hospital. "And for your information, there are such things as green apples."

"Humph," Drew said and went back to whatever he was doing.

Dad seemed agreeable to the green, and he guided my clumsy hand around the fruit, tracing it hard, then softly filling it in. I thought it odd that Dad's tee shirt didn't smell like the Z Club this night. His hand shook a little as he guided me. His other hand was around my waist, holding me close against his chest. Now he was telling Granny that the new baby had red fuzz for hair, "just like a peach," and big round eyes, and that they put casts on his legs today.

"When is Mama coming home?" I wanted to know.

"In a couple of days, Peanut."

"And she'll bring the baby home?"

"Yes. And you'll have to be very gentle with him. Never touch the soft spot on his head."

My eyes wandered to the bedroom where the crib had been set up against the wall by the door, opposite Ma and Dad's bed.

"And this baby gets to sleep in your room?"

"Yes."

I felt the top of my head.

"Why is his head soft?"

"Because it hasn't finished growing yet."

"You mean his head's going to get bigger?"

"Not quite. All the bones aren't together yet."

I thought about that. It made no sense. If the bones weren't together, would there be a peephole into his head? Would things fall out? I was getting the distinct impression of a soft, overripe peach.

"What are casts?"

"They're like hard bandages."

"On his undone head?"

"No. On his legs. They were a little crooked, so the doctor has to straighten them."

This baby was sounding more and more weird. And I wasn't crazy about the sleeping arrangements. Would there be room for me when I had my nightmares?

"Will you lie down with me sometimes?"

"Yes, Peanut."

Satisfied with that answer, I returned to my green apple. One more thing.

"Does he look like a baby doll?" (I had overheard Molly telling her friend Bridie that he did.)

Dad smiled. "Yes, yes, he does."

Well, I had never seen a doll with an undone head and bandages on its legs. Still, I could dress him up in my dolly clothes. This could be interesting.

"Does he have a name?"

"We're thinking about Paul. Paul Christopher."

Christopher was nice, but I didn't like Paul. There was a boy in my kindergarten class named Paul, and he was always yanking on my braids.

"So you've got to be very careful with him, okay?"

"Because he has casts and a soft head."

"Yes."

"And will he love me?"

"I'm sure he will."

"And will you love him?" Granny asked.

I thought about that. A baby doll with fuzzy peach skin!

"Probably."

"Well, I certainly hope so—you're his big sister," Granny said.

I will always remember that day of coloring, the stub of a green crayon, and my father's loving hand over mine, guiding me to stay within the lines.

When Ma finally returned from the hospital with baby Paul, she laid him right down in his crib, as he was fast asleep. I went over and stared at him through the bars. It was like looking at some exotic zoo animal. I reached through the bars and touched his cast. Shocked by how hard it was, I yanked my hand back.

Within a couple of weeks, Molly had nicknamed him Skippy because, she said, whenever he moved his legs it sounded like he was skipping along. The name stuck, and I thought it fit. We never called him Paul. He didn't cry very much, but when he did, he got all bright red, and his legs skipped like crazy. I'd watch the top of his head when he got excited just to make sure the entire inside contents didn't erupt right out of that hole, like a volcano. I liked him.

---

When Dad dressed up proper, he looked like quite the handsome gentleman. He wore clothes well, especially a suit and tie. Growing up, his family lived on Emery Street in the South End, directly up from the beach, and his father traveled back and forth to New York as a clothes buyer before dying at 36, struck down by the influenza epidemic in 1918. My grandfather left behind a fragile wife and seven children, ages two to eleven.

My dad was six at the time. His sister Mimi was even younger, just a toddler, and suffered from ill health. She was sent to stay in Canada with their grandfather, who was a doctor, but she didn't have the strength to survive and died before her third birthday. That left one sister and five boys.

The effect of my grandfather's death on their lives was swift and traumatic. Dad's mother had a breakdown. Somehow, the family managed to stay together, but their financial circumstances were severely reduced. Dad's had been a family of teachers, doctors, artists, and other professionals. Who knows what my father might have become had his father lived. As it was, as soon as they were physically able, the kids all went to work in the mills.

A sickly child, Dad never finished grammar school. His mother, Margaret, never pushed the issue. She enjoyed having her young son at home, helping her to cope with his younger brother and honing his wit as he tried to make his mother laugh. Although she recovered from her breakdown, she never really got over her husband's death. She was a beautiful woman, thin, with classic cheekbones and a broad smile, kind blue eyes, and curly, deep red hair. As an old woman, she was sent to live at Sacred Heart Nursing Home. We would go to visit her on alternate Sundays, and one Sunday a month, she came to our house for dinner. She never said much, and when she did speak, it was in quiet tones.

I remember her sitting there at the table, just watching the controlled chaos of our rough-and-tumble family, smiling. She died when I was young—perhaps 10 or 11—and I have always regretted that I did not know her better. Her influence on my father must have been strong, for despite his relative poverty and dismal work at the mills, his genteel breeding came through when he wasn't drinking. He was extremely witty in a dry, quiet, shy way. People loved to sit next to him at family gatherings just to listen to his running commentary. He'd say a few soft words, and anyone who heard him would break up in laughter.

There was one story he loved to tell, about the time he and his brother Squint went looking for a Christmas tree. Well lit, they went to an old woman's house on Reed Road in Dartmouth—Mrs. Whittle owned several acres of pine trees—and asked if they could fell a tree for his baby's first Christmas. Mrs. Whittle agreed, and off they went, trudging through deep snow, warmed by their own antifreeze, axe in hand. They cut down one tree, but on inspection they noticed a bare spot, so they stuck it back upright into the snow and went on to the next one. Well, that one wasn't quite right either. Neither was the next, or the next, or the next. They lost track of how many trees they had felled before finding the perfect one. Telling the story, Dad would laugh until the tears ran down his face and he had to take out his big white handkerchief to mop his cheeks. All he could think about was the spring thaw and Mrs. Whittle looking out her window, watching as her trees toppled over, one by one.

Ma and Dad met in the Berkshire Hathaway when she was 15 and he 16. They didn't begin courting until four years later. Ma was an unhappy cloth inspector. She'd been forced to quit her freshman year of high school to work, as it was the Depression. Ma had loved school. She still loved reading, reciting poetry, writing, and just about everything else except math. It broke her heart, if not her spirit, to leave, and now here she was, standing at her station, scanning fabric for flaws and imperfections as the cloth passed from one reel to another. The room was dingy, the machines never stopped clack-clacking, and, in the background, was the constant shouting of Sully, the shift boss.

With mid-length wavy brown hair, clear blue eyes hinting at mischief, and a warm smile, Ma was a looker.

One day she came to work and found by her station a small, neatly wrapped piece of fudge. Mysterious sweetness. Another appeared the next day, and the day after that, a small packet of cookies. (Did I mention that Dad's mother was an excellent cook?) One day my mother came in early and caught my shy father in the act. Jack "Red" Kilroy won her heart then and there. His gifts were certainly day-brighteners amid the chaos and noise of the mill. The cookies clinched it. She thought he was handsome, and his gentle shyness had particular appeal. After that, Red began walking Fay home.

When she and Dad were courting, one of their favorite destinations was the Lincoln Park pavilion in Dartmouth. They'd hop the trolley on the weekends to hear one of Dad's beloved big bands play. In the summer, they'd go to "the cottage" every Sunday after Mass.

Somewhere along the line, my grandmother's sister Emma and her husband, Duncan, had acquired a summer cottage on Lake Noquochoke in North Dartmouth, a short ride from Lincoln Park. The lake was small, as was the cottage. The largest room in the house was the kitchen, which overlooked one side of the lake. There was also a small living room, and upstairs were two tiny bedrooms, which were always unbearably stuffy and usually off-limits to my peers and me. There was also a double-seated outhouse, a pier, a rowboat for fishing, a tree swing, and a swimming beach just across the road. Best of all, in my view, was the screened porch, which ran the length of the house.

We have sepia and faded black-and-white photographs of my parents there from the time of their courtship: my mother, with her glowing waves and broad smile, and Dad, dressed sharply in a dark suit jacket and white flannels, smiling shyly at the camera. There they are again in the rowboat. And there, he is pushing her on the swing.

And there are pictures of us, too.

Dad loved to take us out in the rowboat. He'd tell us to be really quiet and listen. He loved the peace and quiet of the lake when the only sounds would be the oars creaking, dipping, rising, dripping, and dipping once again. I remember the muscles of his sinewy arms straining as he pulled, his hair flopped over one eye, his skin reddening and freckled. Ma always got this weird, proud look when Dad took us out, and she'd run for the camera and snap a shot from shore.

It was in the cottage, on the porch and in its rooms, where the generations mingled. As an adult, when I read the John Montague poem, "Like Dolmens Round My Childhood, the Old People," it took me straight to the family cottage. These folks were my dolmens, my old people, the aunts and uncles of my grandparents' generation. They were our family's first Americans, born before the century to settle in New Bedford's South End and eke out a hardscrabble subsistence from the unforgiving textile mills.

While they had little education, they were nevertheless well schooled in America's ethic: Hard work will be rewarded. If they were disappointed by the size or nature of that reward, they seldom spoke of it. Instead they made the best of what they had and formed a tight, protective circle into which later generations would be born.

When my siblings, my cousins, and I were children, the old people were as much a part of our lives as our parents. They lived either in the same tenement house or just around the block, and we all attended the same parochial schools and the same Gothic church on lower County street. The old people were always involved in church things, from making bandages in the St. James guild to running penny sales. Our parents did the same, and so, in time, did many of us.

When I think of the old people, I think of the magic of Sundays in our summers.

The old people had been spending Sundays and brief holidays at the cottage since long before the arrival of my generation, and it continued to be the focus of family outings throughout my childhood and young adulthood. The daylight hours were spent fishing for hornpout, catching frogs and turtles, swimming, playing horseshoes, and any number of variations of tag until our spindly limbs were brown and our faces masks of freckles. When the sun began to dip behind the trees, we'd be blanketed in oversized sweatshirts and allowed to stay out until the mosquitoes drove us in.

It was then that we'd gather on the screened porch with our parents and the old people, sitting on laps or on the floor by black-shoed feet, while the last glow of sunset faded from the lake and our faces grew indistinct in the dark. And Granny or Aunt Emma would say, "Let's have a song," and it would begin, this singing that went on into the night, while the youngest ones dozed and the older children learned how to harmonize with the adults and even the teenagers felt a separate peace. Show tunes and vaudeville skits and songs, so many songs, created the summer soundtrack to my childhood.

Everyone would ask for a favorite tune. Granny always requested "Innisfree," and always, because it had been her mother's song, began to cry as we sang:

*I've met some folks who say that I'm a dreamer*
*And I've no doubt there's truth in what they say,*
*But sure a body's bound to be a dreamer,*
*When all the things he loves are far away.*
*And precious things are dreams unto an exile.*
*They take him o'er the land across the sea*
*Especially when it happens he's an exile,*
*From that dear lovely Isle of Innisfree.*

Uncle Duncan was partial to "Roses of Picardy," while Aunt Emma's favorite song was "The Rose of Tralee," which she'd sing standing up with her hands clasped in front of her like a schoolgirl:

*She was lovely and fair as the rose of the summer,*
*Yet 'twas not her beauty alone that won me;*
*Oh no, 'twas the truth in her eyes ever dawning,*
*That made me love Mary, the Rose of Tralee.*

Toward the end of the night, the songs would get slower, softening with the dark, until finally someone would say, "Well, time to get the kids home." Then we would sing "Now Is the Hour." The adults would round up the children, who had scattered outside under a zillion stars, with the frogs croaking and crickets skreeking. Parents would carry the sleepers, guide the sleepy out to the cars, and collect damp towels and bathing suits, food and bottles, and cartons of spare clothes. We'd tumble in the big old Plymouth, sometimes with a token protest over who got the window seats, but mostly we were content. In the company of the old people we were always safe. And we always made our best harmony on the last note, holding it, unwilling to let it go.

Ma quit the mill after she married and became pregnant with Molly. As each child came along, the number of storybooks increased as well. Ma loved telling stories and reading to us. She grew to be pleasingly plump with a ready lap for any child in need of one. I felt sorry for friends whose mothers were thin. They didn't seem warm or comforting or mother-like. Ma controlled the finances and kept the house running in some semblance of order. She was strong, and she needed to be, with little income, five kids, and a husband who tended to drink.

Together the three women—Granny, Ma, and Aunt Joan—ran the house; they took care of the money, paid the bills, and generally made most of the decisions. My quiet father didn't stand a chance. It was the women who did most of the household chores and dealt with the children, unless Uncle Callan was in one of his rages.

I must add on my father's behalf, though, that he helped with all the Saturday work, such as vacuuming and giving us baths. With no hot water in our tenement, Dad had to heat pot after pot on the Magic Chef stove, lug them into the bathroom, and pour each one into the enormous claw-footed tub for all of our baths. The first couple of bathers had the least amount of water, but it was the cleanest. By the time the last one's turn came, there was a lot of water, but it was decidedly murky. Sometimes Skippy and I had our baths in the shallow pantry sink.

But it was, without question, a matriarchal society. These were stay-at-home women, for the most part (Granny had gone to work at the Cornell Dubilier factory after Grandpa's stroke left him disabled), and it was they who read to us, who handed down the family lore, who faced countless adversities with strength and courage. Granny had lost her 14-year-old daughter and her 21-year-old brother within two weeks of each other to appendicitis and peritonitis respectively. Aunt Joan had endured four stillborn babies. Ma had lost her education—yes, a very real tragedy to her—and married an alcoholic. Still, they smiled together and laughed outright; they sang the old songs; they taught us folktales and poems by heart, and countless days ended with lullabies. They did not take vacations, unless you counted the annual week-long trip to the cottage. They made us feel we were the center of their universe.

This is not to say they never made mistakes or miscalculations (they did), or that the household was a peaceful haven (it wasn't), or that, as we grew older, we didn't chafe under their hovering (we did). It was far from an ideal situation. But what we lacked in terms of privacy or material goods, and what we suffered in terms of tension, in-fighting, and the occasional fractured identity, was balanced by unconditional love and the lessons of perseverance.

But were we poor? I didn't think so. We never went hungry, and if our suppers occasionally consisted of Cream of Wheat, we considered it a treat. Other get-by meals were either oatmeal or bread broken up in warm milk and sprinkled with sugar. I remember, though, inviting a friend over for supper, and she said she couldn't come because we were poor and couldn't afford to feed another mouth. This didn't hurt so much—there was no malice in what she said—but it set me to wondering. As for her family, I thought they were rich. They owned a large motorboat and drove a convertible. But more important to me was that, when I was at her house after school, she served up Coke with ice and potato chips—and it wasn't even a party! I decided that only rich people had ice in their drinks. We never had ice. There was no room in the freezer for something as frivolous as ice cube trays, the freezer being packed with whatever foods were on sale that week. Still, I knew families who didn't have enough to eat, who had no car, and who had to share a bathroom in the tenement hall with everyone else on the floor. That was poor. As for us, if nothing else, we were survivors.

# 3. Origins of Shame

*It was nothing personal, you understand,*
*this moment of her imperfect blooming,*
*immense indifference scratching at the window pane*
*through dust-filtered light in musty cellars*
*against the whitewashed walls.*
*Trees fall.*
*Waves crash.*
*Children hide in the hollows*
*eating stolen apples poisoned with their shame.*

At 7 a.m., Ma would come to get us up for school. We would all line up in front of the stove to get warm. But not this morning—not for me, anyway. I had a raging case of chicken pox and would be staying home. I stayed in my bed listening to the usual morning routine: Ma trying to force Molly to eat something for breakfast, Tom and Drew fighting over the one bathroom, Skippy into everything. Somehow, they all managed to get out on time, except for Skippy, who was only two. I snuggled back under the covers until Ma came in with the thermometer. If the mercury showed a fever—as it did this morning, just over 101—she would return with orange baby aspirin and a bowl of lumpy Cream of Wheat with brown sugar sprinkled on top.

My eyes burned, and my body ached and itched. I was miserable. Though sweat soaked my pajamas, I couldn't get warm enough. The aspirin worked like a miracle, however, at least on my fever and aches, and after everyone had left for school, I asked to be moved to the couch in the parlor. I could watch morning cartoons and *Romper Room* on TV, while Ma went around cleaning up the breakfast things and looked after Skippy before he went down for his morning nap. Then Ma poured herself another cup of coffee from the pot Dad had made. She brought it into the parlor and sat next to me on the couch.

"How are you feeling now, Fiona?" she asked, putting her cool hand on my forehead.

"Better."

"How are the itches?"

"Not too bad."

She cupped the side of my face with her free hand. "You poor kid," she said, her voice full of sympathy. "Do you want me to read to you?"

*I'd love it.* "Sure," I said.

But then, right on cue, Aunt Joan came upstairs with her coffee, and the two women moved to the kitchen and sat down for a chat. It went like this:

"How's Finn this morning?"

"Her fever's already up, and it usually goes higher in the afternoon. If it doesn't break soon, I might have to call Dr. Schwartz. I had a lousy night last night. Couldn't get to sleep till almost four—

"My back is really killing me this morning—"

"—and I haven't had a bowel movement in two days—"

"And I've got this terrible ache in my knee—"

"And there's so much to do. Make out a grocery list—"

"I have laundry all piled up—"

"And pork chops are on sale this week—"

"I don't know how I'll get it all done before Cal comes home—"

"—at First National, but with Finn sick, I don't know when I'll be able to get there."

"The kids leave sock balls everywhere. How much?"

"—yeah, I have laundry, too. At least you have a washing machine and hot water." (A short pause while they sip their coffee.) "Eighty-nine cents."

"That's a good buy. Cal's going to put up the new fence this weekend. He works so hard all week, then he has to do these things around the house—"

Maybe it wasn't a jab at Dad, but Ma defended him anyway.

"Jack works hard, too, but he isn't any good at carpentry. You know that."

"Cal might take me out to dinner Saturday night."

"Anything special?"

"No, he just wants to go out."

It was Ma's turn to complain about Dad.

"Jack never wants to go anywhere. Besides, I can't count on him to be sober."

"I'm glad Callan doesn't drink like that. He's too busy, working all day, working around the house at night. The church wants him to collect on Sunday."

"Well, Jack works 11-hour shifts. They haven't asked him to collect yet, thank God."

"Where are the pork chops on sale?"

"First National."

"Well, better get back to the salt mines. I hope Finn feels better. Thank God my boys are healthy."

Then Aunt Joan went downstairs, and Ma heated the water to do the dishes.

There's something magical about being home sick on a school day. The neighborhood is dead quiet, and the sun streams in through the tall parlor windows, warming the whole room and shining on the Sacred Heart of Jesus nailed to the wall above the couch. It gave me the creeps, like He was looking at me all the time—and not liking what He saw. Still, the room felt peaceful, serene. Even the neighborhood dogs were quiet. It was an afternoon for cats.

At noon, the peace was shattered by a frenzy of activity when Tom and Drew came home from school for lunch. They sat with me for a little while, and we watched *Big Brother Bob Emery*, but they had to leave before a cartoon came on. They were envious.

After they left, it got all quiet again except for Skippy lurching about and getting into everything. There was nothing on TV in the afternoon but soap operas. Ma gave Skippy his lunch, then let him play in the playpen while she heated the water for the lunch dishes. She put them in the sink to soak and came to check on me. Almost immediately, Skippy began making noises to escape from his playpen. He didn't like it when Ma was out of sight.

As for me, I had no appetite for lunch. I was feeling lousy again. Ma slipped the thermometer in my mouth. Skippy started wailing. As predicted, my fever was spiking at 103.

"And how's my little Fiona?" Granny said, coming in.

"Not too good, Gran."

"Her fever's up again," Ma said, showing Granny the thermometer. "I wonder if I should call Dr. Schwartz."

"If it would give you peace of mind, go ahead. I'll stay with the kids."

Ma went downstairs to use Aunt Joan's phone. Granny went out to soothe Skippy. I could hear her talking to him in low tones, and when he stopped wailing, she sang to him "Toora Loora Loora," the Irish lullaby that he loved.

Ma wasn't gone long.

"He says to give it one more day, that chicken pox can go on a while. He said he'd stop by tomorrow if her fever hasn't broken."

"I trust him," Granny said. "He's a good man."

Skippy's wails went up a notch.

"Here," Granny said, "has Fiona had her aspirin yet?"

"Not yet. She's due now."

Granny did the things she did with Skippy when he was cranky. First, she took him out of his cage, cooing all the while, then continued to sing lullabies.

Meanwhile, Ma came in with what I called the sick supplies: aspirin, ginger ale, calamine lotion, alcohol, towel, and facecloth. She washed me and rubbed me down gently with the alcohol, limb by limb. It gave me serious chills. Then she put the calamine on my pox. I was shivering all over, but Ma wrapped me tight in the warm blankets, and it felt soothing. Then she gave me the aspirin, crushed up in ginger ale. She kissed the top of my head.

"How does that feel?" she asked me.

"Wonderful," I said.

She shook her head, sighing and smiling. "Do you have to get every bug that's going around? You've had mumps, measles—"

"Molly calls me 'The Germer.'"

Ma laughed. "She's right."

Granny came in. "Skippy fell asleep, so I put him in his crib. You should nap, too, while he's sleeping."

I started to feel sleepy, too, as the aspirin began working its miracle.

"Do you want your story now?" Ma asked me.

"I don't think so, Ma. I'm really tired."

"Well, you call me if you need anything, all right?"

"Okay, Ma."

"Feel better," Granny said, and squeezed my hand three times. I grinned and squeezed back. Granny had once told me that three squeezes meant "I love you."

The rest of the afternoon went by in a quiet haze: the ticking of the clock, the sun pouring in with dust motes dancing in the rays, the quiet of the street. Sick as I was, I loved the rare peace.

After a while, Ma came in to check on me again. I was dozing. I felt her hand on my forehead, then on my face—it lingered there for a minute—then she was gone. I slept awhile, then was awakened when the boys trooped in, along with Molly and Bridie.

"Dammit!" Ma said. "I just went in to lie down. Go change your clothes and go out to play. Molly, what are you and Bridie up to?"

"Nothing. We're going to take a walk over to Dominic's, okay?"

"Sure, just don't be home too late."

Dominic's was a soda shop on the corner of Rivet and County. It had a nice fountain for ice cream and such and also sold books and magazines. Normally, I'd be whining to go with them.

"How're you?" Molly said, poking her head into the parlor.

"Feeling any better, Finn?" Bridie asked.

"About the same, I guess," I said.

"Want anything from Dominic's?"

"No, thanks."

"Okay. See you."

They tiptoed past Ma's bedroom and were gone.

Drew did as he was told and happily went outside to play with the Twins Downstairs, but Tom came in the parlor and sat with me for a while, talking softly about school and who got in trouble with the nuns that day.

As the afternoon waned, the street came alive with the sounds of dogs barking and the raucous voices of the neighborhood kids playing touch football. Later, Tom and Drew went to deliver their newspapers. When they came back, Drew had a *Green Lantern* comic book for me that he'd bought with his paper tips. It was a rare show of affection.

Ma got up and started peeling potatoes for our supper. When she came in to give me my next dose of aspirin, I could smell dirt and potato starch on her hand. I dozed a bit till 5 o'clock cartoons came on, and my brothers joined me to watch, except for Skippy, who followed Ma around the house. She was fixing supper. I could smell the stew cooking. I hated stew—all those gross chunks of tasteless, fatty meat, and onions everywhere. It didn't matter, though, because I couldn't eat anyway.

Dad came home, late again, smelling of the mill and the barroom. These were smells I liked. He brought me two Chiclets, patted my head, and then the fight began. It went like this:

"Jack, look at the time."

"So?"

"So, you've been to the Z Club. Do you have to come home drunk every night?"

"I'm not drunk. Lay off me."

"You are drunk. You're stumbling."

"I hurt my foot at work. A warp beam fell on it. I'm tired. Just leave me alone, bitch."

"Don't you dare call me that—that's the drink talking."

"Bullshit. I'm tired."

"Eat your supper."

"Don't want no supper."

"Eat. You better eat, or you'll get sick."

There was quiet for a moment. There were sounds of Dad's spoon in the bowl. Then:

"Why did you have to come home drunk tonight? Sick kid and everything."

Sound of the spoon being dropped in the bowl. He rose and took it to the sink.

"Lay off me, I said." There was a dangerous edge to his voice. I prayed my mother would just drop it.

"You're just a drunk," she said, and I cringed.

Unlike more explosive nights, nothing happened this time. Dad just removed his work shirt and settled into his chair in his soft tee shirt and chinos. He had taken his shoes off almost as soon as he came in the house, and now he gingerly slipped off his socks. I passed by him on my way to the bathroom and saw that one of his feet was all purple and swollen. He was half-asleep already.

Molly and Tom did the dishes. Then all settled down to do homework. I was feeling sick and asked to be put back to my bed. But I was still awake long after the boys had gone to bed themselves. Dad was sleeping in his chair outside my bedroom, and Ma and Molly were in the parlor watching *The Honeymooners,* that television comedy show about a working-class married couple living in Brooklyn.

A peaceful evening.

Uncle Callan's heavy boot steps breached our quiet. I could hear his footfall on each stair, feel my stomach clench in time with every step closer. He stepped easily into the tenement. His voice disturbed the air.

"How's Finn?" Uncle Cal asked my mother.

"About the same," Ma said.

Uncle Cal came into my room, as he did most nights, and, in spite of my chicken pox, he went on to do his usual routine. He slipped my pajama pants off. I could see the back of Dad's chair, right outside my door. I could hear him snoring softly. *Wake up, wake up,* I thought hard. But I couldn't talk. I had no words. Uncle Cal fondled me, slipped his fingers inside me, and finished off by licking me. I didn't care. I was too feverishly sick to care. After he left, I called out and woke my father. Not to tell him what happened. I wanted him to stop it, but I never wanted him to know what happened.

"Dad, Daddy, will you lie down with me? Please?"

"Okay, Peanut," he mumbled.

He was asleep before his head hit the pillow. I covered him up tenderly, then pressed against him so we were like spoons. I fell asleep.

---

Uncle Cal had his nighttime routine, but he would manage to catch me other times, too, like when I'd go down to the cellar to get my bike or another toy.

The house had no boundaries and precious little privacy.

Our doors were always unlocked, and we each moved freely among the tenements, no knocking required. Our bedroom doors had latches on the outside, for the '50s version of "time out." (Whenever I was locked in, I would stop throwing my tantrum, then get an envelope from Molly's bureau and slide it up between the doorjamb and the door, unlatching the hook.)

After Aunt Joan's nightly visit—after she would shut me up and shut me in—I'd go on working my way toward my brothers' room through the wall. Then Uncle Cal would come in to "just talk." The contradiction was confusing.

I wondered why they both could just come upstairs and interfere like that, regardless of what Callan was or was not doing. Why couldn't my mother stand up to them? Ma once told me she used to get angry that Callan was keeping me awake. Why, then, did she not just tell him to leave me alone? I'll never know the answer to that. Perhaps on some level, she herself was intimidated by them.

Cal had an uncanny sense of just the right time to come upstairs. He'd appear at a point in the evening when Dad would be asleep and Ma would be watching TV, and he'd come into my room. He was never caught. Even if someone had come by, Cal was positioned in such a way that no one could see exactly what he was doing. He could have been tucking me in. But he wasn't.

Of course, I couldn't say anything.

When he was done with me, Uncle Cal would say, "Don't tell your mother. You should be ashamed of yourself." And then, in an angry voice, "Go to sleep, right now," as if I'd been the one keeping him awake.

Some nights, I was lucky. Once in a while, before Callan came up, I would convince Dad to lie down with me. He'd give in, saying, "Okay, Peanut, but only for a little while." And I would mold myself to his back, happy and secure in the comforting smell of his tee shirt. Uncle Cal stayed away on those nights.

---

Long before I could articulate what might be bothering me, I began running away. When I decided to run away the first time, I was only six. I remember being quite determined. I had to reach a particular park bench at the Joseph Francis Playground to be safe. Grandpa had taken me for walks there, and we would stop at that bench to rest. We'd sit in companionable silence, Grandpa holding my hand. The smells of the cove's brine and the newly mown grass of the park mingled with Grandpa's pungent cigar smoke and Ben-gay. I remember the soft sun shining on my face and the seagulls crying out for food, whirling in the ocean air's currents.

The park was a good five blocks from Winsor Street. I would be safe at the bench.

As soon as the opportunity arose, I decided I would be off. And it came one Saturday afternoon in summer. We were having a cookout in the back-yard. All the others were busy bringing things in and out of the house as I sat quietly playing with my tricycle in the front yard. I had it upside down and was spinning the wheel while holding a playing card to the spokes, as I'd seen my brothers do. Suddenly, no one was there—everyone was in the back getting and serving food.

I quickly flipped my trike over, opened the gate, closed it softly behind me, and pedaled like crazy up the street. As I turned the corner, I could see the water in the far distance, and I could smell its salty air mixed with burning rubber from the Goodyear plant. The sidewalks were cracked and rutted, and I couldn't make my legs go fast enough. I had to get off the trike to go up curbs as I crossed over, block after block, the ocean getting greener the closer I approached. Three blocks away. Four. Five.

Finally, I reached the gas station on the corner of Cove Road and Crapo Street, on which I'd been riding. I could see the bench from there.

But I had to navigate across the very busy and dangerous main road first. I ventured out a little way into the street. A car honked, scaring me. Then a kind man from the gas station offered to help me cross. He took my hand and carried my trike in the other. When he plunked it down on the opposite sidewalk, I let go of his hand and jumped on. I thanked him politely and took off. To my left was the playground and the cove. Everything seemed bright and new. In the distance, the ocean sparkled like bright stars. I briefly considered going into the park and down to the water, where people fished off the rocks. Reluctantly, I decided it would be best to go on to the bench.

The bench: It shimmered in the bright sun like a beacon. The air around me felt pure and sharply clean, alive with promise. Even the stones on the sidewalk were so white that I wondered if they had been cleaned by the ocean and then flung there at high tide. Almost there, almost there...

"Fiona! Fiona!"

I heard my name being called from what seemed like far away.

"Fiona, stop right there, now!"

It was my father's voice, and he sounded angry. I stopped and looked around. Across the street were my father, Uncle Cal, and Tom. Drew and Little Cal were on their bikes. I'd been so close! They ran across the road. Tom was the first to reach me.

"Boy, are you in trouble," he said.

My heart sank. I felt humiliated. I knew I'd be in for a terrible punishment.

Uncle Cal grabbed my tricycle, and Dad grabbed me without saying much that I recall. He was angry and held me tight. Tom said everyone on the block was out looking for me, even our cranky next-door neighbor who had a car.

"Andrew, ride home and tell your mother that we found her," Dad said. Turning to me, he said I'd be punished when we got home, but I knew it wouldn't come from him. It would be my mother, my grandmother, or Uncle Cal. I didn't care about the former two—I just didn't want it to be Uncle Cal, because he'd kill me.

Dad carried me all the way home, holding me close. "You could have been kidnapped," he said. "Or you could have been killed crossing the street. Do you understand? What were you thinking?"

He squeezed me tighter. Uncle Cal seemed to be in a (rare) quiet fury. When we turned the corner to our street, I could see the crowd that had gathered in front of our house.

When we arrived, Ma was sitting on the front porch steps, holding baby Skippy and crying. I hated to see her cry. Dad put me down and took Skippy from her arms. I went over to her.

"I'm sorry, Mama," I said. She grabbed me and pulled me close.

"Oh, Finn, you had us so scared," she said, and her arms were shaking.

"Well, she's never going to forget this prank," Uncle Cal said, coming toward me.

But then the crowd parted, and Granny, not very sentimental, said to me, "Into the house."

So, Granny would have the honor. Ma couldn't have put any strength into a spanking. But Granny sure could. I was sore for a week. Among other punishments, I wasn't allowed to use my tricycle for two weeks, and no cartoons for a week.

None of it acted as a deterrent, however. I'd be off—on foot, if necessary—the next chance I had. I never got as far as the first time, though, when it took them longer to realize I wasn't there. My frequent running-away attempts must have driven my parents crazy. I don't remember how I would answer when they'd asked me why I kept running away. What could I tell them?

Ma used to say, "A child in trouble is a troubled child." She was quite right. Even if I'd had the vocabulary, I was too deeply ashamed, too complicit, too frightened to expose Uncle Cal. Would they even have believed me? What I'd planned to do once I reached that park bench, I have no idea. I just knew I had to run.

By the time I had a two-wheeler, I had a better sense of reality, and I understood there was nowhere to run. I was trapped.

It had been made abundantly clear that the boys did not want me as part of their play group, no matter how hard I tried to act like a boy and do all the things they did. They called me "It" or "Dirt." They hated me. There seemed to be no refuge.

I spent a lot of time looking out the pantry window. Since we were on the second floor, I had a view of the neighborhood backyards, with line after line of laundry snapping in the breeze. I could watch storms move in from the northwest. I could spend an hour or more at that pantry window daydreaming, wondering what all the people in all those tenements were doing, what kind of lives they led. Many of them worked in the "shops" (textile mills converted to garment factories) or the Goodyear tire plant. Were their lives like mine? Was I the only one in the world to be living this way—trapped by my uncle on the one hand, and ostracized by my peers on the other?

The face in the pantry window was at once wistful and very, very lonely.

---

It begins when you are very young, even before you've reached the age to appreciate the story of Adam and Eve, and it begins with bodies. Do not look, do not touch yourself or your brothers; that's dirty and a sin. A bad sin. But there is an adult who does not play by the rules. He looks and he touches and he makes you touch back. Then you are naked from the waist down (at three or four, your chest isn't very interesting; you look just like your brothers and his sons), and he does things—things you know are bad and sinful. When he's done, he says, "Never tell. You'll get in trouble. You should be ashamed of yourself."

The shame settles in and takes hold with another deep dimension. It is huge, a giant boulder pressing down on your lungs, your flat chest, your stomach, and your sex. Sometimes you feel peculiarly warm between the legs, a pleasant sensation that makes the guilt so much worse. Once, to show how a vise works, he puts two of your fingers in its jaws, and he screws it tight, tighter, until you beg him to stop.

You daydream about how you should be punished. You deserve to be punished.

In first grade, Sister Mary Hulga made me sit in the trash can all afternoon for talking, and I felt like trash, like I belonged there. Sister Hulga was tall, young, and very loud, with a piercing voice. She terrified me. One day she made me sit in her bottom desk drawer with my legs hanging out, and by release time I could hardly walk. That punishment was because I got black streaks in my yellow duck because my yellow crayon, worn to a nub, had specks of black in it from a previous user. Sometimes she used her yardstick on the backs of my bare legs when I made a mistake at the blackboard.

I was small for my age and young for my grade. I turned four in June and began kindergarten in September. Thus, in first grade, I had just turned five while everyone else was six, and the one-year difference in maturity was enormous. One day, when I raised my hand to ask permission to use the girls' room, Sister Hulga called me a baby and made me stay in my seat.

I raised my hand again. "But Sister, I need to go bad."

"That's just too bad," she said, and I sat in anguish until I couldn't hold it in any longer. I spent the long afternoon sitting in cold urine while the students around me snickered.

Sister Hulga was an expert at creating punishments. I deserved Sister Hulga.

One morning in third grade, Sister Rose drew an oval on the blackboard and filled it in with white chalk: "This is your soul without sin. Pure. White." She then erased a few small areas: "This is your soul with little sins, venial sins. Can you say that word?"

The class repeated it.

"Good. Now write it in your notebooks—nice, neat print: V-E-N-I-A-L." Then she erased the entire inside of the oval, saying, "This is your soul with a big sin, a mortal sin. M-O-R-T-A-L. Write it in your notebook. If you die, and your soul is black like this, you go straight to hell."

I knew that my soul was tainted with mortal sin, all right, stained with brown, the color of decay, the color of shame.

On another day, having already covered the first through fifth commandments, Sister Rose explained the sixth: "Thou shalt not commit adultery." Sister said that it meant any dirty language, any dirty, bad thoughts, or dirty, impure acts. Everybody knew what "dirty" meant. And now I knew its real name: adultery. Sister added that this was a major sin, a mortal sin—the kind that got you sent straight to hell.

I shifted my gaze to stare out the open window at the Morse Twist Drill across the street—a famous tool company that had been manufacturing drill bits in the old city since the Civil War. I could hear its machines, smell its peculiar smell—a mixture of hot metal and metal dust—as it wafted in on a summer-like breeze, though it was mid-September. I contemplated this sixth commandment. I sighed deeply, embarrassed and ashamed, as if everyone knew.

Ever since school began that year, Sister Rose had been teaching the lives of the saints. She talked mostly about young saints, and the one that stood out in my mind was the young girl who allowed herself to be killed rather than give in to the man who was after her body. That gave me an idea: Maybe I should let myself be killed. I could be a martyr.

No, it's already too late for martyrdom. I have no choice but to live in shame.

But wasn't there always confession?

We were told that if we went to confession and admitted all our sins, God—through the priest—would forgive us. And He would forgive all our sins, not just some. That's what Sister Rose said. I had to be truly sorry and promise to try not to do it again. All would be forgiven, and I could leave the confessional feeling blessedly free. That's how it was supposed to work. And now Sister had given me the name of my sin (adultery, as in the sixth commandment, "Thou shalt not commit adultery," which I assumed covered everything that was dirty). In my mind, "adultery" was defined as anything "impure." All I had to do was muster up the courage for confession.

The following Saturday dawned bright and hot, so Ma decided we should have a picnic lunch at Hazelwood Park. This rare outing was one of my favorites, although I always gave Witch Hazel's house a wide berth. This was actually the caretaker's house, a stone building in the middle of the park, but my brothers had informed me that Witch Hazel lived there. Another stone structure was a public restroom. It was cool and smelled of damp sand.

We spent the first part of the afternoon at the courts, with Dad trying his best to teach us tennis. Drew had a good arm, Dad said. I remember his hand over mine, showing me the correct way to hold a racquet. Holding it properly, I was surprised by how heavy it felt. We had a small set of racquets with handles marked "H" for heavy or "L" for light. Naturally, I preferred the light one, but Dad said you could hit the ball harder with the heavier one. I spent a lot of time shagging balls I'd hit clear outside the courts.

During these picnics, we would play on the swings and other playground equipment, and then Ma would unwrap soggy, warm peanut butter and jelly sandwiches that tasted delicious. She usually brought punch, Fig Newtons and watermelon. Then, an hour after eating and all sweaty from our play, we would plead to go for a sunset swim across the street at Municipal Beach.

It didn't take much to convince her—Dad loved the idea as much as we did. So, we would pack up everything and run like hell down the hill to the almost deserted beach. Dad always swam with us. This late in the day, the water, the color of coral from the setting sun, was calm and inviting, the sand now cool under our feet. We swam until the orange-red sun dipped down behind the Dartmouth hills, and Ma called us all in. We washed the sand and salt off at the outdoor showers with the Ivory soap Ma had brought. Then Ma and Dad wrapped our shivering bodies in hooded terry cloth robes. I sat on the seawall while they packed up, cozy and warm, feeling the breeze through my wet hair, watching the changing sky and the lights on the water and felt content. Ma and Dad were particularly mellow, now that they wouldn't have to go through the ordeal of Saturday night baths.

At times like these, Dad often said, "Look at all we have, look at all we've got here. Who needs fancy vacations?"

We tumbled back into the car.

Ma said, "Brace yourselves, brace yourselves!" and commenced whispering prayers. Scrunched into the back seat, we formed a chorus of voices begging for ice cream. It worked, and we drove to Willow Tree. Ma ordered her favorite—frozen pudding. We sang "Mairzy Doats" over and over again all the way home:

*Mairzy doats and dozy doats and liddle lamzy divey,*
*A kiddley divey too, wouldn't you?*
*Yes! Mairzy doats and dozy doats and liddle lamzy divey*
*A kiddley divey too, wouldn't you?*
*If the words sound queer and funny to your ear,*
*A little bit jumbled and jivey,*
*Sing mares eat oats and does eat oats and little lambs eat ivy.*

When we finally arrived home, we were happy but worn out. We rinsed our bathing suits under the tap and hung them on the line. Often, while hanging out my suit, I would linger at the window just to watch the night sky and breathe in the cool, salty air, looking at the lights in other tenements and wondering what the people were doing, or staring past all the clotheslines, daydreaming about what lay beyond all that—the churches and Ashley Park and the Goodyear plant. This night, I wondered, was there anything for me beyond these boundaries? The sky was infinitely beautiful in shades of light blue with pink and golden orange streaks as it hung over the grimy streets below. I had the odd sensation that I didn't belong here. And why did I suddenly feel so sad?

We didn't get to confession that Saturday, but the next week we had to go. I dreaded it, but Ma was adamant. As we were getting ready, she ran a comb through my hair.

"Go on, now, and don't dawdle," Ma said. "Finn, put a skirt on. Have you got something for your head?"

I went in my room and pulled a stupid skirt on over my shorts. I stuffed a Kleenex into my shirt pocket along with some bobby pins.

"Drew, hold Finn's hand crossing the streets," Ma ordered.

As soon as we were outside, we were met by the Twins Downstairs, who were being sent on the same mission. We all ambled up the street, but once we reached the corner and were out of sight, the boys took off running, leaving me far behind.

I didn't mind. In fact, I preferred to walk by myself to the Gothic church about five blocks away. The only thing I hated was walking by all the men from the Z Club. They sat on stoops or stood in a tight group, spitting in the gutter. I recognized Jimmy-the-Crutch and Manny-Me-Nuts, and I knew the others were around somewhere. I made it past them without getting spit on and kept walking, past Marcoux Pharmacy, Motta's candy store, a variety store on the corner of Rivet at the lights, then past the French church. Storefronts gave way to a few residential homes, some of them very nice.

I tried not to think about what I'd have to say in confession and wondered which priest would be on. I stood at the bottom of the long steps up to the church, pinning my tissue to the top of my head to cover it, as was required by the Catholic Church in those days. I took a deep breath, negotiated the stone steps to the enormous door, and let myself into the cool, dark interior. It smelled of candles and polish and wax. As my eyes adjusted to the light, I looked around the pews and saw Drew and the Twins Downstairs. They were waiting in line for Father Dunne, but I decided to take my chances with Father McCuen. Father Dunne was a gruff man, about six-foot-four, with dark red hair and a fiery temper. Drew was there only because the line was shorter. Father McCuen had a kind look and a soft voice.

I entered the dark box through the heavy, red velvet curtain. Soon the panel slid open, and I found myself looking up at the side of Father McCuen's head leaning into the screen. I could barely reach the shelf to put my folded hands on it.

"Bless me, Father, for I have sinned," I intoned. "It has been two weeks since my last confession. I lied twice, disobeyed my parents eight times, committed adultery six times, fought with my brothers seven times—"

"Wait—wait a minute," Father McCuen said. I froze.

"Repeat what you said."

"I lied, disobeyed my parents, committed adultery—"

"Okay, stop there." He turned and looked down at the top of my head. "What do you mean you committed adultery?"

I felt sick. A voice in my head pleaded with me to tell him. But how? I had no language, no vocabulary for what was happening. Go on, the voice urged. Just say it.

I began: "I let... I let my..."

Father McCuen moved closer to the screen. I was speaking slowly, softly. I intended to say, "I let my uncle do things to me," but then Father McCuen would want to know what things. I couldn't do it.

Father McCuen cleared his throat.

"Yes," he said, gentle, soft.

"I... let... my..." I couldn't do it. I knew, because Sister Rose had told us, that anything dirty fell under the sixth commandment. I opted for dirty language.

"I said s-h-i-t, Father."

He looked down at my face peering up to his.

"You're sure?" he asked.

"Yes, Father."

"Oh," he said, and his voice sounded funny.

I finished up with the Act of Contrition, and he gave me three Our Fathers and three Hail Marys for penance. I emerged from the confessional in time to see Drew leaving the altar, having said his penance, and we passed in the aisle.

"Beat you home," he whispered.

I didn't care. I had a lot to think about on the way home. I said my penance and left the church. The late afternoon sun was going down behind the tenements. Way ahead I could see Drew and the Twins Downstairs horsing around. I waited, without much hope, for that clean, light, and airy sense of relief I used to feel after confession before I learned about adultery. It was a weightless, good feeling, deep inside. But I knew it would not come, not ever again. And now I'd lied to a priest. My sins just multiplied, weighing me down. I felt unclean, defeated, hopeless. I would be dirty forever. My penance was a life sentence. Sister Rose was right: Mortal sins were hell.

I took the tissue off my head and let it float away on the breeze. Then I whipped off my skirt to reveal the shorts I had on underneath. When I got to the corner, I found Drew and the Twins Downstairs waiting for me.

"It's about time," Drew said. "What'd you do, crawl? Or did you have to say a Rosary for penance?"

We resumed walking down the street as though we'd been together all along. Then, just two houses from our own, the boys broke into a run, slamming first the gate then the outside door in my face. I reddened with anger, frustration, and despair. Tears welled in my eyes. I walked up the stairs, hearing the door slam above me. When I went in, Drew was sitting at the table, sniggering. Ma was standing at the stove, stirring something. I don't know where Dad was. I looked at Drew.

"Yes?" he said with sarcasm.

"Why do you hate me so much?" I said, and continued on into my room.

I heard Ma say, "What's that all about?" before I closed my door. I threw my body onto the bed. It continued to amaze me that Ma could be so blind to what was going on with Drew and Little Cal. Did she see the cruelty and choose to ignore it? Or was it that she simply couldn't imagine it could be so destructive and therefore couldn't exist? Is that what this was in the end? A failure of her imagination? Whatever it was, it was plain to see that this was a battle I could never win.

Since it was Saturday, it was the night for hot dogs and beans and baths. Dad heated pot after pot of water. Ma and Dad took their baths first, followed by Molly, Tom, Drew, and me. Skippy was washed in the sink. As I went in for my turn, Drew whispered to me that he'd peed in the tub.

# 4. Biography of a Tomboy

I was a girl among five boys. Molly didn't factor in here—she was too old to be outside playing with us. I was tormented just for being a girl. But at least I got to be Dirt in the Rottenest Sneak Club, for what that was worth.

I was getting ideas. I could feel them, at the pantry window, like a cold coming on, ideas about my birth in this house, of the five boys who'd rather have a sixth but were stuck with me instead. Ostracized, I tried my best to be a boy, eschewing dolls for six-shooter cap pistols, spitballs, and football. I tried to run the fastest, to take on any daring feats that came my way. In the privacy of the bathroom, I wet my mousy brown hair, parted it on the side, and flattened it down to look like a boy. With my straight eyebrows and thin mouth, I could easily pass as male. I cursed like I heard them curse at the paper stop. I walked like they did. People often said Drew and I looked like twins, and this infuriated him. But no matter how hard I tried to fit in with the boys, nothing worked. I was still a girl to them.

I loathed being a girl. What was possibly good about it? I had to wear ill-fitting skirts to school, my legs freezing, when what I wanted to wear were pants. Many of my clothes were hand-me-downs from classmates, and I was the subject of whispers in huddled conversations in the schoolyard. At home, being a girl made it doubly hard to play with my brothers and cousins. If I was included in their play at all, it was only to be the stooge: to be perpetually "It" at tag, to be last in races, to be treated as worthless. Over and over, I had to prove myself worthy of being Dirt in the RSC. The only person to give my female side attention was Uncle Cal. Between the teasing boys and Uncle Cal, I could not escape torment for being a girl.

A tomboy lives in a netherworld—not one, always the other. In this confusion of tides, I eventually turned inward—to read, to paint, to write—where gender did not matter. Developing these inner resources was a lifesaver. Early on, I started thinking of myself as a writer, and it was in many ways my salvation. It offered me an escape, and a place I could go where I controlled the world. On those days when I couldn't take any more of the boys' competitiveness, I had a book or a notepad or a canvas to turn to. It worked a lot of the time. But I was terribly lonely.

There was a group of older girls that hung out on someone's porch on the corner, and sometimes I would slip away to be with them. A girl named Izzy was their ringleader by virtue of age (she was 15) and experience (she was reputed to have done "it"—whatever "it" was). She was, my mother often said, "boy crazy" and "too sophisticated" for me. How could she know this? But it was true. Izzy was always after the paperboys, and her talk was always sprinkled with vague (to me) references to sex.

I was clueless about most things, although to be coldly objective about it, I probably had more experience than the lot of them combined. But that would not have occurred to me then. I had carefully compartmentalized everything that happened to me, from Uncle Cal to the boys.

Still, their porch conversation was different—their whole frame of reference was different—and they made for an interesting diversion from time to time. Of course, if I was caught with them, I was told to get home immediately. I remember wailing at my mother that I had nowhere to go and no one to hang out with.

"I don't care," she said without sympathy. "You're not going to hang around with them."

And that was that.

Ma was way too busy trying to keep house and home together to worry about my loneliness. As far as she was concerned, I had my brothers to play with, and I shouldn't be at all lonely. But Ma was blind to what went on outside, blind to the hazing and shoving and simmering anger. She didn't hear them referring to me as It or Dirt. If we were outside playing, she probably felt relieved, free to do the hundreds of things she had to do to make the household work. Imagine, for example, the impact on housework of having no hot water. Then imagine the daily laundry accumulated by seven people. Think of the ironing and the cooking and just the general picking up after that many people. It had to have been overwhelming from time to time. So I couldn't fault her, really, for not knowing the extent of the damage being done in the name of outdoor play. The boys did and said things Ma could neither see nor imagine. Though I tried to tell her in my periodic outbursts, I didn't tell enough. As usual, I kept too much inside.

Also setting me apart from the other kids was my love of nature. I was very sensitive to the weather and to changes in the sky, changes of seasons, shifts in the barometer. But that was not appreciated by either the boys or the Izzy crowd. I recall one evening hanging out on the forbidden porch with Izzy and her followers and remarking into a rare silence, "Look at the moon—isn't it beautiful?" They nearly laughed me off the block. I ran home red-faced and watched the moon from my own pantry window.

My isolation was complete.

---

"I love Dougie Darling, I love Dougie Darling, I love Dougie Darling," I chanted as I hopped the perimeter of the yard on one foot. I hated Dougie Darling. He was the class troublemaker, an obnoxious sort who had already been kept back a couple of grades. He spent more time in the principal's office (where the spanking machine was rumored to be in her closet) than in class. His mother was my mother's haircutter, and she was—whisper—a *divorcee*. Of course, I was not above borrowing Dougie's *Green Lantern* comic books. He had an extensive collection that I envied. I heard years later that he became a priest.

"I love Dougie Darling." Hop.

It was a typical South End summer: the backyard hot and dusty under the haze of an afternoon sun, the clothesline laden with sheets hanging limp to dry in air heavy with humidity and sea-smell. Oppressive. I would have given anything to be at the beach, but at 9, I couldn't go by myself, and Tom and Molly were working. Drew, at 11, was too young to be responsible. So I was stuck here.

"I love Dougie Darling." Hop.

His name made it all the worse.

There was grit in my sneakers and even in my teeth, and I was thirsty. The sun was full overhead and the tenement cast no shadow. All morning Drew and the Twins Downstairs had me running up and down the stairs getting them drinks. That, plus hopping around the yard three times on one foot while chanting the above was part of The Punishments, for this was Judgment Day for members of the Rottenest Sneak Club.

Drew was the club's founder and president. Little Cal was vice president. Pat and Skippy were official members. Being older, Tom was not involved. My rank was Dirt. I'd have been heartbroken if they'd kicked me out. Even Dirt was better than the isolation of being left out. This was the only game in town.

Periodically, when they were bored, Drew and Little Cal would hold Judgment Day. They'd go over all our infractions: insults real or imagined, cases of assault, battery, and petty larceny of goods. They meted out what they considered appropriate (and imaginative) punishments. Skippy, at five being too young and uncomprehending and given to throwing up easily, usually got a suspended sentence and wandered back upstairs to hang on Ma. Pat, being sweet and good-natured, seldom received a negative judgment, and of course the president and vice president were above reproach.

That left me.

"I love Dougie Darling," I said as I hopped toward the end of my third lap.

"Louder, Dirt, I can't hear you."

I looked up to the pantry window on the second floor. Drew was at the screen, making a great show of drinking a glass of lemonade. I wanted to throw a rock at him, but two things held me back: One, I realized he was too high and far for any of my missiles to do damage, and two, if I stopped hopping, they'd only make me start over again.

"I love Dougie Darling," I said louder and hopped the last step. Thirsty, but not wanting to trudge upstairs, I got a drink of ice-cold water from the outside tap and sat on the cellar steps to cool off. Drew and Little Cal would be out again to mete out the next punishment. Skippy would stay upstairs to "help" Ma peel cucumbers from Granny's garden for supper.

I checked my official RSC bag to make sure all was in order. I didn't want to lose points for having a deficiency. I poured the contents out on the cellar steps: one short piece of wire (which Drew called a "hemoglobinjima" to be used in emergencies—though of what sort I had no idea and didn't ask); a magnifying glass for burning our special identification marks into wood; a peashooter made from a length of dirty pipe; and a ready supply of spitballs, with a few tissues to make more. All seemed to be in order.

I sat for a while cooling off until I thought I heard noises in the cellar. It could be Uncle Callan. I quickly gathered my goods back into my canvas sack and ran up the stairs, almost colliding with Granny on her way to work in her garden.

"Where are you off to in such a hurry?" she asked.

"Upstairs. Need any help in the garden?"

"Aren't you a sweet girl. You can help me if you want."

"Okay, Gran."

"Ka–tee! Mrs. Ka–tee!" came a call from across the street. It was Mrs. Souza, and she was waving us over. She knew my grandmother only by her first name, Katie.

Mrs. Souza was a plump, pleasant woman, always smiling. Her husband was a fisherman, and together they kept a beautiful yard. The grass was perfect, without bare spots, and a variety of flowers grew around the perimeter. These were separated from the grass by a short white fence Mr. Souza had built. Down at the end was a shrine to the Blessed Mother, her statue surrounded by flowers and backed by a piece of plaster painted soft blue and white. The statue held her hands prayerfully and across her arms were more flowers, freshly cut.

Granny and I could see that the woman at the gate was holding a bundle of what appeared to be fruit.

"Finn, run to the garden and pick four good-sized, ripe tomatoes and bring them over."

I took off on my mission. I gently plucked the deep-red tomatoes and ran back to Granny and Mrs. Souza, who were engaged in pantomime conversation. Granny now held a bundle of pears, apples, and grapes from the trees and arbor in the Souzas' backyard. Granny did not speak Portuguese, and Mrs. Souza spoke little English, but they somehow managed to communicate.

"My granddaughter," Granny said, pointing to me, then to herself.

"Pretty," Mrs. Souza said.

I handed over the tomatoes. Mrs. Souza put a hand to her cheek. *"Oh, bonita! Obrigada, obrigada!"*

Granny pointed to the bundle of fruit and tried her best to repeat *obrigada*.

They pantomimed a little more, and we returned to our yard.

"That was nice, Gran," I said.

"She's a good woman," Granny said. "Put the fruit over there, then come in the garden."

I followed her onto the brick path into the garden. Usually Granny didn't allow anyone in her garden, so I felt special as I skipped down her garden walkway. On the right were the tomato plants, with blooming flowers behind them. To the left were the string beans, scallions, evolving cucumbers, carrots, and lettuce of a pale, delicate green that seemed to shine with an inner light. Granny handed me a large saucepan.

"Would you pick the string beans? I'll do the lettuce. Be gentle."

I knelt in the soft, sun-warmed dirt and reached under the broad green leaves for the long string beans that dangled there. When I'd finished, the pan was almost full. The thought of them cooked and swimming in melted butter made my stomach growl.

"That's it, I think, Gran. What about the tomatoes?"

"Okay, but make sure they're ripe. You're a good little helper, Finn."

I went over to the tomato plants. The dirt on the surface was pale and warm, but rich, dark, cool, and moist just underneath. I loved the earthy smell. I plucked six or seven good-sized, red tomatoes and a few that were small but definitely ripe.

"Come on over to the faucet," Granny said.

Carefully, we rinsed all the dirt from our harvest. Granny hummed an Irish tune. It was comforting.

"Here," she said, handing me a small tomato. "Let's have one right now."

She pulled a salt shaker from her apron pocket and grinned.

I bit into my tomato, its juices running warm down my chin, and sprinkled salt on the next bite. Nothing tasted as delicious as a tomato fresh from the garden. Except maybe the red raspberries she had growing on a full bush.

Granny put her arm around my thin shoulders.

"You're good to me, Finny-my-girl, and I won't forget it. Come upstairs after, and I'll give you a little treat."

"Okay, Gran." I kissed her dirt-smudged cheek. It was soft and smooth.

"What were you hopping around the yard for, in all this heat?"

I explained as best I could about The Punishments. Granny's face took on a look that was both angry and concerned.

"Why do you let them treat you like that?"

"If I didn't do it, they'd kick me out of the club."

"It's not right. They have no right being mean to you like that."

I shrugged. How could I explain? It was how things were, that's all.

"And who's in charge of this 'club'?"

"Drew's the president."

"What are you?"

"Dirt."

"I'm going to have a talk with that boy. He's old enough to know better."

"No, Gran—don't. It'll only make things worse."

"How could it be worse? No, I'm sorry, Finn. He needs to be spoken to."

"Granny, if they get mad at me, I won't have anyone to play with."

Granny looked at me hard. Then she hugged me and kissed my forehead.

"No one is going to treat my girl like that. No one. And you shouldn't take it, either."

I sighed. When Granny got mad—which she rarely did—there was no stopping her. And she was mad now.

"Do you want me to water the garden?"

"Not now, love. You have to wait till the sun goes down, then water it well."

"Okay."

We carried our bounty inside, stopping at the first floor to give some to Aunt Joan, then again on the second to give more to my mother.

Ma was in the middle of peeling potatoes for a potato salad. I handed her a small cucumber to peel for me. I loved the smell of cukes on a summer day.

"You've got a good girl here," Granny said to Ma. "She was a big help to me in the garden, and I didn't even have to ask."

Meanwhile, Drew had come into the room and sidled up to me. "Hey, Dirt, are you sure you're finished?" he whispered, but Granny's sharp ears picked it up.

"You," Granny said to Drew. "I have a bone to pick with you. Into the parlor. Now."

"What's going on?" Ma asked. She knew Granny rarely interfered.

"You cannot let those boys treat Finn the way they're treating her. It has to stop, right now. I'm having a talk with Andrew. Ask your daughter what's been going on."

Granny marched into the parlor and shut the door. Ma's eyebrows shot up.

"Well?" she said to me. "What's this about?"

I explained to her about the Rottenest Sneak Club and The Punishments.

"Sounds like he's the one who needs the punishment," Ma said.

"Ma, don't. Don't make a big deal out of this. They're the only ones I have to play with."

"That's not play."

How could I explain that it was just the way things always were? She wasn't going to change them.

"Can I go to the library?"

"I suppose so. Take your other books back, and wash up before you go. Be back by suppertime."

I went and got my books—*The Black Stallion, The Black Stallion Returns,* and *Flame,* all by Walter Farley. I was obsessed with horses. When I came to the first floor I could see Aunt Joan through the screened door. The inside cellar door was open. I flew by it.

"Where are you off to in such a hurry?" Aunt Joan asked.

"Library. See ya!" I called back and ran down the steps to the sidewalk.

"Be back for your supper," Aunt Joan called through the screened window.

"Yeah, yeah," I whispered.

The sidewalks were cracked and smelled like dog crap. It was a relief to get to the corner and smell the aroma of fresh bread from the bakery. I crossed County Street, over to Delano, then down to South Second.

At the end of the street on a straight shot was the face of the library, with its front pillars and portico. I walked quickly toward it. A stiff breeze from the south funneling down South Second Street carried a hint of saltiness. The library was only one block from the cove. Further down were the mills and the beach. Maybe Molly would take us swimming after supper. Or Tom. They'd both be exhausted—Molly worked as a nurse's aide at the hospital, and Tom worked at Gulf Hill Ice Cream Parlor. But the idea of a cool swim after supper might appeal.

I went up the stone steps, returned the books to the front desk, and looked around. Not many customers. A couple of old men read newspapers that were new when the men were young. A few women browsed in the adult section. I headed to the side marked "Juvenile." The place was cramped and smelled musty, the odor of old books.

A few little kids were hanging on to their mothers. I spotted Connie Foster in the science fiction section with her little brother Nicky in tow. I had never delved into the sci-fi section before, but today it appealed to me. I walked over to the shelves, nodding at Connie as I passed.

"Hi," I whispered.

"Hi, yourself," she said back. Nicky ducked behind her legs.

Connie's family lived in a small house on Crapo Street, next to the penny candy store, which made me envious—not only was it next to that store, but it was a cottage, all by itself, and not a smelly tenement like ours. Their house was set way back from the street, and there were always clothes strung on this three-dimensional Y-shaped thing with lots of lines in the front yard. Although we were close in age—Connie was about 11—we were only passing acquaintances. I always felt sorry for Connie because she had kinky hair, and her mother was dead.

She had two older brothers, Freddie and Fremont. I saw them at the paper stop when I trailed after Drew to pick up *The Standard-Times.* On Sunday mornings, I would pull my old wagon to the paper stop so I could help Drew deliver the heavy Sunday papers.

Drew's route was our street. I don't know what streets were Freddie and Fremont's. I guessed Crapo, since they lived on it. Freddie and Fremont called me Dolly. When I asked why, they said it was because of my wagon. I still didn't get it but was too embarrassed to say so.

Connie was a bookworm like me. She'd already picked out a couple of library books.

"What's good?" I asked her.

Connie, surprised, looked me up and down.

"How come your hair's so short in front?" she whispered.

"Because my mother cut it, and she can't follow a straight line, so she keeps cutting it shorter and shorter."

"Can't you go to the hairdresser at the top of Winsor?"

I shrugged. "Guess not. Who cuts your hair?"

"Maybe you can't afford it," she mused. "I don't go to a hairdresser. I have braids."

She twisted her head around, and her long braids flew, one of them catching me across the cheek. They were tied with purple ribbons.

"Ow!"

"Shhh!" said the librarian.

Connie giggled. "Weapons," she whispered.

"You've never been to a haircutter?"

"Not even once."

"Wow... So, what's good?"

"What have you read?"

"Nothing in science fiction."

"Then take this one," she said, plucking a book from the shelf. "It's about these people who live deep inside the earth. They're all short, like munchkins, and look different from us. A group of them, led by Gunnar, has to come to the surface to find water. It's good. Here. And this one I just finished. It's about shadows who talk to a really lonely boy. Read it."

"Girls!" the librarian said.

Connie rolled her eyes.

I was doubtful about the books. I preferred to read about horses. But I took them politely and said thank you.

Without another word, Connie wandered over to the children's section to pick out picture books for Nicky. I brought my new books to a wooden chair and began to read. When I heard talking, I swiveled around to see Connie being reprimanded by the librarian. Connie turned to me and did a perfect imitation of the woman's sour puss. I swiveled around fast so I wouldn't laugh out loud or be caught trying not to. When I dared to look around again, Connie and Nicky had left.

It wasn't long before I was engrossed in the book about the shadows who appear to a lonely boy about my age and help him get out of trouble. After a bit, I went over to the front desk to check the clock. It was a little after six, which meant I was already late for dinner. Ma would be in a fit. I went to check out my two books, expecting a talking-to from the librarian for horsing around earlier with Connie, but she just smiled and imprinted the cards.

Outside, the sun was just going down. I loved this time of day. Most folks were already home eating their suppers, and the streets were quiet. I sucked in the briny smell and watched the clouds turn pink and purple as they scudded across the cove. It felt calm, peaceful. No one was shouting. No cars were honking. The only sound was the distant hum of the Berkshire Hathaway. A soft breeze lifted my hair. I smiled to myself, thinking it would be a great night for a swim. The world at large seemed to be a wonderful place.

"I love swimming!" I shouted into the empty street just for the fun of it.

As I turned the corner for home, I saw Dad hustling along a short distance away.

"Dad!" I yelled after him. He turned around and grinned as I ran up to him.

"Did your mother send you up to meet me?"

"What? No, I was at the library, see?" I showed him my books. "They're science fiction. Got any gum?"

Dad fished in his pocket and pulled out a tiny box of Chiclets.

"Thanks. So, this story is about shadows, and they appear to this lonely boy who's in trouble and—"

"There's your mother. Wave."

Sure enough, Ma stood at the bay window with her rosary beads. She still had her apron on. She shook her head at us.

"Uh oh. Looks like you're in trouble—it's late. What have you been up to?"

"I told you, I was at the library. Reading this book. Guess I lost track of time... You're in trouble, too."

He smelled of hard work and the barroom.

"I know," he said and sighed.

We walked the rest of the way in silence. I took my father's hand. It was rough, and his fingers were thin and bony, except where they were swollen from arthritis. We went up the steps, and Aunt Joan was at the screen door. Her house smelled of beans and *linguiça* (Portuguese sausage)—and it wasn't even Saturday!

"Hello, Jack. Finn, you're late," Aunt Joan said.

"'Lo, Joan, Cal," Dad said.

I ran up the stairs. Ma stood at the door, but her face wasn't as mad as it had been in the window. Before she could speak, I launched into the books, and not noticing the time—

"I saw you take your father's hand," she said softly. "That was nice."

*Ah.* I slipped past her and into the kitchen.

"So, what's your excuse?" I heard her say to Dad, but there was no venom in it.

"Don't start with me, Fay," was all he said. He went to their bedroom and took off his work shirt. He put his shoes under the bed.

"Supper's waiting," Ma said.

We arranged ourselves at the table. Ma took the foil off the pan on the stove, and a plume of steam rose to the ceiling. It was pork chops, the way Dad loved them, cooked in the oven and smothered in onions and thin-sliced potatoes. On the table were bread, butter, and a bowl of cukes sitting in malt vinegar. I stared at the onions. I hated onions. But Dad loved them, so I wouldn't complain. I simply wouldn't eat them.

"I had a hard time at work today," Tom said, but he was grinning, his deep dimples showing. "This guy came in and ordered a banana split, a chocolate cone, and a hot fudge sundae. He left the store, then came back in about five minutes, mad as hell." Tom laughed. "I'd forgot to put the banana in his split. And boy, was he furious. He must have yelled at me for five minutes. Everyone was looking... I was so embarrassed."

"That was pretty stupid," Drew said.

"I think he was trying to get me fired. But my manager just laughed. He likes me."

"Good thing, too," Ma said. "You can't afford to lose that job."

"At least you didn't have to clean bedpans all day," Molly said.

"Eeeoooow. Gross," Drew said.

"Hey, Tom, remember the rag man?" Molly teased.

"Oh, he was *terrified* of the rag man," Ma said.

The rag man used to drive a horse-drawn cart down the street collecting old rags. In the days before leash laws, dogs on the street would often go after the horse, nipping at its heels and causing all sorts of commotion. "Raaaggggs!" the man shouted out over and over as he and his horse came clopping down the street.

"Terrified?" Molly said. "I thought he was going to have a breakdown. Remember the time we did have a bundle of rags to give the man? And they were in a box in the cellar?"

Molly directed her story to the table at large, and though we knew it by heart—it had been told many times—we listened eagerly anyway. "So, here's Tom happily playing outside, when the rag man turns the corner. Tom's ears perk up like a dog's. He takes one glance up the street just to make sure and then goes flying off to hide. And guess where he hides? In the cellar, of course. And when the rag man follows him down, Tom goes nuts."

"How old was Tom?" I asked.

"Thirteen," Molly said.

"Shut up," Tom said. "I was about four, right, Ma?"

"Yeah, about that," Ma said. "You poor kid. Every freckle stood out against your face, it was so white."

"Well, I didn't get much sympathy, as I recall—you were all laughing at me, like you're doing now," said Tom. "It was traumatic. I'm probably scarred for life."

"Poor Tom," Ma repeated, but laughed anyway.

"And then there's the fruit man," Tom said. Molly picked up on cue.

"Yeah, the fruit man comes down the street every day with a truck full of fruits and vegetables. Up at the top of the street, he yells, 'Bananas! Apples! Nice ripe oranges!' But when he gets near our house, he yells, 'Mrs. KIL-ROY!' He even called you Fay once," Molly said.

"Stop exaggerating," Ma said.

"And you go rushing right out so he can show you his melons. Only he's looking at *your* melons. Oh, he definitely has it bad for you, Ma," Molly said. Molly was definitely pushing it, but she liked to do that. She always seemed to know just where the line was at any given moment.

"Don't be ridiculous," Ma said in her no-nonsense voice. "Finn, start clearing the plates would you? Molly, you too."

I think she just wanted Molly to stop talking.

"Humph. A lot goes on when I'm not home," Dad said.

"Who wants to go to the beach?" I put it out there, hoping.

"Not me, I'm beat," Tom said.

"Molly?" I pleaded with my eyes.

"Yeah, let's go swimming, Molly, please?" Drew said.

"It's all right with me," Ma said. "Nice night for a swim."

Molly rolled her eyes. "I hate all this pressure!"

The table went silent, waiting.

"Oh, all right, but not for long," Molly capitulated.

"I'm going out later," Tom said. "So don't be too long—I need the car."

Tom was a very social being who loved going out at night. He'd comb his dark red hair just so, dress up sharp, and use English Leather aftershave, so not only did he look good (he was quite handsome), he smelled good, too. He was the only one who used the car regularly, as Gulf Hill Dairy was in Dartmouth, in the "country," some seven or eight miles away. Everyone else walked, Molly to the hospital in the West End, Dad to the mill, and the rest of us to school. Tom was the one who ran the family's errands and did the grocery shopping for Ma. Molly, for her part, was the one to take us to all our doctors' appointments—and to the beach.

"Don't forget you have to wait an hour after you eat," Ma said. She didn't want us to get cramps swimming.

It would be a long hour for me. I couldn't wait to get in the water.

"Dad, will you go?" I asked him.

"Not this time, Peanut. I'm too tired."

"You're more than just tired," Ma said.

"Don't start, Fay," Dad warned.

"I talked to Connie up the street at the library," I said quickly to ward off any fight.

"You talked to her?" Drew asked. "About what?"

"Books."

"I didn't know she could read," Drew snickered.

"Drew, shut up," Tom said, and his voice held a threat.

"Why?"

"That's enough. Haven't you learned your lesson after Granny talked to you, Drew?" Ma said. "It's too bad about her mother. Must be hard."

"What does Mr. Foster do?" I asked.

"He's a garbage collector," Ma said.

"Poor bugger," Dad said.

"Poor bugger," Skippy repeated happily from the high chair he had outgrown.

"Don't use that word," Ma said.

"But what is it?" I wanted to know.

"Someone you feel sorry for," Ma said. "Finish your supper."

I hurried through my supper, trying to avoid the onions. The chops were good, tender, and sweet. Skippy swirled slices of potato on his tray and made noises. Drew cleared the table. Dad sat in his easy chair by the stove and fell promptly to sleep. Molly and I did the dishes, singing our way through the plates. Tom heated the dishwater on the stove, humming a third harmony to my second. For once, there was no bickering.

When we got to the beach, the summer-orange sun was preparing to dip down behind the trees across the cove. The sea was calm, the colors of jade and amber. I dove in, and the water felt like silk across my body. I couldn't get enough of it, diving down time after time, while Molly swam in leisurely circles and Drew horsed around with the Twins Downstairs, who had come with us. I felt a part of the water, like I was home, like I belonged there, no longer an intruder among the fish.

We swam until the sun was fully and officially down, and a lone star appeared above the smokestacks of the mills. How I regretted having to leave the water. It made me feel all tingly and alive. Coming ashore, I could feel my legs dragging, and I was no longer weightless. I shivered as I snuggled into my terrycloth robe. Molly came at me with a towel and dried the wet out of my hair before doing the same to herself. It didn't matter for Drew and the Twins Downstairs because they all had crew cuts.

We grabbed our things in the gathering dark, and I even felt pleasantly disposed toward Drew. We scrambled into the car without fighting for window seats, and Drew and I commenced whining about ice cream. Molly caved in, and we drove to Willow Tree. All the way home Drew and I sang "Mammy's Little Baby," repeating it again and again while the Twins Downstairs laughed themselves silly:

*Three little children, lying in bed*
*Two was sick an' the other 'most dead*
*Sent for the doctor, the doctor said,*
*Give those children some short'nin' bread*
*Mammy's little baby loves short'nin', short'nin'*
*Mammy's little baby loves short'nin' bread*

Back at home, the tenement felt hot and stuffy. Molly hung our rinsed suits on the line, along with the wet towels and robes, to dry in tomorrow's morning sun. I felt pleasantly tired as we walked upstairs.

"Look at him," Ma said, gesturing toward Dad, who was asleep in his chair. "It's disgusting."

She was putting Skippy into his pajamas.

"Maybe he's just tired," Molly offered.

"He's drunk," Ma said, and that was that.

Tom emerged from the bathroom smelling strongly of English Leather, and his hair was parted in a perfectly straight line. He used Brylcreem to try to tamp down its tendency to curl. I thought he looked sharp.

"I'll be back later," he said, kissing Ma goodbye.

"Don't be too late," Ma said.

"Never am."

I sat in the rocking chair in the parlor and opened my novel about the shadows. I felt perfectly content. And no one came upstairs to disturb me.

"Hey, Finn," Drew called the next afternoon. "Finn!"

I was lying on the couch engrossed in my book. Outside was cloudy and mizzling.

"Finn, look what I've got. It just came in the mail today."

He sounded really excited, which piqued my interest. I put my book down. Drew stood there holding a long, wide plastic strip containing pouches with a frog, a fish, a worm, and two other small animals floating in a yellowish liquid.

"That's formaldehyde," Drew said. "It keeps them from going rotten. Want to help me dissect them?"

"Sure!" I fairly leaped off the couch. When it came to science, I wasn't Dirt in Drew's eyes.

I loved it when Drew played scientist. He always asked me to be his assistant, which thrilled me. This was the real Drew, whose smile was genuine, no trace of the derisive laughter of the previous afternoon. Whatever Granny had said to him must have made some impression. This Drew was sincere, helpful, interesting. And I would remember moments like these for the rest of my life.

Drew chose the frog and put the rest in the refrigerator. He lined up his tools—tools I had helped pay for at Hutchinson's with my 10-cents-a-week allowance. (Other items I'd bought there included Petri dishes, test tubes, and jars of pretty chemicals.) I went and scavenged pieces of white cardboard on which we would mount and label the parts.

"Scalpel," Drew said with authority.

"Scalpel," I repeated, handing it to him.

He made a firm slice down the frog's belly and pinned back the skin, humming as he worked. I felt proud to be his assistant. We worked quietly together until supper, and again after supper, until the complete dissection was done. I surveyed our work: All the parts were cleaned and labeled and mounted with dots of glue on the white cardboard. I was just finishing my last label (Drew's handwriting was awful) when Ma came in and announced bedtime.

It had been an incredible, rare day. We had worked side by side, with Drew removing and explaining each organ and its function, and I marveled at his concentration. It was lovely. With Drew's painstakingly careful work, there hadn't been a wrong cut or slip of the scalpel.

"Ma, can I read for a while before bed?"

"Get ready first. Then you can read for 15 minutes."

Molly came up from talking on the Murphys' phone downstairs.

"Bridie says Father McCuen wants to talk to me after Mass on Sunday."

They both had crushes on Father McCuen. In her scrapbook, Molly had glued a cigarette butt he'd discarded, and she even had the ashes he'd given her on Ash Wednesday, which she'd removed with Scotch tape from her forehead and carefully mounted on the page. Poor man.

"Why? What have you done now?" Ma asked her.

"I haven't done anything. Bridie thinks it's about that college in Vermont."

"The Catholic place? You know you can't go there. It's way too expensive. I don't even know how you're going to afford to go to the state school."

"I'm saving my money. I can make it to Bridgewater State if I commute or carpool with Bridie. I wonder what Father McCuen wants."

She picked up a copy of *Time* magazine she'd bought at Dominic's Soda Shop and went off to the parlor to read. Dad stirred and got up to use the bathroom. He stumbled.

"Isn't that awful," Ma said.

Dad was limping.

"Lights out," Ma said to me.

I came out and said goodnight to Ma and Drew. Then I went to hug Drew, but he stiffened up, so I backed off. I lingered until Dad came out of the bathroom.

"Dad, will you lie down with me, please? Just for a little while?"

"Okay, darl'n'," he said and followed me into the room. He lay down, closed his eyes, and was instantly asleep. I wrapped him in my blankets. When I was covering up his feet, I noticed that one foot was still purple and swollen. I pulled the blanket up carefully.

"Drew, you start getting ready for bed," I heard Ma say. He had gone back to his room to survey his work. Ma went into the parlor, turned on the small TV, and settled onto the couch. *The Honeymooners*, one of her favorite shows, was about to come on.

Without knocking, Uncle Cal entered our kitchen. He went and exchanged pleasantries with Ma, then came into my room. As soon as he saw Dad there, however, he backed out. I kept my eyes shut, hugging my father closer, loving the smell of his soft tee shirt. I didn't want to think about scary things.

The next night, Drew and Little Cal decided to have a Rottenest Sneak Club challenge. Whatever Granny had said, it did not cause Drew to disband the club. To retain my rank as Dirt, I had to sneak to the corner and back, after dark, by hopping fences and traveling through people's backyards without getting caught.

The first yard was easy. It had a chain-link fence and a nice garden with paths, and I crossed the yard quickly and silently to the next fence. This one was wooden and tall. I scrambled up and over, going as fast as my 11-year-old legs would carry me, scraping my knee on the top, and landing hard on the other side. I didn't move, waiting for any indication I'd been heard. Nothing.

The next two houses were simple, but I dreaded the one after. It had a picket fence, and the pickets were old, sharp, full of splinters, and loose. The owners also had dogs, at least two that I knew of. I tried to calm my breathing, put a sneaker against a picket, and heaved myself over. The picket snapped. My leg was momentarily caught between the broken picket and the one next to it. I lay on the ground yanking my leg free, making all kinds of noise and feeling like Peter Rabbit. Then the dogs started barking. I could hear them clearly through the screened windows. Then a screen slid open from one of the tenements. A head appeared.

"Who's out there?" a man's voice yelled down. "I'm letting the dogs out!"

"Shit," I muttered and ran like hell across the dirt yard, vaulting over the fence and landing in bushes on the other side. I heard the dogs barking furiously. No time to linger. I crawled along the bushes that lined the yard, found the opposite fence, and tumbled over. Behind me, a yard away, the stupid dogs barked frantically at the bushes. A light went on in the first-floor window. I heard the screen opening and, crouching low, ran to the next fence. This was a good one. A pear tree in the next yard hung over, its branches low. I pulled myself up on the crossbar, grabbed a branch, and swung into the yard. All the lights were out, and I realized I was in the yard of the four-story tenement, the one that creeped me out even in daylight.

The four floors had apartments on each side of long, dingy hallways and dank toilets at the end of the halls. It smelled funny—not like the usual linguiça or onions or fish, but a bad smell, a smell of something rotten. I knew this because when I helped Drew out with his paper route, he always had me deliver the papers to this house. I'd sneak along behind my brothers when they'd head out to collect their papers a few blocks from our house, where the paperboys gathered. If Drew spotted me getting too close, he'd chase me off some so I couldn't listen to their talk. But I'd get close enough sometimes, and I did listen, fascinated by their boy talk, smoking, jabbing, and spitting.

I ached to belong.

Once the papers came, my brother would drag off their canvas sacks filled with the smell of fresh news. I'd beg to help. For the promise of a nickel, Drew would get me to lug papers to some of the three-story houses and to this four-floor, ugly, smelly one. I'd breathe deep before going in. After flying as fast as I could up and down the stairs I'd meet Drew directly in front of the candy store for my nickel and blow it all on a bag of Fritos, or a blue Popsicle, or two pretzels and a penny candy, or all penny candy, especially the two-fers, or a long strip of white paper with candy dots. The boys would race off home, and I, alone again, would dawdle and daydream all the way back.

I wasn't daydreaming right now though. Crouching in the corner of the yard by the pear tree, afraid to move, I felt a hard lump under my backside. It was a fallen, ripe pear. I grabbed it and took a bite. This wasn't stealing, was it? The pear was delicious and juicy. Then I heard low whispering coming from the direction of the cellar door. I couldn't make out the words, but a match was struck, and I saw two faces in the glow of the light. They were snickering as they passed the cigarette back and forth. The smoke wafted over to where I sat. It was pungent and sweet, not at all like Molly's cigarettes.

When the two boys started giggling, I made my move, hugging the back fence till I reached the other side. This was my last house. It had a low, white fence I could just walk over. I could hear a TV blasting through the downstairs window and was relieved there were no dogs. Emboldened, I walked upright to the far fence and stepped out onto the sidewalk. I was at the corner, across the street from Connie Foster's house. Even at night there were clothes on the line. I heard humming and could see Connie, by the light shining through the screen door, sitting on the stoop, patting a mutt.

I couldn't face going through all those yards again to get home, and it was getting late. I just wanted to talk to someone. I felt alone, tired, and defeated. To hell with the Rottenest Sneak Club. I would walk home on the sidewalk. First, though, I crossed Crapo Street and went to the edge of Connie's property. They had no fence. But, before I could say anything, the mutt came charging down the walk, barking.

"Ambrose! Ambrose! Stop barking! Come back here!"

"Hi," I called out. "It's only me, Finn Kilroy."

Connie ran down the walk to retrieve the mutt, who'd stopped barking and was now wagging its long, fluffy tail. It looked like a bear.

"Where you been? You're all cut up and scratched," Connie said.

I told her.

"Are you crazy? What would you want to do that for?" Connie said, but she was laughing. "Where'd you get the pear?"

"In one of the yards. It's delicious. Want a bite?"

Hesitant at first, Connie took the pear and chomped down.

"Oh my God, that's soooo good! So, why were you out stealing pears?"

"It's the club—a club challenge. The Rottenest Sneak Club."

"What kind of club is that?"

"My brother and the Twins Downstairs made it up. My rank is Dirt."

"You're crazy. Are all white folks as crazy as you?"

The comment took me by surprise. I hadn't thought of myself as white.

"I'm not white—I have freckles."

"You are crazy."

"This your dog?"

We looked at it, now sprawled on the ground between us. It had a curly black coat and a straight snout, like a Scotty. But he was enormous. His ears flopped over.

"Yup. Got him at the pound."

"Wish I had a dog." I was thinking about how nice it would be to have a dog to take long walks with and talk to. I'd never be lonely. "Where'd you get the name Ambrose?"

"I read it in a book."

"You read a lot, don't you?"

"Yeah. Seems like the library's the safest place to be, and the coolest in the summer heat."

*Safe from what,* I wondered, but I didn't ask. The question sounded rude.

"I'm reading that book you showed me. I like it a lot—"

"Hey, Finn!"

I turned around. It was Drew and Little Cal on their bikes.

"You better get home. Ma's in a fit. Hurry up!"

"Okay, but I'm not going through the yards again."

"Then you flunked the challenge," Little Cal said.

"I only half-flunked. I made it all the way to the corner," I insisted.

"Just hurry up home. Ma's in a fit."

"Give me a ride."

"Who are those guys?" Connie asked.

"That's my brother Drew on the black bike, and that's Little Cal—his father is Big Cal and they live downstairs. He has a twin brother, Pat."

"Is that the stupid club?"

"Yeah."

"Finn, move," Drew called. "I'm not waiting."

"See ya," I said to Connie.

"See ya."

I hopped on the crossbar of Drew's bike, and he pedaled like mad down the street. I could smell his sweat through his shirt. It was sweet.

"What took you so long? Did you get caught?"

"No—and that's a lot of houses."

"You've got scratches everywhere. But you did good."

I was so surprised by the compliment I was speechless. All I could do was mutter, "Thanks."

We saw Ma in the window with her rosary beads.

"Where have you been?" she demanded as soon as I came in. "Look at the time—it's almost 8:30."

"Sorry, Ma. I was up the street—"

"With Isabelle?"

"No! I went to the candy store. I had two pennies."

"Where'd you get the pennies?"

"I found them. On the sidewalk."

Ma looked at me suspiciously.

"She was talking to that colored girl on the corner," Drew said, and I was stunned by his betrayal.

"What were you talking to her for?" Ma wanted to know.

"I—I don't know. We were talking about books."

"Books? Look, I don't want you hanging around up there."

"Why not?"

"Because I said so. How'd you get all scratched up like that? Your knee is bleeding."

"I tripped on the sidewalk."

"From now on you be in this house by 8. And no more going up to the corner, you hear?"

Ma put some water in a pan and put it on the Magic Chef to heat.

"Take those filthy clothes off and get into the bathroom so I can clean those cuts. I don't know how you always manage to get so banged up."

Tom and Molly sat side by side in the parlor rockers. They sang along to "Magic Moments" by Perry Como, Molly's new record. They listened to music constantly.

"Ma, that's too hot!" I yelped as my mother dabbed at my cut knee with a gauze pad doused in water from the stove. She added a little cool water from the tap.

"That's better," I said.

Ma got the Mercurochrome down from the medicine cabinet. She unscrewed the cap, dabbed the red liquid on my cut with the wand, then put a plaster over it. "Put your pajamas on now and get to bed. No reading tonight."

"But Ma, why? It's not even 9 o'clock!"

"Next time you be home by 8, when you're supposed to be."

"What's all the noise up here?"

Uncle Cal stood in the doorway. Drew ducked into his bedroom and closed the door.

"Nothing much," Ma said. "Just Finn getting first aid and being sent to bed early for not coming home on time."

"You weren't giving your mother a hard time, were you?"

"No," I said quietly.

"I'll put her to bed," Uncle Cal said to Ma, who was putting the first aid things away.

I quickly changed into my pajamas while Ma heated water for the dishes. On my way past my father, who was asleep in his chair, I deliberately tripped over his outstretched legs. Dad woke up briefly.

"Will you come lie down with me, Daddy?"

"Not tonight, darl'n'," he muttered and fell immediately back to sleep.

"I'll tuck you in," Uncle Cal said, and I knew what that meant.

Ma brought the water to the pantry sink and started washing the dishes. I ran to my room and got under the covers.

"So, what were you doing out so late?" he asked as he reached under the covers and slipped my pajama bottoms down.

"I was just playing," I said.

Uncle Cal continued to make small talk as he rubbed between my legs and slipped his fingers inside me. Then he took my hand and put it inside his pants, making me rub him. When he heard Ma coming out of the pantry, he pulled back and zipped himself up.

"Go right to sleep now," he said sternly and left my room, closing the door behind him.

In the darkness, I lay listening to "Magic Moments" playing for the umpteenth time. I could hear Tom and Molly singing, their happy voices sounding alien to me as I lay in my dark room. As soon as I heard Uncle Cal leave, I got up and opened my door. Ma was sitting in the kitchen opposite Dad, reading a magazine. If she noticed me opening the door, she didn't mention it. I hated the dark. I crept back to the bed I shared with Molly. At some point during the night, she shook me awake from a nightmare. A big black dog was chasing me through a maze of backyards, and I couldn't make my legs run fast enough. I tried to call my father, but couldn't get my voice to work above a whisper. The dog was gaining ground. I could feel its hot breath on my bare legs. I screamed, and Molly shook me awake. She put her arm around me, and in time we slept like spoons.

It was almost a full month later when I saw Connie in the library again.

It was August, hot and humid, and I loved the coolness of the library. I was looking over some new books when Connie came in with Nicky attached at the hip. She went to the front desk to return her books, then saw me sitting there.

"Hey," she said, coming over.

"Hey. Hey, Nicky."

Nicky ducked behind Connie's legs and sucked his thumb.

"Been jumping through anyone's yards lately?"

"No, that was just a special challenge for that night. We had a peashooter fight in the cellar last night, though. It was fun."

"You shoot peas at each other?" Connie's eyebrows arched.

"No, silly, we shoot spitballs. Through a piece of pipe—a peashooter. The only lousy part is that I had to pick up all the spitballs after."

"Gross. Why you?"

"Because I'm Dirt, remember?"

"Oh yeah, you told me." Clearly, she did not approve. "You taking those books out?"

I nodded. Connie looked at the titles.

"This one's good. This one's good. This one's crappy. Put it back."

I went to put it back, and Connie went over to the biography section. While she was making her choices, I picked out three juvenile books—three by Dr. Seuss. I brought them to Connie.

"Here—these are for Nicky."

Connie looked the books over.

"I love the illustrations," she said. "You ready to go?"

"Yep."

We checked out our books and went out into the hot sun. It was very humid, and the air hung heavy with a sluggish brininess. Despite the heat, we decided to take a detour and stroll down South Water Street to see the sights.

I could tell Connie didn't approve of the Rottenest Sneak Club, but I desperately wanted her to think highly of me. I didn't want her to think of me as just Dirt. I searched my mind for something to impress her.

"We're building a house," I announced suddenly.

"Who?"

"Me and my brothers and the Twins Downstairs."

"Where?"

"In our backyard. It's going to be gigunda."

"I'll bet."

"It is! It's almost up to the second-floor windows!"

"You're kidding. Where'd you get the wood?"

"From the lot on the corner. Every night we bring some pieces back."

"You steal that wood?"

"It's free. It's nobody's wood. No one ever goes there."

"So why do you take it at night?"

I shrugged. "I don't know. Want to help tonight?"

"My father would kill me if I got caught stealing."

"I told you, it's not stealing. No one wants this wood. It's old and full of knotholes. It's free."

Connie just shook her head. We crossed Cove Street, passed Fontaine's Pharmacy, and had come to the 5 & 10.

"Come on, let's cut through here. It's way faster."

As soon as we walked in, a woman with blue-gray hair said, "Can I help you girls find something?"

"No, thank you," I said and kept on walking.

The woman followed us down all the aisles as we made our way toward the back of the store, where the notions and knickknacks were.

"Hey, isn't this cute?" I said, picking up a small ceramic kitten. The woman was right there.

"Do you want to buy that?" she asked me.

"No—I'm just looking."

"Well, you better put it back before you drop it."

I did as I was told, and the woman rearranged it slightly. She continued to follow us until we reached the back entrance and went outside. We were across from the City Mission.

"That lady was creepy," I said. "I always cut through there, and I've never been followed before."

"It's because you were with me this time, silly. The old bat thought I was going to steal something. You should see how nervous she gets when I go in with Freddie and Fremont."

I looked at her, puzzled. Connie stopped walking and looked at me dead on.

"How old are you?" she asked.

"Eleven. And you?"

"Twelve. Almost thirteen. You're old enough to know better. Open your eyes."

I did, and it suddenly dawned on me. I felt chastised and embarrassed; my whole body turned red.

"Ever buy candy at Motta's?" she asked.

"Sure."

"Ever buy the two-for-a-penny black licorice shaped like babies?"

I nodded again, and this time I felt ashamed. The licorice candies she was referring to were called "nigger babies."

"You should see the look on your face right now," Connie said. "I don't know whether to laugh or cry."

She opted for laughter, and I tried to join in.

"I'm thirsty," Nicky said.

It was the first time I'd heard him speak. His voice was soft and raspy.

"We're almost home, baby," Connie said.

When we came to my house, I asked if she wanted to come in back and see the house we were building. Connie hesitated.

"I guess so. But I hope I don't get caught."

"Get caught for what?"

"My father doesn't want me going into white folks' yards."

I was about to say, *So?* But I held my tongue. We walked around the house to the back.

"Oh-my-God, look at that thing!"

The house, as I had told her, was almost as tall as our pantry window. Two sides and part of a third were up.

"When it's done, we're going to have couches, chairs, and everything in here. People are just giving us stuff."

"What people?"

I spread my arms to indicate the neighborhood.

"Whenever we're out here working, all these people watch us from their windows. It's like they're cheering us on. Come on up—it's very sturdy."

I hopped up onto the floor, followed by Nicky, handed up by Connie, then by Connie herself. She looked around.

"It's going to be fantastic once the furniture is in. And we'll put pictures on the walls to cover up some of the knotholes."

I twirled around the center support beam. The floor was solid; it didn't make a single squeak.

"Wow. This is amazing."

"Yeah. My mother calls it 'the house that Jack built,' but I don't know why—my father hasn't been very involved in it. Mostly it's the boys and me, and Uncle Cal, who saws the wood. We'll be able to sleep out here when it's done."

Ma came to the pantry window and began hanging clothes on the line that ran just above the unbuilt roof of our clubhouse.

"Hi, Ma," I called up. "This is Connie and her little brother Nicky."

"Hi," Ma said. "Finn, come in now. I need you to set the table for supper."

"Aw, Ma, it's way too early. Why me?"

"Because I said so."

"I have to go anyway," Connie said.

Before they left, I showed Nicky how to get a drink of water from the outside tap. In the end, the whole front of his shirt was soaked.

"Great," Connie said. "Now I've got to change you when we get home."

"When did your mother die?" I blurted out.

"Three years ago. When he was born." She whispered the last bit.

"I'm sorry. It must be hard for you. You must miss your mom a lot."

"I'm sorry too. I miss her every day," she said quietly.

"Hey, you going to help me get wood tonight?"

"No!... Well, maybe. We'll see. Come on, Nicky."

Nicky sucked his thumb with one hand and waved to me with the other. I trudged upstairs with my books.

"Why was that girl with you?" Ma wanted to know as soon as I walked in.

"We met in the library and walked home together. I brought her in the yard to see the house. She's 11."

"I don't want you hanging around with her. Didn't I just tell you that?"

"No—you told me not to go to the corner. And why not anyway?"

"Because I said so. And because—she's too old for you. You're only 9."

"But I'll be 10 soon. And Ma, she's a nice kid, and she reads a lot and helps me pick out books and—"

"You can pick out your own books. You don't need to hang around with her. You've got your brothers and Molly and the Twins Downstairs. You don't need anyone else."

"But Ma, I don't want to hang out with them all the time, and besides, they hate me—"

"Don't say that. Now that's enough. Set the table."

"You spoil everything!" I said, on the verge of tears with frustration and an anger I couldn't name. It wasn't fair. Connie was a great kid. So what if she was a little older than me?

"*Now,*" Ma said. "And do not talk to me like that again."

I looked at what she was putting in the roasting pan. *Oh no. Grumpies.* Stuffed cabbages made me gag.

"I don't like grumpies," I said.

"Then eat bread. *Gwumpkies* are good for you," she replied, correcting my mispronunciation of the word for stuffed cabbage rolls, a favorite of the Polish families in the area.

I finished setting the table, smacking the dishes down. Ma looked at me but said nothing. I flounced into my room and shut the door.

Concentration on my new book was impossible. I found myself reading the same paragraph over and over again. Finally, I just put the book down. My eyes stung with threatening tears. What was going on with Ma and Connie? What was the great secret? I simply had to have another friend to play with. All this time spent fighting with the boys—it wasn't right. The other day Little Cal had slammed me in the back with such force that it left a complete imprint of his hand on my skin.

Their anger toward me was out of control, and it always seemed disproportionate to whatever crime I had committed. For reasons beyond my ken, I was a scapegoat. But I didn't know that then. I needed someone like Connie in my life. I felt happy and free with her, and she taught me so much. Ma and Aunt Joan were blind to what was going on in the yard, but when it came to Connie they had eagle eyes. Even so, they didn't really see her. They didn't see that, unlike Izzy from the other corner, who was boy crazy and silly, Connie was quiet, thoughtful, interesting, and smart.

I decided I was going to disobey my mother. I suspected Connie knew a whole lot more than I did about a lot of things, and I was curious. There weren't many families like the Fosters in our church. Or in my school, for that matter. I wondered why. There were only two black girls in my grade. I didn't know them well; we rarely talked.

So what if she was colored? I knew this was Ma's real objection, and it angered me that she wouldn't say it. It was as though, on some level, even she knew it was wrong, but she didn't dare stand up to Joan and Callan. The odd thing was that they didn't seem to object to Tom's friendship with Fremont, which had grown from their paper routes. I couldn't figure out the mysteries of the universe. But I was going to pursue my friendship with Connie no matter what.

Other trouble was coming, too. My world was about to be upended, and I didn't know how I was going to be able to cope. Molly—my rock, my hero, my roommate—was leaving me.

# 5. Molly

Connie went to the DeValles School on Orchard Street, directly across from Ashley Park, which could be a rough place. On one end, a gravel baseball/soccer field with no fences meshed with open areas where bicyclists, kite-flyers and small pods of kids scrambled around, throwing or kicking balls, swearing in Portuguese and English. A granite ledge in the middle of the park provided play territory for other imaginative groups. At the top of a gentle slope, swings, seesaws, and basketball courts were mostly filled with rough-looking, dark-skinned boys intensely occupied with their playtime business. Caught up in my own personal dramas, I was oblivious to most of these goings-on.

The DeValles School also bordered the Page Mill lot, which I'd hated since I was a small child. When I was about Nicky's age, maybe younger, Molly took me for a walk to Ashley Park, and on the way back we cut through the mill lot. The old weave shed of the defunct textile mill housed the Cove Discount Center, a popular department store. Between the Cove store and the school was a trash landfill. The stench of rotting garbage mixed sickeningly with the smell of rubber from the sprawling, massive Goodyear plant across Orchard Street. A thick muddy odor from low tide in Clarks Cove wafted through the air. As we cut through the lot, overgrown bulrush and elephant grasses towered over my head. I looked around, and Molly was gone. Just like that.

I stood in the grass looking up at the blue immensity of the sky. The mills made steady, low whirring sounds that made them seem alive and dangerous. I was terrified, yet I was afraid to raise my voice. The autumn breeze blew through, bending the grass and making a swishing sound.

"Molly?" I called in a loud whisper. "Molly, where are you?" I called again, then started to cry. Cries turned into sobs. I was utterly abandoned, with no way to get home. Every direction I turned in echoed back the threatening sounds of the mills.

"MOLLY!" I sobbed one last time, bereft.

Finally, after what felt like hours but in reality was only a few minutes, Molly appeared again. She came and scooped me up in her arms.

*"Why did you leave me?"* I wailed over and over, and Molly kept saying how sorry she was. She carried me all the way home, holding me close in her arms.

We were at supper—I was eating Portuguese bread with butter and cukes without vinegar—when Ma dropped the bombshell.

"Well," she said, looking around the table. "We have a big surprise to announce."

We all stopped and looked at her.

"It looks like Molly is going to St. Ann's College in Vermont! She leaves in a few weeks!"

The table erupted with, *What? Where? How?* Ma looked proud, and so did Dad. Only I was silent.

"Father McCuen got her a scholarship to go. So, it looks like you'll be the first one in the whole family to go to college," Ma said, smiling at Molly.

Dad just shook his head. He looked bewildered.

Still in shock, I looked at my sister as if she were some sort of traitor. "Does that mean you'll be going away? Staying away?"

"Of course, idiot, you think she's going to drive to Vermont every day?" Drew said.

I had no idea of where Vermont was, but it sounded far away. I couldn't breathe. I felt a knot form in my throat. I felt stones—cold stones—in my belly. I pushed my chair back and went to the room I shared with Molly, slamming the door shut behind me.

"Uh oh," I heard my mother say.

"What's with her?" Drew asked.

I flung myself on the bed. I couldn't cry. My belly was icy with fear. I would be alone in my bed night after night. Who would wake me from my nightmares? Who would be there for me, as only Molly often was? Who would make me laugh the way Molly did when things were tense?

There was a soft knock on the door as Molly came quietly into the room.

"Go away," I said, facing the wall.

"Don't be mad," Molly said. "I'll be back, some weekends. And you can write to me, and I'll write back. Tell you what, I promise the first weekend I come home I'll take you to the movies, okay? Is there a movie you want to see? We'll go to one of those big movie theaters downtown, like the State or the Olympia."

I said nothing.

"Finn, do you remember that time when I left you in the elephant grass at the Page Mill lot?"

"Yes."

"Do you know why I did that?"

"To be mean."

"No, it wasn't to be mean. It was—well—I wanted to see—to know—if you would need me."

"I did need you."

"I know that, now. Do you still need me?"

It was a long time before I finally answered.

"Yes," I said, rolling over and wrapping my body around my sister. Now I cried.

"I'm not leaving you forever. Just a few weeks at a time."

"What about my nightmares?"

"Ma and Dad are here. They'll take care of you."

I shook my head. I knew better. "They won't even hear me."

"The way you scream? Sure, they will."

"And what about thunderstorms at night?"

Molly sighed.

"Is Vermont far away?"

"A few hours."

"That's far. Won't you be lonely?"

"I'm sure I will. But I'll write."

"To me?"

"Yes. Will you write back?"

"Yes. I don't understand why you have to go so far away."

"Well, it's because it's a very good school, and I'm lucky to be going there."

Inside a voice was screaming, loud: *Please don't leave me.* But I knew she had to go.

Tom came to the door.

"Hey, Finn, we're going to work on the house. Want to help?"

"Maybe."

I disentangled myself and wiped my face on the bedclothes. But I still felt icy in the pit of my stomach, and no number of promises could warm me up. I was devastated. I thought I might throw up.

"When you come in, I'll play you a game of Parcheesi, okay?"

"Okay," I said, the tiniest bit mollified. I went outside with my brothers and helped by straightening old bent nails with a rock. As soon as it got dark, we decided to make our run to the corner for the wood.

"Pssst! Hey!"

I turned around as we left the yard. Connie was standing by the fence.

"Connie! You're here!"

"I am. But if I'm caught, I'm dead."

"You won't get caught. Where's Nicky?"

"I put him to bed. He's asleep, finally."

"That's great. Hey, guys, look who came to help!"

They looked over at her in silence.

Finally Tom said, "Hey, Connie."

"Look, I don't have to go. I was just being silly, is all."

"Are you kidding? C'mon, it'll be fun."

"Are you sure?" she asked, looking over at my brothers.

"Let's go before it gets too late," Tom said.

We trooped up the street to the lot and selected the best pieces of two-by-fours and planks that we could find. We carried them on our shoulders and sang "The Ants Go Marching One by One" all the way home. Connie and I managed to carry a few pieces. The wood was not very good. It was dark and weathered, and many pieces were loaded with knotholes. I couldn't imagine anyone paying real money for it.

When we returned, the boys set up lanterns and flashlights and started putting up the third wall. Connie and I held boards in place while the boys nailed them on.

"This is really cool," Connie said.

"Yeah, it's going to be great when it's done... My sister is going far away to college."

"Yeah? Where?"

"Vermont."

"Wow. I wish I could go to college someday."

"I hate it."

"Why?"

"Because—she'll be away." I suddenly felt myself choking up. Connie looked at me curiously.

"You share a room?"

I nodded.

"Then you'll have a whole room to yourself. Won't that be neat?"

"I don't want a room to myself."

"Scared of the dark?" she teased.

"Yes," I replied seriously, thinking that, and so much more. Connie looked at me but said nothing. We worked side by side in silence.

Then Connie said abruptly, "I've got to go."

"Why?"

"It's late. My father will be mad."

I walked Connie to the sidewalk.

"Sorry you have to go. Thanks for helping. See ya."

Connie gave me a quick, affectionate hug. Then she took off at a trot, her thin, lithe body covering ground quickly. I watched till she safely passed the four-floor house. By then, Ma was calling us all in.

Aunt Joan was sitting by the door when we came in, and I had the impression of a conversation interrupted.

"That colored girl was over tonight," Drew said as soon as we got in the door.

"For Chrissake," Tom said. "Can't you ever shut up?"

"We know," Aunt Joan said.

"Shit," I muttered.

"Don't use that dirty language," Ma said. "Or I'll wash your mouth out with soap. Didn't I just tell you not to be hanging around with that girl?"

"What was she doing here anyway?" Aunt Joan asked.

"She was helping us build our house," I said.

"What's wrong with you? Why are you so disobedient?" Ma said.

"Ma, she's a nice kid. I like her. I don't get what the problem is."

"She's colored, stupid," Drew said.

"So what?" I looked at Ma.

"Drew's right," Aunt Joan said. "White people don't hang around with the coloreds." *The coloreds.* She said it as if they were enemy forces invading our territory.

"You're not serious," Tom said.

Ma looked from me to Tom to Aunt Joan. Finally, she said, "You don't have to go out of your way to be friendly. Stick to your brothers."

"But Ma, you know they don't want me hanging around with them—"

"Don't be ridiculous. Anyway, that's it—"

"No, it's not," Tom said. "I like Connie, and her brother Fremont is a good guy, too. I don't see why Finn and Connie shouldn't be friends. Where are we, down South?"

"Tom, you should know better," Aunt Joan said. "They're not like us—"

"Not like us how? Because their skin is dark and their hair is different?"

"No—they're just not like us," Aunt Joan repeated.

"That's absurd," Tom said.

"Tom! Don't talk to your aunt that way!" Ma said.

"I'm sorry, Aunt Joan. But with all due respect, that's bull crap. If you got to know them, you'd find out they're just like us."

"Tom. You're young. You don't know any better," Aunt Joan said.

I thought Tom was going to explode, but he just slammed out of the kitchen into the parlor.

"That's it, Fiona. Now get washed up and ready for bed," Ma said.

I didn't dare say another word. Anyway, Tom had said it all. I went into the bathroom and ran the cold water to wash.

Through the door, I heard Aunt Joan say to my mother, "You sure have your hands full."

When I was ready for bed, I went and got Molly, who was in our room writing in her journal.

"Ready for Parcheesi?" I asked her.

"Yes—just let me finish this sentence, and I'll be right out. Set things up."

I set up the board, and Ma wanted to know what I thought I was doing.

"Molly said she'd play with me when we got in," I said.

Ma looked at the clock, but said nothing. She was just settling down after getting Skippy to sleep.

"Can I play too?" Drew asked.

"I guess so," I said. It would feel good to bump him off the board.

After the game, I went over to wake Dad up from his sleep in the chair.

"Dad, will you lie down with me?"

"Sure, darl'n'," he said, but he fell back to sleep again.

"Just go to bed," Ma said.

"But Ma—"

"Go!" she said and sat in the chair opposite Dad's to read. I felt panicky.

"Molly?"

"No."

My heart sank.

"But I'll read you a story," Molly said.

Yes!

I hurried to my room and climbed under the covers. Molly went to the bookshelf that hung on the wall above the bed.

"*Little Women*?"

"Read it."

"*Eight Cousins*?"

"Read it."

"How about *Five Little Peppers*?"

"Okay."

"Just one chapter, though."

That should be enough, I hoped. I heard Uncle Cal's footsteps coming up the stairs. The layout was not to his liking.

He talked to Tom about getting nails for the house, then said to him, "And I don't want you giving your mother any more trouble about the coloreds." I couldn't hear Tom's response. I wished I could see his face.

Uncle Cal went downstairs, and in a while I heard Tom say to Ma, "I'm going out," and he left, closing the door sharply behind him.

Molly finished the chapter.

"Will you read to me every night till it's done?"

"Maybe. We'll finish the book before I leave. I promise."

She turned out the light, and I grinned into the darkness. Then Ma came in and sat on my bed.

"Fiona, I need to talk to you about Connie."

I sat up against my pillows. I had no idea what was coming, but I didn't feel like fighting. Every time we got in the car, Ma would say, "Brace yourselves!" I braced myself now.

"I like Connie," she said slowly, surprising me. "In fact, they seem like a very nice family."

"So, what's the problem?"

"You know what the problem is. White people don't…hang around with colored people."

"Why not?"

"Because they're… different."

"Different how?" I wasn't trying to be snarky. I really wanted to get to the bottom of it. Aunt Joan had said the same thing. "As far as I know from Connie, the only thing different is the color of their skin."

"Oh, Fiona. You're so young. You'll learn as you get older. They *think* different. And they don't like white people."

"But Ma, Connie likes me, and Fremont likes Tom."

"You don't know that, Finn. They might say one thing, but they're thinking another. They could be using you. I just don't want you to get hurt, that's all. You can't trust them."

"But how can you know this? How do you know what they're thinking? You think Connie is using me? How? For what? Ma, I just don't get it. In fact, if I were Connie, I'd be afraid of me—white people do bad things to colored people." *Go ahead, Finn, say it,* I thought. *Say it. Say, "You're wrong, Ma."*

"I know you don't get it, and I'll tell you a secret: I don't get it either. It's just the way things are, that's all."

"Ma, it isn't right. When I'm with Connie, we have a great time. She's really smart, and knows a lot about books and—everything. She's a good friend and she is *not* using me. She's just like us."

Ma sighed and ran her hand through my hair.

"Finn, you're very trusting. I'm not saying you have to be mean to Connie. Just don't go out of your way to be with her, that's all. To be honest, I don't feel as strong about it as Aunt Joan and Uncle Cal. But if they see you with Connie, it could… cause problems."

She took my hand and held it. We were quiet for a while. Finally, Ma said, "I do like Connie. She seems very nice—"

"Ma, if you got to know her better, you'd see she's not… what you're worried about."

"Maybe," she conceded. "But around the country, coloreds are turning against whites… I just don't want you hurt, that's all."

"If I run into Connie at the library, can I still walk home with her?"

"I—I suppose so. But leave it at that." She sighed again. "Come on, now, go to sleep."

I slid down into the bed, and she tucked me in.

"Close your eyes, and I'll sing you a song."

I nestled against her, and she began: "Skeeters are a-humming on the honeysuckle vine…"

---

Sunday morning Mass was said by Father McCuen. Drew was one of the altar boys. Father McCuen was tall and thin, with glasses that gave his face a gentle look. He had dimples and an easy smile. Not in appearance, but in demeanor, he reminded me of Bing Crosby. I stared at him, my expression glum. Ma said she wanted to talk to him, so we all traipsed into the sacristy behind the altar after Mass. Drew was still putting things away. He looked downright angelic in his altar boy robes. Father McCuen was wriggling out of his alb.

"Hello, Mrs. Kilroy—and clan," he said, smiling. He shook hands with Dad and Tom and gave Ma a hug.

"Father, I don't know how to thank you for what you did for Molly," Ma said.

"Well, she deserves it, and she is very bright. She should go to a good school."

Molly blushed.

"You know, my family—cousins, aunts—are telling me she should stay home and go to work, that college is wasted on a girl," Ma said.

Father McCuen winced. "An education is never wasted, especially on someone with Molly's potential. People can be so shortsighted. You stick to your guns, Mrs. Kilroy. Don't let them rattle you. What about you, Tom? Any thoughts for your future?"

"I don't think I'll be going to college. I'm not the school type. But Drew is. He wants to be a scientist."

"Good for you, Drew. You follow your dream. If your sister can go to college, so can you."

"Yes, Father."

"And what about you, Finn? Any dreams for you?"

*Only nightmares,* I thought, and turned bright red. I was extremely shy. I just shrugged.

"She loves books," Molly told him.

"Think you'll follow in your sister's footsteps?"

"Maybe," I whispered.

"And what about you, young man?" he asked Skippy, bending down to see him eye-to-eye. But Skippy immediately ducked behind Ma. "Going to be an altar boy like your brothers?"

Skippy poked his red head around Ma and smiled, nodding.

Just before we left, Dad shook Father McCuen's hand and muttered, "Thank you." He was just as shy as I was.

"You're welcome, Jack. I can't think of anyone more deserving of this chance."

At home, Ma and Dad made our Sunday breakfast of fried eggs, toast, Scotch ham, and coffee. The house smelled delicious.

"Bridie's coming over later to help me clean out my stuff," Molly said.

"Clean your closet," Ma said.

Molly rolled her eyes.

"What about the cottage?"

"You'll have to go without me."

"Oh, that's too bad," Ma said, looking at Dad. "We won't have you to drive."

"Tom can drive."

"No—we have to drop him off at work."

Molly thought about it. "Well, I guess I could go—I've got three weeks to pack. Can Bridie come with us?"

"I guess so."

After the breakfast things were washed and put away, Dad walking back and forth between the kitchen and the pantry with a dish cloth slung over his shoulder, we got ready for the cottage. Molly went downstairs to use the phone to tell Bridie to bring a bathing suit. I went outside and sat on the porch to wait and brood over Molly's leaving.

I was sitting there with fat tears sliding down my cheeks when Bridie appeared.

"Hey, Pip, why so blue?" Bridie said, startling me. She always called me Pip. I didn't mind. It was better than Dirt or It, and Bridie wasn't being mean.

"Nothing," I said, wiping my eyes and nose on my sleeve.

"You're crying over nothing?"

"Just lonely, that's all."

"Yeah, it's going to be hard on you with Molly gone."

*No kidding.*

"At least you have the rest of your family to hang out with."

The hair on the back of my neck prickled.

"You mean the boys," I said with sarcasm. "In case you hadn't noticed, they hate me, and I'm sick of them."

"Oh, I'm sure they don't hate you."

I looked at her. Not her, too.

"When are you people going to get it?" Were they all blind and deaf?

Bridie didn't answer. The street was quiet on a Sunday afternoon. I turned away from Bridie. It was all getting to me.

"I'm sorry," Bridie said and tried to put her arm around me. I shrugged it off. I didn't want her sympathy. I just wanted them all to open their eyes.

I flung myself off the porch and went to sit in the car, an ancient, gray Plymouth with a roomy interior and cloth seats. It was hot and stuffy, so I rolled the windows down.

Molly and Drew came outside carrying boxes and paper bags to put in the trunk. Tom followed with the heavy cooler.

"Hi, Bridie. I didn't know you were here," Molly said.

"Yup. All ready. I've been having a chat with Pip. It didn't go so well."

"You mean 'It,'" Drew corrected and smirked.

"Shut up, Drew," Tom said.

Bridie said, "I'm beginning to see what she means."

I sat there steaming.

"Yeah, she has a rough time of it with the boys. She really needs a girlfriend her own age," Molly said.

The conversation might have continued, but Ma and Dad came out.

Going to the cottage was a complicated affair. There were boxes of food for lunch, supper, and snacks; bags of bathing suits, towels, and robes; other bags with nighttime clothes like sweatshirts and jeans; games to play; and the giant cooler with the refrigerator food and drinks. Aunt Joan and Uncle Cal and the Twins Downstairs had already left ages ago.

The car finally packed, we all piled in, with Dad in the driver's seat. Molly would drive home.

"Okay, brace yourselves," Ma said as we pulled away from the curb and went jolting up the street. Dad was a very nervous driver. On the corner, I waved to Connie, who sat out in front with Little Nicky and Ambrose. She didn't see me. Ma took out her rosary beads and commenced whispering the Rosary. The car was still hot and stuffy. I sat squished between Molly and Bridie, while Drew and Tom had the windows. Skippy sat on Molly's lap.

"You sure you can get a ride home?" Ma asked Tom as we dropped him off at Gulf Hill Dairy.

"Yeah, Ma, I'm all set," he said. He waved once and disappeared inside. The smell of fresh fertilizer from the dairy farm wafted through the open windows.

"Oh, gross," Drew whined, covering his nose and mouth.

"Look at the little nalfs!" Skippy said, referring to the calves across the street with their cows.

"Calves," Molly said.

"Nalfs," Skippy agreed happily.

We continued on from South to North Dartmouth, Molly and Bridie singing in harmony.

"That sounded good," Bridie said. "Let's do it again."

They launched into another round of "But Tonight You Belong to Me."

Drew looked pained.

"Cottage Street," Ma said as we turned down Reed Road. "Cottage Street, Cottage Street, good ol', good ol' Cottage Street," Ma sang off-key as we drove down the windy road. We pulled into the yard at Aunt Emma's cottage, where other cars were already parked. Several cousins were scampering about. Granny was already there, having ridden in with her sister Theresa and brother-in-law Bib.

As soon as the car was unpacked and the food put away, we got into our bathing suits and went for a swim in the lake, which was the color of strong-brewed tea. Bridie and Molly swam out to the raft, where they sat and talked nonstop. Drew and Skippy and I played in the shallows with Dad, jumping off his rounded shoulders into the water. We swam until lunch, and after lunch Dad took Drew and me out in the rowboat to go fishing. I loved the look of my father's arms, reddened from the sun, pulling the oars, his arm hair turning golden in the summer light. Dad loved this part of the day best. He loved the gentle waves, the peace and quiet, the clean air, the warmth of the sun on his freckled shoulders. Drew proudly caught a hornpout, and I captured a couple of turtles in my net.

When we got back, Drew put his ugly hornpout in a bucket of lake water. Then we set turtles to racing. Mine won. When that ceased to amuse us, we played horseshoes and tag and other games with the cousins. Cousins, aunts, and uncles were everywhere. Bridie and Molly went blueberry picking. For supper, we had a cookout of hamburgers, followed by a sunset swim. Dad gave us baths in the lake water with Ivory soap. I loved seeing the bar of soap float in the lake. Then we got dressed in sweatshirts and jeans and played hide-and-seek until the mosquitoes drove us in.

By then, most everyone had gathered on the porch to begin the singing as the darkness gathered outside. I sat at the feet of my grandmother as we sang all the old songs. Even Drew joined in, and we all harmonized. I felt safe, loved, warm. In the end, we sang "Now Is the Hour," holding the long last note an extra beat, sending it echoing across the lake. In the distant summer air, a cheery round of applause resonated from some of the neighboring cottages.

Then, sleepy and content, we piled back into the car for the long drive home, back to the stifling tenement and another work week for Dad, who sat pleasantly potted in the back seat and hummed all the way home. I cuddled between Bridie and Dad and dozed fitfully. Skippy was fast asleep in Ma's lap.

The summer was winding down. Dad had a week's vacation coming to him, beginning Friday night, and that meant one thing: We would be going to Lincoln Park.

When we were young, we had this annual outing to the local amusement park. On the afternoon and evening of the day we were to go, my brothers, sister, and I would be in a frenzy of anticipation. We would have eaten an early supper so we'd be all washed and ready to go as soon as Dad came home.

My mother called me. "Finn, go up to the corner and meet your father."

"Why?"

"So he'll come straight home. He won't go into the club if you're with him."

"Geez, Ma, I don't want to do that. It's like spying or something. Can't Drew or Tom go? Why does it have to be me?"

"Because the boys are doing the dishes, your sister is busy, and because I said so. Period. Now go before it's too late. And take Skippy with you."

"Ma, do I have—"

"Yes, you do. Now go!"

"I don't want to go," Skippy protested. "I want to stay here with Tom and Drew."

"Skip. Stop whining and go with your sister. If you miss your father, I swear you won't be going to the park tonight. Go now and hurry up."

I clumped down the stairs of our tenement with Skippy in tow, muttering, "I'm not going," at every step.

When we began our walk up the cracked sidewalk, we looked back and saw our mother standing at the second-floor parlor window. Skippy pulled his hand free from mine and clung to the picket fence, looking pitiably back at Ma. She made a shooing gesture, and I gave him a yank. So we made our slow progress to the corner, Skippy grabbing at pickets all the way up until we were out of our mother's sight. When Skippy realized he was no longer being watched, he let go of the fences and took my hand.

"What ride do you want to go on first?" he asked me. "I want to go on the big roller coaster."

"You're nuts. You don't mean it."

"Yes, I do. Drew said I could go."

"Then Drew is teasing you. You have to be this tall,"—I illustrated—"to be allowed on, and you're not half that size. Stick to the little roller coaster. I'll go on with you, and we can sit in the front seat. Besides," I added, as an afterthought, "if you went on the big roller coaster, you'd throw up, and we'd all have to go home."

Skippy agreed that was probably true and asked what my favorite ride was.

"The Dobby Horses," I said immediately, "the merry-go-round." I gave a little skip of delight. "I love the horse that's all black with a white mane and tail. I LOVE horses," I shouted to the world at large. "Hey, maybe Dad will have some gumballs for us."

We stood together on the corner of our street and the very busy County Street, which I had been allowed to cross alone only this year—and I was 9. I hated it; the traffic whizzing by scared me, made me feel small. I hoped I wouldn't have to cross the street to intercept Dad. All along the sidewalks were men smoking, sitting on stoops, spitting into the street and gutters. I thought they were gross. A small clump of men—my father's cronies from the Z Club—gathered across the street. They were standing at the club entrance, and I was charged with keeping my father from getting close to them.

With every passing moment, I became more and more anxious. We had to go tonight. It was a promise. Next to Christmas, this was our happiest time of the year. The trip to Lincoln Park happened just once each summer, and usually it was on the night before my father started his vacation from the mill. My father was able to get a pass for all the rides from Tillie, his friend from the mill who worked a second job handing out tickets for rides at the park. I never met her—Dad always went and spoke to her alone—but I thought she must be a saint. Lincoln Park was only a few acres, but, to us, it was paradise.

The whole fantastic trip began when Dad drove down a back road to the back entrance to the park, which faced the roller coaster. As soon as he turned the car into the driveway, we faced the enormous wooden tracks and heard its signature clack-clacking as it climbed the highest peak. Then there was a moment's pause as riders read the "Please Hold onto Your Hats!" sign at the top, before the coaster plunged down the hill with a great roar melded with the screams of its passengers. The screaming continued throughout the ride, but the volume increased and waned as the string of cars moved close to and away from wherever you stood. Whenever I heard that sound, all my insides turned to jelly.

We would ride them all—the coasters, the Scrambler, the Ferris wheel, the Dodgem cars, the Tilt-a-Whirl, and of course, the merry-go-round. We would go through the Fun House, although I was afraid of the clown mannequin that stood by the entranceway and laughed mechanically, an evil sound in my ears. Inside, it was the maze of mirrors that frightened me the most. I hated banging into myself. But I always went in anyway, mostly to avoid my brothers' teasing. After the initial burst of our frenzied run from ride to ride, we would take a short break to eat: French fries soaked in vinegar in cardboard boxes, clam cakes, linguiça on Portuguese rolls, cotton candy, and candy apples. And if one of us got lucky at the booths, we'd get to take home a box of chocolates. Young men took chances on winning large stuffed animals for their girlfriends, and the whole mood of the park was festive.

All summer long we had dreamed of this night, and it was finally here. I told Skippy to wait at the corner and keep his eyes peeled while I ducked into the laundromat to see the time. I pushed the door open and was hit in the face with a blast of humid heat and the smells of starch, detergent, and bleach. I saw the clock read 5:45. It was getting very late—he was out of work at 5, and it didn't take more than 15 minutes to walk home. So where was he? How could we have missed him? I went back outside into the balmy air of early evening. It was a perfect night for the park. The air tasted of salt from the cove.

"Five forty-five," I announced to Skippy.

"How much is that really?"

"Quarter of 6. Fifteen minutes before 6 o'clock. An hour and a half before your bedtime."

"But not tonight!" he shouted, dancing about.

"Quit it, Skippy. You look like an idiot."

Skippy stopped bouncing and said, "It's late, isn't it?"

I nodded.

"Oh Gawd, it looks like we missed him."

"Don't swear. That's a sin. I don't know how we could have missed him. We better go back. Ma will be in a fit. Oh geez."

"Don't swear. It's a sin," Skippy mimicked.

"I didn't swear, pea-brain. 'Geez' isn't a swear. It isn't 'Jesus.' It's just a bunch of *g*'s together."

"What does it mean?"

I looked at Skippy's freckled face. Deciding he was being sincere, I said, "I really don't know. It's just something we say, that's all. It's a sound thing. Come on, let's go—Ma is going to be SO mad."

"At us?"

"Of course at us, who else?"

Skippy took my hand and held it tight as we walked down the street. As soon as we passed the halfway point, we could see the house. I could see Ma looming large in the parlor window. From one hand dangled her long rosary beads. She still had her apron on.

Before we reached the top of the stairs, she stood in the doorway, waiting for us.

"It wasn't our fault!" Skip shouted and immediately ran off to be with Drew and Tom.

"Well, where is he?" she demanded.

"I don't know, Ma. We waited and waited, right on the corner, the whole time."

"You must not have been looking."

"We did look, every minute," I protested.

"You let him get by you! Can't I count on you for anything?"

Drew, Tom, and Skippy watched from the pantry. Molly peered out of the room she shared with me.

"I didn't let him get by. I don't know where he went. Maybe he's just late."

"You know where he went, all right—to the bloody Z Club. Well, you can forget about going to the park tonight."

"NO!" Skippy wailed.

"Why?" Drew asked.

"You're old enough to know the answer to that, Andrew. The park will just have to wait for another day."

Molly closed the bedroom door. Skippy just stood there in tears with Drew and Tom. Then the three of them went into their bedroom and closed the door.

"It wasn't my fault," I repeated. "He just wasn't there."

I wanted to crawl under the bedcovers and never come out, but Molly was in there, and I didn't feel like talking to her. Instead I locked myself in the bathroom. Through the crack in the door (the crack had been repeatedly covered with contact paper and torn again), I could hear my mother's furious mutterings.

"Bugger probably knows another way in," I heard her say, and suddenly I went all red and hot. I sat on the edge of the claw-footed tub and cried: It was my fault because there *was* a back way in, on the other side of the street. I'd suddenly remembered that, once, when I was very small, my mother sent me with him to pick up the boys' Sunday newspapers for their route. After he had picked them up, we drove around some side streets, and he parked the car. He brought me in with him, telling me not to tell Ma. I must have been around three or four.

I remembered tables with red-checkered tablecloths and a long, huge wooden bar that glowed in the morning sun shining through the back window. Mostly I remembered the smell. It was the same smell that was on my father every night he came home.

I never told my mother about it, and I wouldn't now, either. I heard Dad's footsteps on the stairs, and my stomach went into knots. It wasn't very late, maybe there was still a chance—

"Where have you been?" my mother began as soon as he opened the door.

"Don't start with me, Fay. It's been a long day."

"You went to the Z Club, didn't you, after I begged you not to go today. I begged you. And you promised you wouldn't. Did you see the kids? I sent Finn and Skip up to meet you. You must have seen them."

"What's the idea of sending my own kids up to spy on me?"

"You saw them, didn't you? And went in some other way. I know you. You can't fool me. Do you even remember what day it is?"

"Of course, I remember. Look, I only had one lousy beer—"

"Only one?"

"That's right. One. And Tillie said to meet her between 6:30 and 6:45."

"Why did you have to go in there? You know we can't go if you've been drinking. And I don't believe you had only one. Your face is all red. The kids are in their rooms. Heartbroken."

"Jesus Christ. I had one goddamn beer. One. There's no reason we can't go."

"You smell like a barroom. I don't believe you."

Dad's voice took on the edge that scared me the most. I wished my mother would just shut up.

"Okay, you want to hurt me by punishing the kids? You don't want to go. All right, then. We won't go. But don't you blame me, you hear? Don't you dare tell the kids it's my fault. You're the one ruining everything, bitch."

I heard Dad slam into his bedroom. How I hated those fights. Why hadn't I just intercepted him?

Silence. I peered through the crack. I could just see my mother, sitting in the cozy chair next to the window, her hand on her throat. She always did that when she was upset. Then she got up and moved out of my field of vision. I listened to her moving about. I heard the clank of silverware, heard her lift the lid off the stew pan on the Magic Chef stove—she was putting my father's supper out.

My father came out of the room. "Who's in the bathroom?"

"It's me. I'll be right out," I said, drying my eyes quickly.

"Are you sure you can drive?" my mother asked him in a tight voice. For a minute, I thought my father wasn't going to answer her at all.

"God, you're miserable," he said finally. "One goddamn beer. I can drive. There's nothing wrong with me," he said, punctuating each word with a slap on the table. "Finn, are you coming out of there or what?"

I opened the door and slipped out. I put my arms around my father's waist. He smelled of the mill, of hard work, of his soft cotton tee shirt, of the Z Club. Dad fished in his pocket and handed me a tiny box with two Chiclets in it. I smiled up at him and hugged him harder.

"Your supper's getting cold," Ma said to him.

Dad went into the bathroom to wash his hands.

"Get the kids ready. We have to meet Tillie by quarter of 7."

Miracle of miracles. We went. And I won a box of chocolates.

Sunday night of Dad's vacation was special, too. Instead of going right home from the cottage, we went to the Dartmouth Drive-in on Route 6. *Swiss Family Robinson* was playing, and we were all together, including Bridie. Tom had the bag of goodies Ma had packed so we wouldn't have to go to the concession stand for food. Dad hooked up the speaker to the window.

"Tom, give me a couple of red jelly beans," Ma said.

"Ma, it's too dark back here. I can't see the colors."

"That's all right, Tom. Give me two black ones then."

---

Tuesday was Molly's last day at the hospital. It had been a scorcher of a day, and it was still in the low 80s when she left work at 5 to come home. But to surprise her, Tom and I were there to pick her up. Tom was off for the day.

"You look like the Wreck of the Hesperus," Ma said when Molly walked in and slumped into Dad's chair.

"Yeah, I feel like it, too. Anyone want to go to the beach after supper?"

"Yay!" we all chorused, including Skippy.

Ma had made French meat pie for supper—it was Molly's favorite—and the tenement was steamy with heat. We decided to eat outside in the shade of the house. I recalled how, when I was very small, Dad would fill an old, small porcelain tub with cool water for me to play in on hot days, and I would splash and watch while Granny tended her garden.

We cleaned up after our impromptu picnic, changed into swimsuits, and piled into the car. We collected Bridie on the way. A few other people were on the beach on this balmy night. We plunged into the water with wild abandon—except for Dad, who made his way in a little more slowly—while Ma yelled from the beach, "Don't forget to bless yourselves!" We dived off Dad's shoulders, did somersaults, played water tag. Ma went in the shallows with Skippy, then Dad took him out into deeper water and twirled him around in it. He loved it. We couldn't seem to get enough of the cool pleasure of the sea. It was almost full dark by the time Ma called us in. Never had we been allowed to stay in the ocean so late before. It was pure magic.

We stopped at Willow Tree for ice cream, and all the way from there to the house we sang "Mammy's Little Baby" over and over until it drove Dad nuts. The tenement was still hot and stuffy. Tom and Drew and the Twins Downstairs decided they would sleep in the house we had finished building in the backyard. It had two couches, and the boys set up sleeping bags on the floor to accommodate them all. I was jealous that I couldn't join them and had to stay upstairs in the hot house with Skippy. I stood at the pantry window with a flashlight, listening to their chatter, shining the beam on the house like a bright moon. How I longed to be with them.

Since Bridie was over to help Molly sort things out, it was decided that I would sleep in the boys' bed with Skippy, and Bridie would sleep with Molly. I was pleased with the notion of sleeping in my brothers' bed and made the announcement to them from the pantry window.

"Hey, you guys! Guess what—I get to sleep in your bed tonight!" I yelled down.

Drew's disembodied voice floated up. "Oh no—what if you've got cooties?"

"I don't have cooties!" I yelled back, insulted.

"Finn, get out of the window and scoot to bed. And don't keep Skippy awake all night. Come on, now," Ma said.

Dad was outside with the boys making sure they were all set. I slipped into my shorty summer pajamas and climbed into bed next to Skippy. He was already asleep. The kid could sleep through anything. Then my heart sank. I could hear someone coming up the stairs and prayed it was Dad. Ma had gone in the parlor to watch TV. The door opened. It was Uncle Cal. He greeted Ma and asked where Jack was (did he really not know, or was he just getting the lay of the land?), and Ma said he was outside with the boys. Uncle Cal then poked his head into the middle room, where Molly and Bridie sat amid a pile of books and papers.

"Where's Finn-o?" Uncle Cal said, entering the room. "Under all that stuff?"

I couldn't hear what Molly replied, but I heard him coming toward the boys' room. In my panic, I was about to wake Skippy to be my protector.

Uncle Cal leaned in and whispered, "Get ready." But suddenly Molly was right behind him.

"Finn, I almost forgot—you want to read the next chapter in the book?"

"Yes!" I stage-whispered. Skippy stirred.

"Come on, then. We'll sit in Ma's chair."

I skipped quickly out of bed and brushed past Uncle Cal.

"Don't keep her up too late," he admonished Molly, who stiffened—she did not take kindly to the remark, I could tell. He left the room and went back downstairs. I couldn't count the times Molly had saved me recently. It made me wonder if she knew something.

We settled together in Ma's easy chair. Bridie came out of the bedroom and sat on the chair's broad arm.

"Hey, don't leave me out!"

I felt safe and happy and terribly, terribly sad.

The rest of the week was spent sorting and packing and making multiple trips to White's Laundromat. Ma packed what she called a care package for Molly that made me jealous. It included cookies and Nab crackers and, best of all, jars of baby food apricots and peaches. Molly loved the baby food fruit. So did I, but Ma would never buy them. She thought it was ridiculous. But she gave in and got them for Molly's care package.

Finally, Sunday arrived. We all went to 8:30 Mass. It was rainy and mizzling out. After Mass, we went into the sacristy so Molly could say goodbye to Father McCuen. He gave Dad the directions to the college and handed a white envelope to Molly.

"Good luck," he said. "I know you'll make us all proud. Try not to get too homesick." He gave Molly a hug, and we left the church, with me clinging to Molly's hand.

Right after breakfast we packed up the car. Molly said goodbye to Granny and Grandpa, Tom and Drew, and the Murphys downstairs. Tom and Drew would be staying at home, as there wasn't enough room in the car. I knew that, as soon as we turned the corner, they'd be having a spitball fight in our tenement. Then we were off, collecting Bridie on the way.

"Brace yourselves," Ma said automatically. Dad was clearly very nervous driving to an unfamiliar place. His hands shook on the wheel, and each time he shifted, the car stuttered and threatened to stall out. We were all very quiet. Ma sat in front with Skippy in her lap and said her prayers. She had a whole stack of prayer cards to get through, which took well over an hour. I sat in back between Molly and Bridie. The trip involved navigating downtown Boston, which was very confusing to an anxious driver like Dad. But Father McCuen's directions were excellent and intuitive. Molly suddenly remembered the envelope Father McCuen had given her after Mass and pulled it out of her bag. She read the note aloud:

*Dear Molly,*

*As you begin this new, important phase of your life, know that our thoughts and prayers go with you. We will all miss you terribly; I for one will miss your strong voice in the choir and our after-Mass chats. I know in my heart that you will do very well at St. Ann's—they're getting a rare gem. But—and this is important—if you feel that St. Ann's is not the place for you and you must return, then come back to us with your head held high. There is no shame in trying; there is no failure if you have done your best. As you know, St. Ann's is an all-girls school, and girls can be catty at times. You are likely to encounter many girls who are very wealthy. Just remember that money isn't everything, and where the real things count, no one is better than you. No one.*

*We will always be here, supporting your every decision. Your parents are very proud of you. So am I, and I'm happy to have been somewhat instrumental in sending you on your way. Here is a little something extra to have for a rainy day—or if you ever need to take the bus home. Take good care of your valuable self. The best of luck to you.*

*Fondly,*
*Fr. Steve McCuen*

Folded into the note were five, crisp 20-dollar bills.

Molly started to cry.

"Oh, isn't he a wonderful man?" Ma said. "Aren't you lucky to have a friend like him? I'm going to pray for that man every day."

"What am I going to do without you in the choir? I'll have no one to laugh at Mousy with," Bridie said. Mousy was a quavering soprano of about 45 who walked with her shoulders all hunched over.

They rode for a while until Bridie said, "I can't stand this quiet. Come on, let's sing." Bridie began "Tonight You Belong to Me" by Patience and

Prudence. Then they segued into "Magic Moments," "Catch a Falling Star," "I'll Be Seeing You," Bridie and Molly alternating harmonies. Dad visibly relaxed at the wheel, and they sang all the way to Wallingford, Vermont. But they grew silent again as they approached the college.

"I wish you were coming to Bridgewater with me," Bridie said.

"And I wish you were coming to St. Ann's with me," Molly countered.

The campus was a canvas of woodlands, farmlands, and fields. The buildings were very old and ivy-covered. In the distance were the mountains of the Green Mountain National Forest. The rain had given up, and the sun was doing its best to poke through the fast-moving clouds, rays of sunlight isolating this or that part of the campus. It was breathtakingly beautiful.

We pulled in front of a building where others were parked and students were all unpacking trunks and suitcases. The sign above the portal read "St. Francis Hall." Molly had only one suitcase. The rest of her belongings were in cartons and paper bags. Two students with nametags and clipboards approached. They took Molly's name and introduced themselves as Senior Big Sisters. It was their job to help Molly find her room and roommate and get settled.

Molly's room was on the first floor of what appeared to be the smallest and oldest building.

"Looks like they knew you were invading the place," Bridie said, pointing to the nameplate on the door of the room next to Molly's, which read, "Dean of Students, Sister Albert Catherine," who, according to the seniors, was called "The Ace."

Molly's roommate was already there. She sat on her bed surrounded by children of all ages.

"Hi, I'm Blaise, your roommate. These are some of my brothers. I'm one of 12, so there's a lot of us poking around the place."

"Hi, I'm Molly." She introduced Ma and Dad and me and Bridie and Skippy. "I have two other brothers who are at home."

Blaise was flat-out beautiful, a tall, willowy Audrey Hepburn, with a wide, welcoming smile and perfect teeth. Her brown eyes shone with warmth and humor.

"Dump your stuff, and I'll show you to the lounge. Need help? Exie, Max, Charles—go help Molly with her things."

The boys happily complied, making short work of it. Then they all went to the lounge.

"This is the only place where men are allowed in the building," Blaise said. "And these are my parents, Lee and Judy Warren."

Handshaking all around.

"What a beautiful little boy!" Judy said, approaching Skippy, who clung to Ma's thigh. His red hair was all tufted from sleeping in the car, his blue eyes wide with a combination of anxiety and curiosity, his face a mass of freckles from the summer sun.

"What's your name again?" Judy asked him, kneeling next to Ma to be at eye level.

"Skippy," he whispered and smiled shyly, his deep dimples showing.

"He looks like a little Irish cherub," Judy said.

"Where are you from?" Molly asked Blaise.

"New York, upstate. My father's a judge. And you?"

"Massachusetts—New Bedford—"

"Oh neat, the old whaling port, Herman Melville and all that," Blaise said.

"Yeah."

"Can I have a soda please?" I asked Ma. There were vending machines all around.

"Sure, you can," Blaise said before Ma could say a word. "What about you, Skippy? Want a candy bar?"

Skippy nodded. Blaise took his hand, and he allowed himself to be led away, though looking back to Ma for reassurance.

Bridie and I went with them. Ma and Dad stood awkwardly, not knowing what to say to this judge and his wife.

"Say, Jack—interested?" The judge removed a silver flask from his inside jacket pocket. Dad's eyes lit up.

"Sure," he said.

"I'll bet you could use the women's room after your long trip," Judy said kindly to Ma. "Come with me."

"Jack—you have to drive home, remember," Ma said to Dad before they left the room. He nodded and raised his eyes skyward.

"Dad, don't let the nuns catch you—I'll be expelled," Blaise said.

"This place is a prison," the judge said, but he was smiling. "Our daughters will be safe here."

Like his wife, the judge was tall, trim, and well-tanned. I could see where Blaise got her eyes—and her stature.

"Maybe I should unpack," Molly ventured.

"Jack—you play Ping-Pong?" the judge asked.

"Love the game," Dad said.

They went over to the Ping-Pong table and started a volley.

"We're going upstairs. You guys be good," Blaise said to her father and brothers. "And remember, no wandering around."

"Finn?" Molly asked.

"I'll stay here with Dad and Skippy," I said. It would be more interesting with the other kids around. Besides, Exie was kind of cute. Bridie went with Molly and Blaise.

I watched the game, interested. My father was very good at it.

And so the afternoon passed. The Ace came in and introduced herself and explained some of the dorm rules.

"We'll keep your daughters safe here," she said. "But now it's time for you to say goodbye. The girls have a meeting at 6 o'clock, and then dinner."

We trooped out of the lounge and into an upstairs parlor. The Ace ushered in Molly, Bridie, and Blaise. Molly hugged Dad, then Ma. She scooped Skippy up and nuzzled his neck, making him giggle. But when she came to me, I could not let go.

"It'll be all right," Molly said. "Time will go by fast. Write to me."

I nodded, not trusting my voice.

"Come on, now, Finn," she said gently.

I peeled myself away. Ma tried to hug me, but I shrugged her off. I felt devastated.

Molly and Bridie were both crying, promising to write and stay close.

"Come on, Pip," Bridie said. "We'll console each other on the way home."

Blaise was lost among her clan. Lee came over to Dad.

"Good games, Jack. You're aces. We'll have to play again—but I have a lot of practicing to do!" He laughed heartily and went back to his family. Then Blaise's brother Exie came over to say goodbye to me. He was round-faced with clear brown eyes and dark hair that kept flopping over his eye. A cowlick shot up in back, reminding me of Alfalfa from *Our Gang*. I was surprised he came over, and I turned suddenly very shy.

"Nice meeting you, Finn," he said in his best manly imitation.

"Same here."

"See ya."

Finally, we all departed. Molly stood in the road waving until the car turned a bend. In the back seat, Bridie put her arm around me. I was crying softly.

"I'm going to miss her too, Pip. A lot. Can I come over and visit you sometime?"

"Sure," I said, not believing for a minute that she'd really come.

The ride home was quiet and dark. Eventually I cried myself to sleep.

When we dropped Bridie off, Ma said, "Now don't be a stranger, Bridie. Come over any time."

"Okay, I will," she said. "Bye, Pip."

Back at the house I was slow to get into my pajamas. I dreaded going to bed knowing Molly wouldn't be following me.

"Dad, will you lie down with me, please?"

"Sure, Peanut. I'll be there in a minute."

Dad went off to change from his good clothes into his chinos and tee shirt. Then he produced several 20-dollar bills from his pocket. Ma's eyes widened.

"Where'd that money come from?"

"Ping-Pong. The judge doesn't play very well," Dad said, grinning. Then, as promised, he came to my room and lied down on his side. I wrapped myself around him and eventually fell asleep, bereft.

No one really knew how distraught I was over Molly's departure. For weeks, I felt lethargic, with no appetite and little energy. In school, I did the work I had to do to get by, but no more. The nun called Ma and told her I was lazy. Truth was I had a hard time concentrating. I worried about Molly all the time because I overheard Ma telling Aunt Joan that by the time Molly was finished doing the dishes after dinner (a condition of her scholarship), it was late and she had to walk across campus alone in the dark.

After school, instead of going outside to play with the boys, I retreated to my room, where I would try to read or draw. I still went to the library but rarely took out books. It was mostly to see Connie. Uncle Cal continued with his routine of abuse with one less threat to worry about catching him. I seldom spoke. During the day I avoided him, steering clear of the cellar.

It was Connie who finally brought it up.

"What's going on, Finn?" she asked one Saturday afternoon on our way home from the library. The weather was changing, and today it was a mix of clouds and sun, with a very brisk wind. I longed for summer.

"You haven't taken a book out in ages. Why do you bother even going there?"

"It's quiet. And I get to see you."

"Ah—so you brood better in the library. And you want to see me why?"

"Because."

"And?"

"Because I—I need you in my life."

"Are you going to tell me what's wrong, or do I need to pry it out of you with a wedge?"

I stopped walking. We had just exited the 5 & 10, and I leaned against the rusted fence of the City Mission.

"Out with it, white girl. I'm all ears."

I looked at her eyes—concerned, compassionate—then looked away.

"Are you sick?"

"Yeah—sick at heart. Connie, I really, really miss Molly."

Connie waited. Finally, she said, "That's it?"

"What do you mean, 'That's it?' Isn't it enough?"

"I'm sorry," Connie said softly. "I didn't realize—"

"No. Nobody does."

"So...why are you hurting so bad?"

How could I tell her? Molly meant so much. It was not only the occasional protection from Uncle Cal, but also that Molly and I had shared a bed together my entire life. She comforted me after nightmares. She read to me. She played board games with me. She took us to the beach. She listened when I was down. She paid attention. I couldn't get it all into the right words, but I tried to explain it to Connie, omitting references to Uncle Cal. I told her about my school and about being labeled as lazy.

"Connie, I'm not lazy. I'm just—"

"Grieving," Connie said.

"What?"

"Grieving. Like a death. It's as plain as the freckles on your face. It's something like how I felt after my Ma died. But you're only 9 now, and your sister's not dead. She'll be back. You can pull out of this. I'll help you—if you'll let me."

I nodded, too choked up to speak.

"The first thing I want you to do is make a calendar, starting with October. Cross off all the days that have passed so far. Then cross off each new day as it passes. Circle the date when she'll be coming home to visit. Ask your Ma when that is. Then you can watch as the time gets shorter and shorter. You'd be surprised at how fast it can go. Really. Then make goals. Take a book home from the library and mark on the calendar the date you think you can finish it by. And really try to stick to it. Mark the date in red crayon. Add other goals—school projects or whatever. Use a different color for each goal. Can you remember all this?"

"I think so."

"If you bring your calendar and crayons to the library, I can help you with it."

"This sounds like a great idea, Connie. How come you're so smart?"

"I'm not that smart. I've just had more experience than you. I've learned a lot," she said with a wry smile.

We walked on, chatting amiably. This was the most animation I'd shown in weeks. When we got to Division Street, two streets before Winsor, we split up, so no one would see us walking together. As soon as I got home, I retrieved my box of crayons, pencils, ruler, and a pad of large drawing paper that Molly had given me. I set to work, humming softly to myself.

# 6. Holidays

Excitement was in the air: Molly was coming home for Thanksgiving, and she was bringing Blaise with her. Father McCuen was picking them up and driving them home, to save Dad the trip. Tom was picking up Bridie to bring her over to the house.

I couldn't keep out of the window, even though Ma said, "A watched pot doesn't boil," whatever that meant. Finally, the black car turned the corner. I flew down the stairs and swished outdoors just as the car pulled up at the curb. Father McCuen leaned over and kissed Molly on the cheek. I grabbed the door handle and flung it open, wrapping myself around Molly as soon as she emerged from the car. I was speechless all of a sudden. Blaise climbed out of the back seat and stood on the sidewalk. I was struck again by her beauty. At five-foot-seven, she was stunning, with brown shiny hair in a bob, prominent cheekbones, and a wide, generous mouth in a broad smile. Drew, Tom, and Bridie came out to greet them and to help with the bags. Father McCuen left quietly.

"Well!" Ma said as soon as they walked into the kitchen. "It's good to have you back home. Eat."

"We're not hungry, Ma. Father McCuen took us to dinner on the way home."

We walked into the bedroom we shared.

"Finn, we've got presents for you," Molly said, handing me a plastic bag.

"And this is from me," Blaise said.

I opened Molly's bag first. It was a white sweatshirt with the school emblem on it in purple. Underneath it read "Graduate 19??" I put it on immediately.

"Perfect fit!" I said and gave her a hug. Then I opened Blaise's bag. Inside was a flat, plush tiger face with a zippered opening in the back. He wore a bow tie in the form of a purple A.

"He's a pajama bag. Whenever you sleep over someone's house, you can put your pj's in it."

"Can I use it at home?"

"Sure, I guess so."

I got my pajamas from under my pillow and put them inside the tiger. "This is great!" I thanked them both, then sat down on the bed, just grinning at them. I felt absurdly happy.

"And guess what we're doing Friday night?"

"What?"

"We're going to the movies, just as I promised you. What would you like to see?"

"I don't know what's playing."

"Well, go find the paper. Come on, Blaise, I want you to meet my grandmother and grandfather."

They went upstairs to Granny's tenement, Bridie following. I poured over the paper. After an hour or so they came back down, each one munching on a cookie.

"Find a movie, Pip?" Bridie asked.

"Yeah—*White Wilderness* is still playing. It's a Disney movie, and it's at the Empire."

"Sounds good."

"Ma, Granny doesn't seem too good to me," Molly said. "She all right?"

"Well, she seems to be failing a bit lately. The doctor says she has congestive heart failure, and there's nothing to be done for it."

"Why didn't you tell me?"

"I didn't want to worry you."

"Ma, please—I'd rather know. Where's Dad?"

"He hasn't come home yet."

"Isn't it kind of late?"

Ma looked at the clock and shook her head. Molly and Bridie exchanged glances.

"Yes, it is, even for him. And he knew you were coming home."

Ma rose and went to the parlor window, picking up her rosary beads along the way. Time passed. Then she called out, "I see him—he's coming down the street... Oh no."

"What?"

"Tom—Tom, go out and help your father."

Tom looked at Molly, shrugged, and went down the stairs. Ma came back to the kitchen. She looked embarrassed.

"What is it, Ma?"

"He's staggering."

Molly raised her eyebrows. "Dad hardly ever drinks that much."

"Well, he has this time. In fact, it's the third time since Sunday."

"What do you think's going on?"

"Molly, I have no idea. Blaise, I'm so sorry—"

"Don't worry about it," Blaise said. "Both my parents drink."

"They do?" Ma was shocked. Not that judge and his beautiful, classy wife!

Blaise nodded. "Not all the time—but enough. You needn't be embarrassed, Mrs. Kilroy."

We heard Tom and Dad trying to negotiate the stairs. Drew went out to help. Together Tom and Drew shepherded Dad to the bedroom. Dad was muttering something about a young punk. They removed his shoes and socks and shirt and somehow got him into the bed.

"He's really bad," Tom said, coming out of the bedroom. Drew said nothing. He went into the parlor and threw himself into one of the rocking chairs.

"I'm going up to the Z Club," Tom said.

"The Z Club? Why?" Ma asked him.

"See if I can find out what's going on. Something has to be up, Ma—he's never this bad, and he knew Molly was coming home—with company. Drew?"

"I'm coming with you," I said.

Tom smiled. "Sorry, Finn, they don't let kids in there."

"I'll walk to the corner with you," Bridie said.

"Drew?"

"No, thanks—I'll stay here," he said, and Tom and Bridie left.

Into the awkward silence that followed, Molly said to Blaise, "Welcome to my house!"

Blaise laughed.

"Come on, let's unpack and settle in."

"Drew, do you want to play Monopoly?" I asked him.

"No."

"Parcheesi?"

"No."

"Chutes and Ladders?"

"NO! Go away!" he yelled and went off to his room, slamming the door behind him.

I went back to the paint-by-number kit I'd been working on before Molly's arrival. It was a closeup of a horse's head and neck. I tried blurring the lines so the paint would seem more natural, less fragmented. Ma just sat in her chair, saying the Rosary with one hand on her throat. About an hour later, Tom and Bridie returned.

"You were gone a long time," Ma said. "I was getting worried."

"I wasn't in the Z Club all that time. We've been outside talking for a while."

"So?"

"Yeah—hey, Molly, you should hear this."

Molly and Blaise came into the kitchen and sat around the table. Drew appeared at his bedroom door and stood there. Tom was too agitated to sit.

"So, I talked to the bartender—Louie, if you want to know—and I asked him if he knew if anything was up with Dad. And he said yes, he did. He said Dad came in on Monday after work all upset. Louie said it took two boiler-makers to get Dad to talk. So, Dad told him they'd hired a new foreman in the weave room, a young guy, cocky, full of himself. So, Dad's working, and this guy comes up to him and he says, 'Better keep up the pace, Jack. You don't want to lose this job. Where would an old guy like you get another one?' or words to that effect. And of course, he's the new boss, so Dad can't say a damn thing."

"What a little bastard," Blaise spouted.

"Yeah, so every day this week he's gone to Dad and said, 'I'm watching you, Jack.' Louie says the guy is a ball-breaker—'scuse the language—and he needs to learn a thing or two. Louie says Dad's a great guy. All the guys at the Z Club like him. So, I'm talking to Louie, and this other guy comes up to the bar and says, 'You're one of Jack's boys, aren't you?' I tell him, 'Yes, I'm Tom,' and he says, 'Well, Tom, you tell your father not to worry. We're going to take care of things.' Whatever that means. This guy's name is Small Change. And he's a cop."

"Sounds like the ball-break—um, the guy in the shop—better watch his back," Bridie commented.

"Poor Jack," Ma said, shaking her head. "Poor bugger. He's a hard worker, your father. He's never missed a day of work in his life."

"Ma, tell Blaise and Bridie what he used to do when you first met," Molly said.

Ma smiled. "Well, Jack was very shy. Still is. And I kind of thought he was sweet on me, you know. Then I came in to work one day—I was a cloth inspector, checking the cloth for imperfections, and he was a loomtender—anyway, I came in, and at my station, wrapped in waxed paper, is this piece of the most delicious fudge I'd ever tasted. The next day the same thing. This went on for weeks! Then he finally got the courage to ask if he could walk home with me."

"Did he live near you?" Blaise asked.

"Oh no. He lived on Emery Street, down by the beach. To come here was way out of his way."

"He came here, to this house?"

"Yes, this is where I've always lived. I was born in this house. Upstairs. I've never lived anywhere else."

"Wow. That's amazing. What a terrific story. How old were you then?"

"Well, I started working at the mill when I was 15. It was the Depression, you know, so they had to pull me out of school to go to work. I hated to leave—I loved school."

"What grade were you in?"

"I had just started ninth grade at Holy Family High School. I loved it," she said wistfully.

"What about your husband? How far did he go to school?"

"Fifth grade, if I'm remembering right."

"Feel like playing whist?" Molly asked Ma.

"Yeah, I guess so."

"You'd better watch out. Blaise and I play all the time at school, and she's pretty good."

Molly got the cards, and they set up at the table. It was Ma and Bridie against Molly and Blaise.

Ma hadn't finished high school herself, and that may be why she was so strict with us about studying. She was determined, even overbearing sometimes, that we would get—and appreciate—an education. Next to church, school was the most important focus of our lives. Good grades or awards were cause for great celebration, and it was unthinkable that we would not do well. Doing well in school was one sure way to earn her approval. Skipping out on homework was not an option; she'd be sitting at the table with you until it was done. I think she liked learning alongside us.

But she also enjoyed a good board game or a game of cards, like tonight.

I continued on with my painting. I loved painting, and I loved horses, so when you combined the two, I couldn't be happier. Periodically, we could hear Dad snoring. When the game was over (Bridie and Ma won), Tom gave Bridie a ride home. And I slept that night very happily wedged between Molly and Blaise.

---

Thanksgiving Day was cloudy, cold, and spitting snow. The various aromas began seeping through the house early. Upstairs, Granny was making pies—mince and pumpkin—while in my house the turkey had been put in the oven at 6 a.m., so the scents of turkey, nutmeg, dough, and cinnamon mixed deliciously as they wafted through the house. Dad, who must have been hungover, didn't show it. He helped Ma as much as he could with the meal, lifting the turkey, smashing the carrots and turnips, mashing the potatoes. The stuffing, made from a recipe that had been in the family for generations, was eagerly awaited by all. Ma made an enormous pot of gravy, and Dad put out the cranberry sauce.

At 2 o'clock we gathered around the table, including Granny, who said grace and presented the toast. We all had a shivering sip of some horrible, sweet wine. Then Granny took two plates full of food upstairs so she could eat dinner with Grandpa.

After dinner, Dad and the boys cleared the table. Dad heated the pots of water, and Molly, Blaise, and I did the dishes, singing as we went along. Dad complained that if we didn't sing songs with a quicker tempo, the dishes would never get done. A couple of hours after dinner, Granny served up her desserts while Dad made the whipped cream for the pies. I had my dough cookies—cookies made from scraps of dough left over from trimming the pies, sprinkled with sugar and cinnamon.

After we'd cleaned up once again, the fun began. We stripped the table—long now, with its leaves in—and put up the net, while Dad got the Ping-Pong paddles and balls. The Twins Downstairs came up, and each person had a turn playing the winner of the previous game—who was usually Dad, though Tom gave him a run for his money.

While the players played, the rest of us went upstairs to Granny's tenement for the party. Granny served up soda in small multicolored glasses in a colorful display of orange, lemon-lime, root beer, and sarsaparilla. Aunt Joan and Uncle Cal came upstairs, too, and Uncle Cal brought his guitar, on which he only played one song: "Frankie and Johnny." Then we sang all the other old songs, from "Little Harry Hughes" to "Ten Cents a Dance" and "She's More to Be Pitied Than Censured" (an interesting little ditty that I never understood until I was an adult). The day finally ended around midnight, when everyone drifted back to their own tenements. In my house, the leftovers were brought out, and we had turkey sandwiches with stuffing and cranberry sauce and a little gravy poured over the top. I sat in the broad chair by the stove with Molly, drifting as the adults talked softly about the world outside, forgetting my presence or assuming I was asleep.

The only light came from a small lamp on the kitchen table and from the fire in the Humphrey. I caught phrases about race and riots, about Dad and the mill, about layoffs and textiles moving to the South. The fishermen seemed to be doing okay, though. In the flickering light, I took in what I could and tried to understand. The world they talked about was a scary place, and dark, and I wanted no part of it. I let myself drift off to sleep. They tucked me in on the parlor couch so Molly and Blaise could get a better night's rest.

They slept till noon. I couldn't wait for them to get up. When they finally did, I had the Parcheesi board all set up, and we played the game over coffee. Then I was instructed (by Ma) to "Leave the girls alone for a while," so I went outside. I decided to borrow Tom's bike—I could hardly reach the pedals—and went for a ride to the corner. I hadn't seen Connie in weeks, and I was going to be brave. I hopped off the bike and left it lying in the dirt while I went up the walk to Connie's door. I knocked.

It was answered by Fremont, a tall young man about Tom's age with the lightest brown eyes I had ever seen. They were the color of cashews. He stood at the door looking at me. I looked back, all the spit gone from my mouth. What if Mr. Foster were there and came out and yelled at me? Too late now.

"Hi, Fremont. Connie around?"

Fremont raised one eyebrow.

"I'm Tom Kilroy's sister," I added.

Fremont smiled. "Dolly!" he said. He then turned and called Connie. The house was dark, and I couldn't see too far into the interior. Connie came out of another room carrying little Nicky, who wasn't that little any more, still in his pajamas.

"What are you doing here?"

"I came to see you. Want to come out and play or something?"

"Didn't I tell you my father hates white folks?"

My eyes widened. "Is he here?"

"No—lucky for you. Lucky for me," she added as an afterthought.

"Well, then?"

"I don't know. Wait a minute."

She left me standing there while she went back inside, calling Fremont. I could hear conversation, but not the words. Presently Connie came back.

"I can go out for a little while, but I have to get Nicky dressed first."

When she came back she was alone. "Let's go," she said.

"Want to go to Ashley Park?"

"Okay."

"Hop on the bar."

"You'll get us killed."

"Will not. Hop on."

After a few wobbly false starts, we were off, arriving at the park within minutes. It contained the usual eclectic mix of people. While several soccer scrimmages took place at one end, a bunch of older, scruffy-looking boys gathered on the basketball court at the other end. One of them took a knife from his pocket, opened the blade, and began flipping it into the air, catching it by the handle. We steered clear of them, playing on the monkey bars, slide, and then on the swings. We twisted ourselves around in circles, then let ourselves go. We sat there, dizzy. Then we went and lied down on the smooth granite ledge in the center of the park, taking in the rays of a warm, late-autumn sun.

"Did you ever play that game as a kid where you stare at the clouds and pick out the animals?" I asked Connie.

"What? No."

"It's fun. Look, there's a camel."

"One or two?"

"One."

"That's not a one-humped camel. It's a turtle. On its back."

"That one's a mashed potato."

"Not an animal, white girl."

"So?"

"So if that's mashed potatoes, then that is a rutabaga."

"What's a rutabaga?"

"I have no idea," she said and collapsed into giggles. We rolled down the rocks, laughing like fools.

"I'm hungry," Connie said when we'd caught our breath.

"How was your Thanksgiving?"

"All right."

"Do you like turkey?"

"Love it. But we had ham and rice."

I was horrified. "No turkey? Hardly seems like Thanksgiving without a turkey." Then I had a bold idea. "Come to my house, and I'll give you some leftovers. You can make a sandwich."

Connie hesitated.

"It's all right. My sister's home for the weekend, and she has her roommate with her. Ma won't be saying anything." I knew I could be punished for this, but I didn't care.

Connie had her doubts, but she hopped on the bike, and off we went.

As we were climbing the stairs, Connie said, "It smells funny here. Good funny, just not like our house."

"It's the pies my grandmother makes."

"Are you sure this is okay?"

"Sure, I'm sure," I said, though I wasn't sure at all, and I opened the door. Molly and Blaise were still in their pajamas, drinking coffee and talking. God, could those two talk. Ma was in the pantry doing dishes.

"Hi. This is Connie. Connie, this is my sister Molly and her roommate Blaise."

"Hi, Connie," they both said.

"How's your brother Fremont?" Molly asked.

"He's good," Connie said softly.

"You wouldn't believe how handsome this boy is," Molly said to Blaise. "Eyes to die for."

"Wow, what long braids you have," Blaise said to Connie.

"They've never been cut."

"Never?"

"Nope, never."

Ma came out of the pantry wiping her hands on the dishcloth.

"Hi, Ma. You know Connie."

Ma seemed surprised, but only said, "Hi, Connie."

"Ma, can we have some turkey? Connie loves turkey, but at their house they have ham," I explained.

"I—I guess so. Get it out of the ice box."

"Ma, get with it. It's a refrigerator," Molly said.

I unwrapped the turkey carcass, and Molly got a knife.

"I'll do it," she said. "Get the bread, please. Mayo? Stuffing? Cranberry sauce?"

"Yes, yes, and yes, please," Connie said. She was practically drooling.

We brought our sandwiches into the parlor to eat. I showed Connie the painting I had almost finished.

"You should try painting without the numbers," Connie said. "That's what I do, and it comes out...interesting."

We both laughed.

As soon as we were done eating, Connie said she had to go. Fremont was waiting to go to work, and Connie had to look after Nicky. Plus there was laundry to do.

"Ma, I'm walking Connie back," I said.

"Thank you, Mrs. Kilroy. That was delicious," Connie said.

"You're welcome, Connie."

"Say hi to Fremont," Molly said.

"Hey, come here a minute," Blaise said. "Mind if I play with your hair? Have you ever put your braids up?"

"No. I don't know how."

"It's easy. I'll show you—it won't take long."

Within two minutes she had Connie's braids wrapped around her head like a crown, using Molly's bobby pins.

"Go look. See if you like it."

I led Connie to the bathroom mirror. She grinned broadly.

"I love it!"

"See? It's real easy."

"Thanks. I'm going to wear it home like this."

Connie smiled at me, and we headed down the stairs.

"Your sister's friend is real nice."

I nodded. I had a full-blown crush on Blaise. "How was the turkey?"

"Scrumptious."

"Do you think Molly has a crush on Fremont?"

Connie laughed. "I'm not going to tell him she thinks he's handsome. He'll get a big head."

We reached the corner. Outside Connie's house a garbage truck was parked.

"Oh shit! Shit!" Connie said in fright. "Get out of here—Go! Shit, I hope Fremont didn't say anything. Go, will you? Run!"

I turned and took off down the street. I didn't pause till I reached my house. I sat on the porch, out of breath. I wondered what kind of trouble Connie would be in.

I caught my breath, then went inside. When I opened the door, the room went silent, though Molly, Blaise, and Ma were all sitting there. It was obvious they had been talking about me.

"What?" I said.

"Connie seems like a nice kid," Molly said.

"She reads a ton of books."

"That's great—isn't it, Ma?" Molly said.

"Yes, yes, it is. Finn, what have I told you—"

"Ma," Molly said.

"What?" I asked.

"I told Ma it would be nice if you had a friend of your own without having to hang around with the boys all day."

I looked at my mother.

"Just don't—"

"Don't what, Ma?"

"Don't get too close, that's all."

"Why not?"

"Because. You could get hurt."

"Hurt how?"

"Ma, they're only kids," Molly said.

"I know. It's just... I worry, that's all."

"Ma, there's nothing to worry about," I said and went off to finish my painting.

I was grateful to Molly. Ma often listened to her advice. If Molly could turn her around on the issue of me and Connie, well, that would be terrific. I could hear snatches of the conversation still going on in the kitchen.

Molly said, "Ma, she's getting older. She needs girls to be around, not the boys. It would be good for her." I couldn't hear Ma's reply. It would be great to have Ma accept Connie. But now I had to worry about Connie's father. I wondered what would bring him around. I wondered if Fremont would step in and defend Connie, the way Molly did with me.

That night, right after supper, Molly, Blaise, Bridie, and I took the bus downtown. Blaise and Bridie went shopping while Molly took me to see *White Wilderness*. Molly treated me to popcorn, soda, and a box of Sno-Caps. I couldn't have been happier. And snow was in the air.

Father McCuen came by late Sunday afternoon to drive Molly and Blaise back to St. Ann's. I couldn't believe the weekend was over already. Bridie came by to see them off. Blaise gave me a big hug before getting into the car, and I went red all over. They waved from the car all the way down the street until they turned the corner. Of course, I was heartbroken. I sat on the front porch to brood.

"Mind if I sit with you?" Bridie asked.

"Sure."

We sat in silence for a while. Snow flurries flew around us. Then Tom came out to the gate.

"Oh, there you are. I thought you'd left," he said to Bridie. "Do you want a lift home?"

"Sure." Bridie gave me a hug. "I'll see you soon," she said, but I didn't believe her, really.

As they walked toward the car, I overheard Tom asking Bridie if she wanted to see a movie. Bridie was in the car before I could catch her reply. They drove off into a shower of snowflakes.

Despite the cold, I didn't want to go back inside. The house would feel especially empty without Molly, Blaise, and Bridie. I tried to console myself by thinking Thanksgiving had passed, so Christmas would be here soon, and Molly would be home for an extended stay. I worried about Connie. I hadn't seen her on the street since Friday, although that wasn't unusual. I'd go to the library tomorrow to see if she was there. As for Ma, all she'd said to me since Connie came over was to be careful around Aunt Joan and Uncle Cal.

When I could no longer feel my toes or fingers, I finally decided to go inside. It was getting dark already, and snow was flying down in thick, soft flakes.

Because we'd had our big meal in the early afternoon, Sunday's supper consisted of Cream of Wheat and hot cocoa, which I ate on a tray in the parlor so I could watch the *Walt Disney Presents*. Later, Drew and I would prevail upon our father to make us homemade French fries. He finally agreed. There was nothing like Dad's French fries, with salt and vinegar. Dad peeled potato after potato until we were all satisfied.

We heard the sound of a shovel scraping outside. Sure enough, it was our next-door neighbor, who always started shoveling at the first flake. But this time, there were many flakes. I was shocked by how much snow had already accumulated. The street and cars were thickly covered.

"I should go out and get a jump on it," Dad said.

"I'll go with you," offered Tom.

Drew and I looked at each other.

"Can we go out? Please?" we whined. It was 8:30.

Out came the long underwear, the galoshes, the sweatshirts, the mittens, the hats, the scarves. We could hardly move. Drew and I went to the cellar for our sleds. Pausing now and then to throw snowballs, we brought our sleds out to the middle of the deserted street, which was very slick. I hopped on my sled, and Drew gave me a whopping push. I was four houses down the street before coming to a stop. Drew took off at a run, then leaped on his sled, passing me. We went up and down the street in this fashion, while Ma watched, smiling, from the parlor window. Skippy was long asleep, but he'd have fun tomorrow.

After an hour or so, Dad called us in. He and Tom had made short work of clearing our sidewalk, but the snow was coming down very heavy now. We all trooped upstairs and shed our sopping wet clothes. Ma put all the mittens, gloves, hats, and scarves on top of the Humphrey to dry. For the rest, she opened up the clothes rack on the wall. The tenement soon filled with the smell of wet wool drying. Dad rubbed his swollen, red hands over the heater. We were all red-cheeked and happy. Ma ordered us into pajamas and bed, as it was past 10 o'clock. She wasn't too concerned about the hour—it was obvious there would be no school tomorrow.

I went to bed and pulled the book I'd been reading with Molly off the shelf. I lay at the end of the bed, reading in a shaft of light that slid in from the kitchen. Then I heard the front door open, and Uncle Callan came in. I quickly hid the book under my pillow and pretended to be asleep. Dad was sitting in his chair right outside my bedroom door, listening to his favorite radio station, and eating his own new batch of fries. He was quite wide awake.

"Say, Jack," Uncle Cal said. "Think we'll get much more snow tomorrow?"

"They said five or six inches, but who knows."

They went on chatting about nothing, and Uncle Cal finally left. I smiled and set to work picking at the hole in the plaster wall. It went quite deep. This time I reached the wooden laths that held the plaster together. I hadn't counted on that. Then I hung a picture of Molly over the hole and went to sleep.

It was Christmastime before Molly came home again for an extended stay. As promised, Bridie had been stopping by to visit, but I suspected she came as much to see Tom. They had been out to the movies two or three times since Thanksgiving, and I saw the way Tom got ready to go out: nice clothes, ruler-straight part, and... something else. After he left, I snooped in his room. Next to the English Leather stood a beautiful green bottle. I opened it, and it smelled wonderful. I read the label: Jade East. I had also seen the way Bridie looked at him when he wasn't looking. I wondered if Bridie had written Molly about it.

As for me, I saw Connie whenever she was able to sneak down to my house without being caught. The first time she came by, I was stunned.

"Connie, your braids! You cut them off! Why?"

"I didn't cut them off. My father did."

Apparently, although Fremont had never told her father about the post-Thanksgiving visit, little Nicky had. He told his father that Connie had gone off with the "library girl." Her father had been furious. When he noticed Connie's hair all done up, he demanded to know who had done it, and when she told him, he went and got the scissors. She undid the "crown" that Blaise had made, and in two quick snips he cut off each braid. Connie had spent the better part of a week alone in her room, crying. She retrieved the braids from the trash and kept them under her mattress in a plastic bag.

It only made Connie more determined to stay friends. But it was an enormous risk she was taking. My heart ached for her. Even Ma was upset when I told her what had happened.

When the snow came, Connie came to my house to help build a snow fort, various imaginative snow people, and a snow maze for tag. We had walked intricate paths in fresh snow, then shoveled them out. With each new snowfall, the path grew deeper. Even Drew had fun playing tag in the maze, along with the Twins Downstairs. This was done, of course, when the men were at work—in particular, Connie's father and Uncle Cal. Aunt Joan said the less Callan knew about Connie, the better.

Molly took me downtown with her to go Christmas shopping. After hitting all our favorite stores, we sat at the counter of the downtown 5 & 10. I had French fries and a vanilla Coke. Molly had coffee and pilfered fries from me. After, we stood in front of the bank to wait for the bus.

The air was crisp with heavy, snow-laden clouds, and my nose filled with the aroma of peanuts from The Peanut Store a few doors down. The main streets were decorated with lights and wreaths, and from a church somewhere the bells pealed out Christmas carols. With Molly's financial help, I had bought a new chemical for Drew's lab, a model battleship for Tom, shaving soap for Dad, and a nice smelling body powder for Ma. For Granny, I bought a new pair of garden gloves. A velveteen rabbit and book by the same name for Skippy completed the list, except for Molly. I would have to depend on Ma to help get her gift. So we stood at the bus stop, happy, our breath coming out in white plumes, full of the magic of Christmas.

We had waited for Molly to come home to get our Christmas tree, so right after supper we trooped up to the lot behind the bakery to pick one out. Ma stayed behind to help prepare the space for the tree in the bay windows. We picked out a good one with no bare spots and carried it on our shoulders, singing "O Tannenbaum" all the way home. I carried the front end with Skippy, Dad brought up the rear with the trunk, and Molly, Tom, and Drew carried the middle. When we got home, our hands were sticky with pine sap, and I had to scrub with borax powder to get it off. While they put the tree in its stand, I made stencils on the windows with pink window wax. Someone put Bing Crosby's Christmas album on the hi-fi, and we sang as we decorated the tree together.

Molly remarked to Tom that Dad appeared to be fairly sober.

"He's been pretty good lately—not great, but better than he was at Thanksgiving."

"That was bad."

"Yeah—but did I tell you what happened?"

"No, what?"

"Remember what Small Change told me that night at the Z Club? About the guy who was on Dad's back all the time? Well, it seems this guy had a run-in with the cops. The cops beat the crap out of him, locked him up for the night, and when he started crying about 'police brutality,' they came and released him, apologizing. The cops said it was a case of 'mistaken identity,' that the guy resembled a drug dealer they were looking for. And they warned him, somehow, to be a better boss at the mill. Dad said he was banged up pretty bad, with a broken wrist and cuts and bruises everywhere. He was out of work for a week. Dad was thrilled. He said the guys on his shift cheered when they heard the news. And he's been very nice to Dad ever since."

"Nice to have friends like that," Molly said, laughing.

They looked over at Dad, who sat in the rocking chair, watching them decorate the tree and humming to the music.

Christmas Eve, however, was another matter. Dad came home from work well lit from celebrating at the Z Club. A nasty fight broke out between him and Ma. Molly, who had been trying to read the traditional *Night Before Christmas* to me and Skippy (and Drew, though he pretended not to be listening), finally stopped reading.

"For God's sake, it's Christmas Eve!" she yelled at both of them. They stopped their shouting, but the fight went on without words—pounding steps, things slamming, looks given, dishes crashing in the sink.

I went to bed early, both to escape the fight and to try to fall asleep fast so Christmas morning would come sooner. But sleep would not come. Dad finally fell asleep in his chair, but I was still awake when Uncle Cal came upstairs. He came into my room while Molly and Ma were in the parlor cleaning up. Uncle Cal had just zipped his pants when Molly came into the room.

Unflustered, he just said, "Now you go right to sleep," in a stern voice to me. Molly was the one who was flustered, as though she had interrupted something but wasn't sure what. She didn't know what to say. Callan just brushed by her and went back downstairs.

"What was he in here for?" Molly asked me.

"I don't know. Just to talk, I guess."

"Are you all right?"

"Yeah. But I can't fall asleep."

"I'll close the door a little so it's not as bright in here. Dream about your presents."

Molly went out, and my heart began to slow to its normal rate. Molly had almost caught him. What would have happened if she had? It was unthinkable, unimaginable. I was still awake when Molly and Tom left at quarter past 11 to pick up Bridie and go to the church for midnight Mass. The choir sang carols from 11:30 till midnight.

I didn't know what to do about Mass tomorrow. The children's Mass was at 8:30, and we each had to sit with our grade. What was I going to do when it came time for Communion? How could I receive Communion with a mortal sin on my soul? Yet, if I didn't, I would be the only one in the whole class still kneeling in my pew when they all went up to receive, and everyone would know I had committed a mortal sin. Sister would be furious at me. Suppose she asked me why I didn't go? How could I not go to Communion on Christmas?

These thoughts, not sugar plums, were what danced through my head until I fell asleep. Before I did, though, I managed to pull out a few more pieces of plaster from the wall.

I awoke to the smell of fresh coffee commingled with the piney scent of the tree. Christmas! I crawled over Molly, trying not to disturb her, and went into the kitchen to stand in front of the Humphrey heater to get warm.

"Merry Christmas!" Ma said, putting her arms around me and kissing my forehead.

"Merry Christmas, Ma. Merry Christmas, Dad." I hugged my father. "Merry Christmas, Drew," I said and kissed his cheek, which he immediately wiped off.

"Come on, get ready for Mass now."

"Oh, Ma, can't we open just one present?"

"Not now—after Mass."

At church I sat squirming in my pew. I didn't know what to do about receiving Communion. I tried to pay attention to my surroundings—the beautiful flowers, the poinsettias, the wreaths that adorned the altar, the crèche, the priests in their elaborate robes, my classmates all dressed up. I, too, was wearing a dress, about which Drew and the Twins Downstairs teased me unmercifully. I could hardly wait to get it off. As the time came closer, my heart beat faster. I glanced over to where my parents were sitting with Skippy. Ma was saying her Rosary instead of following the Latin. Next to them in the same pew sat Uncle Callan and Aunt Joan. Little Cal and Pat sat with their grade. At the Offertory, Uncle Cal got up and went around with the basket, collecting. He wouldn't miss Communion. He never did.

Then it was time. The students in my row stood to line up. I forced myself to remain kneeling—until the last possible minute, when I caved in to the pressure. I stood and joined the rest. I'd made my decision. Now I'd be damned forever.

Molly and Tom were still in bed when we got home. I couldn't understand how they could possibly stay in bed late on Christmas Day. Dad began making breakfast while Ma, Drew, Skippy, and I went into the parlor. Skippy was so excited he could hardly sit still. Ma doled out the gifts, but I was somewhat subdued after my recent damnation. I cheered myself up thinking that maybe I'd be able to make a deathbed confession and all would be forgiven.

The first gift Ma gave me was a large paint-by-number kit of a lovely mare roaming the pasture with her foal. I couldn't wait to get at it. I thanked Ma with a big hug.

"Go thank your father," she said.

I found him in the pantry, getting dishes down for breakfast.

"Thanks for my painting kit, Dad. I love it," I said, wrapping my arms around his waist.

He hugged me back awkwardly and mumbled, "You're welcome."

Ma seemed delighted with her powder, Dad loved his soap, and Drew appreciated his new chemical. Skippy was very happy with his stuffed rabbit, which he dragged around by the ear with him everywhere. He was so happy with everything, from the rocking horse Ma and Dad gave him to the box it came in. Drew gave me a set of different colored gimp, enough to make many bracelets. I would get gifts from Tom and Molly when they ever got up. I felt rich.

We ate breakfast to the smell of the turkey roasting. Molly and Tom eventually got up and opened their gifts quietly over coffee. Tom said he loved his model and couldn't wait to get to it, while Molly was happy with the pretty stationery I gave her so she could write home. Tom gave me the newest Walter Farley book, and Molly gave me a set of paints, brushes, and paper so I could paint my own work. I felt overwhelmed.

Dinner was a repeat of Thanksgiving. As usual, after Ping-Pong, we all went upstairs for dessert. Grandpa, who hadn't been well lately, seemed in great spirits as he tried his best to tell his favorite jokes. Granny sang "Little Harry Hughes" and served up her pies and sugar cookies with her multi-colored glasses of soda. But I didn't spend much time upstairs. Right after dessert, I went back downstairs to start my paint-by-number kit. I put on Dad's radio and sat there painting the rest of the day. Molly came downstairs a few times to get things for the party—more desserts, more utensils—and urged me to come upstairs and join them. However, I was very happy and perfectly content painting. How rare it was to have the tenement to myself. It felt magical. But I would later regret that decision, as it turned out to be Grandpa's last party.

During that school vacation, Tom drove us all, including Bridie, to the Dartmouth cottage for ice skating. All the cousins were there. The men made a big fire in an old oil drum by the shoreline, and the aunts made brownies and hot cocoa in the kitchen overlooking the lake. Tom laced up my skates good and tight, and I slid onto the ice.

Aside from swimming, ice skating was my passion. For one thing, I could do it without having to depend on the boys, though I did try to play hockey with them for a while. Although I was a strong skater, I really didn't understand the game, so whenever the puck came my way, I simply pounced on it. Eventually I tired of it and went off to skate by myself. Here, I entered another world; everyone else was far, far away, their voices diminishing in the thin air. The only sounds were the groaning, settling, echoing of the ice and the scrape of my blades. I practiced skating backwards, twirling, humming a song that would be the music for my astonishing Olympic program. For nearly two hours I practiced, determined to beat gravity and leap, gazelle-like, into the air. Okay, so I didn't make it more than four inches off the ice, and maybe my landings were a little rough. But, in my mind, I was flying, and cars going by on Reed Road would stop to watch in amazement at my skills. My brothers would be stunned. And jealous. And secretly very proud.

"Hey, let's see a double-axel!" Bridie called out. She and Tom were skating with Skippy between them. He was doing well on his double-bladed skates.

"I wish!" I called back. And I did wish. Hard.

I noticed that the hockey game had ended, so I went to rejoin the group. With all my cousins, we had wild "sled" races. (How to make a "sled": Skater 1 crouches down, facing forward, knees up, and grabs onto Skater 2's skates behind her. Skater 2 leans over Skater 1's body and holds on to her knees in order to steer. Skater 3 positions himself behind Skater 2 and pushes, while Skater 2 steers the knees of Skater 1, and Skater 1 holds onto Skater 2's skates for dear life.) At the signal, we raced across the ice, laughing like fools until one by one the sleds collapsed into a heap. The last sled still standing (more or less) won. Discerning that there were no bones broken, we then made long whips and flew into the clean, clear air.

The pale sun was long gone, and now a lone star shone with the moon above the lake. We skated wearily to shore. I took off my skates, my feet feeling strange and light in boots, and went inside for a brownie and a cup of cocoa. Aunt Emma put mounds of Marshmallow Fluff into my cup.

We were all exhausted, and I knew I would suffer tomorrow for today's exertions—my legs would be all stiff and achy. I would ask Dad to make me a bath tonight so I could soak my sore muscles. On the way home, Molly, Bridie, and Tom sang "Moon River" and a spate of Perry Como songs. I loved the crowded warmth of the old Plymouth. I loved Tom's third-part harmony. I suppose I even loved Drew. The day felt that good.

---

On January 7, Grandpa had a massive stroke. He died at home at a quarter to 5 in the afternoon, just as the cold sun set on the city of New Bedford. Ma wouldn't allow me or Skippy to go upstairs and see him. I don't know why. So, I sat in our tenement holding Skippy and crying as everyone else went upstairs. Molly came down to use the phone and had to convince the others on the line to let her cut in.

"Please, could you hang up? We've had a death in the family," she explained. We shared what we called a "party line," so you'd pick up the receiver and almost always find yourself in the middle of someone else's conversation. A while later the undertaker arrived. They took Grandpa's body down those narrow, steep stairs, banging our door open as they passed. Grandpa was covered with a gray blanket. They put him in the hearse and drove off, taking him down streets he hadn't been able to walk for years.

At the wake I could not cry, as much as my throat ached. I felt numb inside. It was my first real encounter with death, and Grandpa just looked asleep. He was wearing his old, gray suit with a white shirt and gray tie. The last time I had seen him in this suit was at my cousin's wedding reception, the night of his first stroke. I would have gone on thinking of his death as sleeping until I reached out and touched his arm to give it a squeeze. Shocked by its hardness, its coldness, I snatched my hand back. That told me in a visceral way that he was truly dead. I went and sat in the lineup of chairs, shaken. I don't remember Ma or Dad or any of my siblings being around me. I felt lost and alone. But I could not cry.

The last night of the wake, as we were leaving the funeral parlor, Granny finally broke down and wept. She went over to the casket and tried to hold his head in her arms, crying, "Tommy, Tommy, what will I do without you? Oh, Tommy, come home with me." My heart broke. We had a difficult time leading her away. But, when we got to the coat rack, Granny whispered to me through her tears, "Grab me some of them wooden hangers—I need them to crochet for Christmas presents."

As indomitable as Granny's spirit was, she mourned my grandfather deeply. They had been together since they began stepping out when she was 16. She had never faltered in her care of him since he had become an invalid. I can't help but wonder, though, if after his death, she felt a certain relief. Taking care of him 24 hours a day had been demanding—he was demanding, and her respite would be well earned.

A month or so later, on a Saturday night, we heard all sorts of commotion upstairs and went running up to investigate—only to find Granny dancing a polka with an imaginary partner to Lawrence Welk. It was strange to see the big chair empty, to go upstairs and not hear Grandpa call out in his booming voice, "How's my little Finn?" I thought back to Christmas, when he'd had such a good time, and I'd stayed downstairs, painting, missing my last opportunity to laugh with my grandfather. And, in my young mind, I thought my sin-filled life was the cause of Grandpa's death. The sins—heavy, powerful—just continued to multiply like weeds in a wet garden.

And so went the winter of my damnation.

In June of the following summer, I turned 10. That summer also brought my first experience as a patient in a hospital.

I'd caught some unscrupulous germ—or perhaps it had been given to me by Uncle Callan. It began with severe cramping and diarrhea. I'd never felt so sick or in so much pain. The cramps put me in a full-body, ice-cold sweat, and several times I was close to passing out. For a week, I sat curled in a fetal position in Ma's easy chair, as it was the only place I could be even slightly comfortable, and I even slept there at night.

Molly, who was home for the summer and back working at the hospital, tried her best to tempt me into playing cards and other games with her, something that ordinarily would have thrilled me. But I felt way too sick to move from my position on the chair. By week's end, the diarrhea had turned to blood. The pediatrician sent me to St. Luke's Hospital. Thinking I was only going in for some tests, I was shocked to discover I was going to have to stay there indefinitely.

They set me up in a bed in the children's ward—there were about 15 beds in one long room—and the doctor tried to insert an IV line into the tiny veins of my foot. When that didn't work, he tried the veins in my hands. I remember the doctor was sweating. I began to cry silently. Finally, he got the line in my left hand and taped it in place. Granny sat on the other side of the bed holding my free hand and stroking my arm. She looked on the verge of tears herself. I remember begging to go home with them when visiting hours were over at 7. The thought of spending the night in that long room with 14 other sick kids terrified me.

The family left.

I was alone. I had to call the nurse for the bedpan, which I hated and felt totally embarrassed by. I even felt bad for the nurse, who had to collect samples for the doctor to study. There wasn't much to collect; most of it was blood. The nurses were very busy. One time I was left sitting on the bedpan for two hours before the nurse finally came back. Molly came in to see me every morning before her shift started. She came by again at her lunch hour, and again at the end of the day. She made sure I always had a supply of bendable straws, which I loved, and ginger ale to drink. Ma, Dad, Granny, and sometimes Tom came during evening visiting hours.

In the children's ward, lights went out at 8 o'clock, and they played soft music for an hour or so—the minstrel song "Jimmy Crack Corn" got played over and over. It drove me crazy. I found myself longing for Perry Como.

The long ward was scary, with no light on except from the nurses' station at the end of the hall. One young girl was very ill, I think. After the stupid music stopped, all I could hear were beeps and pongs from the machines that cast an eerie green glow around her bed. Some children cried. How I hated it.

I couldn't sleep. Each time I dozed off, I was awakened with cramps and had to call for the bedpan. And every time I heard a siren go by, I worried that there was a fire at home and no one could get Granny out. The house was going up in flames, and I was utterly powerless to stop it or to help. Off and on, in fits of sleep, I worried for my family's safety. Away from them, in this ward of shadows and strangers, I felt lonelier than I ever had before.

It was another week before they finally got my illness under control. In the end, they shrugged their shoulders and called it a virus.

Ma brought me new sneakers to wear home—they were red plaid and I loved them—and Drew presented me with three new *Green Lantern* comic books he had bought himself with his paper money.

Although I had been in the hospital for only 10 days, it felt like months had passed. Once at home, I was set up in Ma and Dad's bed. I remember vividly the softness and the fresh smell of the clean, white muslin sheets that had been line dried after washing. The pillows were deep and soft, with crisp white pillowcases that were cool against my head. It was the ultimate of safety and comfort, and I was grateful beyond measure.

Aunts Emma and Theresa came to visit me at home and brought me a book of paper dolls, which I found endlessly fascinating. Granny was a constant presence at my side. Looking back, I wonder if my illness reminded her of losing her own daughter, for whom I was named. She doted on me, tempting me to eat bread broken up into warm milk with sugar, or creamy oatmeal, which was her specialty. She held my hand and told me stories and sang lullabies. I was so happy to be home.

It took a long while for me to regain my strength and my weight. Granny began force-feeding me a tablespoon of Scott's Emulsion—cod liver oil—every day after supper. It was indescribably horrible tasting, and I would put up a huge fuss about it. It became a nightly ritual. All my siblings would gather around to watch me gag. Quite dramatically, I would refuse the spoon, my mouth shut tight, while my parents bribed me with all manner of desserts. Granny was relentless. I can still see that tablespoon full of white, thick, foul-smelling liquid coming at me. They'd all watch, coming in closer to see—Would she take it? Would she throw up?—and as soon as it was finally in my mouth, they'd back away a bit, just in case. I'd commence gagging, and my mother would shove some form of sweet in after it. By the time the ordeal was over, we'd all be in a sweat. But Granny insisted it would make me well.

It took some time, though, to get over the trauma of my hospitalization. I had nightmares about it for over a month. But for three whole weeks, I was not bothered by Uncle Cal.

# 7. Transitions

*It is as if they know*
*their time is short, so*
*this evening*
*the crickets and peepers, giving*
*it their all, sing to the start*
*of a dying season, the heart's*
*yearning, as when the new young teen*
*sitting alone on the backyard swing*
*learns—sudden and sharp—*
*a new kind of loneliness, deep*
*within her sex but abstract as water*
*a pure pain that has no color*
*—she has not yet learned the name*
*of this solitary awakening*
*in the song of the crickets and the peepers,*
*the beginning of an end, griever*
*alone and sighing in the backyard swing.*

It was the end of September, 1963, and the sky was a clear, bright, deep blue without a cloud, but there was a distinct nip in the air telling us summer was over. I was 12.

I was bringing Skippy to the library for his first visit and, at seven, to get his very own library card. He clutched my hand as we walked and had a fine time looking all around.

Skippy had a list of recommended books from his second-grade teacher, but I had my own agenda: I couldn't wait to introduce him to Dr. Seuss, one of my favorite children's authors.

"Is it far?" he asked.

"Not very. You can see it from here. See?" I pointed. "Are you tired?"

"No, but I might be on the way back home."

"Planning ahead, hey?"

He grinned.

"That's good. I like a boy who plans ahead. Want to run to the corner?"

He agreed, and we took off. I allowed him to beat me by a freckled nose. I grabbed his hand again, and we made our way across the busy street.

Inside the library, we went up to the desk to apply for his card. The librarian, smiling at Skippy as though she wanted to devour him, gave him a temporary card and an application for Ma to fill out.

As we passed the juvie section, a voice whispered, "Finn! Over here!"

I looked, and it was Connie.

"Big day for Skippy?"

"Yeah—I can't wait to get him all the neat books."

She smiled, remembering. "Those Seuss books were great."

"What are you into now?"

"Biography. I'm reading about Langston Hughes. I really like his poetry."

At 14, Connie had filled out. Her once-boyish form had new curves. I, on the other hand, remained (as Granny told me) flat as a pair of fried eggs.

"Go get your books. Then we can get out of here and talk. What are you reading now? Still sci fi?"

"Yeah—a little of that, a little of horses."

Connie shook her head. "You should branch out, try something new. Try biography. I'll bet you'll love it."

"Okay," I said and brought Skippy over to the children's books. We picked out the Seuss books for starters. I left Skippy there, surrounded. Then I went to biography and picked out Eli Whitney and one on James Watt. Inventors intrigued me. Then my eye caught a new book called simply *Amelia Earhart*, so I grabbed that one too.

We checked out our books and walked slowly down South Water Street.

"Cut through the 5 & 10?" Connie asked.

"No, let's go around."

"Why? Because of what happened before? No way, they're not keeping me out. That means they won. Uh-hunh, we're going in."

And we did.

We trooped through the store, and Connie made a point of stopping to look at different items as we made our way toward the back. We were followed this time by the blue-haired woman and a nondescript older man. They watched us carefully. When we finally exited the store, we laughed so hard I nearly wet my pants.

"Did you see the look on that old bat's face when I picked up that sewing kit and looked through it? And that man—I'll bet he's the manager—he looked like he wanted to push us out. His face kept getting redder and redder the more time we took. It was great."

"What's so funny?" Skippy wanted to know.

We looked at his earnest, freckled face, and then at each other, and burst into laughter again. Skippy joined in the laughter, but his face was quizzical. We walked the rest of the way home, stopping now and then to erupt into giggles. When we were about halfway down Winsor Street, a car drove by and honked. I recognized it as Uncle Callan's car, but instead of waving, he pointed a jabbing finger at us. He looked mad.

At my house, we separated, Connie giving me a big hug. I opened the back door and had started up the stairs when a loud voice boomed from below.

"Fiona! In here, now!"

Uncle Cal sounded furious. No way was I going in there.

"Run!" I whispered to Skippy, who was behind me. I grabbed his shirt and tried to pull him up faster.

I heard the downstairs door open, and Uncle Cal shot out, yelling, "Get back here! I'll teach you a lesson for being so disobedient!"

I ran faster, tripping up the steps and trying to hold on to Skippy, whose eyes were wide with fright.

"Skip, come on!"

Uncle Cal chased me, cursing and shouting racial slurs. I was terrified.

"MA!" I yelled, and Uncle Cal knocked Skippy out of his way, roughly banging him into the railing. Library books went flying everywhere. Skippy fell back a few steps, and I was afraid he'd fall backwards down the stairs. I wanted to stop and help him, but one look at the blind fury on Uncle Cal's face kept me going. Skippy was crying, and at the top step Uncle Cal grabbed my foot. I fell, whacking my shin against the stair, but when he lunged for me, I hit him in the face with *Amelia Earhart*. It made him pause long enough for me to regain my footing, and I flew. Ma was at the door.

"What's all the commotion? What's going on here?"

"Mama!" Skippy wailed.

I flew by Ma into the tenement and dashed into the bathroom, the only door with a lock on the inside. He reached the door just as I slid the bolt into place. I could hear Ma getting Skippy up the stairs. I felt bad about abandoning him and hoped Uncle Cal would leave him alone. He pounded the bathroom door, making the crack wider.

"Callan! Stop!" Ma yelled, and through the crack I saw that Skippy was pressed into her body.

"You stop crying, or I'll give you something to cry about!" Uncle Cal turned and tried to grab Skippy's shoulder, but was stopped by Drew.

"You keep your filthy hands off him!"

"Callan, stop it! Stop! Get control of yourself!" Ma yelled.

It was chaos, with everyone yelling and Skippy crying.

"She was with that nigger girl again, and I'm going to teach her a lesson she'll—"

"You'll stay away from her," Drew said, coming forward.

"What? What did you say to me?"

Through the crack, I saw Drew standing next to Ma, his face a mask of barely controlled fury. Skippy had his face pressed into Ma's apron. I could see even from the opposite side of the door that he was shaking. Uncle Cal took a step forward, but Drew held his ground.

"You're not too big for me, boy. You better—"

Aunt Joan rushed in.

"Callan!" she said in her sharpest tone. "Callan—go downstairs, now!"

"These disobedient, disrespectful brats need a lesson," he shot back.

"Callan, it's none of your business. Leave them alone." She lowered her tone. "Downstairs, Cal. Now."

For a moment, no one moved. We could hear Granny coming down the stairs. Then, with a glare toward Drew and another toward the bathroom, he slammed out of the tenement. Skippy was still shaking, holding onto Ma's leg.

"Are you hurt?" Ma asked him.

Skippy pointed. "Right here."

He had a swelling red welt under his right eye.

"Did he hit you?" Aunt Joan asked him.

"No. When he pushed me, I banged it on the rail."

Granny came in. "What's going on here? What's all the shouting about?"

"Uncle Cal went berserk and went after Skippy and Finn," Drew told her.

"Are they all right?"

"Skippy's got a bruise under his eye. I think Finn's okay. Finn, you okay in there?"

"I hurt my shin. But I'm okay," I called out.

"I'm so sorry, Fay," Aunt Joan said. "I don't know what to say—"

"You'd better be careful, Joan. He's out of control. You should have seen him—he was wild. You tell him not to go near my kids again. I mean that, Joan. If he thinks there's a problem, I'll deal with it. Not him."

Aunt Joan nodded. "I better get downstairs. I don't want him looking for excuses to go after my boys."

"And Joan," Ma said, "maybe you should think about getting him some help."

Drew came over to the bathroom door.

"You all right in there?"

"I guess so," I said, my voice quavering.

"You can come out now. They're both gone."

I realized with a shock that I was all wet. "I can't come out. I wet myself."

"Here," Ma said to Granny, handing her some ice wrapped in wax paper. "Put this on Skippy while I go get Finn some clean clothes."

Ma came back with dry jeans and clean underwear. I cleaned myself up with the cold water from the tap. It made me start shivering, and I couldn't stop. I was cold all over. I unlatched the door and peered out.

"It's all right. Come on now," Granny said.

Ma was applying the ice to Skippy's face, and I flew into Granny's arms, shaking.

"It's all right, it's all right," she said, stroking my hair.

But it wasn't all right, not at all.

"Where's your shoe?" Granny asked.

"On the stairs, I expect."

"Can you tell me what happened?"

"Yeah. We met Connie at the library and walked home together, that's all. Uncle Cal drove by us and honked the horn and pointed at us. Then when I came in the house, he went crazy. Ma, he was ready to kill me!"

Ma shook her head. "He's really out of control. Joan better do something about him," she said to Granny.

"I would have helped you," Drew said to me.

"I know, Drew. Thanks."

Drew pulled out from behind his back his wickedly sharp scalpel. "If he had caught you, I would have cut him to ribbons."

"I don't know what's going on with Callan," Ma said to Granny. "He seems tense and angry all the time. You all steer clear of him, you hear me?" she said to the three of us.

"Yes, Ma," we chorused. It was a warning she would not need to repeat.

---

The November day was bright, sunny, and cold. I was still trying to adjust to eighth grade. At 12, I felt my classmates were so much older. I was wearing a dress that was a hand-me-down from Susan, a classmate. That afternoon, as we stood in the schoolyard talking and waiting for the bell to ring after lunch, another girl came by.

"Where'd you get that dress from? Susan?"

I didn't know what to say, so I just nodded. But Susan was shocked.

"You shouldn't ask questions like that!" she said to the girl, but I wondered. Even though Susan came to my defense, how could the other girl have guessed the dress was from her, if Susan hadn't said something to her about it? Did everyone know?

The bell rang, and we trooped inside. I couldn't stop myself from blushing. I wondered if anyone else had overheard the conversation.

I tried to concentrate on Sister Rosalina's lesson on parsing sentences, but then Sister Mary Frances, the principal, came in.

We all stood automatically and chorused, "Good afternoon, Sister." She waved us down, then spoke quietly to Sister Rosalina. When she left, Sister Rosalina slumped into her chair and just sat, staring at nothing. We could tell something serious was up and refrained from the usual talking. Sister Rosalina was young and pretty. History and politics were her favorite subjects, and she managed to inject them into every lesson. Finally, she stood up and surveyed the class.

"President Kennedy has been... shot," she announced quietly.

We sat in stunned silence. Some students gasped. I knew how much my mother loved the young, handsome president. I wanted to ask questions—How? Where? Who?—but didn't dare.

"Classes are dismissed for the day," she went on. "And it might be nice if you stopped by church and said a prayer."

She then sat down in a daze, not moving. We gathered our things together quietly and lined up two-by-two without being told. Sister Rosalina rose and opened the door to let us out. All the other grades were leaving at the same time, but the silence on the stairs was eerie.

I walked home alone, chilled to the bone. I thought I would never be warm again. When I came to St. James Church, I climbed the massive granite steps and went into the darkness. Several people were in the pews, some crying openly. I said a few prayers for the president's recovery—it was unthinkable that he would die. And yet, at that hour, he was probably dead already. I didn't stay long. I wanted to be home with my family.

Ma was sitting in the parlor with the small TV on. Her eyes were watery and red-rimmed. The black-and-white pictures showed a repeat of Walter Cronkite announcing that the president was dead. He was in tears. Ma took my hand.

"It's terrible, just terrible," she said, tears streaming down her face.

From Thursday till Sunday, we sat in the parlor watching events unfold. Ma was washing the lunch dishes as I sat and watched as Lee Harvey Oswald, arrested for the assassination, was being escorted out of the police station. Suddenly a man stepped out of the crowd with his arm outstretched and a gun in his hand. He pulled the trigger. And Oswald went down, a horrible grimace on his face. For a moment, no one moved. Then chaos erupted. A man had just been killed before my eyes. I called for Ma to come in. They replayed the scene over and over again. I was stunned.

The next day was a day of national mourning. Then there was the long funeral, with images that were seared into my mind and would stay with me all my life: the riderless horse Black Jack, boots reversed in the stirrups, acting up and frisky all along the route as if he were mad as hell; young John Jr. saluting his father's casket; the widow, grief-stricken behind her black veil, walking the long way to Arlington with the president's brothers flanking her; the presentation of the flag at the graveside ceremony. For a long, long time, these were the last pictures in my head before I fell asleep at night—drums beating in the background.

That June, I turned 13 and graduated from grammar school. In the fall of 1964, I became a freshman at Holy Family High, and my transition from grammar school was a dismal failure. Emotionally and physically immature, I was so much younger than the others. I noticed that some of the boys in my class were shaving already. Connie was still my best friend, but I had no one at the high school. I was frequently unkempt, as the once-a-week bath no longer sufficed to keep my oily hair and body clean.

As for my classes, I failed every course at least one quarter (except for religion, for which I earned a steady 70). Ma and Dad were in a state of agitation over me, and I didn't know how or what to tell them. That constant feeling of being out of place, of deep loneliness, of something close to despair, haunted my daily routine as I daydreamed my way through all my classes. My secret also made me different, dirty, and ashamed. I lived a solitary life of writing, painting, and reading novels.

One time during the winter, I had been outside until 7 or 8 o'clock, skating on the ice that had formed over the blacktop in the backyard—a 28-foot by 7-foot stretch of concrete that led to the garbage coop. (All right, I'd actually flooded it with water from the outside tap two days earlier.) I was twirling and practicing techniques on thin ice with abandon under the stars and loving every minute of it. School was not on my radar.

"Finn!" Ma called from the pantry window. "Finn. Upstairs. Now."

This was a Ma voice I knew not to ignore.

One of my teachers had called to complain about how poorly I was doing, not just in her class but in all of them. "Is her father alive?" she asked. When Ma said yes, the nun replied, "Then he should beat some sense into her." Ma was mortified. (Dad was asleep.) She had never in her life been spoken to like that by a nun. Ever. As for me, I had other things to think about, from Uncle Cal to my dad's drinking to my friendlessness at school. What cared I for homework? I was going to be a champion skater. Needless to say, there was no more skating for me that winter—a punishment that nearly killed me and sucked all the joy out of my life for months.

In school, kids teased me for being poor and ugly, and only my blue-plaid school uniform kept me from the torment of being out of style. Teasing isn't quite the right word. When class pictures came out, Kenny Hyde, who always sat behind me, tapped me on the shoulder and asked for one of my pictures. I couldn't believe it. Flattered and surprised, I felt a flush in my cheeks. I wrote a nice note on the back, signing it "A Friend Always, Finn," and passed it back. I asked for one of his pictures, but he said he didn't have any more.

*Of course,* I thought. He was popular, so it made sense that he'd given all his away. After a while, I heard snickering behind me. I turned around and saw Kenny, in front of a group of guys, drawing a droopy mustache and beard on my picture, along with zits and spiky hair. Deeply humiliated, I wanted to crawl home.

So, these were the things on my mind that year. Studying was not on the list. I limped along, in the end passing all my courses for the year, but just barely. The contrast between my performance and Molly's couldn't have been sharper.

When school let out, finally, Molly and I moved our room upstairs, both to keep Granny company and to ease the overcrowding downstairs.

Our former room became Tom's, and Drew and Skippy stayed together in their old room. The new room had a steeply slanted ceiling and walls that dripped sweat with the humidity in summer. Just outside my window, I could step onto the roof of the second-floor bay windows. I frequently sneaked out to look beyond the tenements to the cove. I would listen to the sounds of the night—the humming of the mills and the moaning foghorn, inhaling the tidal smells of the cove and roasting rubber from the Goodyear plant. But if Granny caught me, she'd be furious.

"You're making this house look like one of them slums in New York! Get inside!"

Although we still shared the room, we had separate beds, Molly a double, me a twin. We shared the deep closet that was in Grandpa's bedroom, since there was no closet in ours. We each had a bureau, and I put some bookshelves up along the wall above my bed. Molly had her own bookcase and a desk. She tended to stay up well past two in the morning, and I quickly adjusted to sleeping with the lights on. Periodically, Molly would wake me at 3 by sitting on my body and pinching me.

"Wake up, Finn. C'mon, pea-brain, wake up!"

"What? What is it?"

"I've written a new poem. Listen. Are you listening?" (Pinch!)

She would read her poem while I struggled to stay awake.

"Well?"

"That's good. I like it."

"Okay, now tell me what it means."

"No, I want to sleep."

"Tell me what it means!" (Pinch!)

"No! Cut it out!"

"I will. I'll stop. Just tell me what it means." (Pinch!)

"Hey, that hurt!"

"Tell me—"

"Okay, okay, you win!"

And I would do my best, on short sleep, to interpret the poem.

Satisfied finally, Molly would say, "Okay, now you can go back to sleep. But not like that, with your arms folded across your chest—you look like a dead person. Laid out. In a coffin. Roll over or something."

On other occasions, I would be asleep, and into the darkness would come a voice:

"Water."

A pause. Then:

"Water!"

She would keep this up, getting louder and louder, until I got up and fetched her a glass of water. I was afraid that if I didn't, she would get too loud and wake Granny. Sometimes she would say, "Bring sauce for the mongoose!" which was code for "Bring me cheese with my water."

Molly could be a real brat. But I loved sharing a room with her.

Being so close allowed for many discussions about poetry and writing and life. As we were moving into our new space, I was helping Molly unpack a box of magazines she'd saved and I came across a copy of *Time* from May 1963. It had a portrait of the black writer James Baldwin on the cover. Intrigued, I stopped unpacking and read the article sitting on the floor surrounded by books and papers.

"Hey, Molly, what do you know about James Baldwin?"

"Baldwin? He's brilliant. He wrote a book called *The Fire Next Time,* basically warning that our cities would go up in flames if we don't do something soon about racism. I have it in here somewhere. You should read it. You're old enough now."

"What's the title mean?"

"It's a biblical reference, I think. And it's also in a Negro spiritual, something like, 'God gave Noah the rainbow sign. No more water—the fire next time.' When his book came out, they were calling Baldwin a prophet. And he was right. Look at all the rioting. New York, Harlem, is exploding. So are other places around the country."

"Why? What are they rioting about? I mean, I know there's racism. But why destroy their own neighborhoods?"

"You have to look at the conditions they've been forced to live under for so long. Do you know the Langston Hughes poem, 'A Raisin in the Sun'?"

"Yeah, Connie read it to me one time."

"Well, you put people under so much stress and there's bound to be an explosion."

Molly started to put her books on the shelf.

"So many people are forced to live in slums. They have no place else to go, no opportunities, no way to get good jobs, or go to good schools. They have no way out. They can't move out because white people in white neighborhoods won't rent to them.

"In the South, they can't even vote, or use the same restaurants or bathrooms or even water fountains as whites. You need to read about what's happening to those people. They've been horribly beaten by the cops and white people. Read about it—you'll find it in one of the magazines floating around here somewhere."

I stared into James Baldwin's eyes on the cover of *Time*.

"God, that's horrible. How can we let this happen? Do you think there will be riots here, in New Bedford?"

Molly sighed. She leaned back against the bed.

"Honestly, Finn, I don't know. It's possible. What's been happening to black people—it's not new. It's been going on for centuries. It's unbelievable that it's taken this much—the rioting, the marches—to open white people's eyes. But prejudices run deep. It's hard to change."

I thought about Connie, and the trouble when we were kids from Ma and Aunt Joan and Callan. I thought about what I had learned from Connie and knew now that it was the least of it. I felt embarrassed and ashamed to be white. And I thought, if the rioting does start here, I'd do anything to help Connie and keep her safe.

In the coming days, I read *The Fire Next Time*. It changed me in ways I couldn't express, and for that, I would be forever grateful to Baldwin. The book reminded me also that words matter. One thing was clear: that the truth, written plainly, had the power to affect lives and to effect change. It was a lesson I would never forget.

---

They said that the hurricane dike had been built to protect the South End and the harbor, but what they really built it for was to protect the mills. An enormous pile of rock, it was flat on top, and it ran all along Cove Road, from the Dairy Queen at one end all the way past the Kilburn Mill, ending just before our beach. On the other side of the peninsula that was the South End, it extended from the Cornell Dubilier factory, past the Berkshire Hathaway, and into the harbor. The tip of the peninsula, which ended at Fort Rodman, was left exposed to the elements. Residents there didn't mind; they didn't want their view of the ocean or their beach destroyed by this monstrosity.

Drew said the walls of the dike were home to thousands of rats. If there was a hurricane, where would all the rats go? No doubt into all those tenements across the street from the dike. Before the dike was built, it had been lovely along Cove Road, where even the poorest people could enjoy a million-dollar view of the ocean and the long, lush green of Joseph Francis Playground. Now they looked out to giant boulders.

The dike did, however, provide an interesting path to the beach. Connie, little Nicky, Skippy, and I got to the top of the dike via a service ramp we picked up on Cove Road. From there, we walked along the dike's flat top all the way to the exit ramp next to the beach. It was a pretty walk with a stunning view, and if you actually climbed down on the other side of the dike, where there was a long stretch of grass, you could almost forget the tenements and the mills existed.

Connie's father didn't mind Connie taking Nicky to the beach, as long as she was home in time for his supper. Of course, he had no idea that she was meeting me and Skippy, and Nicky was old enough to understand Connie's admonition for him not to tell. Nicky adored his sister, and had grown to like me, and he loved playing with Skippy. He wouldn't want to get any of us in trouble. However, little boys are not always trustworthy creatures.

Unless it was actually pouring rain, we went to the beach every day that summer. The only problem Connie and I faced was which side of the segregated beach to put our gear on. For a while, we alternated. When we were on the "colored" side, I felt acutely uncomfortable. No one ever said anything, but I felt occasionally that a few people looked at me as if to say, "What are you doing on our beach?" I felt like I didn't belong. And I wondered, for the first time, if Connie felt the same way on the white beach. Then I wondered how she felt being the only black family in the neighborhood. I remembered Connie saying that she went to the library because it was "safe" there. Was she afraid of white people? I was beginning to understand her father's hatred. Who wouldn't hate people if they made you feel afraid all the time? I felt as though I'd stumbled onto some great truth, but that its full meaning and implications were just outside my vision. At 14, I was just beginning to recognize that there was a world outside myself, and I wasn't liking what I saw.

In the end, we finally chose a spot of real estate near where the two groups seemed to mingle by the showers near the pavilion. Although we were more on the white beach, Connie didn't seem at all bothered by that, so we stayed.

I had a small transistor radio that Ma and Dad had given me for Christmas, and it was a gift I cherished. It went with me everywhere. Most afternoons after school I would swing in the backyard and listen to it until the sun went down and it grew damp. Sometimes Skippy joined me for a little while, but usually my only friend was my radio. So, of course, it tagged along when we went to the beach. We listened to our favorite station, WPRO, and at the moment, the Rolling Stones were singing "Satisfaction." Connie and I sang along while Skippy and Nicky played in the sand.

"Come on, let's go swimming."

"I can't," Connie said, face in her towel.

"Why not? Did you eat late or something?"

"No—it's that time of the month."

"What time of the month? What are you talking about?"

Connie rolled over and looked at me.

"You serious?"

"Of course, I'm serious. Why can't you go in the water?"

"Oh Gawd," Connie moaned and flipped back down on her towel. "Don't you know anything? Hasn't your mother...talked to you yet?"

"About what?"

"You better sit down, girl. You're in for a shock," she said, and launched into her version of what periods were all about. I was utterly shocked.

"You have got to be kidding," I said to Connie.

"No joke, girl."

"How long have you done this?"

"It's not something you do. It's something that happens to you, and you...take care of it. I started about four years ago."

"Four years...wow. And you never told me."

"I figured your mother would tell you. I thought you had it already."

"How did you find out? Who told you?"

"By accident. I thought I was dying—I thought I was going to bleed to death."

My eyes widened.

"So, I told Fremont that there was all this blood in the toilet and it came from me and I thought I was dying," Connie said, laughing. "Poor Fremont. He didn't know what to do. All he kept saying was, 'You're not dying. It just means you're a woman now.' And I thought, okay, this is some mileage marker or something. That it would stop and never happen again. But who wants to be a 'woman' at age 12? So, he called my aunt and told her she had to come over right away.

"My aunt rushed over and gave me this big hug—and this big ol' pad and a weird belt to attach it to. 'Put this on,' she told me. 'Then we'll talk.' We talked, all right. I could hardly believe her. Then she took me to the drug store and bought me all the supplies I'd need. I told her I felt sick. I had bad cramps and a backache, and I felt fat. She told me that was normal! I said, 'You mean I got to get sick every month from now on?' and she said, 'That's why they call it the curse.' The curse!

"My aunt waited around till my daddy came home and took him into the kitchen and told him. I thought I'd die of embarrassment. It was bad enough I couldn't look Fremont in the eye. But all Daddy said to me was, 'Connie, you're a woman now. That means you got to take good care of yourself.' And that's all. But every time I have my period, if he sees evidence of it in the bathroom trash, he gets all gentle with me. It's weird. And you know what? He never hit me again, not once, since that day."

I chewed over this information. At least now when it happened to me I wouldn't think I was dying. Still...

"How come I don't have it yet?"

"Maybe you're just not ready. How old are you? Fourteen? I dunno. It's different for everybody."

"Maybe I'll never be ready." I glanced down at my body in my bathing suit. Fried eggs. Then I looked at Connie. She had curves and breasts.

"I'm going in the water."

"That's right, rub it in," Connie said, but she was smiling.

I swam for a long time by myself, wondering if Uncle Cal had done something to me to make me not have periods. Connie said having periods meant your body was capable of having babies. Maybe my body decided it was safer not to have periods. Maybe I should talk to Molly about it. It was all too confusing.

Looking back at Connie on the beach, I saw that a boy had come over and was talking to her. He was very good-looking, with dark skin and not-too-long straight hair that had a startling streak of gray in the front. It gave him a mature look, and it flopped over one eye as he spoke. He sat in the sand next to Connie's towel. I felt awkward. I didn't want to interfere, but I was getting chilled. So I splashed up through the small waves, and, instead of going to my towel, I sat down with Nicky and Skippy, who were building a sand castle. In a few minutes, Connie called me over.

"Finn, this is Courtney. Courtney, this is Finn, my best friend. Courtney goes to my school. He's a senior."

"Nice to meet you," I said.

"I gotta get back to the guys. See you later, Connie. Bye, Finn."

"Wow!" I said after he left. "He's something!"

"Yeah, I know," Connie said, looking embarrassed.

I looked at her. "You like him, don't you?"

Connie grinned.

"Has he asked you out?"

"Not yet."

"But he's going to."

"I think so."

"Wow."

"He's really sweet. And smart. He's going to apply to all these colleges in the fall, and for scholarships."

"But—what about your dad?"

"I think Courtney can pass as mixed blood. It's what he is, after all; his mama is white, his dad is Cape Verdean. Dad shouldn't have a problem with it."

We walked back slowly on the dike, each lost in our own thoughts. My mind was going in circles. I wondered what it would be like to have a boyfriend like Courtney. I wondered if anyone could ever like me. I didn't think it was likely. I felt too dirty. No one would want someone with my history. Even if he didn't know about it, I would. I wondered, too, about periods. They sounded positively gross. Maybe I'd be lucky and never get one.

After a few weeks of beach meetings, Courtney began a habit of walking Connie home. They talked at length about their classes and their futures, their high hopes of going on to college. They held hands. As for me, I held Skippy's hand and talked to him and Nicky about the Red Sox.

When it was time for Dad's vacation, my aunt Emma offered to let us stay at the cottage for the week, while she stayed in her city tenement. I loved the idea. Come that Saturday morning, I packed up my transistor and other gear and brought it outside. Then I sat on the porch to wait while the car got packed. Connie came down the street with Nicky. She'd been to the bakery and had a fresh loaf of Portuguese bread. Nicky was munching on a *malasada*. It was almost as big as his face.

"Hey. What are you doing out here?" Connie said.

"Waiting. We're going to the cottage for a whole week."

"Sounds like fun."

I nodded. Then I brightened.

"Hey—you want to come? I can ask my mother." I knew damned well that she would never agree to such a thing. But I wanted it to happen so badly I believed it could.

"No. My father would never let me go. He doesn't let me hang out with white folks. You know that."

"Geez."

"He says it doesn't make sense—says white folks always want something from you."

I was beginning to get irked by this white folks/black folks thing. I had never thought of myself as white or any other color, for that matter, before all this trouble, and said as much to Connie.

"Of course, you did. You just never acknowledged it before."

"I did not!" I protested.

"Oh really? And when you went to the beach and saw all the black people on one side, you didn't say to yourself, 'I'm white, so I belong on this side'?"

I thought about it, reddening, and realized she was right.

"I don't want anything from you—except friendship," I blurted.

"Yeah, you 'accept' me. Think you're pretty brave?"

I didn't understand her sarcasm, and it stung.

"Did you even stop to think about what a risk this is for me? You're clueless, Finn. If we go someplace together, who will be watched? Not you. And if we're seen hanging out together by my black friends, some might see it as a betrayal. And pretty soon I'd be the outcast—unaccepted by my own people, spit on by white people. So where does that leave me? With your friendship?"

I thought I was going to throw up. How could I know all these things? I started to cry.

"Connie, I was only thinking of the fun we could have together, fishing and swimming and—" My voice cracked, and I couldn't go on.

"Right. Look, I have to go—the man wants his bread. I'm sorry if I hurt you. But you have to learn. There's another side to this, that's all, and it would be good if you thought about that." Connie sighed. Then she put an arm around my shoulders.

"Don't worry, white girl. I still like you. I forget, sometimes, that you're only 14. It's a crazy world we live in, though, and you don't get to hold on to your innocence for long. That's the trouble with white people. They think that if they personally didn't lynch someone, they're innocent of all the rest. Innocence. It ought to be a crime for all folks over 10."

"Connie, I—"

She waved her hand dismissively. "Forget it. You and I—we're fine. I mean that."

Connie squeezed my shoulder and headed up the street to her house. I sat there feeling sick to my stomach. I didn't know how to solve all of these problems, and I would have to depend on Connie to guide me. I was determined not to let our friendship end, and I would do whatever it took to keep my eyes and ears open to life as Connie lived it.

Tom and Molly trooped out with boxes and bags. I went over to put my stuff in the trunk.

"Hey, It, open the gate for me," Drew said.

That was it. I was over the edge.

"You know what, Drew? Fuck off," I said.

Drew was momentarily stunned.

"Finn!" Molly said.

"I can't wait to tell Ma—" Drew began.

*"You will shut your mouth, Andrew,"* Tom said, standing nose to nose with Drew. The threat hung heavy in the air.

I helped Molly put her boxes in the trunk, then sat in the back seat, steaming. I'd had it.

Our time at the cottage was a lazy week of swimming, fishing, reading, and just hanging out. Tom and Drew were both working at Gulf Hill that summer and would drive to the cottage after their shift. When Molly wasn't taunting me, she read or wrote in her journal. Sometimes she, Skippy, and I played Parcheesi.

The three of us were seated at the kitchen table. Molly and I were drinking coffee while Skippy was just hanging out, waiting for some action. Molly and I had been up for only an hour or so, and it was early afternoon. Dad was on the screened porch listening to the ball game on the transistor, a bottle of Dawson beer by his side. Ma was outdoors saying her prayers in a chair under the shade of the enormous oak.

With nothing better to do, Molly put her bare foot on my forearm. The only bare feet I liked were baby feet and my own. Everyone else's grossed me out.

I gagged dramatically and said in my most melodic voice, "Get oouutt!" I shook her foot off. She laughed and did it again. Skippy watched, fascinated. "GET OOOUUUTT!" I sang out, louder. Skippy giggled, egging her on. She did it again. And again, and each time she did it, I yelled louder. Then we heard cursing coming from the porch. Hearing how mad Dad was getting only made Molly worse. She did it again.

"GET OOOUUUUUUTTTT!" I nearly screeched, and Skippy said he was going to wet his pants.

"Goddammit," Dad said.

Molly laughed and did it again. It didn't take much to amuse her.

"Goddammit, stop!" Dad yelled from the porch, and that finally worked.

We muffled our laughter, and Skippy, when he could recover himself, asked if we would play Parcheesi.

"Oh sure, why not," Molly said, and Skippy ran off to get the game. I wiped my laugh-tears on my pajama sleeve and told Molly I had to talk to her, but not now.

"About what?"

"Stuff. I'll talk to you later."

"Yeah, but what kind of stuff?"

"Later," I whispered as Skippy came whizzing in with the game. He set it up, and we played for a couple of hours.

"I don't believe it," Ma said, coming in to make her lunch. "Still in pajamas!"

"And driving Dad crazy," Skippy added.

"Well, it's not like we're going anywhere," Molly said.

"I don't care—it looks like Tobacco Road in here. Stop playing games and get dressed. Now," she ordered.

I sighed and went upstairs with Skippy in tow. There were two rooms up there, the larger of which had a double bed for Ma and Dad. The second room was smaller and had a curtain dividing it into two sleeping areas. The boys shared one half, with Skippy and Drew in one twin and Tom in the other. On our side, Molly and I shared a three-quarter bed. Skippy went on his side now to get his clothes from a paper bag with his name on it. I thought about it for a minute, then went over and tackled Skippy onto his bed, where I tickled him till he couldn't catch his breath.

We both lay there, still half-giggling, till Skippy asked, "Do you want to go fishing? We could catch turtles and have turtle races."

"I don't know. I'm not really in the mood for fishing right now."

"What about picking booberries?"

"Yeah—maybe later. And they're called blueberries, not booberries."

"Booberries," Skippy repeated. I gave up.

The air up there was heavy with humidity and a thick, musty smell. It was conducive to secrets and ghost stories. I was thinking up a story to tell Skippy while he babbled on about what he wanted to do that day. Neither of us heard the footsteps on the stairs.

"WHAT'S GOING ON IN HERE?" Ma's shout was so sharp and loud in that tiny, quiet space that we both jumped. I'd still had Skippy half-pinned to his bed from my tickle attack, and now I leaped up, scared. My heart was pounding.

"What?" I said, feeling somehow guilty.

"We weren't doing anything," Skippy said. "Finn was just tickling me and..."

"Tickling you where?" Ma demanded.

Skippy looked confused. Finally, he said, "Everywhere."

I knew I was bright red and looked guilty, but for what I didn't know. What was Ma suggesting?

"Finn, what were you doing to Skippy?"

"For God's sake, Ma, I was only tickling him. What did you think I was doing?" I felt defensive, as if I were being judged.

"Get over to your own side now and get dressed," Ma commanded.

I shuddered while walking past her and ducked behind my curtain.

*Be careful, Skippy,* I thought. *Careful what you say.*

From behind the curtain I could just hear Ma saying, "Did she touch your private parts?"

"What? No!" Skippy said indignantly.

I could hardly believe what I was hearing. I felt suddenly sick to my stomach, and furious at my mother. She made me feel dirty and ashamed. How come she never questioned what Uncle Cal was doing in my room? I squirmed quickly into my clothes and stormed down the stairs. Molly was still at the kitchen table.

"What's going on?" she asked me.

I just waved her off and ran out the back door down to the dock. I untied the boat, got in, and pushed off. I rowed quickly, my arms straining against the oars, out to where the lake turned a bend. The cottage got smaller and smaller until it just blended in with the scenery. I rowed further until I was well out of sight. Then I pulled the oars in and let the boat drift on the current.

Why was she so ready to accuse me? I knew I was dirty inside, but I would never do anything to my little brother. And why weren't her antennae up when it came to Uncle Cal? I kept hearing that loud, accusatory scream in my head. *What's going on here?* And the one word kept coming back to me: dirty.

The boat rocked gently, and I sat there and wept bitter tears, tears that tasted of the sea, as clouds scudded in from the west, and the shy turtles poked their bullet-heads along the lily pads.

After wearing myself out, I threaded the oars into the oarlocks and headed back to the cottage. I had drifted quite a ways out, and I rowed slowly. I was in no hurry to get back, but I didn't want to get in trouble for worrying them. Sure enough, as soon as I rounded the bend I could see Dad and Molly standing on the dock. Ma must have been in the house with Skippy. I waved to them, and they waved back. Dad didn't look mad. I picked up the pace a little, noticing the blisters developing on my palms from the rough oars. When I got to the dock, Dad tied the boat up for me and gave me a hand getting out.

"Where were you all this time?" Dad asked mildly.

"Just around the bend there."

"We were beginning to get worried," Molly said.

"Well, I'm fine," I said. Now what? I didn't know where to look or where to go. "Where's Ma?"

"She walked up to Thibeault's to buy Skippy a Popsicle."

Good. Then I could go up to my room. I grabbed a tall glass of water from the kitchen and went up to sit in the stifling attic heat. But Molly followed me up.

"Moosh over," she said, climbing on the bed with me. I moved.

"So, what happened?" she asked.

"What happened? Nothing happened. I was tickling Skippy, and we were making plans for the day when all of a sudden Ma screamed at us. I didn't know what was wrong. She said, 'What's going on in here?' in this real nasty voice that made my skin crawl. What did she think we were doing?"

"I don't know," Molly said, not looking at me.

"Well, she made me feel real dirty, by the way she talked and looked at us. I don't know what Skippy thought." I could feel myself getting choked up again. Molly worried a hangnail, and I struggled for control.

"You said earlier you wanted to talk to me. Do you want to talk now?"

"I don't know—I'm awfully tired."

"Well, now's a good time—no one's around."

I just shrugged. She waited. Finally, I said, "I don't want to go back to school next week."

"I'm not ready to go back to teaching next week, either," she said.

"No, I mean it. I... I don't fit in. None of the kids like me. They're all way ahead of me, and they have these cliques—"

"What do you mean, way ahead? How?"

I thought about that for a minute. Then I finally said it.

"Why haven't I started...you know...periods yet?"

"Is that what this is all about? It's perfectly normal not to start till later—"

"Everyone else has. And how come Ma never told me about it?"

"Where did you find out about it?"

"Connie."

"What did she tell you?"

I told her. She thought about it.

"Yeah, that's pretty accurate. Maybe Ma doesn't realize you're growing up. But if you haven't started when you're 15, we'll get it checked out."

"Some boys in my class shave...No one ever talks to me. I eat lunch by myself. I hate school."

"You'll make friends. You'll see. And you'd better get your act together and do well this year. You're smart. There's no reason not to do well."

"I hate it."

"Stop whining. It will get better. Anything else?"

I shook my head.

"Then I'm going downstairs to read my book."

She left, and I flopped over on the bed. All I could think of was my lack of a period and the new school year. I felt like crying all the time. I felt like a little kid. And I was jealous of Connie and Courtney, who were acting like they were in love or something. I liked Courtney. He was polite, a little shy, smart, and he always tried to include me. He had plans for his future. But everything depended on scholarships. Without those, he couldn't go to college, and if he wasn't in college, he'd end up getting drafted and shipped off to Vietnam.

The same was true for Drew. He was trying to save enough money to go to the state college. Tom was working his way through the local textile college, but it was obvious that he didn't like it. He spent more time with Bridie and at frat parties. But Drew was brilliant in science; it was entirely possible that he could get a scholarship. Drew and Courtney had a lot in common. They both wanted to get out of the South End, and they both chose the same route out. The options for other kids, kids who didn't like school or have the capacity for it, were limited. There were the streets—or the Army. Or the seminary. Connie's brother Freddie would have been a street kid if the Army hadn't snatched him up. Now he was in Vietnam, and Connie didn't like the tone of his infrequent letters. He sounded angry, confused, sometimes almost desperate. I wondered what he would do when his hitch was up. Fremont, on the other hand, had joined the Navy and loved it. In his letters to Connie, he talked about making it a career. He loved the ocean, its constancy, its many colors and moods, its cradling movement or terrible rolls. Connie said it was the first time she had ever known him to be really excited about something.

I could hear downstairs that Ma and Skippy were back from Thibeault's. I decided to go for a swim, to wash the dirtiness off me, despite the clouds, and take Skippy with me—if Ma would let me. I changed into my bathing suit, grabbed a towel from the towel bag, and went downstairs.

"I'm going swimming," I murmured to anyone within earshot. "Skippy, you want to come?"

"No—I'm eating my Popsicle."

With the sticky mess he was making, he'd need a bath by the time he was done. Ma came out of the kitchen.

"I don't want you swimming by yourself," she said. I felt frustration creeping up my neck. But I didn't want to get into another argument.

"Molly, will you come? Just for a little while? You can read your book on the beach."

"Oh, for God's sake. All right, I'll come."

She went upstairs to get a towel to lie on.

While she was gone, Ma said, "I'm sorry, Finn, for before. I overreacted."

*Damn right,* I thought, but I said nothing. I didn't know what to say. But then Molly came down, and we left. I walked ahead.

"Hey, wait up, Finn," Molly said, and caught up to me. "You shouldn't slump your shoulders so much, you know. Stand up tall. It's better for you, and it makes you look better too."

Everyone was always after me for hunching. I didn't care. Sometimes I just wanted to hunch myself away and for everyone to leave me alone. What did I have to stand up tall about?

I swam out to the raft, dived off it a few times, then headed back to shore. Though the water calmed me, as it always did, it really wasn't much fun swimming alone. I told Molly I was ready to leave.

"Already?"

I nodded and picked up my towel.

"Okay, then. Suit yourself. Or unsuit yourself. Aha! Get it?"

I raised my eyebrows heavenward and trudged off across the street.

After supper, we got out the cards and played whist till bedtime.

Drew tried to get undressed for bed, and Molly looked over the divider.

"Ma, she's looking at me!" he whined.

"Okay, I'll stop," Molly said. Then did it again.

"Ma—she won't let me get undressed—she keeps looking!"

"Molly, will you stop?" Ma said from the other room.

"She's doing it again!"

"Molly, go to sleep and leave him alone," Ma said.

"Heeheehee," Molly said and did it again.

"Maaa!" Drew whined.

"Goddammit," Dad said.

"Heeheehee," Molly said, but finally gave over when Dad sounded really mad and not just annoyed. Drew struggled to put his pajamas on under the covers.

"Aaarrggh!" Tom said. "Drew farted!"

"I'm going to throw up," Skippy said and gagged for effect.

"Goddammit," Dad said.

Things finally quieted down, and I drifted like the rowboat into my sleep. Molly got up and slipped downstairs to read.

The next day was Tom's day off. He dropped Drew off at Gulf Hill, then went to run some errands. He was gone the entire day. When he came back, he'd picked up Drew, and Bridie was with him. They seemed subdued and spent a lot of time out on the dock talking quietly. After supper, instead of whist, Tom dropped his bombshell.

"I've decided not to go back to school," he began. He took Bridie's hand and said, "I'm joining the Navy. So I won't get drafted."

We were all stunned.

"It's really hot in here. Can we go out on the porch?" he said.

That got everyone moving and thinking. It wasn't surprising that he would quit school. But joining the Navy came as a complete shock.

"I think it would be best right now for me," he said as we settled in. "Who knows—after my hitch is up, maybe I'll go back to school on the GI Bill."

There was silence on the darkened porch. Finally, I went over and gave him a hug.

"Tom, wait. Have you really thought this through?" Ma asked him. "Don't they send ships to Vietnam too? Tom, I wish you wouldn't do this. Why don't you stay and finish school—it's only a couple more years—"

"Ma, I've given it a lot of thought. Yes, they send ships to 'Nam, but they're way off the coast. And as to school, I hate it. I'm just wasting time and money."

"Oh God, Tom," Ma said, her hand at her throat. "You've done this already? You enlisted?"

Tom nodded.

We all thought about this for a bit.

"When would you be leaving?" Ma asked.

"I leave in two weeks for boot camp. After that I'll go somewhere else for training in my specialty. I put in for signalman. Then I'll have a little time before they ship me out. If I were to leave school, or flunk out, then I'd be drafted into the Army, and I don't want that. That's a sure ride to Vietnam."

"Two weeks," Ma said softly.

"Are you sure this is what you want?" Dad asked him.

"Yeah, I'm sure. I've been thinking about it all summer. I knew I didn't want to go back to school, and I don't want to be drafted. This is all that makes sense."

"How long are you in for?" Ma asked.

"It's a two-year hitch, then I'll be in the reserves for another couple of years. Bridie thinks it's a good idea, too."

Bridie nodded.

"I can't believe this," Molly said. "It's hard to absorb."

"You'll believe it when you see me looking cute in my uniform," Tom said.

It was Saturday evening, our last night at the cottage. Bridie was spending the night, as she'd done the night before, squeezed in with me and Molly. The three of us walked to Thibeault's, Molly for cigs, Bridie for a candy bar, me for a frozen Zero bar. The night was balmy, a perfect summer's evening, and the sun had gone down on a mirror-smooth lake in shades of pink and purple. When we returned, we all sat around the porch, and Molly started a song:

*Now is the hour, when we must say goodbye*

*Soon you'll be sailing, far across the sea...*

Everyone joined in, and we continued to sing song after song, the mood nostalgic and sad. Tom would be the first to break up the family. And we would hold the circle open until he returned.

No one wanted to leave the next morning. We would stretch out our vacation by having a Hazelwood Park picnic on Labor Day, but we were all glum.

---

The first day back to school, I felt silly in my school uniform—a navy blazer with a blue plaid skirt and white shirt and stupid saddle shoes. I felt wretched. I had a very bad lower backache, and my stomach and abdomen felt like they'd been pummeled. I felt shaky and nervous. I emerged from the bathroom white-faced. I called Molly over.

"It's started," I said.

"What? Why are you whispering? What's the matter with you—are you going to throw up?"

"I might," I said and pointed to the toilet full of blood. Thank God for Connie.

"Oh! Oh my God!"

"What?" Ma said, coming over. She looked, then called, "Has anyone thrown ketchup into the toilet?"

"What?" Drew asked.

"Ma, for God's sake, it's Finn," Molly hissed at her.

Ma was taken completely by surprise. She looked over at me, and I just stood there, embarrassed.

"Oh, Finn—I didn't realize—you never—" Ma just shook her head. Then she hugged me. "You're a woman now," she said.

*What a stupid statement,* I thought. "Great. I don't feel like a woman. I feel like shit."

"Don't use that word. Wait here," she said and disappeared into her bedroom. She reemerged with a package and a booklet that was yellowed with age. "Put these on. And read this. Then, if you have any questions, come and ask me."

"Do I have to go to school today? I feel lousy."

"I'll get you some aspirin. It's your first day of school. Of course, you have to go. Finn, I'm so glad...thank God..."

"What did that mean?" I asked Molly later in the car.

Molly sighed. "I have no idea." She gave me a look to remind me of Drew and Bridie in the back seat. She pulled up in front of Holy Family High.

"Drew, you look after Finn today, you hear?"

"Yeah, yeah," Drew said and got out of the car.

Molly drove off to New Bedford High School, where she taught with Bridie.

"You all right? You look real pale," Drew asked. He looked uncomfortable.

"I'm okay, I guess."

"Come on, I'll walk you to your homeroom."

I sat in the back of every class and drifted in and out of daydreams. I took no notes, wrote down no assignments. There was no way I could concentrate. I hated being a girl—excuse me, *woman*—especially if this was what periods felt like. At lunch, I was expecting to take my usual solitary walk down to Souza's Pharmacy for a Coke. But Drew showed up, and he had a couple of friends with him. Usually seniors went to Goggin's for lunch.

"Feeling any better?" Drew whispered.

I nodded.

"Finn, this is my friend, Robert. And this is his sister, Angie. Angie is a sophomore, too."

"Hi," I said. I recognized Angie from some of my classes. As far as I knew, she didn't belong to one of the cliques, but I didn't think she'd want to be friends with me. No one did. I didn't know what else to say. I just wanted to disappear, but Angie wouldn't let me.

"You're in my bio and Latin classes," Angie said.

"Right. Thecla scares the hell out of me," I said, not really thinking, just saying what came to me first. Sister Thecla was our Latin teacher. She was very tall and Germanic. And she generally picked on me a lot.

"She's not so bad, if you're prepared. I have a study in Kempton House this afternoon. You want to work on our Latin homework together?"

"Sure," I said, pleased.

We chatted the rest of the lunch period, and I went to my afternoon classes feeling considerably better. Angie was nice, and funny, too. It would be great to have a friend at school. For once, I was grateful for Drew. Angie and I met at Kempton House for last period, and she helped me with my

Latin translation. It wasn't as daunting as I'd thought. I just hadn't memorized the vocabulary and given it a chance.

---

Drew had taught himself to play guitar, and he played beautifully, his long, slim fingers able to stretch and reach even the most complex chords. As it turned out, Angie played guitar as well, a nylon-string, and she had a sweet soprano voice. So I was determined to do the same. I began by sneaking into Drew's room when he was out or at work and borrowing his guitar. I used his music sheets to learn the chords. Of course, I had been "trained" in harmony since I was a young child, so the sounds of the chords were familiar to me. The hardest part was growing calluses on my fingertips. Having to keep practicing while the calluses formed was agony (Drew's guitar had steel strings), for if I stopped playing to rest my fingers, the fledgling calluses would soften, and I'd have to start all over again. So I kept at it. Sometimes I'd practice till my fingers bled. But, over time, my fingertips hardened, and once they did, I was able to develop a repertoire of simple folk tunes, which I played by ear. Ma and Dad admirably put up with hearing the same songs over and over again.

Then, after a few weeks, there came a major breakthrough: almost entirely intuitively, I learned how to fingerpick songs, instead of always strumming them. This gave the songs a whole new dimension and extraordinary range. I was so thrilled I called up Angie and asked her to come to my house right away for a practice. We went upstairs in what had been my grandfather's bedroom and played till midnight. It was a tangible milestone.

The only problem occurred when Drew came home from work to find his guitar missing. He stormed upstairs and was ready to light into me—but he stopped in the doorway and listened. I was playing Simon & Garfunkel's "The Sounds of Silence," and Angie's voice was mellow and touched by my harmony. At the song's end, Drew turned and went back downstairs without a word.

By mid-October, Angie and I had developed a strong collection of folk tunes, and the beginnings of a friendship that would last the rest of our lives.

---

Nineteen sixty-six was a banner year: We got both a phone and hot water! At first, I thought I could make tea from the tap, but I soon discovered it didn't work that way. Having hot water meant that I could wash my hair in the sink on a regular basis instead of just once a week at bath time. I went to school better groomed.

Studying Latin with Angie helped me to improve my grades, and Sister Thecla stopped harassing me. For biology, I had a ready tutor in Drew, who was only too happy to explain the double helix and other concepts I was having trouble with. He was not only patient but also a brilliant teacher. I never—even into adulthood—forgot the things he taught me. He relayed concepts in a way that was understandable, that made sense to me.

Soon all my grades were improving, as I settled into a routine of studying and playing guitar. Without the constant disapproval of the nuns, I found myself actually enjoying school. It was a truly remarkable turnaround from my first-year disaster. My bio teacher, Sister Dianne, had taken me under her wing, and, at my urging, she helped me, Angie, and a few other acquaintances form the Depression Club. We had membership pins made from Creepy Crawlers, and I made up a slogan: We're in the depression, and we're not progressing from the depths of despair. We met in Sister Dianne's classroom after school, and we would stay on talking for hours. Poor Sister Dianne was probably dying to get home after a long day, but she never seemed impatient to leave. She encouraged and supported me and helped me to deal with the bullying Kenny Hydes of the world. And I would soon need that support more than she could possibly know.

Near the end of October, Tom left.

I ironed his whites while he sat in the parlor spit-shining his shoes and singing along with Johnny Mathis on the hi-fi. Boot camp and his leave were over. He would be flying out from New Bedford Airport today to join his ship, the aircraft carrier *America*, in Norfolk, Virginia. Ma was all in a flap. Dad would be coming home at two, having worked an 8-hour instead of 11-hour shift. Ma kept looking up the street, praying he wouldn't stop in at the Z Club. There was no time—Tom's flight was at three.

Dad did come straight home, a measure of how important the day was to him. Tom, dressed in his bright whites, looked so handsome it made my heart ache. Bridie drove over. She was going with us to the airport, and we needed her car as well as Molly's to accommodate everyone. I wondered how Bridie and Tom would weather the split.

At the airport, while waiting for his flight to be called, I held one of Tom's hands, and Bridie the other. His hand squeezed mine. Skippy sat on his duffle bag. No one had much to say. Not out loud.

Inside my head, though, I was having a kind of private conversation with Tom, fondly rehashing a parade of memories starring my biggest brother. I stood there remembering the times Tom would bring me to Gulf Hill for a Brown Derby ice cream cone, and the times he defended me during Drew's torture-Finn phase, and even the time when we were all walking home from grammar school and I tripped, landing in a pile of dog crap. No one leashed their dogs then, and no one picked up after them. Stepping in dog crap happened a lot. But falling flat on your bottom in the pile was a rare spectacle. The other kids were in hysterics, pointing and laughing—except Tom. He found a crumpled tissue in his pocket and did his best to wipe me off. He took off my soiled coat and gave me his own jacket to wear home. Tom might not remember these things. But I did. I always would.

"Write often," Molly said. "Every day. Every week. Whenever you can."

Ma came and stood close to Tom. "Tom, be very careful," she said, not in her usual strong voice. It was more a weak whisper.

Drew and Skippy were subdued. Dad said nothing, but stood with his gnarled hands folded in front of him, rubbing his thumbs together and looking anywhere but at Tom. Finally, the last boarding call came. Ma hugged Tom and started to cry. Drew shook his hand, then looked away. Skippy jumped up on him and hugged his neck. Molly and I held him close. Dad didn't know what to do or say. He reached out his hand, but Tom pulled him close, hugging him tight.

"I love you, Dad."

"Take good care of yourself," Dad managed.

"I will. And I know you love me too."

Dad nodded and turned away, too choked up to say anything more.

Finally, it came to Bridie. They walked a few feet away and said some words in private. They hugged, and Tom kissed her mouth gently.

Tom walked to the tarmac and boarded the small plane that would take him to far-off ports, the first to leave the family's warm embrace. That night, in a poem, Molly would write:

*Now in the nest it is still womb-warm*
*but all the feathers are growing.*
*And you are the first to fly.*

For weeks, the house was too quiet. The first letter we received from Tom excited us all. We sat around the kitchen table while Ma read it aloud. He said the *America* was enormous, with over a thousand sailors on board.

> *It's like a city on the sea, and it's easy to get lost. We're shipping out tomorrow for the Mediterranean. I'm glad we won't be anywhere near Vietnam. I miss you all like crazy. Please write soon. Give my love to Bridie when you see her. And love to all of you.*
>
> *Your son, Tom.*

Later, I brought the letter up the corner to Connie's house. I knew Connie's father would not be home at this early hour. Connie was almost as excited about the letter as I was. Fremont was stationed on the *Forrestal*. With both Fremont and Freddie gone, Connie was very lonely at home. I had been meeting her on Saturday mornings at the new library, where we would both write letters to her brothers, and now to Tom. The new library had been built just a block away from the old, which was now a police station. Built of stucco and brick in a modern design, the library was airy and wonderfully cool in the summer. It had long tables and, best of all, four futuristic-looking contour chairs, which I loved. I could curl up, enfolded, and read while also swiveling around. It was a perfect place to meet Connie, where we could sit at one of the long tables and write. Fremont was good about writing back, but not Freddie. In the weeks that passed, whenever a letter arrived from any of the boys, Connie and I pored over them.

I spent a lot of time that fall of '66 sitting on the backyard swing late in the day after school, listening to my transistor in the waning hours of daylight, filled with sadness and nostalgia. Something inside me was changing in ways I did not know how to describe. I felt different somehow. My relationship with the world had shifted in some fundamental way, the way the world changes when you see it reflected, refracted, in water. Many afternoons I wanted to cry, and I didn't understand why. Sometimes I felt a deep loneliness, a disconnect from family and friends. Skippy was often the only one I wanted to be with. I wanted to hold him in my arms even though, at nine now, he was too big for such things.

Then came that Sunday.

# 8. Sunday Bloody Sunday

Some Sundays are hard to face, and this was one of them. Though it was only fall, outside it was in the mid-30s, raw and rainy. The weather darkened the house, and I went around putting all the lights on. Unable to get warm, I wrapped myself in a quilt Granny had made and propped myself up in bed to read, though no doubt I would fall asleep after a few pages. It was that kind of day, where sleep was your only protection from the gloom. It made me think of death and new graves and unquiet spirits. When it felt like something was crawling up my arm, I pulled back my sweatshirt sleeve to see. Nothing was there except for the crawly sensation. I stared at my arm hairs against my white skin. They didn't stir. I peered closer. Nothing was there. I gave my forearm a good scratch anyway and pulled the sleeve down. Opening the book to where I'd dog-eared the page, I tried to focus. At the moment, I was reading Carson McCullers's *Member of the Wedding*, which was strumming chords deep inside my young heart. I didn't know where Molly was, downstairs or over at Bridie's. Granny was visiting her sister Emma and her brother-in-law Duncan. I closed my eyes and had just begun to doze off when I heard my name being called from downstairs. Grudgingly, I disentangled myself and tripped over my own feet on the way to the door.

"What?" I called.

"Come down here—now," Molly called back.

Her voice had a serious timbre, giving me a chill of premonition. Or maybe it was just the cold of the stairway. I trudged down the stairs, and everyone except Skippy was in the kitchen when I entered. Ma and Molly both looked upset. This was more than Molly discovering I'd worn her suede jacket. Dad's face was red but otherwise inscrutable. My insides quivered.

"Sit down," Ma said, indicating a chair at the table. I sat. I had the sensation of a trial beginning.

"Where's Skippy? Is he all right?"

"Skippy's in his room," Molly said.

"He's asleep now," Drew said.

"Is he sick?"

"No," Ma said, but simultaneously Drew said, "Oh, he's sick, all right."

I looked from one to the other.

"What's going on?" I asked, feeling very afraid.

"I have to ask you some questions—serious questions—and I want honest answers," Ma said, pausing and taking a deep breath. I shivered. I knew where she was going, and I did not want to follow her there.

"Has Uncle Cal ever... done anything... to you?" Ma asked.

*Oh God, oh God, here it comes.* My stomach flipped, and I could feel my bowels loosen.

"Like what?" I said in a small voice. I felt the heat in my face. I couldn't breathe right. Ma looked afraid of my answer. And she looked mad. Sweat formed on my upper lip, and I gazed down at the floor.

"Has he ever... touched you?"

"Yes," I whispered.

There. It was out.

There was no retreat, nowhere to hide. My answer hung in the air above us.

"How? Where?" Ma wanted to know.

I looked around desperately. I caught Molly's eye. *Help me.*

"Did he ever touch your private parts?" Molly asked, her voice gentle.

I nodded. I could hear Ma's sudden intake of breath.

"He didn't... put anything into you, did he?" Ma asked, her tone sharp-edged. My hands trembled, and the strength was sapped from my legs. My spine tingled as though it might collapse on itself. I didn't know what to tell them. I didn't know how to tell them. The tension in the room sat on my chest, choking me. Drew was looking at me from the doorway to the parlor. I couldn't read his face. Then he turned away. I blushed to the roots of my hair. Without making eye contact with anyone, I whispered. My voice was hoarse.

"His fingers... and... his tongue."

Ma, who had leaned forward to hear me, suddenly snapped back in her chair. "*What?*" her voice hit a high pitch and broke.

Dad swore and punched the wall. The plaster dented under the blow. Drew slipped into the parlor. Molly was biting her bottom lip and looking down at her hands.

"Oh, my God," Ma said, her hand at her throat. Her face was bright red, as red as I imagined mine was, and tears welled up in her eyes. It was a long, long minute before she spoke again. She looked at me closely.

"Did he put anything else into you?"

I shook my head no.

"Did he do anything else?"

"He made me touch him...squeeze him..." I could not bear to look over at my father.

He kept saying, "Bastard. I'll kill the bastard."

"When did he do these things?" Ma persisted. Ma took my hand in hers and held on tight.

"When? I don't know—all the time, I guess."

"What do you mean, 'all the time'?" That edge in her voice was searing me. "Since when?"

"Since I was little—I don't remember the first time. Since before I can remember."

A terrible strangling sound came from over by the door. It was Dad, and he was crying, his head leaning into the wall. Never in my life had I heard my father cry, and it made me feel terrible. I felt I had let him down.

"Where did he do these things?" Ma's voice was dry and stern.

"In my room at night, in the cellar, sometimes in his house."

Ma's shoulders slumped. Her body sagged back into her chair. For a moment, she seemed lost, defeated.

"Everything you told me is true? Is there anything else?"

"No."

"Finn, why didn't you tell us?"

Ah, there it was. The question. The accusation. I knew I was to blame.

Into a terrible stillness, I finally said the truth as I knew it: "I don't know...he told me not to...he said I'd get in trouble." And he was right.

"You should have told us," Ma said, and I knew I was in the deepest trouble I'd ever been in. My heart pounded. Tears of embarrassment and shame formed in my eyes. Why were they asking all these questions now? Had he been caught?

"Why didn't you tell me?" Ma repeated. She put her hands on my shoulders.

Aloud, but softly, I said, "I was afraid of him."

"Finn," Molly said finally, "he tried something with Skippy."

This took me by surprise.

"What happened? Is Skippy all right?"

"He's okay," Molly said. "He came upstairs and threw up. Then he told me what had happened. We needed to know if it happened to anyone else."

Skippy. He had told. He had done the right thing. Uncle Cal hadn't gotten to him early enough.

"Did it? Besides me, I mean?"

"Drew says he doesn't remember anything. Of course, we can't ask Tom. I remember some... incidents," Molly said.

"Finn, think now... how often did this happen?" Ma wanted to know.

Would the questions never end?

"Ma—I don't know. How often did he come into my room at night? You would know that. It was all the time when I was small. Kindergarten. First grade..."

*A child in trouble is a troubled child,* I recalled Ma saying long ago.

"To think I used to get mad at him for going in there and keeping you awake," Ma said quietly.

"Lately it's been—I don't know—maybe twice a week."

"Where?"

"In the cellar, mostly."

"What were you doing in the cellar?"

"Getting my bike, or other things. He follows me."

There was a long silence, into which Dad said, "I'll kill the bastard. I'll..."

Ma stopped him. "No, Jack—we have to think about this."

I still sat sweating in my chair, not knowing what to do or where to look. Tears were threatening to spill over.

Ma continued.

"Jack, if Joan finds out, it will kill her. Her whole life would be destroyed. And Ma—my mother—she could have a stroke. We have to think about this... I wish you had told us," Ma repeated.

"I told you, Ma—he told me not to tell. He said I'd get in trouble."

"How could this have happened? Where was I when this was going on?" She spoke half to herself.

"Usually you were in the parlor watching TV."

"But I could have come out at any time...Finn, I'm so sorry. How could he—how could he take such chances like that?"

I didn't know the answers. I remembered the note he had recently shoved into my hand, asking why I had been avoiding him. I'd torn it to tiny pieces before throwing it away.

"Can I go back to my room now?"

Ma looked at Molly, who nodded. "I suppose so. But lock the door, and if he comes up, don't let him in."

I unstuck my thighs from the chair and stood up. I walked, slouched, head bowed, past Dad. Dad put his hand on my shoulder briefly and squeezed.

As I left, I heard Ma say, "We've got to protect Joan and Ma..."

Upstairs, I locked the tenement door and went to my room. I threw myself down on the bed and cried. I had never been in so much serious trouble before. I had hoped to feel some sense of relief when it all came out. Instead, I felt deeply humiliated, and my stomach went into spasms. Cramping, I curled in a fetal position. I gulped the air but still could barely breathe through the sobs.

*My family must hate me for not telling.* Skippy, of course, had done the right thing. He told right away. But I had gone along with it all. I was just as guilty as Uncle Cal. What would happen to me now? Was there a punishment big enough to match what I had done?

I thought of Dad. All his married life he had been unfavorably compared to Callan, if not outright, by implication. He could do none of the things Callan did around the house and yard. He couldn't build things. He wasn't an electrician or a plumber. He drank. But now it was clear he was the better man, a good man. He would never hurt his children or anyone else's. He was gentle and kind and, when he wasn't drinking, he was very much a gentleman. I hoped he felt good about himself. I hoped he felt vindicated. So what if he didn't have a white-collar job? His frayed blue collars were clean, and so were his hands. And at that moment I loved him more than I ever had.

Ma, on the other hand, was unfathomable to me. She was usually warm, she read and sang to us, she had a ready lap for any child in need of one. But her anger and contempt in the kitchen made me feel dirty. Her disgust felt as if it were directed at me. All my life I had sought her approval, all the while knowing that as long as things were going on with Callan, I would never deserve it. Growing up ashamed of myself, of my body, of my gender—I knew I was unlovable. If people knew how bad I was inside, they would never love me. Well, now Ma knew the real me, and she seemed inscrutable. Would she ever love me again? Could she hold this violated body in her arms and not feel repulsed? The very core of me felt bad, as in rotten, spoiled, decaying. I loved my mother. I wanted desperately for her to love me back.

A memory suddenly flashed in my head. I was in fourth, perhaps fifth, grade. A girl in my class, Maria, was walking home from school with me, and it was a lovely fall afternoon with the leaves changing.

We left St. Mary's and walked down to Washington Square, when Maria said, "Hey, my uncle lives here, above his shop. Do you want to stop by with me?"

I hesitated. Ma had frequently warned us not to talk to strangers. She had drilled into us that they were dirty, which I took literally to mean that they were scruffy and smelled bad. But this wasn't a stranger. He was Maria's uncle.

And, having nothing better to do, I said, "Sure."

The shop was a cobbler's, and when we entered I was hit with the commingled smells of shoe polish and leather. I loved it. Strange-looking forms sat on a wooden counter top, some with shoes or boots perched on them. Maria's uncle was standing at one of these forms putting black polish on a shoe that looked brand new.

"Hi, Uncle Tim. This is my friend Finn from school," Maria said.

Uncle Tim said he was delighted to see us, and from her book bag, Maria pulled out two paintings she'd done in art class. I thought they were excellent. They were of leaves, and Maria had used strange mixtures of colors in fascinating ways. I was jealous. Maria's uncle looked them over carefully and pronounced them beautiful, telling Maria she was a real artist. He was short, almost Mickey Rooney short, and a little stout, though not what you would call fat. He had white hair in a fringe around his head, and he wore wire-rimmed glasses. I thought he looked like a cobbler, the expression on his face gentle and impish.

"Wait here," he told us, wiping the black polish from his hands onto his long apron. He clomped up a nearby staircase.

I looked around the shop. Finished shoes and boots were aligned in pairs on a broad shelf with tags on them. I inhaled deeply and saw all the old shoes lined up to be repaired. Some of them looked like they were falling apart, but I had every confidence that Uncle Tim would make them like new.

He returned with a Milky Way bar that he had cut into halves and gave one to each of us. Then a customer came in carrying shoes with holes on the bottom, and Uncle Tim said we had to leave now. Before we left, however, he slipped each of us a quarter. I was thrilled and thanked him. A whole quarter to spend! We left the shop and ran to the variety store on the opposite corner of the square.

Oh, the choices one could make with a quarter. I got a nickel bag of Fritos, some two-for-a-penny red-licorice shoelaces, some red-and-green coconut watermelon slices, a Bonomo's Turkish Taffy bar, a pair of Wax Lips, five Squirrel Nut candies for my father, and a Bolster bar for Ma. I felt rich.

Maria and I parted ways on Fair Street, and I dilly-dallied the rest of the way home.

When I got there, Ma wanted to know why I was so late. I grinned up at her with my Wax Lips in my mouth. She laughed, but then she noticed the paper sack of candy in my fist.

Her face changed.

"Finn! Where did you get all that candy?"

I gave her the Bolster bar and the five Squirrel Nuts for Dad. She thanked me and put them aside.

"Well?" she demanded.

I took the Wax Lips out of my mouth. You can't talk with Wax Lips.

"From Uncle Tim, the cobbler."

*"Who?"*

I explained about Maria's uncle, the half Milky Way, and the quarter. The more I told her, the more furious she became.

"How many times," she yelled, "have I told you not to talk to strangers?"

"He's not a stranger. He's Maria's uncle," I said. "And he's a very nice man."

I could not fathom why she was so angry.

"Did he do anything to you?"

*Do anything?* "Like what?"

"Finn, for God's sake. Did he touch you?"

I thought about that. Did he pat my shoulder on the way out? Ma took my chin in her hand and looked at me hard.

*"Did he touch your private parts?"*

"*What*? Of course not." I was indignant. "I told you he was just a nice man."

"Give me that bag."

I handed it over.

"And the lips."

She put them on the table.

"I should throw them away."

"Ma!"

"Go to your room. And think about what I told you. Never, ever, talk to strangers or take candy or money from them."

I flounced into my room and slammed the door.

She gave me my candy bag back after supper. And Dad was happy with his Squirrel Nuts.

Sitting in my room after telling my parents about Callan, I wondered at the fact that my mother had been so adamant about staying away from strangers when, in fact, the "stranger" was living in the house.

After some time—An hour? Two?—there was a knock on the door. Oh God, what if it was Uncle Cal? I got up and walked cautiously across the kitchen. The knock came again, then a voice.

"Finn? It's me. Open up."

Molly. Relief flooded through me. It occurred to me that, like my parents, Uncle Cal and Aunt Joan also had a key to this tenement. Would I ever be safe? I undid the lock and slumped back to my room.

"What's going on?" I asked Molly as I sat on my bed.

"We've been talking in circles about what to do. I think Dad's going to have a talk with Uncle Cal. Poor Dad."

"That's right?" I asked. "He's going to stay in this house?"

"What are the alternatives? Joan worships Callan. I don't think she'd ever recover. It's just too complicated... And I'm afraid of how Callan might react—you know what his temper is like. And what if Joan didn't believe us? She'd want to talk to you, Finn, and I don't know how you'd feel about that..."

"It would be an interrogation," I said.

"She'd have to believe us. Why would we make this stuff up? Besides, it's not just you. He went after Skippy. And, lately, he's been after me, too."

"What?"

"Yeah, trapping me on the stairs, rubbing up against me, trying to tongue-kiss me, saying lewd things. Sick bastard."

"So it's not just me," I murmured.

"No. But think about it. He's gone after you, after Skippy, after me. Joan would have to believe us. I think he's having some sort of breakdown," Molly said.

"Molly, what about the twins? Do you think he's been after them too?"

"It wouldn't surprise me."

"He'd beat the crap out of them if they threatened to tell."

"That's how he's been able to get away with it all these years. Everyone is terrified of his temper," Molly said. "Ma doesn't know what to do. If she tells Aunt Joan, it could be a terrible uproar. Possibly a complete rift between them. And if Ma and Dad insist he move out—I can't imagine the blowout there'd be."

I didn't answer right away.

"I—I don't want to be responsible for tearing the house apart," I said softly. My guilt would be multiplied a thousand fold. I didn't think I could live with that.

"You wouldn't be responsible, Finn. It wasn't your doing," Molly said.

Oh, but it was. I let it go on. I didn't tell. I was the co-conspirator. I didn't think anything could erase that guilt.

We sat for a few moments in silence.

"Molly?"

"Yeah?"

"Do you think Ma still loves me?"

"Of course she does. It wasn't your fault."

"But I didn't tell."

"Finn, Ma loves you. All that anger? It's for Callan, not you."

I wished with all my aching heart that I could believe her.

In the end, they decided Dad would talk to Callan and threaten exposure if he went after any of us again. At the earliest opportunity, Dad followed Uncle Cal down to the cellar. Drew came upstairs and told me. He had sneaked down after Dad—he told me he was afraid that Uncle Cal might hurt Dad. Drew sat on the cellar steps and listened, occasionally peeking around the corner. He said that Dad was so furious that he choked up. But he controlled himself. He told Uncle Cal that if he ever went anywhere near his children again, he'd tell Aunt Joan and call the police. He said Uncle Cal should get psychiatric help. For his part, Uncle Cal denied everything. He told Dad that he loved us like his own children and would never hurt us. Then Dad told Uncle Cal that if he ever so much as touched one of us again, he'd kill him. Drew said his fists were clenched and there could be no doubt that he meant it.

I thanked Drew, both for watching out for Dad and for telling me. Drew was uncomfortable and embarrassed, but he gave me a quick hug before going back downstairs. I went back to my room and pulled the quilt tightly around me, wrapping myself in Granny's innocence. I had thought at first that the long nightmare was finally over, but now I realized it would never end for me. In my heart of hearts, I believed I was responsible. I was to blame for not telling, and I was quite certain that Ma hated me for my complicity.

Ma was angry every day. I would come downstairs in the morning to find her sitting in her chair looking out the window, her eyes red-rimmed, one hand around her coffee, the other at her throat, her rosary beads puddled in her lap. She would glance at me and quickly look away. Her facial expression held a mixture of anger and contempt, and in the absence of anything to indicate otherwise, I assumed it was directed toward me. I felt like a pariah.

For weeks on end the house was subdued. We ate dinner in awkward silence. There was no singing during dishes. If we heard footsteps on the stairs, we stiffened, then fled to our rooms. If Uncle Cal was forced to come upstairs on an errand for Aunt Joan, he now knocked on the door first before coming in. Ma would turn her face away. Dad would get whatever he had come up for, and Callan would slip silently back down the stairs. The usual family gatherings for birthdays and special events were torture. Each of these was soured by the tension of having to interact with Callan socially without letting on to Granny or Aunt Joan that anything was amiss. The discomfort was extreme, and the former joy of such occasions was sucked out until nothing was left but the motions.

I couldn't see how we could go on with these charades. Whenever I looked at him I felt sick. And what must Ma and Dad have felt? Imagine them trying to tamp down that rage, swallow the bitter bile, and live behind a mask of pleasantry. I was sitting on brambles, waiting for someone to say something that would cause the whole world to explode. But a somber inner silence prevailed, time moved on, and we grew accustomed to our masks. And I sat in the midst of this heavy silence with the word "GUILTY" flashing through my mind like a neon sign.

On the other hand, Dad came home earlier now. If he stopped in at the Z Club, it was for the briefest of visits. At night, he was more alert. Meanwhile, Skippy and I weren't allowed to go in the cellar anymore. If we needed anything, we had to wait for Dad or Drew to get it for us.

I spent as much time away from this toxic atmosphere as possible, mostly by going to the library. Connie wanted to know what was wrong with me, but I couldn't tell her. She soon stopped asking what was the matter and instead tried to be supportive. She was affectionate and greeted me with a hug when we met, and again when we parted company. She could have no idea how much those hugs meant to me. With Connie, I didn't feel like a pariah. She gave me affection that I desperately needed. Other than meeting Connie, I kept more and more to myself. Angie had acquired a boyfriend, so she was unavailable most of the time anyway. As for school, I poured myself into my studies. I remember Sister Dianne stopping me after class one day and asking me why I frowned all the time.

"What's going on?" she asked. "Look at your posture—you're walking all hunched over, like 'I am a worm and not a man.'"

I had no answer for her, though I longed to talk to her about it. I said nothing, though, because it seemed that would have been a betrayal of my family. I resigned from the Depression Club—it all seemed so silly now.

And so we went on, somehow, each of us in her own private prison where the air was rank and foul and no light shone through the bars. Gradually, the days got shorter, the nights lengthened, and the tenement grew colder. Color seeped out of the world as the leaves turned brown and left the trees, making mounds of leaf-meal in the gutters of tree-lined streets. By late November, the rains were raw and seeped into my bones. And, though I increased the wattage in the light bulbs of our room, nothing seemed to chase out the gloom and shadows. Even the music was muted. No one sang anymore. Molly rarely played her records.

Into this silence, a call came from Father Jeremy Farringdon, the young, newly-assigned priest at St. James. He asked to speak with me.

"Hullo?"

"Hi, Finn. I'm Father Jeremy. Your friend Father McCuen suggested I give you a call. He told me you're a good singer and guitarist, and I'm looking for people to help me start a folk Mass for the 10 o'clock slot. Do you think you might be interested?"

"I—no, I don't think so—"

He caught me off-guard, and I had no excuse ready.

"May I ask why not?"

"Well, I'm—it's just that I haven't played in a while, and I don't even own a guitar—"

"That's okay—you can borrow one of mine. Want to give it a try? Why don't we meet and talk about it? I can pick you up at, say, 6:30, and we'll go out for pizza. What do you say?"

He was a hard sell. "I—well, yeah, I guess so."

"Okay, I'll see you soon."

"For pizza?" Ma said.

"That's what he said," I replied, squiggling into my jacket. "I'm not planning on saying yes. I'm really not up for it. Anyway, I'm not sure what time I'll be home, okay?"

"I suppose so."

It was the first time I'd gone anywhere since what I privately referred to as the Inquisition. I was surprised that the idea of a night out actually appealed to me. It would be good to get away from the tension for a while, and the giant, unspoken accusation that floated through the house.

Father Jeremy was at the house a few minutes before 6:30. He introduced himself all around. Though he wore a black shirt, his plastic collar was sticking out of his pocket instead of in place around his neck. His eyes were twinkly—literally—and a soft blue. His long hair was a nondescript brown, but his mustache had grown in reddish in spots and gray and brown in others. I put him at 25 or 26.

"All set?"

"Ready," I said.

I had never ridden in a real sports car before, and I had to admit I felt pretty cool riding in Father Jeremy's "baby," a gold GTO. We drove past the beach, and then came around to a pizza place on Brock Avenue called Me & Ed's.

"So," Father Jeremy said, sipping the beer he'd ordered while we waited for our food. "Father McCuen has told me some interesting things about you. Let's see. He said you are 15, that you love to read and paint, that you're a sophomore at Holy Family, and that you sing. You have a brother in the Navy, an older sister who teaches at the high school, another brother who's a senior at Holy Family, and a younger brother who's at St. Mary's. Have I got it right so far?"

I nodded, still too shy to speak.

"I'm willing to bet—but I'm guessing now—that your favorite bands are Simon & Garfunkel and the Beatles. Right?"

I finally smiled. "Right so far."

"Who else do you listen to?"

"Joni Mitchell, Joan Baez, Judy Collins, Leonard Cohen, and Peter, Paul & Mary. And the Rolling Stones."

"That's a great list. Pretty much matches mine. I was wondering if you'd be able to help me. I'd like to start a folk group at church for Mass—I play guitar, too. Would you be interested? I know you said no over the phone, but have you given it any more thought?"

"I don't know. Maybe."

"That's better than no. Why do you hesitate?"

"Well, most of the church songs I've heard in English are—"

"Crappy. I know. But there's finally some really good music coming down. I'd like you to hear it. I think you'd really like it. Really. I wouldn't tell you it was good if it wasn't."

"There's only one problem. I don't own a guitar. I sneak into my brother Drew's room and borrow his to practice on when he's out, but he'd never let me use it. It's his baby."

"Not a problem. I have two Martins. You can use one of them."

*Two Martins? Sold!*

"Look, when we're done here, why don't you come with me to the rectory, and I'll play a few of the new songs for you. Then you can decide."

"Okay."

At the rectory, Father Jeremy led me up the stairs to a room cluttered with guitars, music sheets, stereo equipment, and amps. Records and tapes were everywhere.

"Welcome to my den of iniquity," he said.

I was astonished. I'd no idea that priests could live in anything but Spartan accommodations. This room was a music lover's dream.

Father Jeremy picked up one of the Martins.

"Let's just jam it up for a bit," he said and launched immediately into Simon & Garfunkel's "The Sounds of Silence." After a few seconds, I couldn't help myself; I began to harmonize with him, and our voices sounded great together. He handed me the other Martin, and we sang Judy Collins, Joan Baez, and song after song by Peter, Paul & Mary. I had forgotten how nice it was to have music in my life. And the sound coming from those Martins was incredible. Two hours had gone by, and we still hadn't touched on any of the songs for the folk Mass.

"That will have to wait till next time, I think," he said, glancing at the clock. "Your folks will be worried if I don't get you home soon. Hang on to the Martin—you can practice on it." He put it in a velvet-lined hard shell case.

"How come you have all this equipment?" I asked him. He laughed.

"I've always played in a group. During the seminary, I used to sneak out late at night and play gigs in Boston."

I didn't know what to say. A Martin—I had a real Martin in my possession! Drew was going to be so jealous.

"Want to meet again next Saturday night?"

"Sure."

It was almost 10:30 when I got home.

"My God, look at the time!" Ma said when I walked in. I gave her an abbreviated version of the evening.

"He's got a great voice—wait till you hear it. So, I guess we're going to start a folk Mass."

"Oh, brother," Dad said.

"Sounds like fun," Molly said.

Ma wasn't convinced.

"It won't be like the choir."

I rolled my eyes.

"Well, he sounds like a good man," Molly said.

"Yes, he is. I'm going to bed."

"Okay."

I lay in my bed and pondered the evening. Father Jeremy was a good man. I wondered if I could ever have him hear my confession. For the first time in weeks, I fell asleep naturally, without crying myself into exhaustion.

The next week, I brought Angie along to be another voice and another instrument in our fledgling group. Her boyfriend had a job now and was working that night. We practiced in the empty church, and the acoustics were incredible. Downstairs, in the parish hall, some meeting was taking place. Soon, Father Jeremy would be holding programs and mini-retreats for young people, and that staid parish, which till now had hosted only Bingo nights, started to revive. Vatican II had brought in a sweeping gust of fresh air, and the young priests were eager to get on with it.

As winter approached, we were becoming a tight group, and we always went out for pizza after practice. I began to feel safe. We sang our songs, lamenting Vietnam in verse, but the world outside didn't really matter, not to me. I was beginning to feel a sense of belonging, of being home.

In December, we played our first Mass, and it was a resounding success. Attendance picked up measurably, especially among young people. Even the old folks—even Dad—liked us. The new songs were rich in meaning, appealing to young angst. Father Jeremy and I began performing weddings, a welcome source of income for me (Father Jeremy never accepted anything). Ma and Dad seemed pleased.

Every now and then Father Jeremy and I would drive to Boston to see a movie. He had graduated to a gold Corvette by then. The ride was thrilling. I discovered that movies were another of his passions. On the long drive home, we would discuss things that mattered to me—Dad's drinking, our relative poverty, the ubiquitous textile factories, and the factory milieu. One day I would tell him about Uncle Cal, but that day was years down the line.

The tension in the house was very gradually dissipating. At least Ma wasn't crying every morning.

Uncle Cal rarely came near any of us, and for our part, we avoided him as much as possible. None of us wanted to be caught alone with him, especially poor Skippy, who felt guilty, of all things, for blowing the whistle. Even taking the laundry down to the cellar was forbidden. We now had a washer and dryer—but Dad had to sit on the washer during its spin cycle or it would roll off its platform.

Dad was extra sensitive toward me. If he saw evidence that I was having my period, for example, he'd just say quietly, "You sit down and rest. I'll fold your clothes."

That Christmas, I was finally old enough to be able to join the choir and attend midnight Mass. For half an hour prior to the ceremony, we sang Christmas carols. The church was beautifully decorated, and the brightness of the candles and lights made a magical space in stark contrast to the dark and frigid air outside. Such color! The light danced off the poinsettias, the stained-glass windows, the priests' red-and-gold vestments, the crèche. I was surrounded with music and light, and the words to "O Holy Night" resonated so deeply it gave me gooseflesh: *"A thrill of hope/the weary world rejoices/for yonder breaks a new and glorious morn…"* I actually felt the thrill of hope deep, deep inside. I was heady with candle-scent and incense. Darkness was kept at bay; it was all about the light and a glorious lightness of being. The totality of the experience took me out of the mundane, dark world outside, and I left the church elated and grateful.

When we got home, we stood shivering in front of the Humphrey heater, which Dad turned up high, and once we were warmed up, we drank spiked eggnog and sat down to open our gifts. I went to bed that night feeling good. Christmas dinner was its usual chaos, but the feelings were warm. We all agreed it wasn't the same without Tom, the first time the family was not all together. And Granny had dinner with us, but for the first time in my memory, we did not go upstairs afterwards for the party, as Granny was feeling too tired. She'd had made her pies and cookies, but it had worn her out. I was secretly relieved—I didn't know how I was going to handle the party with Uncle Cal there.

Before going to bed that night, I went over and kissed my mother good-night, saying, "I love you, Ma."

She looked at me, tears forming in her eyes.

"I love you too," she said.

Then I went to my father.

"Thanks for the presents, Dad. I love you."

He was very embarrassed, but managed to say, "I love you, too, darl'n."

And, for the first time in weeks, no voice inside me rejoined, *Why didn't you tell?*

# 9. Upheavals

### Late 1960s

January 1967 was a month in monochrome. Mornings broke dark, and afternoons stretched gray and white with long purple shadows on the snowfall. The sky was either overcast or held a dim, anemic sun that gave no warmth. Daytime temperatures hovered in the single digits.

Dad and I were in the street shoveling out a parking space one Saturday morning when Ma came to the window and called us in. Her voice quavered. When we went upstairs, Ma was standing there with her hand at her throat. She wasn't breathing right. She told me to stay put and brought Dad up to Granny's. I looked at Drew and Skippy.

"What's going on?"

"I think it's Granny," Drew said, almost in a whisper. I could hear sirens in the distance. Then Molly came downstairs. She was crying.

"Granny is... Granny has... passed away. She never got up this morning..."

The sirens came closer.

"We called the paramedics—just to... make sure."

The sirens stopped.

"I'll take them upstairs," she said and went down to meet them.

I sank into Dad's chair, stunned. She'd seemed fine last night. We had played whist—which she and her partner, Ma, won. Not believing, I couldn't cry. Skippy came over to me, and I moved over to make room for him on the chair. Drew retreated into his room. I listened as the paramedics made their way upstairs. Maybe Molly was wrong. Maybe Granny was just unconscious. But the paramedics didn't stay long.

Molly came back.

"Can I go upstairs?" I asked. She thought for a moment, then nodded.

"Drew?" she asked as he came out of his room, his eyes red-rimmed.

"No—I don't want to go."

"Okay, stay here with Skippy, then." I followed Molly upstairs. She took my hand and led me to Granny's room. Ma sat on the bed, patting Granny's still face. Aunt Joan was on the other side, holding Granny's hand. Dad stood by the window, looking out on the backyard. Snow covered Granny's garden.

I went to Ma and hugged her. Then the tears came. I cried as though my heart would break. Granny lay peacefully in her flannel nightgown, her lace ruffle framing her face. Her eyes were partially open, and her pupils were enormous. I touched her arm and felt the chill of cold skin.

The wake and the funeral were remarkably well attended—so unusual for a woman of advanced age to have so many survivors and friends! At the church, the ladies from the guild formed an honor guard on either side of the center aisle, their hands on their hearts. Molly's eulogy moved everyone to tears, and I sang a song in Irish called "*Smointe,*" the Gaelic word for "thoughts." We led her out of the church with a bagpiper. She was our matriarch, our last connection to Irish soil.

We buried her as a snow squall flew around us. Ma wept bitterly, saying how Granny hated to be cold. Before the limo pulled away, I saw Connie through the snow, standing at the edge of the scattering crowd. I was deeply touched.

Many years earlier, on white-hot afternoons, a child-sized enamel tub was my pool, filled with cool water and set in the shade of the tenement in the spare quarter-acre of our backyard. I'd sit facing the bush with purpling, plump red raspberries growing in the bright sun and Granny's garden, where the baking stalks of green beans leaned, and the dusty warm leaves of tomato plants, pale lettuce, and cucumbers grew, half the perimeter splashed with the colors of blooming marigolds, dahlias, and impatiens. When Granny would water the plants, the sun would make rainbows between the garden and the tub, her feet padding in the dirt where we kids had made roads with a push-broom for our matchbox cars.

When I think of her, I can almost see her stooped, plucking weeds. Granny lived just shy of 90 years. She is in her garden. There is dust again between us.

Granny, your things are still here, set up in the pantry, waiting for your breakfast. The tenement echoes your presence. There is no more Lawrence Welk. I can still see you, getting up in the middle of the night, your body ricocheting off the doorway jamb, the TV, the kitchen table, the refrigerator, before you finally made it to the bathroom. I see you offering me tea in your saucer. I hear "Little Harry Hughes." Granny, yesterday the Portuguese couple across the street brought over homemade custards and sweet bread. All around us, neighbors have come out to express their sympathy. I want to feel your gnarled fingers around my hand, squeezing three times. How can it be that your all-embracing love for life, for us, your unconditional acceptance of who we are have vanished? How much I depended on that, even you could never know. The canyons of my heart echo the loss. *Granny, where are you now?*

---

The year 1967 ushered in harsh economic times for our family. The cold snap dominated the news for several days, trumping murmurs about the Berkshire Hathaway being in trouble. We had heard about problems with foreign imports and about the advent of synthetics. Still, we thought we had a good union—the Textile Workers Union of America, AFL-CIO—and the name Warren Buffett kept popping up. And then it happened: Berkshire Hathaway, once a thriving enterprise with 1,500 workers spinning yarn and weaving cloth 24 hours a day, had a massive layoff and a temporary shutdown. Hundreds of workers, including Dad, were thrown out. Dad had been working there since he was 14 years old. His coworkers were family. Now a 55-year-old loomfixer, where would he find work? Where would they all go? These people had skill sets geared for spinning cotton into fine yarns and weaving cloth. Worse, none of the workers was given a penny in severance pay. Many families lost more than one income. Where was the vaunted union now? Many workers were within months of retirement, and now they had nothing. It felt like betrayal. What would happen to the workers? Cast aside like so much flotsam.

Businessman Warren Buffett's economic model may have made hard economic sense. Wall Street praised him—but he was a villain to us. He bought the mill not to keep it going but to eventually liquidate it and get as much cash out of it as possible. The Berkshire Hathaway lasted longer than most, cutting corners and making do with old looms and outdated equipment, meticulously repaired, in no small part because of the dedication of workers like my father. But it couldn't compete forever without investment in modernization. When the mill finally shut down altogether, it was one in a chain of premier New Bedford factories that closed after decades of supporting the city and its residents. In a span of several decades, tens of thousands of city workers were left without jobs, causing a terrible tear in the fabric of the community. There were not enough businesses to offer jobs, so many people could not find work. The city spiraled into a depression from which it is still trying to recover.

I was devastated by what happened to my father, and furious, and it pained me to see him treated so shabbily. My father, for his part, said very little about it, and it was very strange to have him home on workdays. We were all worried about where and when he would find new work with such limited skills.

Dad was out of work and out of sorts. Part of him was delighted to have some free time. But he had to be scared. And he had to be kept from spending his time at the Z Club. So, Ma created a list of things to do around the house. There was a spring cleaning unlike any other. The enormous glass closet was opened, and every dish and knickknack was removed, washed, and dried. New cloths were put down on the shelves before everything was put back, looking shiny and new. All the woodwork in the house was scrubbed clean. The linoleum was replaced with tiles. We were all kept busy, our worries set aside under a fresh coat of paint. Inside the closet of my old bedroom, Dad painted his whimsical sketch of Kilroy. His cartoon droopy nose always made me giggle.

Still, we were worried sick. Only Molly was working full time. She had graduated from St. Ann's *summa cum laude* after a stellar academic career: She had been chosen for Phi Kappa Phi and had been the editor of the student newspaper. She had been elected president of her class and St. Ann's Outstanding Woman of the Year. She had done everything that was expected of her and so much more. We celebrated with a huge party for her when she came home. All the clan was invited to honor her achievement of becoming the first of her generation to finish college. Now she was teaching English and Spanish at New Bedford High School while she waited for a position to open up in editing for a publishing house.

I was a junior at Holy Family High School, Skippy was still in grammar school, and Drew was in college. Molly's salary wasn't enough to keep us afloat for long. As weeks went by, Ma and Molly resorted to praying novenas to St. Jude, trekking to church every Tuesday night for nine weeks petitioning for relief for our family. Dad stopped going to the Z Club. I would often try to talk to him about his layoff, sometimes at night, when he'd be sitting there listening to big band music on the radio or Bing Crosby on the hi-fi. But he refused to be drawn into the conversation. Sometimes, when he wouldn't answer, I would take my case to Ma.

"Ma, why can't we fight the nonseverance deal? Some of those workers were only months from retirement. What happened to his union?"

"We can't fight it, Finn. There's no recourse. The union leaders—I don't know what's happened to them. They've done nothing to help out."

"What, did they just roll over and die? Then someone needs to rile up the membership and—"

"And what? Those people still working—they're terrified that they'll be next to be laid off. They wouldn't dare to protest."

"Bastards," Dad interjected.

"No, Jack. They're just afraid. It's the leadership that's rotten."

"Got that right. They're in somebody's pocket," Dad said bitterly. And he would say no more.

When it came to being laid off, Dad was one of the lucky ones. He wasn't out of work for long, not like some of the other folks. It was only about two-and-a-half months before my godfather, who knew someone who knew someone else, offered Dad a job at another mill. This company was a middleman: It took in shipments of things like hats, scarves, gloves, mittens, seasonal clothes, and other novelties from around the country, boxed them, and shipped them off to area retail stores. Dad's job was to pack boxes all day. It wasn't much to live on, but with Molly's help and Ma's magical economics—she knew how to stretch a dollar beyond its snapping point—we survived.

March seemed to go on bleakly till forever when I noticed a patch of bare ground in the backyard near the swing. Finally, a harbinger of spring, but then a blizzard struck on April Fool's Day—some cosmic joke—and we were plunged back into more than two feet of snow again. In the cold months, Dad would walk to work without gloves or a hat. At the end of his shift, the boss would say, "Red—it's too cold out. Take a hat and some gloves." So, Dad would come home, hatted and gloved and looking about 20 pounds heavier. He'd unzip his jacket and remove a stream of scarves, hats, and mittens, like the Banana Man on TV. They just kept coming.

"OOOH, Jack!" Ma would say, horrified. But then, one look at Dad's impish grin, and she would end up laughing. I loved when he could make her laugh. As long as Dad had that job, he kept us well supplied in woolens.

Hundreds of men and women were not so lucky. Those who did not know someone who knew someone were left to fend for themselves, losing not just an income but also their pride and dignity when they were forced, finally, to apply for welfare.

The city took on a look of abandonment.

As New Bedford was failing, outlying towns were building enormous malls and other commerce. With surprising speed, almost all the stores that had filled downtown and made it such a vibrant hub were closed, shuttered, as the malls sucked away their business. Lofty plans for new industry, harbor development, and neighborhood revitalization were part of a massive "urban renewal" scheme that would span more than a decade and change the face of New Bedford forever. Most of the movie theaters were razed or boarded up, and people now drove out to the multiplex.

Downtown died a death so sudden it made my head spin. Only a few anchors and a small Historic District remained. Years later, the Seamen's Bethel and the Whaling Museum were the cornerstones for the city's revitalization and the establishment of the Whaling National Historical Park. But in the late '60s and throughout the '70s the demolition crews continued to advance into the South End until the business district and most residences along South Water Street were wiped out. Only the shuttered Orpheum Theater escaped.

How I had loved movies at the Orpheum, with its ornate cherubs on the ceiling and the onstage organist. Built by a French group called the Sharpshooters, it opened the same day the *Titanic* sank. It was a fancy place with a ballroom, but even when we went there as kids the Orpheum's elegance was in decay. It had a musty smell and, in winter, a cold draft that froze your legs and feet the entire time.

South Water Street vanished, and the aroma of Eight O'Clock Coffee was replaced by the smell of decay as buildings were razed to prepare for the new four-lane highway leading nowhere. And, despite the modern highway, some neighborhoods had the feel of an area cut off from the main part of the city, an area of neglect, a magnet for desperation, drug dealers, users, and other unsavory characters. The once-lovely Hazelwood Park went to seed. The folks who owned the nicer properties along the shore hung on, increasingly surrounded by an atmosphere of despair.

The exodus of manufacturing, along with urban renewal and the building boom in outlying towns, had the impact of a large bomb. In many places, all that remained were the craters, the rubble, and the rat-infested hurricane dike.

One night, late, when Connie and I were leaving the new library, I suddenly had an urge to strike back at the Berkshire Hathaway.

"See that goddamn mill?" I said when we got outside. "I've got a brilliant idea."

"Yeah—?"

"Well, I'm going over there, and I'm going to throw a brick through a window."

"You're not."

"I am. You stay here and hold my books. I don't want you to get in trouble."

"Are you crazy, white girl? The police station is right there," she said, pointing to where it stood a few blocks away. I shoved my books into her arms.

"I'll take my chances," I said and headed across the street. Connie reluctantly followed.

"Go back, Con."

"No. Someone has to look out for you. I'm coming."

We ducked down Harbor Street, which ran between the mill buildings. No one was around. I looked up to the white-washed windows on the second floor. This wasn't going to be as easy as I thought.

"Dammit, I'll never be able to throw that high."

"Good thing," said Connie, relief filling her voice.

Still, I scrabbled around for rocks. Finding a half-broken brick, I heaved it at the window as hard as I could. It hit the wall a foot shy of its intended destination.

"Here, let me try," Connie said, maybe realizing how much I needed this, how tired I was of being cowed, of feeling helpless. She put the books on the ground, found a rock, and let it fly. This one hit just below the windowsill.

"Hey, not bad—for a girl," I said.

Picking up another stone, I put all my strength into the throw. Still no luck hitting the window.

"Fuck it," I said and began hurling rocks one after the other.

"Bastards!" I yelled.

"Cheats!" Connie echoed.

We carried on in this fashion, cursing and throwing, for several minutes.

"Shit! Cheese it, the cops!" Connie yelled.

I saw the flashing lights, but there was no siren.

"Grab the books. Let's go!"

We ran around to the back of the mill complex. The paved alley ended in rubble. I peered around the corner.

"He stopped... maybe he's backing out... no, he's getting out of his car with a flashlight. Run!"

We ran and turned right into a second alleyway. About half-way down, there were several big vats against the wall.

"Here, behind here," I said to Connie, knowing we couldn't run fast enough to make it to the street. We ducked behind the vats and held our breath. We saw the beam of the flashlight pointing down the alley, coming closer. Closer.

Caught.

"Get out here," the cop said. He looked to be in his 40s and had a paunch. He was puffing.

"What the hell—what are you girls doing here?"

"We're on our way home from the library," Connie said.

The cop looked her up and down.

"That supposed to be funny? I ought to take you both in for malicious destruction of private property."

"We were only throwing rocks," I said. "We didn't damage anything."

"Well, you sure tried hard enough," he said. "May I ask why you were doing this?"

Connie looked at me.

"It's my fault. I was mad."

"At who?"

"The Berkshire. For laying off my father. He's 55, worked here all his life. And no severance pay, either."

My anger flared, then dissipated. I felt like crying.

The cop said nothing for a full minute.

"What were you trying to do, tear the wall down?"

"No, sir. I wanted to break a window. But I couldn't throw that far."

Connie looked at me, her eyebrows somewhere up around her hairline. But I saw a smile beginning on the cop's face. Then it was gone.

"Where do you two live?"

"Winsor Street, number 85," I said.

"Crapo Street, near the corner of Mosher," Connie said.

He led us to the squad car. "Get in," he said, opening the back door. He turned the lights off, and we drove away.

"I'm sorry, Connie," I whispered.

"Do you think he's taking us in?"

"I don't know, but I don't think so."

Sure enough, he passed the police station and headed down County Street, turning left onto Winsor. He stopped in front of my house.

"Go on. And don't let me catch you around there again."

"Yessir," I said.

"I'll get out here too, if that's okay," Connie said.

I was about to close the door when the cop added, "Sorry about your father."

"Thank you," I said. He drove off.

"Remind me never to go along with another of your cockamamie schemes again," Connie said. "Imagine what my father would have said if he saw a cop dropping me off..."

We contemplated that for a second. I looked at Connie. Then we burst into laughter until our knees were weak and our bellies hurt and tears dripped down our faces.

---

Besides the deconstruction of the city, 1967 was memorable for the revolution in rock and folk music. I could shut out the unforgiving world around me by spinning 45s and albums (mostly borrowed from friends) on the hi-fi. I learned to play the songs that so moved me and defined my generation.

With the advent of spring in 1968, the presidential campaign gained momentum. I was heart and soul into Bobby Kennedy's race for office. He was young, he was handsome, and his eyes seemed to express an enormous compassion. Then, in April, Martin Luther King Jr. was gunned down by a white assassin. Fear was everywhere. Ma was certain that the West End of

New Bedford would erupt. I could tell she wanted to say something about me spending time with Connie, although she didn't.

The world felt charged. Bobby Kennedy, in what would be one of his finest moments, got up on a makeshift platform in Memphis and called for calm. He reminded the audience that he, too, had lost a brother to a white assassin. People wept openly and held on to each other. Bobby emerged as a courageous, thoughtful, and kind leader, and it was clear to me he should be everyone's choice for president. I wanted to watch King's funeral with Connie, but her father was home, and she didn't want to come to my house.

A week after the funeral, we had a letter from Tom:

*Dear Ma, Dad, and Everybody,*

*You won't believe who's been transferred to the* America*—Fremont Foster! He just got here yesterday, so his own family probably doesn't know it yet. Isn't that great! Now there's someone on board from home, someone I can really talk to when I'm homesick. It makes a big difference. Fremont's a nice kid. He's very worried about Connie being left alone with just Nicky and her father. He's worried about Freddie, too. Has anyone at Connie's heard from him? Anyway, me and some of the guys are going to have a little welcoming get-together for Fremont tonight. I can hardly believe it.*

*We've been tailed by a Russian ship for the past three days. Since I'm a signalman, I signaled him over me eating ice cream. He signaled me back that he was drinking a beer! I think people are alike everywhere. Anyway, after a few days of cat-and-mouse, we went our separate ways without incident.*

*We're off the coast of Greece, and it's beautiful here. I haven't had a shore leave yet, but I'm hoping to get over there soon. I'll bring Fremont with me.*

*I miss you all very much. Please give my love to Bridie when you see her, Molly. Drew, stop being a pest to Finn. Skippy, listen to Ma. Fremont says to tell Connie thank you for her letters—they mean a lot to him, and he'll try to write back soon. And thank you all from me for all your letters—Finn, Molly, Ma, keep writing.*

*Love to all,*
*Your Son, Tom.*

I called Connie right away to share the news. She was so excited she screamed into the phone. She ran all the way down to my house, and when we met we jumped up and down in place. We decided to go to the library to write letters to our brothers while Skippy and Nicky read books.

Connie was thrilled to hear of the transfer. She thought it was great that our brothers could look out for each other. Molly, after hearing Fremont was on board the *America,* decided to write to him as well. Finally, a couple of weeks later, Connie had a letter from Freddie. He said the firefights were the worst, and he wondered what was going on back in The World. A lot of what he'd written had been blacked out by the censors. Though he didn't write much, he loved getting Connie's letters, and could she please send him socks? He was getting trench foot.

---

On June 5, 1968, I was happily looking forward to my 17th birthday and volunteering at the local campaign office to elect Robert Kennedy president. Suddenly, my world was turned upside down. Now, for the second time in my brief life, I watched a live TV event where a man was murdered. I stayed up late to watch the election returns from California. Bobby had won and had given a moving speech at the hotel. Then he headed out, going through the hotel's kitchen instead of the lobby to avoid the crushing crowds. Suddenly, shots rang out. There was mass confusion; people were hysterical. Bobby had been gunned down. Shocked, I couldn't believe this was happening again—only two months after MLK's assassination and five years after JFK's assassination. I ran to wake Molly and my parents. The next morning, video and photos showed him lying on the floor, his arms outstretched, blood pooling around his head.

The whole nation was stunned. A few days later, Connie came over, and we all watched the footage of the funeral train as it made its slow progress from New York to Washington, DC. When the train pulled in to Philadelphia, a group of mostly black Americans along the tracks sang "The Battle Hymn of the Republic." Just as we had watched King's funeral only a couple of months before, and John Kennedy's funeral five years earlier, we watched Bobby's funeral now. And when the voice of the last Kennedy brother, Ted, cracked during his eulogy, we all wept.

Assassins were destroying our country, and it was a country in chaos. We watched the footage from Vietnam every night on the news, Connie hoping to catch a glimpse of Freddie. Here at home, boys grew their hair so long that someone even wrote a hit off-Broadway musical about it. Everyone was either talking about or taking drugs. Monks immolated themselves to protest the war. Every week brought a new protest from somewhere. Two priests were jailed for setting fire to draft records. Unrest was everywhere, and I was scared.

The world was falling apart, and the only people who might have been able to fix it had been murdered. Peace in our family was also threatened. Dad came home from the Z Club ranting about "young punks who think they know everything." More and more, he fought with Drew, who was vehemently against the war. Dad had done his stint in the Navy in World War II, and stood behind the war, calling anyone who didn't want to go to 'Nam a coward. For her part, Ma was against any sort of military fighting. She just wanted her sons to be safe. It was all a bloody mess, and it frightened me badly.

In my English class, we studied a poem by W. B. Yeats called "The Second Coming," and its lines rang too true: The "best" were either too afraid or too discouraged to seek public office, while the worst—to me, Nixon—were filled with a "passionate intensity." Decades later, evidence surfaced that suggested Nixon's campaign worked to scuttle the Paris peace talks, promising South Vietnam a better deal if they waited until Nixon was elected. Nixon didn't want the Democrats to get credit for ending the war. The war continued for another five years, at the cost of 28,000 more American lives.

But the lines of the Yeats poem that really got me were:

*"Things fall apart.*
*The center cannot hold...*
*And what rough beast, its hour come round at last,*
*Slouches toward Bethlehem to be born?"*

Another major upheaval in our lives was Vatican II. When the sweeping changes filtered down to our church, it felt very personal. The Latin Mass was gone. I'd known the translation, yet it was very odd to hear, "Eat my Body, Drink my Blood." The beautiful hymns in Latin had been replaced by songs in English that had all the depth of greeting card verses. When Father McCuen transferred to a parish on the Cape, Molly became inconsolable. It was obvious that he didn't want to leave his parish of 22 years. To me, the changes made it feel like the magic and majesty were gone. There was no more mystery, and the cadence of the Mass in English hurt my ears and bothered my heart. In English, the Consecration—so powerful, so mystical—sounded like so much cannibalism. The only upside was the folk Mass, which continued to be very popular. I did enjoy that.

Many of the other changes were disconcerting and confusing. I was now being taught that God is love, instead of God is the one who will punish you for your wrongdoings, especially against that sixth commandment. Things were not black and white anymore; there was now an element of choice. You listened to your informed conscience, not what Sister Mary Something said was sinful.

As Molly complained, "For years they kept us in fear, following set rules like moral children. Now they want us to make our own choices like moral adults. I wasn't trained for this freedom!"

The whole concept of sin, the nature of sin, had been radically changed. As the shifts continued, I began to wonder if there might be some forgiveness here for myself. But I didn't really hold out much hope.

---

Late one June afternoon, I was sitting in the swing outside with my transistor on, enjoying a perfect summer day without responsibilities. High school graduation was over, and I would begin my first full-time job at the Kilburn mill in a couple of weeks. In the fall, I'd be starting college at Southeastern Massachusetts University (SMU) in Dartmouth, but I didn't want to think about that now.

Ma's sheets flapped in the breeze like bright white semaphores against a clear, deeply blue sky. Then Molly came to the pantry window.

"Hey, Finn. How about going up to the corner for me? I need cigs."

"Go away," I said cheerily.

"C'mon, please? I'll give you a nickel."

"A nickel? A whole nickel? What am I—five? Forget it."

"Okay, a quarter. But that's my limit."

"Plus a game of Scrabble."

Molly sighed dramatically. "You drive a hard bargain."

"Well?"

"Okay! Here, I'm throwing down a dollar."

She clipped a clothespin to a dollar bill so it wouldn't fly away and tossed it out the window to the ground.

I took my sweet time walking down the street. All the ragamuffins were out playing. I narrowly avoided getting smacked by a baseball. I wished I'd taken Tom's bike, but Callan was home, and I hadn't wanted to ask Dad to go in the cellar. While Callan's visits had stopped, now everyone in the family knew my deep shame. I didn't want to keep reminding them of it.

So I walked to the store and bought the cigs for Molly and a Milky Way bar for myself, which I was opening as I left. Taking a bite, I glanced over at Connie's house. Her father's truck was there. So was a shiny black car, and two military men climbed out. My stomach knotted. I stood and waited. Then, from the depths of the house, came a wild, high-pitched wail. I dropped the candy bar and ran as fast as I could.

"Ma, Molly—I think Freddie Foster has been killed!"

"What? How do you know?"

I told them what I'd seen—and heard.

"Oh, my God," Molly said. "They must be devastated. Poor Fremont."

"Poor Connie."

"I'll bet they send Fremont home, to attend services."

I felt frustrated. I wanted to go to Connie, but with her father home, I didn't dare. Our separation seemed so stupid. I wondered how long it would take to get her brother's body home.

In a couple of days came a letter from Tom. Ma opened it and read it aloud. Molly, Drew, Skippy, and I sat around the kitchen table to hear.

*Dear Ma, Dad, and Everybody,*

*I don't know if you've heard the sad news or not, so this may come as a shock to you. Something terrible has happened. There's no easy way to say this, so I'll just say it. Fremont Foster was killed Friday night in a freak accident on the ship. The pilots were practicing night landings, and one of them overshot the cable. He missed the hook. The plane skidded down the deck, and Fremont, who had been signaling, got caught by the wing. They told me he died instantly. Since he had opted to be buried at sea if anything happened, we held a funeral service for him this morning. The band played the Navy hymn as his body slid from the flag-draped stretcher. Because I was his closest friend on board, I had to say a few words. It was tough—I had a hard time getting through it. The Navy is going to send me back home with his things and the flag that had covered his body. I'm sorry to have to tell you this. I can't imagine the shock to his family—everyone was so worried about Freddie, thinking Fremont was safe and out of danger. Now this.*

*I'm not sure when I'll be back. I'll call you as soon as I'm stateside. Please tell Molly that Fremont kept all her letters. I found them in his locker, tied up with string. I think he was falling in love with her; I know he sure loved getting her letters.*

*I'll see you all soon. I love you very much.*

*Tom*

We all sat around the table, stunned. Molly was crying quietly.

"Finn, those military men you saw, what color were their uniforms?" Drew asked.

"They weren't khaki—they were dark. Black, maybe."

"Probably Navy. Those were Navy personnel, not Army."

"Oh, poor Connie. She was so close to Fremont."

"It wasn't Freddie," Molly muttered. "Oh God, it wasn't Freddie."

"Tom's coming home," Ma said.

Tom was home at 6 on Thursday evening. A service was planned for Fremont at the Bethel A.M.E. Church, near downtown, on Saturday.

Tom looked exhausted. His eyes, which had that faraway look that sailors and seamen get, were red-rimmed and bloodshot.

"It was such a freak accident," he told us. "The pilot missed the cable. Fremont was part of the deck crew, and the wing just clipped him...it was horrible. I have to go up there," he said, referring to Connie's house.

"Now?" Ma asked. "You just got home."

"I know. But I have to go."

"I'm going with you," Molly said.

"Me, too," I said. "I've got to see Connie."

We walked to the corner. I held Tom's hand. In his other hand, he carried a medium-sized box. He was wearing his dress whites.

We went up the path to Connie's. She opened the door before we had a chance to knock. No one said a word. Connie showed us into the living room, which was sparsely furnished. Mr. Foster sat in an easy chair by a dead fireplace. I let go of Tom and went to Connie, hugging her.

"Connie, I'm so sorry. I don't know what to say."

We heard voices from the kitchen. Tom went over to Mr. Foster and introduced himself.

"I was Fremont's best friend on board, Mr. Foster. I can't tell you how sorry I am. Fremont was like a brother to me."

Tom handed him the box.

"These are Fremont's things. I thought you might want them."

Mr. Foster finally stood. He looked Tom up and down. Then he reached out his hand, which Tom shook firmly.

"Sit down. You live down the street."

"I'm Molly, Mr. Foster, Tom's sister. Fremont and I—we used to write to each other. He was a terrific guy—he—he had a lot of—he loved the Navy..." Her voice trailed off as she started to choke up.

"Please sit down. Connie, get some chairs from the kitchen, and get your brother in here."

"Mr. Foster," Tom said, "Fremont and I used to talk a lot, you know, coming from the same neighborhood and all—anyway, he told me a lot about you. He said you worked your—you worked hard. He was proud of you, sir. He loved you very much."

Mr. Foster's eyes filled. Tears threatened to spill over, but he held them in check.

"He said that? My boy said that?"

"Yes, sir. He said he was proud of what you did in the union, and he told me what you did in the big strike."

"Mr. Foster, I'm Finn. I'm a friend of Connie's." I hesitated, not knowing what to expect. This was a man who cut off braids. But if Tom could be a friend of Fremont's, and Molly too, then maybe we had entered some new territory. I hoped.

Mr. Foster was a big man with a broad face and a sprinkle of freckles across his light skin. His eyes were deep-set and intelligent. He looked at me.

"I know. Connie doesn't know I know. But I've known it for a long time. She thinks I don't know you two go to the beach all the time. Walk along the dike."

My eyebrows crept up. *So, Nicky had told?*

Connie came back in, carrying a straight chair. Connie's boyfriend, Courtney, followed, then Freddie, still in his Army uniform. Each carried a chair. Freddie looked at Tom, and they nodded to each other. Nicky came over to me and stood by my side. I put my arm around his thin shoulders.

"Little rat," Connie said gently.

"It's all right, Connie. I used to see you—drive by the beach on my lunch hour, see you girls there. I know," Mr. Foster said. "So." He turned to Tom.

"Tell me how my boy died, Tom."

"Didn't the Navy—"

"I want to hear it from you."

Tom told him what he'd told the family.

"Freak accident. That's what they're calling it. What happened to the pilot?"

"He's still in critical condition, sir."

Mr. Foster nodded and closed his eyes, as if trying to imagine the scene. He sat in the stillness of his grief, his large hands gripping the arms of his chair.

"Makes no sense," Freddie said, speaking for the first time.

Freddie's eyes were awful to look at. They were sunken in, full of grief, suffering, and something else I couldn't put my finger on. His hands were never still, twitching all the time. He walked around the room, sat, stood again, wandered, sat. Courtney sat next to Connie, holding her hand.

Mr. Foster inhaled deeply, then opened his eyes.

"There's a memorial service on Saturday at the Bethel Church. Since you were close to my son, would you mind saying a few words?"

"I'd be honored to, sir."

"Mr. Foster," I said. "Would it be all right if we—my family—came to the service?"

Mr. Foster looked at me a moment. Then he said, "Yes, Finn. Fremont would have liked that."

The service was at noon. Tom carried the flag he would present to the Foster family at the end of the service. We sat in the back, Ma and Dad looking acutely uncomfortable. Dad kept tugging at his collar. Tom sat with the Fosters.

The minister swooped in, singing as he entered the church from a side door. A woman played a small organ. The congregation rose, sang loudly, and clapped along with the music. Then they sat, and the minister, standing behind a podium, commenced his sermon. He cited verse after verse dealing with loss, grief, and the promise of the Resurrection. Even from the back, I could hear Connie sobbing. After close to an hour, the minister wrapped it up, then led the congregation in singing a song. Then he introduced Tom.

Tom stood tall before the congregation. He looked around the church before finally letting his gaze fall on the Foster family.

"Fremont Foster was the best friend I ever had. A ship becomes your home, and your shipmates become your family. Fremont was my family. He was my brother. Whenever we talked, we talked of home—it was incredible luck that Fremont and I, from the same neighborhood, should be stationed together on the *America*. Whenever we were homesick or lonely, we had each other to turn to. He was always talking about his family—about how hard his father worked, how proud he was of him, and of Connie, who did so much at such a young age to help keep the family together when Mrs. Foster passed away. And he was proud of Freddie for bravely going to fight in a war none of us understands. And he was proud of little Nicky, growing up fast and strong with so much potential. Fremont loved his family with all his heart.

"Fremont had a dangerous job, working with the deck crew of an aircraft carrier. He faced danger every single day. He knew the lives of the pilots depended on him doing his job right. He was brave. He never complained. Next to his family, the love of his life was the Navy.

"One thing about Fremont—he was always singing or humming to himself. He actually had a wonderful baritone voice. One of the songs he used to sing often at night when we'd all be settling in for rack time—which someone had the foresight to record—was 'Precious Lord.' I think he'd like it if we stood and sang it with him."

Tom reached down and put on the tape recorder. Fremont's voice reverberated in the silent room. One by one, the people joined in. When the song came to its shivering conclusion, Tom went to Mr. Foster and presented him with the tightly folded flag, "On behalf of a grateful nation." A young Navy man in full dress whites, standing at the back of the church with his bugle, played "Taps." When it was done, the minister and the congregation sat in silent contemplation for a few minutes. Then the minister rose up and launched into "When the Saints Go Marching In," and the choir and congregation joined in. We all filed out, the song spilling into the street.

We had all been invited back to the Foster house, and Ma brought some sort of casserole. Connie, with help from me, Molly, and Courtney, put out a spread of sandwiches and rice and beans and breads from the corner bakery. We ate, chatted awhile with Connie and Courtney, then rose to leave. We went to pay our respects to Mr. Foster.

"I don't know what to say," Skippy said nervously to me. I understood shyness. And I knew the only way through this was to do it.

"All you have to say is, 'I'm sorry for your loss.' That's all. Can you shake his hand?" I coached him.

"That too?"

I gave him a look, and he sighed. Mr. Foster was standing with Connie's aunt, talking quietly. I hated to interrupt him, but he saw us and stopped talking.

"Go ahead," I whispered to Skippy.

Skippy gave me an I-might-throw-up look but went forward.

"Sorry for your loss," he mumbled to the floor. Then he stuck out his hand. Mr. Foster shook it and looked at Skippy gravely.

"You seem to be a good boy. Be like your brother, and you'll do fine."

Skippy didn't know what to say to that, so he just nodded and stepped back. Ma then approached.

"You have a fine boy there," Mr. Foster said of Tom. "I—I hope you'll come around some time, when you're home on leave," he said to Tom. "And Miss Finn, you don't need to hide your friendship with Connie anymore."

"Thank you, Mr. Foster," I said.

Drew and Dad shook his hand and said they were very sorry, and we left to walk back down the street on this beautiful, balmy evening.

Tom had a few more days before he had to go back, and he spent as much time as he could with Bridie. On Monday, he borrowed Molly's car and asked me if I would like to go shopping with him.

"I'm going somewhere special, and I need your help," he said without further explanation. He drove out to the mall in Dartmouth, and we went inside to the jewelers.

"I want you to help me pick out a ring," he said, grinning.

"A ring? A ring! Oh-my-God, a ring! Wow!"

"Calm down, crazy girl."

"When? When will it be?"

"Finn, she hasn't even said yes yet. But if she does say yes, it will be when I get out of the Navy."

"In a year and a half—wow."

"Well, we'll see what Bridie says, okay?"

We looked at section after velvet-lined section of diamonds before finally deciding on one in a teardrop shape. It glistened as if it had fire inside.

"Oh, she's going to love it," I gushed as we left the store.

Tom smiled. His dimples were very deep, and the red highlights of his hair shone in the sun. "Think so?"

"Yeah, I do."

Tom took Bridie out for dinner that night and then for a ride to the beach, where couples in cars went parking, or as some kids called it, watching the submarine races. When he drove home, they came into the house. Bridie was wearing the ring.

"Bridie, this is great! You're going to be my sister-in-law!" Molly said.

There was a palpable air of excitement in the Kilroy house that night. It was such a relief from the heavy sadness of the past week.

But then, Tom had to leave. First, we walked up the street to say goodbye to Mr. Foster. I went with him to see Connie.

"My father's not home," Connie said. "He's out doing his route."

Freddie was there, sitting in a tee shirt and khaki pants, drinking a beer.

"Good luck, man," Tom said, shaking his hand.

"I can't go back there," Freddie said, slightly slurring his words. "I can't go back. You have no idea, man. The firefights. Razing villages. Little kids being killed, and horse—50 cents a packet. Numbs the pain, you know?"

Connie gave me a look. Knowing I was clueless, she whispered in my ear, "Horse is slang for heroin." She was clearly scared.

"You don't want to get into that shit, Freddie," Tom said.

"No? What do you know about it?"

Tom was silent. He knew Freddie was a tortured soul. Going back would be hell, not going would be too. Then he said, "Don't go AWOL, Freddie. Do that, and you're screwed. You got guys depending on you. They need you, man."

Freddie took another swig of beer, and for a while we just sat in silence.

"Don't let your guys down," Tom said quietly.

Freddie looked at Tom with bleary, frightened eyes.

"You must be on short time now. Finish your time and come home with your head high—and I don't mean on horse."

Freddie half-smiled. "I know you're right, man. I know it. It's just so—you're so damn scared all the time. And I can't let the guys see that."

"They're just as scared as you are, maybe more. You got to be strong for them. They'll follow your lead. Just keep your head down, and do your job. Then come home to us."

Freddie nodded.

"I got to go. Connie, take care of yourself. And little Nicky. Freddie, you take it easy."

Freddie stood, and they shook hands.

"I'll call you later," I said to Connie, and I walked out with Tom into the afternoon sun.

"Tom!"

Connie came running down the path.

"Yeah?"

"Can I write to you?"

"Sure, I'd like that. Keep me posted on what's happening—especially with Freddie."

Connie gave Tom a quick hug, and we went on our way down the cracked and pitted sidewalk.

# 10. Beginnings and Endings

Freddie made it back from Vietnam with shrapnel in his legs, but no smack in his system, which was a great relief to all. But he was a profoundly changed man. He had an aura of desperation. He limped about the house like an unquiet ghost. Connie urged him to go to the VA hospital for help, and Courtney offered him rides. Freddie shrugged off all talk of help. He wanted to be left alone. I thought I recognized the signs of guilt. In his withdrawal and his refusal to seek treatment, I saw a man who felt his sins were unforgivable. With Connie's permission, I called to ask Father Jeremy's advice. He had an idea.

"I have a friend—Charles Jennings—who was a chaplain in Vietnam. Do you want me to contact him and see what he says?"

"Sure, that's a good idea."

Father Jeremy called me back within 20 minutes.

"Charles says he'll go and visit Freddie. He says no doubt Freddie can't talk to any of us because we weren't there. We don't know what it was like. But because Charles was there, maybe Freddie would open up to him. It's worth a shot, I think. Why don't you ask Connie about it, and then you can call Charles directly and set up a time?"

So, I called Connie, who said, "Let's try it." I called Father Charles to arrange a time. His voice was deep and gruff, but I could hear the kindness in it. I told him about my guilt theory, and he wanted to know how I'd come by such knowledge. Without warning or a second thought, I spilled the entire story of my history to him. It was as if I had no control; it had to break out. I think it surprised me even more than it did him.

"I see," he said. "Does Father Jeremy know this?"

"No—I've never been able to tell him. You're the first real person I've ever told outside the family. And I can't talk to them about it much."

"That's a lot of weight on your shoulders. We can talk about it when I come to see Freddie, if you'd like."

I told him okay, surprising myself again. I had long since compartmentalized all that stuff, but I could always feel it there, just under the surface. It would be interesting to hear what Father Charles would say about it all. I hung up the phone feeling oddly free.

Connie called a week later to say that Father Charles was there.

"What's he like?"

"Well, he's got this voice like a giant—but I'd be surprised if he was taller than five-five. He has a military haircut. His eyes—wait till you see them—they're blue-green, the color of the ocean at full tide. But they look kind. He's wearing a camo jacket over a tee shirt. And get this: sandals."

I laughed.

"Anyway, they're in the other room with the door shut. Sometimes I hear Freddie shouting, but I can't make out what he's saying, and beneath it all is this steady rumble of Father Charles's voice. So, anyway, he said he'd call you after they're done, and you can go with him for lunch. What's all that about? Is he going to tell you about Freddie?"

"No, I doubt that," I paused, not knowing exactly what to say. "No, I, well, I wanted to talk to him about something else. We agreed to meet, to discuss a problem from the past."

Usually I told Connie everything, but I wasn't ready for her to know this.

"Can you tell me what it is?"

"I, well, not now. But someday. I promise."

"Okay," she said slowly. "I'll hold you to that."

It was well past lunch when Father Charles called. I told my mother we were going out, and I wasn't sure what time we'd be back.

"Wow," Molly said, "another ecclesiastical boyfriend!"

"Shut up, Molly," I said sweetly, and went downstairs to meet Father Charles just as he drove up in a Volkswagen bug. He was as Connie described, only his tee shirt was wet with sweat.

"I'm not dressed for anything fancy," he said. "But there's a seafood shack in Westport, just off Route 88, that has good food. Want to go there?"

"Sure. How did it go with Freddie?"

"It went...well. That boy has a lot of shit to go through. Sometimes I wonder how any of them came back with their sanity intact. But it was good.

He got a lot off his chest. Still, there's so much more. We're going to meet again next week."

We drove in a comfortable silence for a few miles.

Then he said, "So. That was some story you told me about your childhood. How did it all end?"

I told him about the Inquisition and the aftermath.

He shook his head but said nothing for a few minutes. Then he said, "You blame yourself."

I looked away. "Yes," I answered. My voice was so low I could barely hear myself, but he heard me.

"Why?"

"Because I was complicit. I never told on him, the way my brother did. He did the right thing."

"And you didn't tell why?"

"I was afraid to. Afraid I'd get in trouble. Afraid of him."

"And?"

"And what?"

"Were you also afraid of losing his attention?"

The statement took me by surprise. I didn't know how to answer it or what to say.

"Think about it. Your mother was too busy. Your father—did you get much attention from him?"

"Not really," I said and told him about his drinking.

"So, he was out of the picture. Your sister?"

"No—she was too old and into her own thing."

"Your other siblings?"

I laughed at that and told him about the Rottenest Sneak Club.

"It's really not funny. They treated you like the rank they gave you—like dirt. So, you craved attention, especially adult attention, and your uncle singled you out. Did he hurt you?"

"Physically? No."

"In fact, I'll bet when you were real small, it even felt good?"

I turned bright red. Unbidden tears sprang to my eyes.

"It's only natural that it would. And you reacted as any normal child would to a pleasurable stimulus. Operative word: normal."

This was more than I could handle at the moment. He let me cry.

Then he said, "That's why you felt like an accomplice. That's why you took in all the blame. It was the one unforgivable sin."

"Mortal sin," I choked out.

"Finn. It wasn't your fault. Your reaction was beyond your control. The sin is solely your uncle's, for introducing sexual pleasure to a young child, when it is wholly inappropriate. He destroyed your innocence. He gave you attention, and it felt good on some level, even if overall it was negative and you were hurt by it. And of course, you couldn't tell—did you even have the vocabulary to describe it? You were too young to understand, and he'd taught you that this was just the way things were. You turned on yourself when you grew older and became aware, on some level, of how inappropriate it was... Do you hate him?"

"No."

"Do you hate your parents, for their reaction?"

"Hate? No. But I was hurt and angry."

"Do you hate your brothers?"

"No, of course not. We were kids. I don't hate anybody."

"Yes, you do."

I looked at him sharply, ready to deny.

"You hate yourself," he said gently. "And your body for betraying you. And self-hatred turns to depression and low self-image."

He turned the car into the parking lot at a small take-out place called Handy Hill. A few people there were getting ice cream. He parked a distance from the other cars.

"Still feel the need to be forgiven?"

I nodded. He reached into the backseat and pulled out a box. It contained everything he would need for hearing confession or administering the Last Rites, now called the Sacrament for the Sick. He removed his stole and put the rest back. Putting his stole around his neck, he turned to me.

"God forgives all sins. All. Not some. Do you believe that?"

I nodded again.

"Finn, I want to hear your confession."

"Now? Here?"

"Why not? Go ahead," he said and made the sign of the cross.

"Bless me, Father, for I have sinned," I began, the words rolling off my tongue as if I'd said them yesterday. Then I stopped. How could I phrase this? He waited.

"Just say it. Use your own language. Don't try to fit it into a formula."

I took a deep breath and began again.

"I have been complicit in sexual acts for years as a child and teen. And, despite my sins, I received Communion... Is that enough?"

"You left one out."

"What?"

"Self-loathing."

"I am guilty of self-loathing and believing my sins were unforgivable."

"Do you resolve never to commit them again?"

"I do, Father."

He said the prayer of forgiveness, blessed me, and told me to go in peace, for my sins were forgiven.

"And for your penance," he added, surprising me, "I want you to resolve that you will stop hating yourself. Amen."

I turned to Father Charles, and he held me while I wept. Then a peace settled over me like a warm blanket.

"It isn't going to happen overnight," he said. "It's a process, and it will take a lot of work on your part. Promise you'll try, and not fall back to the status quo."

"I will do my best."

"That's all we ask."

He removed his stole, folded it neatly, and put it back in the box while I pulled myself together.

"I'm starved," he said. "Let's go look at the menu."

We got out of the car and strolled over to the hand-painted panels hung on the restaurant's wall. I didn't feel especially hungry, but I felt an obligation to eat something. I ordered a stuffed quahog and a Coke. Father Charles ordered clam cakes, a hamburger, and a Mountain Dew. We ate at one of the picnic tables scattered around the property. I noticed for the first time what a lovely day it was—puffy clouds, light blue sky, temps in the 70s. It was, I felt, extraordinarily beautiful. We weren't far from Horseneck Beach, and I could sense the ocean air. It brought me instantly back to the cove and the dike. I looked down at the gray wood of the worn table, its grain, knotholes, texture, the finest details.

Then I looked at Father Charles munching away as if it were an ordinary day. He had a remarkable gift, to make me feel, well, just ordinary. I would never forget this. I found comfort in the memory of this afternoon for years, and would draw on it for strength.

"Where'd you go to school?" I asked him in order to change the topic.

"To Boston College for an undergraduate degree in psych, then on to a PhD at Notre Dame, also in psychology. Then seminary training. Why don't we meet whenever I'm down to work with Freddie?"

"Sounds perfect. Where is your home parish?"

"I guess you could say Boston, St. Anthony's, but my work takes me all over the place, from the VA hospitals in Brockton and Holyoke to soup kitchens and halfway houses. Just about everywhere."

We left the parking lot, and, instead of taking Route 88, we took the back roads, down long, winding country roads with farms selling fresh produce roadside, passed cows and horses, bales of hay. The smells were rich and earthy. It was worlds away from Winsor Street.

"I want to thank you for all you've done—for me, for Freddie. You're remarkable."

He actually blushed. "Don't mention it. All part of a day's work. Do you plan to tell Jeremy about your background?"

"Should I?" I began to panic about who I should tell.

"I don't think you should or shouldn't. That's entirely up to you. The thing is, I don't want you to feel like it's some deep, dark secret you have to hold in all the time. It takes a lot of energy to do that. You should feel free to tell anyone you feel is trustworthy. I realize your parents don't want it to leak out, and I can see their point. I may not agree with them. It's the big silence that protects these predators. They hide behind their reputations as do-gooders, as community leaders, as good providers, even, sadly, as priests..."

I was shocked to hear him say that, although I'd heard the rumors.

In the decades to come, the Catholic Church was rocked by sexual child abuse scandals itself, and New Bedford didn't come away unscathed. Children, victims of those they trusted, were left devastated in the wake of priest pedophiles betraying their young wards, just as Uncle Callan had betrayed me. For me though, it was a priest who nudged me along to begin the journey of healing, disjointed and never-ending though it has been.

"Does your uncle have children?" he asked.

"Twin boys, a little older than me."

"Were they victims too?"

"I have no way of knowing that."

He nodded. "It would be unusual if they aren't suffering from his abuse too. It's an awful situation. By protecting the adults—your aunt, your grandmother—the children are left vulnerable."

It wasn't a pleasant thought.

We arrived at my house, and I hopped out.

"Thanks again, Father Charles. I'll see you soon."

I waved him off, shouted up that I was home, and went to sit in the backyard swing. I knew my face looked puffy and splotchy, and I wanted time to try to look normal before going upstairs. I didn't need more questions. I needed time to think.

---

My college years went by in a blur, with academics intruded on by events taking place in the world. I enrolled at SMU. Nothing was quiet or simple, certainly not the lovely bucolic setting of Molly's college years. I stumbled around, trying to steep myself in my English major, trying not to let the outside world in too deep. But it was difficult. Nixon was lying to us through his teeth, telling us, for example, that we were not bombing Cambodia or Laos, when we knew, from the returning vets on campus, that we most certainly were.

It became impossible to ignore the world when four students were gunned down at Kent State by our National Guard. Now we realized that even our campuses were not safe. We held a mock funeral for the Kent State victims, using four life-sized black coffins.

When six of our favorite professors were summarily fired for "subversive activities," the campus exploded. A strike was called. Sit-ins and teach-ins were held, presided over by the ousted professors. Tensions were extreme. Everything was politicized. I never knew from one day to the next if my classes would be held or if I'd be left sitting in the cafeteria playing whist.

After all this activity—the protests, the strikes, the vigils—we needed a break from all the tensions. Organizers put together a three-day concert featuring bands that performed on the large lawn behind the academic buildings. Billed as "The Woods of Dartmouth," after the Woodstock celebration the year before, the event was attended by 100,000 young people. Bands included The Byrds, Manfred Mann, The Guess Who, Rhinoceros, and The J. Geils Band. A group of our friends rented an RV for the weekend and parked it on the access road to the stage. We were lucky to have decent bathroom facilities and a place to store our gear and to hang out between sets.

The field was thick with the aroma of pot, and many took advantage of the free-for-all atmosphere and made love on their blankets in the grass, or in sleeping bags or tents. Food, drink, and joints were freely shared by all. My friends and I drank sangria under the stars and enjoyed the suspension of the university's strained mood, although I never truly let go, and I felt more than ever a bystander when it came to the social ins and outs of life.

I hadn't dated in high school, but tried a few times in college. It never lasted. I always seemed to end up back inside my hunched self.

Awkward, and believing intimately in my own ugliness, I stayed away from mirrors, and had a hard time rising above my own lowly self-image. I had difficulty getting close to anyone. Eventually, I just avoided interactions with the opposite sex. More and more, I filled my life with isolating pursuits and activities that I could do to avoid being with others, burying myself in my writing or painting. I made little effort to join in or break out. I had few new friends, and those that I did have often had to carry the social weight, seeking me out as I sought to fade away. While I could care deeply about others, I didn't believe I was worthy of their love and concern.

---

Family continued to offer me a place where I belonged, even as Callan lurked on the edges. Tom was honorably discharged from the Navy. He married Bridie on a sweltering hot day in August with Father McCuen presiding and me singing. I was a bridesmaid, and Molly was the maid of honor. Drew was best man, and Skippy and Freddie Foster were ushers. One of the songs I sang that day was "One Hand, One Heart," from *West Side Story*: "One hand, one heart, even death won't part us now." Years later that song would come back to me in all its aching poignancy.

We celebrated the reception in an enormous barn, with all the doors thrown open. It was great fun. Whenever the band took a break, we all sang, and the dancing, especially by the older folk, was hilarious. Connie and Courtney were among the guests, and I spent much of the evening with them and Freddie. Connie had just graduated *summa cum laude* from SMU, and Courtney was working his way through graduate school. I was still working on my English major, and surprised myself by actually doing well.

Just before Tom and Bridie left for their honeymoon in Bermuda, I got together with the band and sang "Sunrise, Sunset" for them. Everyone crowded around and formed a circle with the bride and groom in the center. I sang my heart out, and there were few dry eyes in the house. Music was one of the things that could bring me center stage without self-doubt, allowing me to overcome the crippling self-consciousness that so often plagued me. Then, while the last note still hung in the humid air, the heavens opened up, the rain poured down, lightning crackled across the sky, and thunder shook the barn. We crowded around the doors, both to watch the storm and to breathe in the wet, fresh air with a taste of grass in it. Steam rose from the road like sighs. Mr. and Mrs. Tom Kilroy waited till the storm blew over, then left to the cheers and well wishes of the crowd that did not want to let them go.

I drove home with Molly, Skippy, Ma, and Dad in the car. When we got to County Street, however, we were pulled over by state troopers. There had been minor riots in New Bedford in recent days, and we were supposed to have abided by the ten o'clock curfew (it was now eleven). Apparently, we had just missed a shooting nearby, and the police were edgy. They were unimpressed by our wedding attire and were giving us a hard time until, fortunately, one of the wedding guests in the car behind us, who was a well-known attorney, got out and spoke quietly to the police, who then allowed us to move on.

Riots and unrest were commonplace that summer of 1970. Sometimes it seemed the country was going up in flames. Writer James Baldwin's predictions had come true: It was the fire this time.

In 1972, at the urging of my mentor in the English department, I applied for graduate school at University College in Dublin, Ireland. I thought the very idea of it was crazy—even if I could make that emotional leap to live in another country, how could I afford to live in Ireland and pay my tuition? It was a fantasy. But she made me believe just enough, and I applied. The letter of acceptance into the program made it very real. My mentor offered to pay my plane fare, and I worked long hours all summer at a supermarket to earn my tuition. Between that and a student loan, I was able to board an Aer Lingus 747 in September, tearing myself away from my family.

Molly, in a farewell poem, promised to "wait, the circle broken, until you come again." I was scared, flying to a country I knew very little about. I didn't even know the currency. I wouldn't be able to phone home, as the rates were prohibitively expensive, and given my shyness, the idea of meeting new people was terrifying.

As for Ma and Dad, they could hardly believe it was happening. Through some instinct, I knew Dad was afraid, and not just for my well-being. This was during the heat of "The Troubles," and in these months, Belfast, in Northern Ireland, was victim to some of the bloodiest bombings in the decades-long religious and political conflict that was tearing at the country. Dublin, too, had its strife. Despite that danger, though, I think he was more immediately and personally afraid that I would come back feeling superior, that I would have outgrown Winsor Street in general and himself in particular, that I would think less of him. He needn't have worried. In my heart, I could never leave them, and I felt sad for my father's insecurity.

I understood that, as desperately homesick as I felt, my parents, too, were missing me. This came as a revelation to me through their letters. Molly and Ma wrote to me often, and in her letters it came through that she was proud of me, amazed that I had the sheer guts to do what I was doing—Ma, for whom a trip to downtown New Bedford was an adventure.

In one remarkable letter, she wrote:

> *Your father talks about you every night. He misses you so much. So do I. Do you remember when you were small, I used to call you my little Dark One? It was from a poem I read in the paper. You seemed so secretive and withdrawn sometimes. I didn't know what you were holding inside. I love you very much, Finn, and so does your father.*

In an odd way, my being half-a-world away brought us closer together through the honesty and revelations of those letters. And being so far away meant I had the chance to examine the trauma of my childhood without the trappings of family, which I found liberating as well as frightening.

In Ireland, despite my shyness and the tumultuous politics of the times, I met some amazing people.

One Friday evening in mid-October, I boarded the bus and headed to O'Reilly's Pub in downtown Dublin to listen to Irish music. Assuming I'd be having a pint or two, I'd left my bike at my bedsitter in Rathmines. Folks squeezed in wherever they could find a space, and at the bar they lined up four deep. Under the spotlights, sweat reflected off the skin of the musicians.

The crowd sang along and clapped in time to the music. The band finished the set on a serious note with Tommy Makem's song "Four Green Fields." The song gave me chills, and by the last verse I was softly singing a harmony:

*What have I now, said the fine old woman*
*What have I now, this wise old woman did say.*
*I had four green fields*
*Now one of them's in bondage*
*In strangers' hands*
*Who try to keep it from me.*
*But my sons have sons*
*As brave as were their fathers!*
*And my four green fields*
*Will bloom, once again, said she.*

The crowd, more than half with tears in their eyes, exploded into cheers, some of them shouting, "Up the Rebels!" as the political song riled their sympathies.

Above the roar, the bandleader shouted, "Thanks very much. Back in 15!" exhilarating the crowd into more applause. It was thrilling. The din abated as people scrambled to the bar for refills.

Suddenly a male voice close to my ear said, "You have a lovely voice. That harmony was great."

I turned, my face warm with embarrassment. He was smiling, his eyes the color of blue autumn sky, and he put his hand on my arm.

"Do you want a fill-up?" he asked, pointing to my empty glass.

Surprised, I said yes and searched my pocket for a pound note. He waved me off.

"It's on me," he said and made his way to the bar. My arm still felt the warmth from his touch. He wore a short, neatly trimmed beard, and his smile had deep dimples. He was of medium height, with cute buns in loose jeans. Black hair over his collar. Sleeves rolled. In the time it took for him to make it back to the table, I was smitten. I'd never experienced this feeling before.

"My name's Liam. Liam Quinn," he said as he put two frothy pints down. He held out his hand and I shook it.

"Finn Kilroy, and thank you very much for the pint. I owe you one."

"Ah, an American. Where from?"

"A city about sixty miles south of Boston. And you are—let me guess—from Cork?"

He raised his eyebrows. "You're not far off! How did you know?"

"Because I hear everything's from Cork."

He laughed. It had been a gamble, based on a standard joke about the rivalry between the two major cities. I was glad it went over well. We made small talk, but then the band started up and it was impossible to be heard. I felt happy and relaxed. Must have been the Guinness.

Spirits were high. The crowd clapped and laughed and sang along, tapping feet to the rhythm of the *bodhran,* an Irish goat-skin drum. A palpable sense of tension released as the band played. The fighting up north during this time of The Troubles was fierce, and although we were an hour's drive from the Belfast border, the anxieties stretched throughout the country.

I glanced at my watch.

"Oh my God, I've got to go!" I said, standing. "The last bus! I can't miss it!"

The last bus came at 11:00 p.m., only ten minutes away.

"I'll go with you to the stop," Liam said.

"No, you'll miss the music. It's okay. Thanks for a great night."

I headed for the door. He followed, putting on his jacket on the way. I had no time to argue.

"Come on, then," he said. He grabbed my hand and we started to run. We were crossing the O'Connell Bridge when the bus ambled by us. I stopped short, out of breath. Leaning on the stone wall, I looked down at the Liffey. The water was murky.

"Dammit, dammit, dammit," I said. I didn't fancy a long walk home at night.

"Sorry," he said. "Where were you going?"

"My bedsit in Rathmines."

"Sure, that's not far. Want to hoof it?"

I hesitated. Did I have enough money for a taxi?

"Not by yourself, of course. I'll walk with you." He watched for an answer, a smile playing on his mouth.

"And where do you live?"

"I live over—oh, gobshite! I'm after leaving my push-bike at the pub! God, what am I thinking? Wait—wait here, I'll be right back. Don't talk to strangers!" he flung over his shoulder. I laughed. What a sweet man.

The streets weren't crowded, but there were people about, and I didn't feel afraid. I turned back to the River Liffey. It had a peculiar smell, and suddenly I missed my beaches back home. Engrossed in my memories of Municipal and Horseneck beaches, I barely noticed that someone had stopped beside me.

"Your chariot is here," Liam said.

I turned, startled. He sat on the bicycle, grinning, sweating, and thoroughly disheveled. I had to laugh.

"Hop on," he said.

The closer we got to Rathmines, the more rattled I became. It would be the polite thing to invite him in to rest up before his ride back to his flat on the north side of Dublin. But I was afraid of what signal that might send. What would he think? I hadn't known him long enough to gauge his reactions, although he seemed a good sort, if a little off balance on the bike. The arrival at my bedsit was a soft crash landing that left us sprawled together in a heap on the sidewalk. After quickly determining neither of us was hurt, we sat on the curb laughing at the awkward stop.

I invited him in.

I put the kettle on for tea, laid peat bricks in the fireplace, and lit them.

We sat together on the couch and talked. For hours. This felt special to me. I learned he was a few years older than me, and a third-year grad student at Trinity aiming for a PhD in archaeology. He described the dig in County Meath that he'd be doing next summer, and I could feel his passion. But he was also interested in my program at UCD, and also in writing and literature. He could quote Yeats. He was the only child of a single mother, whom he described as courageous and "gutsy." His father had run off just before he was born, and he'd had an impoverished childhood that included a great deal of torment and gossip regarding his unwed mother. He asked about my family, and I filled him with funny anecdotes and family lore, which he seemed to enjoy.

But when he stopped laughing, he said, "Finn. What are you leaving out?"

I searched his eyes and face, but said nothing. He pulled me closer, put his arm around me, took my hand in his. Then he kissed the top of my head. We sat like that for a long while. My mind was filled with questions, fears, and a very strong attraction. But I still could not speak. I wasn't sure where to go with this, although I thought his honesty and gentleness deserved an answer. I leaned into him, and he did something I never would have expected. He sang me a soft lullaby.

I woke to the sound of Liam's heart beating, to sunlight, to a blanket around my shoulders, and to a feeling I'd never had before. I wanted nothing but to be with him.

In the days after, we were together. I would pick him up on my motorbike, and we would explore the Dublin mountains. Once, we found an icy, sparkling brook overlooking the city and stopped to rest by its bank. We lay on his jacket holding each other close, and he cupped my breast ever so gently. I had never met a man like this before, so sweet, almost innocent. It was hard to imagine that he could possibly love me. Boys I had dated in college seemed so immature and clumsy, mostly interested in drinking and sex, not in me. I hadn't had sex with any of them. I hadn't wanted to. Liam, though, was different. He was patient and kind. Even after I'd told him of my past, even when he knew all my shame, he still loved me. It frightened me badly. I was certain he didn't understand just how bad I was underneath it all. Everything in me wanted to make love with him yet at the same time push him away. I never felt so happy, nor confused. I think he sensed this.

For months we enjoyed each other and our young love. In March, during our break between terms, we rented a car and drove west, first to Galway, then to Sligo—Yeats country, where we stopped by his grave *(Cast a cold eye on life, on death / Horseman, pass by)*. We went to the desolate, wild province of Connacht. We stayed in youth hostels along the way. On the way back we meandered through County Clare, the Cliffs of Moher, the stark and haunted area of the Burren, all stone and dolmens. We went to Limerick and stopped off in the town of Doolin, where we listened to some of the most moving music I had ever heard.

Doolin had no youth hostels, with their separate dorms for men and women. Instead, we rented a room in a bed and breakfast. And it was that night, the last of the trip, that we spent making love—long, gentle, astonishing, slow, terrifying, urgent, utterly loving.

I returned to my bedsitter the next day profoundly changed. We spent April together, but in May, Liam had to leave for his dig. Although we acted as if we would stay close, I knew it was not likely. Much as I loved him, I could not live permanently in Ireland or any other country, and I knew that Liam would follow his own dreams around the world.

For months after he left, I mourned. In early September, I took my comprehensive exams. It was time to return to Boston. As the Aer Lingus

747 lifted off, I wept. I had been loved. As Ireland receded, I remembered the last day we went to the brook. Liam sang:

*We'll meet again,*
*Don't know where, don't know when,*
*But I know we'll meet again some sunny day.*

Ireland had given me a newfound courage and independence. Although I could never escape the past, I felt lighter and freer being away from home. Slowly, I was learning to trust myself. And I was finding that there was this vast world out there, a world outside of my inner secret shame, outside of the confines of Winsor Street. And I could be part of it.

When I returned to the States, older and wiser, the Vietnam War had finally ended.

Nixon resigned before he could be impeached, and the country went quiet. Very quiet. No one was protesting, no one was burning himself or his draft card, no one was shouting. The previous few years had been the most tumultuous era since the Civil War: The country had been ripped apart, and many wounds would never heal. The Vietnam vets came home to a very different and often hostile world. Many would end up homeless and suffering from mental illness. Many would never be able to kick drug addictions that had begun during their tours of duty. No cheering crowds or parades welcomed them home. But in all our minds and for years to come would be the sounds of helicopters and visions of desperate people reaching up and up as America fled from Saigon. And the field nurses—those unsung heroes—returned to their families, or got married and divorced, and compartmentalized their war into mental strongboxes that many would never again open. They, too, were quiet.

An era that began with civil rights marches, assassinations, and protests ended in utter, profound silence.

---

Molly never made it into publishing, primarily because she could not type. In those days, the typical way for a woman to enter into the publishing business was to start out as a secretary, and this was definitely not in her skill set. But she would have made a fine editor. Her own work as a poet showed a keen ear for rhythm, her poems lyrical, airy, and wise.

I read my sister's work with open admiration for its depth and music, and we continued our middle-of-the-night critiques as long as we lived together, the only difference being that I, too, was writing, so the explications went both ways. We grew together as writers and sisters, a truly extraordinary bond that ran as deep as our collective memories. Through two-dimensional surfaces and the power of words, we learned each other's hopes and dreams, fears and nightmares, love and pain—and laughter. But our words also showed our differences, and I learned with a great sense of loss that, as much as I wanted to be like her, as much as I idolized her, we would never be the same.

We were fundamentally different, and how much of that difference was due to the abuse I never really knew. Where Molly was graceful and bright and pretty, I felt clunky and average and ugly. I imagined myself the shadow to her light. I was damaged. But the shock of this epiphany led me to love and appreciate her more—I felt protective of her, lest anything or anyone hurt her as I had been hurt. The sisterhood between us ran deep and strong and true.

We rarely talked about Callan. We didn't know what to do with the conversation.

And as odd as it sounds, my uncle didn't loom large as a physical presence in our house after the revelation, as we all thought of him with contempt. His stature had diminished. He avoided me, and I him, and we rarely crossed paths. When we did, when it was unavoidable, he seemed shrunken somehow, less of a commanding person, and more inconsequential as time went on. But his memory haunted me still. His larger-than-life character from my childhood never left me alone, often coming at me out of the blue when I turned a corner or put my head on my pillow.

I wondered if I would ever be rid of him.

Abandoning the dream of a publishing job, Molly kept teaching, though it was not a good fit. Every September, she would begin the new school year by having to stop her car and vomit on the way in. By all accounts, she was a firm but fair teacher who enjoyed her students, but deep inside she trembled. Grading papers was a painstaking job for someone like Molly, who was a perfectionist with a conscience. An A- or B+? D- or an F? These were moral dilemmas that kept her awake most nights, and marking periods were fraught with tension. However, she'd find time to go places with a group of friends, one of whom was Richard McElroy, who taught history. Over time, the group faded into the background, and Molly and Richard became

Molly-and-Richard. I thought they were well matched, with harmonizing moral convictions and a similar sense of humor.

So, when Molly walked in with Richard one Valentine's evening sporting a lovely ring, I was not surprised. Instead, I was devastated. As much as I liked Richard—and I did—and as happy for Molly as I was, my tears that night were equal parts joy and sorrow. Molly would be leaving me again, this time permanently. There would be no one to share midnight readings with. Our room would be bare without her overflowing desk and bookcases. And who would be there to break the tension when parental fights were going on? What would I do without her madcap humor? Without her constant support?

For his part, Richard appreciated and apprehended the nature of our relationship. From the very beginning, he did his best to include me in their lives, inviting me for sleepovers and bringing me with them on outings to the theater or movies or picnics, and I was grateful for his efforts. But, marching up the aisle as Molly's maid of honor, I couldn't stop crying.

As I passed Ma's pew, she whispered, "Finn! Pull yourself together!"

Molly quit teaching when they started having babies, and I was present at the birth of each one—three boys and a girl, in rapid succession. I offered babysitting services whenever I could. I was finally able to come to a comfortable compromise: Instead of losing Molly, I was sharing her. And the bond remains, made so much stronger by crises and life experiences and time.

I went off to finish another graduate degree and teach at a writing program at an Ohio university. Eventually I returned to New England to teach in Rhode Island, and later moved back to the New Bedford area.

Skippy finished his BA, the last of the five of us to earn a degree—remarkable when I think of it, since our parents had never even taken a college course yet all of their children had gone on to college. Skippy did a year of graduate work in professional writing before being offered a job as a technical writer with a small high-tech firm. He stayed with them, as they were a division of a Fortune 100 company. Eventually, he climbed the ranks to vice president of human resources in a worldwide, multi-million-dollar corporation. He travels around the world, dealing with whatever human resources crises arise, be they in Japan, Israel, China, Germany, the UK, Poland, or another spot. Think about it: freckled, shy Skippy at board meetings, traveling with bodyguards, taking charge, and making his mark in a company that appreciates his brilliance and ability to find compromise in a corporate culture. I am so proud of him. He lives not too far from New Bedford, is married, and has three lovely children, all of them redheads.

Drew was the only one to really break away geographically. The rest of my siblings all live within an hour's drive of each other. But Drew landed on the West Coast. He had dreamed of this profession since we were kids, and now he has it all. After earning a PhD from Harvard and completing post-doctoral research at Yale, he became a neurophysiologist, teaching medical students and running his own lab at UCLA. He is wedded to his Alzheimer's research.

I remember when, as kids, we briefly had guinea pigs, and mine, which I had named Sandy, suddenly became ill and died. Too intrigued to let it go, Drew—with my permission—performed a necropsy. I assisted. Drew found that Sandy had died of an intestinal blockage. He was 14 at the time.

Drew and I became very close as adults, despite our rocky childhood. Unlike the others, he talked to me over the years about our uncle's sexual abuse and its toll on my life. Even though we live on opposite coasts, Drew and I are in constant contact.

*I dreamed of dreaming in our mother's house,*
*of poking holes in the plaster wall separating my room from my brothers,*
*where Drew grew blue crystals in Petri dishes and dissected mail-order*
*frogs and fish that came sealed in formaldehyde.*
*I can still smell it.*
*We spent our 10-cent allowance on test tubes and quarter jars of pretty*
*chemicals.*
*Now the old house is emptying, like a bottle rocking on its side,*
*spilling its life into the artificial landscape*
*where the difference between recording and reliving is a blurred line*
*stroked in the dark.*
*Smudged thoughts fly upward like startled birds,*
*hang in the cluttered air, waft down to the worn rag rug.*
*I am dancing with scarecrows.*
*We share the bottle, the experiments,*
*the inarticulate dreams of dark rooms and musty cellars:*
*this wastebasket bulges with the crumpled scraps of distress.*
*And if I call you long-distance, the connection will be clear.*

# 11. Back to the Future

**September, 1995**

Ma sits stoically next to me in the car as we drive away from the house. Her eyes are far away. At the top of the street, I stop the car, hop out, and tell those in the caravan behind me to go on ahead to my house. We'll follow in a little while.

Back in the car, I turn right onto County Street. The others turn left.

"Where are we going?" Ma asks.

"Just for a ride," I tell her and head toward Cove Road, then right on Rodney French Boulevard. First, we pass the Kilburn Mill complex. Then we pass through the hurricane barrier floodgates to the beach. I park facing the ocean, across from the entrance to Hazelwood Park.

"Why are we stopping?" Ma wants to know as I turn off the motor.

"I just thought... we had a lot of good times here."

She nodded.

On this fine September day, a few people are walking the shoreline. A man is fishing off the jetty. The tide is out.

"Your father loved it here. Remember what he used to say?"

I smile. "'Who needs a fancy vacation when we have all this?' We loved it here too. I loved it when he came in the water with us, swinging us around, letting us dive off his bony shoulders—"

"And I'd be on the beach wall, counting heads," Ma adds. "I loved watching you all play together. It made your father so happy."

"And you?"

She smiles wistfully. "Oh yes."

We watch the seagulls soaring, circling, landing on the sand, foraging for food, squawking at each other.

"I miss him," Ma says softly.

*Soft waves lap at the shore, measuring time, time, time...*

It was just two years ago that I was on the phone with Ma.

"Your father isn't feeling well today. I don't know what's wrong with him. He's not right." She sounded worried. "He's pale and—oh God, oh God, Jack!"

The phone clattered in my ear as Ma dropped it. When she came back on the line, her voice was strange and panicked. She said Dad's eyes had rolled back, and he was vomiting blood.

"Call an ambulance," I said. "We'll meet you at the hospital."

I telephoned my siblings and ran to my car. I flew down the highway, making the 50-minute trip from Rhode Island in 27 minutes flat, and met them all in the waiting room. Dad had blown an enormous ulcer.

He survived the surgery but developed aspiration pneumonia, followed by a stroke that left his arm paralyzed, and he was unable to speak clearly. We all went to the hospital as often as we could so that he'd never spend a day alone. By April, he had developed *c. difficile,* a gut infection they could not cure. He was transferred to a nursing home, ironically called the Hathaway Manor, and was fed through a J-tube in his abdomen, which often became infected.

I would sit with him, afternoons or evenings, watching him waste away. In my mind, I would see him clearing the table from supper, a dishrag thrown over his shoulder. Shy, inarticulate, uncomfortable with strangers and favors and affection, he avoided the spotlight.

Dad finally succumbed after several months, passing away on January 7, 1995. We were all with him when he died, including the grandchildren, Aunt Joan, and the Twins Downstairs. We held his hand, told him how much we loved him. His eyes were open, and at one point a single tear made its way down his gaunt cheek. We gathered closer.

"I love you, Dad." *I have always loved you, Dad. Did you know it?*

"I love you, Jack. I'll see you soon," Ma said.

He stopped breathing.

Ma and I sit in the car, listening to the gulls. I know we need to head out, to make our way to my house in Westport, and settle Ma into her new home. But I don't want to leave. We sit mulling over our own thoughts for a few moments.

"Sometimes," Ma says, "I wish I could bring it all back. I wish I could bring back just one more supper, with all of you sitting around the table talking, sometimes squabbling, pleading for an after-supper swim—"

"With a bowl of Granny's cucumbers and tomatoes, and Portuguese bread from the corner," I add.

Ma takes my hand. "We did our best," she says, her voice quavering, almost a question.

"We know you did, and how hard it must have been. But we all turned out okay."

"Are you okay, really?" she asks. But she doesn't wait for an answer. "And I worry about Tom. His eyes have that look... I wonder if he'll ever get over losing Bridie."

I know the look she is referring to, and it's a deep, unquiet grief. Bridie died too young, just a few years ago, of cancer. I remember her at this beach with Molly, or sometimes with the whole family, laughing and carefree. I remember Tom and Bridie's barn wedding, where the generations all came together.

"He'll be okay, Ma. He has two kids to look out for, and we're here for him."

As mothers, we can't protect our children from so many of the hurts that life brings. Over the years, I have begun to understand this.

Ma nods.

"We'd better get going," I say. "They'll be waiting for us."

I start the car and head back on Rodney French toward Cove Street. When we get to the intersection, we can see the Berkshire Hathaway a block to the right.

"Finn, I'm very grateful that you're taking me in," she says.

"It's okay," I say. Although I wonder if it will be okay. We're fine, Ma and I, as long as there is some distance between us. "I have to say, Ma, that I'm a little worried that you won't like it at my house. We're very different in many ways. You know that."

"I know. But I think I might be a help to you, with the kids and all."

I don't share her optimism. I see troubled times ahead, and I feel trapped. But I can't tell her that, this woman who has just lost so much, and I feel guilty even thinking that. And the guilt makes me feel even more trapped. Suddenly, I wonder about my mother's own feelings of guilt about my childhood, and how trapped and helpless she must have felt in the situation.

"I don't want to be a burden to you," she says. She seems so small.

I shake my head. "Don't worry about that, Ma. You won't." I squeeze her hand three times, and together we begin the long journey to my house, a world apart from the city and the neighborhood she has loved, a journey that is bound to take us to strange, unexpected places of the heart.

As we drive past St. Mary's cemetery, where all our family is buried, I wonder at the confluence of events that brought us to this point.

Uncle Callan died several years before my father. He had a particularly aggressive form of bone cancer. I knew he was dying, so I wasn't overly surprised when Molly called me one morning (I was teaching in Ohio then) to tell me he was dead. What shocked me was the way he died: not from the cancer, but from a fiery, one-car crash down by Fort Rodman. He had told Aunt Joan he was having a good day and wanted to go for a short ride around the beach. He drove past Municipal Beach to the end of the peninsula, and where the road curves at a 90-degree angle, Callan's car picked up speed and rammed straight into the concrete beach wall, according to witnesses. The car burst into flames. Since there were no skid marks, the police speculated that he dozed off at the wheel due to his medications. I didn't believe for a minute that he had fallen asleep. I'm quite certain that the crash was a deliberate attempt to escape from the ravages of the cancer. Or perhaps from something else haunting him.

At the time, I was in my mid-20s. I thought Callan's death would put some things to rest for me. But it was actually more confusing than it was settling.

Molly picked me up at Logan Airport in Boston when I flew home for the funeral.

"Ma says she feels like she should forgive Uncle Callan after all he went through with the cancer and then the crash," Molly said as we got onto the Southeast Expressway heading back to New Bedford. Traffic was blessedly light.

"But?"

"But she's not sure she can."

"Hmmff."

"She asked me if I could forgive him, and she's going to ask you the same thing. I'm just warning you."

"Do you forgive him?"

"No," Molly said without hesitation. "What about you?"

I shrugged and shook my head. "Molly, it's a moot point. As far as I'm concerned, he got his just desserts. As for forgiveness, I'm the one in need of it."

"You? Why?"

"Because I was a co-conspirator. I didn't tell on him all those years it went on." I wonder, if Ma is thinking she can forgive Callan, could she maybe forgive me?

"That's absurd. You were brainwashed. You were a kid, for God's sake. You were the innocent victim."

"Then why can't I shake the feeling that I'm guilty, even after all these years? Ma couldn't even look me in the face when she found out. Don't you remember?"

"Ma was in shock. But I know for a fact that she didn't blame you."

"How?"

"She told me. She blamed him completely. Anyway, if you feel that guilty, then maybe it's time for you to see a shrink. I'm serious. This isn't right. You shouldn't be living with that in your head."

I allowed as how she was probably right. Fact was, I never felt good enough, no matter what I did or what I accomplished. Nothing I could do would be enough to erase my lack of self-worth. Molly was wrong about one thing, though: It was not in my head. Intellectually, I knew perfectly well that I was—had been—innocent. But try telling that to my heart.

Ma and I never did have that conversation about forgiveness. The funeral was a mere formality for me. I watched with detachment. It was, of course, a closed-casket affair, so I was spared looking at him one last time. But it didn't matter. His face was not something I would easily forget. I was not there to pay any respects to my uncle anyway; I was there strictly as a witness. Aunt Joan sat throughout the proceedings looking stunned. I tried my best to stay out of the past, but it was impossible. I thought that when my monster was dead that the past would die with him. I was beginning to understand that that wasn't going to happen.

But I knew where Skip's head was. He told me later that day that he had returned to the cemetery after the burial—and pissed on Callan's grave.

---

When everything had settled after the funeral, I decided to give Connie a call. I hadn't seen her for quite a while, although we'd stayed in touch and had been writing regularly since I'd moved to Ohio. She now lived in Dartmouth.

"Connie, hey, it's me." My voice took on a strange, low rasp, threatening to choke up on the way out of my mouth.

"Hey, you. What's wrong?"

"Nothing."

"Liar."

"You're right. Something. I'm home for a few days, and I wondered if I could come and see you."

"Of course! Why are you home? Is your family okay?"

I told her about Callan's death and funeral.

"I didn't know your uncle had died," Connie said. "I would have gone to be there for you. I'm so sorry."

"Don't be. When do you want me to come?"

"Anytime. Right now would be fine."

I borrowed Molly's car and drove out to Connie and Courtney's apartment in Dartmouth.

Fittingly, Connie was working as a librarian in town now, and Courtney had a job at the local hospital while they were both finishing up their graduate degrees. Theirs was one of four nice apartments in a big, very old house on Tucker Road, my favorite road in the whole town, especially at that time of year, with all the autumn leaves changing into vibrant reds and golds. It had been very cold at the cemetery, and even warm coats couldn't stop a biting wind chill. Just one town over, though, here at Connie's, the wind was much calmer. It felt more like sweater weather.

The door swung open before I had a chance to knock. Connie threw herself at me and twirled me around.

"Look at you," she said, genuinely happy to see me. I never doubted that with Connie. We had that kind of friendship, and it was something I don't think I ever replicated with any other friend.

"White as ever," she teased, pulling my shoulders out of my slouch so she could look me in the eyes.

"One of these days my freckles are going to merge, and I'll look just like you. Wonder what you'll say then."

"I'll say you look like a palomino. Come in. Sit down. What are you drinking? Still bourbon and soda?"

I nodded. While Connie was off getting the drinks, I looked around at the prints she had hanging on the walls in interesting arrangements. Several were by Beauford Delaney, but I didn't recognize the other artists. One of the Delaney prints was of James Baldwin, whom I admired immensely. The prints were bright and colorful, lending a charming air to the room. I thought uncomfortably of the chaos of my own room back in Ohio. Connie had created a home, but I still hadn't mastered that art.

She returned with our drinks and munchies.

"Where's Courtney?"

"Over at the lab. He'll be gone till late, so you may not get to see his handsome face this time."

"Tell him hi for me. You look great, Connie, truly. Married life must suit you. Who knew?"

Connie laughed. I took a very long sip of my drink.

"I'm thinking that we might move into a bigger place next year, when we're both working full time. My father is getting older, and he's lonely, rattling around by himself in the old place. We'd like him to live with us."

She paused. I took a long sip of my drink. "But that's not why you came, is it? I can tell by the look on your face. Finn, what's going on?"

I took a deep breath. The couch was comfortable, but I felt the need to get up and move around. I let my breath out through my teeth.

"Connie, do you remember a time when we were kids, and you knew I was upset about something but I wouldn't tell you why?"

She nodded. "There were a few times like that. I remember one time when you were 13 or 14, and I could tell something was very wrong. It drove me crazy. You were so... sad, in another place, like you had the weight of the world on your shoulders. I kept thinking you were in some kind of serious trouble, but you would never tell me. It felt like every time I tried to help, I only made it worse, so I stopped asking you all the time. You wouldn't believe the thoughts that would run around in my head. I wanted to help, but there wasn't a damn thing I could do about it. I figured you'd tell me when you were ready."

I stopped pacing and stood in front of her. "But you did do something. You were my friend, you supported me, and you hugged me when I needed it desperately."

Connie took my hands in hers. "I don't want to pry, but I want you to know that I'm here to listen. When you're ready."

"Yeah, well, I know it's been a lot of years, but I'm here to tell you that story. The only person who knows it outside my family is Father Charles."

I resumed pacing. Then I flung myself back on the couch.

"It's about my uncle, Callan…and me."

"He had a wicked temper—"

"Connie. He was a predator."

Connie's eyebrows shot up. "Oh shit," she said.

In a monotone—so many emotions swirled in the retelling, and I couldn't let them get the better of me, so I folded them into a drone—I went on to tell her the entire story about Callan, beginning before I even had memory in my early childhood and ending with that day's funeral, including the part about Skip.

When I was done, I looked down at my shoes, noting that the hole in the toe of my loafer had grown slightly. I knew all of my shoe details well, since I spent so much time avoiding people's gazes. Connie said nothing at first, and when I looked up, her eyes were brimming. Without a word, she came to me and wrapped me in a tight embrace. Neither of us wanted to let go. Then she went and refilled our drinks.

"Christ, no wonder you were upset, Finn. It's a wonder you didn't have some sort of psychic break from reality. I wish you had told me then. Maybe I could have helped you."

I shrugged. *Who could have helped me?* I still hadn't figured that one out.

"So, now he's dead, and I don't know how to feel about it. It's plunged me back into a past I've kept at bay for all these years, and I feel, well, I don't know how I feel, and that's the truth. I do know one thing. I've got to get it all back in the box, or I won't be able to work at all. I need to be able to concentrate on my writing—I can't let myself be distracted by this." I could feel my heart beating itself into a panic. What if I couldn't get away from it? What if everything I'd built just couldn't stand it? I'd been struggling to keep above it all, but what if I couldn't? What if Callan could still reach me, even from the grave?

"Bullshit, Finn. This should be an incentive to write. But, even if you can't write about it, maybe it's time you got yourself someone to help you through it, professionally, I mean," Connie said. "Having something like this happen to you, I'm sure it stays with you. In your letters, you told me you want to sleep a lot, and that you keep getting sick, that you're stuck in your room for days at a time. That's depression, Finn."

I had wanted to think I was coping just fine, but I knew I wasn't.

"Go to the university's counseling center and get yourself a shrink. Don't make up excuses. It shouldn't even cost you. You get that free as a graduate student, right?" she said. "Check it out when you get back. Promise you'll do this. Promise. Promise me."

"Okay, I promise." I didn't have the will not to promise, and I wanted to believe in it, but I wasn't sure I had the energy for the follow through.

"You've been so strong dealing with this on your own, but you don't have to go through this alone. Something like this, there's a lot to work out, Finn. Even I know this, and I'm not a shrink," Connie said. She looked worried. "This has been with you for a long time, building up. It's hurting you. I can see you're slipping into depression. You have a lousy self-image. I've known that for years, and could never figure out why, unless it was from that crazy Rottenest Sneak Club and being told you were Dirt. Seriously, though. I mean, how many degrees are you going to get before you're good enough?"

"Ever the perceptive Connie. What would I do without you?"

"Wow. Nothing happened to this guy. What's that like for you? How did that make you feel?"

"Like a co-conspirator." Even if I knew intellectually that I wasn't to blame, deep in my soul, I still felt that I was.

The stain wasn't so easily removed.

"Look, I'm glad you told me. Secrets like that—they fester, like cancer. But I don't like the look in your eyes. They look haunted, wary. The bastard is dead, Finn. It's high time you focused on yourself."

I was in a cold sweat. Connie was right. Now that the past had all come fast-forward, I could no longer deal with it alone.

"I'm worried about my writing, if not my sanity," I said.

"You know what? I'm willing to bet that, if you get some help, your writing will be better, stronger, more insightful. You told me once that you wanted to be an honest writer. Have you been? So far? Or have you been masking everything?"

I thought about that. I wasn't really sure. I hadn't written about any of this, though. I didn't want words to give it form.

"I wish I had been able to be there for you when we were younger," Connie said. "Well, now that you've told me, I'm not going to let you down. I'm sticking with you on this, and I'm going to pester you until I'm satisfied that you've got some professional help."

"Connie, thank you for listening, for being here for me. I'll never be able to thank you enough."

Connie's face reddened. "Knock it off. You don't owe me anything."

"I have to go and pack. I'm leaving for Ohio early in the morning."

"Keep writing to me, okay? I want to know everything. I'll never let you down, Finn. Count on it."

I nodded and felt tears stinging my eyes. Relief flooded through me, relief that Connie hadn't recoiled from me.

She hugged me again.

"Go," Connie said. "Go before we both end up in puddles."

Connie followed me out to the car. She stood there waving until my car turned the corner.

---

I flew back to Ohio. I thought a lot about my conversation with Connie. But I didn't—couldn't—act. At the house I shared with a few other grad students, I retreated to my room, rarely coming out, not even for the classes I was supposed to be teaching. My housemates didn't notice that I'd nearly disappeared. We weren't friends; we were more like boarders, each going our separate ways without interference or even much conversation.

My retreat into depression and isolation barely registered with my housemates. But my family started to worry, and so did Connie, whose flurry of letters arrived over the next several weeks.

> *Dear Finn,*
>
> *I just got your note. You don't have to thank me for being there for you, just count on it. I do worry about you. Please keep your promise about getting help. You need it and deserve it. And please put yourself into your writing. It's important.*
>
> *I just read Baldwin's latest book,* If Beale Street Could Talk. *Have you read it? It's different from his other stuff, but I'm not sure if that's good or not. I'll reserve judgment until we can talk about it.*
>
> *Hard to believe it's October already. I hate leaving summer behind. Remember our summers? Going to the beach every day? The long walks along the dike? Nicky and Skippy playing in the sand? Me meeting Courtney? Traipsing home late for supper? Spying on Fremont and your brothers doing their paper routes? Fremont. I don't want to go there.*
>
> *Write back soonest and let me know you're okay. Keep your promise.*
>
> *Love, Connie*

*Dear Finn,*

*Why haven't I heard from you? I hope it's because you've been too busy. I hope it's because you're working on your own writing. I hope it's because you're spending lots of time with your shrink. I hope.*

*I'm sitting at my desk in the library. Halloween decorations are everywhere. Out near our apartment, folks have hung ghosts and skeletons from their trees. Creeps me out. Makes me think of lynchings. Strange fruit indeed. I hate Halloween.*

*Dig this: I'm pregnant. Yeah. I haven't told Courtney yet. I just got the test results. I'm not sure how he'll react. I'm not sure how I feel about it myself. We want children, but we weren't planning for this right now. Next year's going to be the hardest in the degree program for both of us. We'll have comps to deal with, and I'll have a fellowship, so I'll be teaching, which means less time at the library and less income. Shit, Finn. Why now? I think I'm in shock. Shitshitshit. I can't deal. I'm two months along, so a decision will have to be made soon. Shit. Christ, Finn, I have a baby growing inside me.*

*Write to me, dammit.*

*Love, Connie*

*Finn,*

*What is going on?? You've got your whole family worried, and that includes me. Molly says you don't answer your phone. She called the house phone, and one of your roommates finally picked up and said she hadn't seen you for days. She was supposed to leave you a message to call home, but nothing yet. Where are you? Why are you not in touch? Stop being an idiot. Your family doesn't deserve this. Neither do I. Make the effort and call somebody. I'm serious, Finn. Get in touch.*

*With love and concern,*
*Connie*

*Dear Finn,*

*Your note arrived today: "I'm in a dark place. Hope to come out of it soon. Love you all. Pass it on." What the hell is that supposed to mean? I called Molly. She's beside herself. Get off your skinny white ass and call her. And while you're at it, call health services.*

*All that being said, I'm not giving up on you. I love you. I want to help. Don't block us out. Call us.*

*Love, Connie*

I knew Connie was frustrated with me, and I couldn't blame her. But I couldn't seem to do anything to get out of the deep hole I was in. The day after I received that note, Connie showed up knocking and calling at my door. I thought at first I was hallucinating, but she was so persistent that I finally realized I had to answer. I opened the door. We stared at each other, myself in the darkness of my room, Connie backlit by the light behind her. She seemed to glow. I broke her gaze and saw my room through her eyes: total disarray, with clothes, books, student papers graded and ungraded strewn about in utter chaos. Empty bottles of Coke, plates with moldy, half-eaten toast.

The first thing Connie said when she entered the room was, "My God, what is that smell in here?" Then she said, "You look like hell."

She waded into the mess and embraced me silently. I could barely lift my arms to hug her back. I couldn't talk. We stood like that for a very long time. She would not let go, whispering over and over again, "It's going to be all right. I'm here. I love you. It's going to be all right." My body trembled. Her arms tightened until she was literally holding me up. After a very long time, she settled me into the recliner I had been sleeping on.

I realized through my haze that tears were slipping down my face. Connie started the bathwater running and led me into the bathroom, where she gently removed my stinking clothes and put me into the tub, then left me to lie there soaking for a long while. Returning later with some relatively clean clothes, she sponged away the accumulated grime and sweat. She washed my hair. Gently toweling me dry, she said she wasn't leaving any time soon. Back in the room, she lifted the shades, opened the windows a few inches, and gathered the dirty clothes into a heap. She went through my mail, finding official letters from my director, first expressing concern, then increasing alarm, and finally notifying me that I was about to lose my fellowship and could be dismissed from the program. I just sat in my recliner, watching her.

"Sit tight. I'll be right back," Connie said and left the room. When she returned, she told me she had called Molly, health services, and my director. She set up an appointment for me with the school psychiatrist for that afternoon.

Connie brought me to my appointments, grocery shopping, the pharmacy, until she was sure I was out of the woods. She left me in the compassionate care of the shrink, who prescribed anti-depressants. Over the course of the semester, we'd have many sessions and talk for countless hours.

When it was time for Connie to go home, I drove her to the airport. She had used up a week's vacation on me.

"I can't believe you came all the way out here for me," I said.

"Course I did. Don't you get it Finn?"

She hugged me.

As Connie was leaving, I suddenly remembered Connie was going through a crisis of her own. The baby. I asked her what she was going to do.

She smiled. "You're going to be a fairy godmother." Then she boarded the plane.

Slowly, I became stronger and was able to work out a routine of teaching my classes and finishing up my thesis.

The therapy sessions were difficult, taking me back to places I had resisted exploring, but they helped.

I poured myself into my work and earned my graduate degree, then got a job teaching back in New England, at a small Catholic college in Rhode Island.

After the move back to the East Coast, and yes, at Connie's urging, I didn't wait for the depression to take over again, but started seeing a therapist. On good days, I started to wrest control back from Callan. I began to realize this wasn't ever going to go away, but I also realized that I didn't have to abuse myself in his stead. I tried not to let him control me again and again in my memory. He was dead. Dead. I was here. I was the survivor. It wasn't a victory, but there was some satisfaction of sorts.

The depression hung over me always though, breaking back and forth. Sometimes, it almost felt as if it held the properties of a tide, complete with waves and dangers of flooding, and even, at times, a rhythmic comfort.

Rhode Island was close enough to home that I could visit often while keeping some distance and independence. I had changed. New Bedford had changed. We both struggled on.

---

Cal's death, and then Dad's, left Ma and Aunt Joan as the only ones in the entire tenement, two sisters alone in their childhood home. The loneliness must have been intense, with no one upstairs, no husbands to rely on, no children's antics—just, for Ma, the echoes of songs during dishes, of laughter and Friday night fights, of stories told and retold. The connections among three generations had been forged in that tenement and our love for each other. The threads of our individual lives, while occasionally strained, were drawn from this family and this neighborhood, woven together like the fabric of the mills, the whole cloth durable and of an intricate, colorful, and comforting design. Granny had been strong, Ma had an inner steel core, and although it would take me a while to believe in my own strength, it turned out I too had it in me.

January crawled by, with heavy snows that continued through till March. Then, in mid-April, I got a phone call from Ma.

"Joan is dead," she said baldly.

I actually staggered to my chair. The light in my house seemed to zoom out, then in, and I couldn't catch my breath. I was no longer living in Rhode Island. After my divorce, I'd moved a little closer to home. I had a house near the ocean in Westport, where I lived with my kids, one a late teen and the other a young adult. My marriage had ended in disaster, except for my children. We had salvaged a family and forged a close love that I had come to cherish deeply.

A breeze whipped through a crack in the window and its salty cold was a relief. Oddly, it brought back the warmth to my face and the room steadied.

Had I heard my mother correctly?

"Finn? Are you there?"

"Yes, Ma—Oh-my-God."

"Oh my God is right," Ma said, and there was something off, something odd about her voice. It was without affect. I recognized the tonal emptiness of grief.

"What happened?"

Ma told me she had tried calling Aunt Joan on the phone that morning. Getting no answer, she took her key and went downstairs to investigate. There, in the middle room, Joan was lying dead on the floor. The TV was still on; she had not been to bed the night before. To this day, Ma is haunted by the fact that, sometime shortly after she spoke to Joan at 11 p.m., Joan had died, alone, and had lain there all night. Ma said she felt a strong pull to go downstairs that night because Joan had sounded confused on the phone, but she didn't go, resolving instead to call her in the morning. Ma still has terrible guilt over this, but we tell her there was probably nothing she could have done. Joan had suffered either a massive heart attack or a cerebral hemorrhage, nothing Ma could have prevented. Still, she says, she might not have had to die alone.

After I hung up the phone, I drove down to New Bedford as quickly as I could. Ma was in a state of shock. She was pale, and she seemed almost angry.

"It's different when you lose a sister. I've known Joan all my life, my whole, entire life. Longer even than I knew your father." That was all she said.

I sat with my mother and thought about what it would be like to lose Molly.

Ma sat in her cozy chair looking off into the middle distance. I don't think she even noticed that she was crying.

That was the end of Ma's household. She tried living in the house alone for a while, and we all tried to make it work for her, but it was too much.

And now she is moving to mine.

We have come to this great turning point in our lives. I look over at Ma as we drive down the highway. Her eyes are closed, but her lips are moving. Her frail hands are bunching up the rosary beads in her lap. She is reciting the prayers that have given her strength and comfort all her life, and I know she will survive this latest trauma. As she has done so many times in the past, she will pick up the pieces and go on. We will go on. And I think again of writer James Baldwin, who wrote in *Giovanni's Room*, "I must believe, I must believe, that the heavy grace of God, which has brought me to this place, is all that can carry me out of it."

# Epilogue

Ma is sitting in her cozy chair in her new room, a room that, until a few days ago, had been my office. I don't feel resentment as much as displacement. We're almost done unpacking the cars. She is surrounded by her things: her dressers, nightstand, a new bed, and her TV perched atop my father's bureau. She looks mildly shell-shocked. I wonder if I do, too.

We've been here well over an hour, and she still has not removed her jacket, as if that would imply permanence. Her face is etched with a sorrow I can barely look at.

I repainted the room the softest of yellows with white trim, and hung new sheer curtains. Sunlight floods the space. Tomorrow, I plan to cover one wall with all her favorite pictures. Next to her bed is one of Granny's colorful rag rugs. She would save every scrap of cloth and weave rugs with the green-blues, with the rain and the grass and the sea in them; bits of an immigrant's life, of seven children orphaned young, of a few years of school and then the mills—all here in these pieces of rag transformed by her twisted fingers tugging and teasing beauty from the scraps of a long life.

Skip, Tom, and Richard, aided by my kids and Richard and Molly's boys, are still bringing in things from the truck. My mind is in a whirl; I have no idea where I am going to store everything. Needing a break, I go to my new office, which is in the three-season back porch. It is surrounded by windows overlooking the backyard with its stately maples, solid oaks, pines, and a singular, beautiful, deep-red Japanese maple. Maybe, while the weather is good, Ma would like to sit outside on the lawn chair. It is beautiful out there in the fall.

I think to myself: *Ma is a strong woman, she'll be okay.* She has weathered many crises with her indomitable spirit intact. Looking back, I wonder at what we've been through.

Is it really any surprise that she reacted to the exposure of Uncle Callan as she had? Over the years, I have often wondered at my mother's decision to shield her sister and her mother from Callan's abuses. How could she have put her sister and mother before me?

But what resources did she have, beyond an inner strength? She knew nothing about the long- and short-term consequences of sexual abuse. She had no one to turn to in her time of need, no one to tell her what to do or what to expect, no one to help her handle the situation. Perhaps she could not imagine how Joan would have reacted to these events if she'd found out. It was so horrific as to be beyond her imagination. She only knew that her sister would be destroyed. And, possibly, her daughter. What would happen to a girl sullied this way? If it all got out, the world as we knew it would fall in on itself. All Ma could envision was the disintegration of the family. It would have blown the house apart. For that matter, as a young teenager, I'm not sure I could have handled being the one responsible for such devastation.

Even as an adult, it took every last bit of courage for me to blow up my own family. My marriage—what I thought would be my salvation—nearly ended up destroying my entire family and myself. But as destructive as my marriage was, I didn't want to end it.

Bernard was 15 years older than me, a large man who filled his suit with satisfaction. While I always was tortured by decisions, he always knew what to do, what to say. He was well respected and so sure of himself. A tenured professor at a nearby college, he struck up a conversation with me at a conference in Providence. I never would have been so bold. But Bernard—never Bernie—had confidence. Enough confidence, I thought, for the two of us. It wasn't romantic, and he didn't pursue me. He just assumed, and I fell into the role he set for me. Soon we were a couple.

We shared some interests and could talk for hours about books, movies, poetry. Or, really—and I didn't realize at the time but could see it in retrospect—it was he who would drone on and I would hang on. He didn't want my opinions so much as someone to chime in at the right time so he could use it to launch into more of his own theories. I was a prop, unaware of my role. As time went on, he became more of a blowhard, and a bully. But who else would have me? And I was grateful, for the marriage gave me the two loves of my life—my daughter and son.

I'd learned how to deflect Bernard's unpleasantness, maybe even thought I deserved it, but after the children came, it hit me that he had become abusively bullying. It crept up on us and into us. I had to shush the children against setting off his bad moods. If my daughter, Elizabeth, spilled juice at the dinner table, he would storm off with his dinner to eat alone. Every day became about making sure we didn't upset him and set off a tirade.

Bernard knew about some of my childhood abuse. I'd told him once, and he never wanted to talk about it again, as if it was something that traumatized him, not me. He made me feel worthless, but craven for his affection, making me think no one else would have me. I wonder now at his own demons, just as I wonder at Callan's sometimes, but with a cold detachment. I feel no sympathy for either of them.

James, my youngest, was two when I knew our marriage was done. Clumsy and chunky, he was learning how to walk and tripped on his own feet, as toddlers do. He collapsed on the rug and cried. Bernard grabbed him roughly and stood him up by his shoulders. He shook him, an oversized monster toying with its prey. James's cries pitched higher.

"You're pathetic." My husband spit the words at him. My son choked on his own sobs in fright at his father.

Seeing my child this way, I made a decision. Protect my children. End this marriage, blow up this toxic family.

When I had given birth to my children, I felt deeply that motherhood was my chance—not for forgiveness, but for a version of redemption. I knew I had to salvage this.

The divorce was ugly and mean. And it meant my children grew up poorer and without a father, since Bernard left and rarely contacted them. My daughter and son were better off, I believe, without him, but that doesn't mean they weren't scarred. Despite my love, I had placed them in harm's way and could only save them with an imperfect solution, one that hurt. They would carry some of this with them for the rest of their lives. I'd made the best choices I could, and the three of us made a loving unit. I feel blessed with them in my life.

As I think of that, it leads to an epiphany: What if—*what if*—Ma had that same ferocious need to protect her children and to retaliate that I'd had when my children were born? That animal instinct to save the young and destroy the predator? What if Ma had had all that, but because of the circumstances and the times, did not have the luxury of being able to act? She could not vent her feelings about Callan without destroying her sister and mother. And maybe me. It was an untenable position to be in with no good solutions. Consider, then, the enormous strength and courage it took for her to choke it down and hold back—to choose not to blow the family apart. That she did not indulge in the desperate need for revenge was, perhaps, an unselfish act.

In this way, I was not collateral damage: Had she chosen otherwise, I may not have felt vindicated after all. Rather, I might have felt responsible for the dissolution of the family, and I could not have lived with that. I think that, at 14, I could have become suicidal. That I did not see Callan as the responsible one was a direct product of the abuse. He had trained me from very early on to accept my role as co-conspirator, before I'd even developed a sense of self.

Father Charles had granted me forgiveness. For a few moments then, I felt as if maybe I had been forgiven, but I soon realized forgiveness and absolution were more elusive states than I had imagined. *Who do you hate?* His question echoed in my mind. Myself? My mother? My father? My uncle, my aunt? Ma had asked Molly about forgiveness for Callan after his death. I still didn't know how to answer. Not for him. Not for anyone.

Still, I had started to untangle some of it. For years, I had continued with therapy, fortunately finding a kind and caring woman to counsel me. She listened. Yet, I kept feeling frustrated. I couldn't in conversation get across what I had been through. One day, before we were to meet, I started writing out my thoughts. Earlier, I had been afraid that describing my abuse in my writing would make it all the more real, the more difficult to push out of my mind. But I found the release cathartic, and as a writer I could come at it from different angles. I could allow my young self to talk to my more grown woman, and my more adult self could guide the child within me. I wasn't ever going to make sense out of it, not in a logical way. But by writing about it, I could feel some power over my own story.

Ma and I had never been able to really talk about the abuse, but I realize now that she and I are not so unalike.

The world continues to throw things at Ma that are beyond her ability to imagine. Still, she refuses the easy, perhaps earned, cynicism and goes on. Our lives are her lifeblood.

Earlier this year, at a birthday celebration for her, Ma sat amid us all and said to Skip, "I'm so lucky."

Skip said, "How can you say that after all you've lost?"

And Ma replied, with strength and firmness in her tone, "Look at all I have." She waved her hand to include all those present, dozens of family and friends.

Skip said, "We're all here because of you. You created this." And she had. We are a strong, loving, tight-knit family, and she, the matriarch, is our anchor.

As I look out over the copse of maples and hardwoods, I think of what is past. While my abuser stole parts of my childhood, and my adulthood for that matter, I work hard at trying to keep alive those things from my young years that matter most. I draw strength, still, from the feeling of sitting in a dark porch circled by the clan, safe and loved—long, sweet nights of summer warmed by song, the soft lapping of the lake waves, the collective heart beating close, the harmony of the last shivering note. Callan usually begged off, saying he had too much work. While nothing kept me totally safe from his abuse and its aftermath, on those nights on the porch I was in my family's warm embrace. He couldn't get to me, and I cherish those moments deeply.

My cousins are scattered now, living with their own concerns, private griefs, and personal celebrations. We gather now and then for funerals, as the old-timers pass on, and sometimes for milestone birthdays, and many times we sing. But, with the passing of Ma's generation, the context, too, is gone, and we do not seem capable of creating another quite like it in this new world.

As I think of my mother, I realize that my brothers, my sister, and I, along with our children, had woven our own tight-knit, warm, embracing cloth of sorts, bound together still by Ma's love.

Despite my troubles, I too feel lucky. I have much: two wonderful children, several degrees, a home in a nice town with the ocean nearby, a good profession, family, and a few close friends.

Slowly, I walk down the hall to my mother's room.

Ma is sitting there, perhaps contemplating her new life, remembering the old.

She's relived a lifetime today. She has no idea that I've been doing something of the same. I miss my father, and Granny and Grandpa and Bridie, with a great, unrelenting ache. But the rest of the family is here, and Ma is here, 80 years old and still going. And so am I. Survivors. I will go to her now, and I will tell her it will be all right. And I will tell her, and mean it with all my heart, that I love her.

## A Conversation with Catherine McLaughlin

**Why did you choose *Blue Collars* as the title for your novel?**

*Blue Collars* felt right for the story of the Kilroys, a working-class family living in this blue-collar neighborhood in the South End of New Bedford. The novel speaks to the strides and the struggles of blue-collar workers in general and this blue-collar family in particular. The word blue also symbolizes depths of sadness, which Finn fights throughout the book.

**How personal is the story? Is this story drawn from real life experiences?**

This is a book of fiction, and the Kilroys are a family of fiction. But of course, every writer draws from her own life experiences. And yes, I was abused as a child by a trusted family member. That betrayal definitely informs my writing, but this is Finn's story. I have my own.

**How did the trauma of the abuse affect Finn in her adult life?**

Finn's accomplishments were driven by a need to prove herself worthwhile, but they were never enough because she never felt as if she could be worth much in anyone's eyes, least of all her own. She sought validation through her studies and work. However, validation has to come from within and that wasn't easy. She shied away from intimate relationships, and had trouble getting truly close to anyone. When she did marry, it was to a man who was cold and emotionally abusive. The marriage, after two children, ended in divorce. Although she intellectually knows the abuse was not her fault, she internalizes the blame, feels she can never be lovable, and is eaten up by guilt.

***Blue Collars* seems to be a timely story to tell right now, considering the public allegations surfacing today of sexual abuse and child sexual abuse. Do you see this newfound public willingness to talk about abuse as a positive development?**

Yes, I see it as a positive development. In Finn's time, it was the public shame and secrecy and lack of support that allowed this kind of abuse to thrive. Victims today still struggle with that. But the more we talk about it, the more we teach our children how to protect themselves, and the more open we are about it—the more difficult it is for abusers to hide and get away with it. Also, in Finn's time we were less aware of sexuality and more naive.

**Your characters navigate some difficult racial issues and you also use some racially charged language. What went into your decision-making process?**

It wasn't a conscious decision. Rather, I envisioned that one of Finn's friends was African American, and given the time period and the novel's setting, I just followed that lead to its logical conclusion. In the course of their friendship and coming of age it was inevitable that Finn and Connie would encounter issues of race but this was not a conscious plan. Readers may find some of the language offensive and maybe even inflammatory. However, it's an accurate and honest representation of the common vernacular used at the time. We whitewash the past at our own peril.

**One of your mentors was James Baldwin, who was a writer-in-residence at Bowling Green State University in Ohio when you were a graduate student assigned to assist him. How inspirational was your association with him?**

He had a tremendous influence on me. One part of that was his acceptance of me as a friend, even though he was world famous and I certainly was not. The friendship gave me confidence and a sense of worth. On another level, he taught me many things about the racial conflict in the United States. From a writing perspective, he once wrote on the fly leaf of a book he gave to me, "Go the distance. Love, Jimmy." Writing *Blue Collars* was my answer to his encouragement in that comment. He also taught me that being an honest writer was paramount. My relationship with Baldwin made me more sensitive to Connie's issues in the book.

**Education seems important in the Kilroy family, despite the fact—or perhaps because of it—that neither of Finn's parents finished high school. How did they raise five children who went on to pursue higher education and professional careers?**

The Kilroys raised their children to respect education. It was important. Education was redemption. As with many working-class immigrant families, the Kilroys saw education as the way to success, a way for their children to do better than they had. Finn's family was also unusual in their support of Finn's sister Molly going away to college rather staying home to help out the family. This continued with Finn.

---

Visit Catherine's website at www.creativelycatherine.com.

## Book Club Discussion Questions

1. In *Blue Collars,* Finn Kilroy's hometown of New Bedford, Massachusetts, sees drastic changes in the 1950s and '60s. What transitions have our small American cities witnessed since the mid-1950s? How have shifts in industry, population, urban renewal, politics, and economics shaped our lifestyles today?

2. Connie and Finn share the same South End neighborhood in New Bedford, and a love of the beach, the library, and reading—a natural foundation for friendship. Yet Finn's Irish family and Connie's African American family actively discourage the girls from becoming friends. What do you see as the reasons for Finn's parents' racial bigotry? Do you think it's different than Uncle Cal's and Aunt Joan's? Are the Kilroy children less prejudiced? How does Connie's father's feelings about the girls' relationship differ from Finn's parents? How do the girls navigate these troubles within their friendship? Would the same barriers exist today?

3. As in Finn's story, child molesters often are trusted members in the family circle. That trust provides cover for abusers to exploit children even when caring adults are nearby. How did Uncle Cal "groom" Finn to accept the abuse? What contributed to the abuser being able to get by Finn's siblings and parents without being caught? What events led to him finally being caught?

4. The Vietnam War is a looming backdrop to Finn's teenage years. How did it shape her? How do individual members of the Kilroy family see the war? The war pushed family and friends apart, such as with Finn's father disagreeing with his children, but tragedies sometimes brought people together, as with Connie's brother's death during the war. Why did it take a death for the two families to connect?

5. Finn comes close to divulging her uncle's abuse to a priest at the Catholic Church during confession. Why does she feel that she is the one who needs to be forgiven? How does her Catholic upbringing play into her interpretation of who is to blame? What holds her back from revealing the molestation?

6. Despite the burden Finn carries with her from an early age, she experiences great moments of joy during her childhood: secretly reading her treasured books by the sliver of light coming into her bedroom from the kitchen; taking evening swims with her siblings in Clarks Cove; and building a fort in the backyard. What scenes touched you and evoked moments from your own childhood? Finn also encounters some of the classic cruelties of childhood: being bullied, teased, shamed, and left out. How does she deal with that? Who helps her get through these times?

7. What did you think would happen once Cal's sexual abuse of Finn is revealed? Do you agree with Finn's parents' decision to keep quiet? Would the family have different options today? What do you think would have happened if the abuse was revealed publicly? If they'd taken the abuse to Aunt Joan or Gran? What would you like to have happened to Cal?

## About the Author

Author and artist Catherine McLaughlin grew up in New Bedford, Massachusetts. She received graduate degrees from the University College Dublin in Ireland and Bowling Green State University in Ohio. As a graduate student at Bowling Green, she was an assistant to Writer-in-Residence James Baldwin, author of *The Fire Next Time*. Baldwin mentored McLaughlin, and they developed a friendship that continued through the last ten years of his life.

McLaughlin earned her bachelor's degree from UMass Dartmouth, where she later returned as a visiting lecturer. She taught English and writing for 40 years at Framingham State University and UMass Dartmouth. In 2015, she released *Under a Circus Moon*, a book of her poetry. *Blue Collars*, published in 2018 by Spinner Publications of New Bedford, is her debut novel. Now retired, McLaughlin is a professor emerita of Framingham State University. She lives in Dartmouth, Massachusetts, with her two cats.

## About *Blue Collars*

Set in the South End of New Bedford, Massachusetts, during a transformational time in American history, *Blue Collars* is Catherine McLaughlin's debut novel.

Young Fiona "Finn" Kilroy grows up in a devoted, yet dysfunctional, Irish American family during the late 1950s, '60s, and '70s. Theirs is a working-class, immigrant neighborhood, where Portuguese, Irish, French, African American, and Cape Verdean families live side by side in three-decker tenement houses distinct to industrial mill cities.

Finn's hardworking and hard-drinking father labors as a loomfixer at the Berkshire Hathaway textile mill, while her resourceful, Catholic mother holds the family together. Her life seems carefree and idyllic, her days and nights filled with family, singing, reading, swimming, playing board games and building forts. But a terrible secret haunts Finn's childhood and its revelation only deepens her pain and confusion. Her determination to survive—and forgive—in the face of betrayal is as heartwarming as it is heart wrenching.

*Blue Collars* is a timeless story of a family's enduring love triumphing over poverty, abuse, and heartache.